E. V. Thompson was born in London. He spent nine years in the navy before joining the Bristol Police Force where he was a founder member of the Vice Squad. Later he became an investigator with BOAC, worked with the Hong Kong Police Narcotics Bureau and was Chief Security Officer of Rhodesia's Department of Civil Aviation.

Over two hundred of his stories were published in what was then Rhodesia, and he returned to England committed to becoming a full-time writer. While pursuing this goal he supplemented his income with a variety of jobs, from sweeping floors in clay works to working as a hotel detective in London. He then moved to Bodmin Moor, the powerful background for *Chase the Wind*, published in 1977 and the book that won him the Best Historical Novel Award. Its success has been followed by many other historical novels, including the acclaimed saga of the Retallick family and the popular Jagos of Cornwall series.

E. V. Thompson continues to live in Cornwall, where he shares a charming house overlooking the sea near Mevagissey with his wife, two sons and a wide variety of family pets.

Also by E. V. Thompson

Lewin's Mead
Ruddlemoor
The Tolpuddle Woman
Mistress of Polrudden
Blue Dress Girl
Wychwood
Cassie
Lottie Trago
God's Highlander
Becky
The Stricken Land
Polrudden
Cry Once Alone
The Restless Sea
Singing Spears
The Dream Traders
Ben Retallick
The Music Makers
Harvest of the Sun
Chase the Wind

And writing as James Munro

Homeland

Moontide

E. V. Thompson

HEADLINE

First published in 1996
by HEADLINE BOOK PUBLISHING

First published in paperback in 1997
by HEADLINE BOOK PUBLISHING

10 9 8 7 6 5 4 3 2 1

ISBN 0 7472 4824 9

Typeset by Palimpsest Book Production Limited,
Polmont, Stirlingshire
Printed and bound in Great Britain by
Cox & Wyman Ltd, Reading, Berkshire

HEADLINE BOOK PUBLISHING
A division of Hodder Headline PLC
338 Euston Road
London NW1 3BH

Moontide

Prologue

Alice Rowe and her friend Charlotte Jane were returning home from Tregony fair in a very happy frame of mind. Even the cold, grey mist, billowing inland off the sea, could not dampen their high spirits.

It had been a good fair. The best either of them could remember. They had flirted with young men they would probably not see again until the autumn fair; enjoyed the many entertainments on offer, and were returning home with small presents for each member of their families.

'Did you see that Tregony boy, Charlie something-or-other? The one with the lame leg. He climbed that old oak tree to prove he could do it, then couldn't get down. They had to keep passing drinks up to him until he was so drunk he fell out!'

Charlotte went into peals of laughter. Alice, who had been genuinely concerned for the boy from Tregony, said, 'It was a good thing his friends were there to catch him, or he'd probably have broken his good leg.'

'And what about that girl from Mevagissey? She went off to the fields with more than half-a-dozen men to my knowledge – and in broad daylight too!'

The two friends had very different natures. Charlotte loved to gossip and was an incessant talker. Alice was quieter and the more thoughtful of the two, but they chattered happily as they walked along the narrow country lane. The mist, sometimes dense, more often wispy, kept the early-spring moon hidden from view, but both girls knew the road well. The sound of the sea, heaving itself over the rocks at the base of the nearby low cliffs, was a familiar and reassuring sound.

They had walked the four miles to Tregony fair from their coastal homes that morning and were almost home now, having enjoyed a full day at the fair. Friends since early childhood, the two girls worked together making fish nets in a small business at Portloe, a short distance to westward along the coast.

Their homes were on the vast Porthluney Estate, home of the Bettison family. Alice's father was a gamekeeper, Charlotte's mother the widow of an estate worker who had been in charge of the large stables.

Suddenly, Charlotte put out a hand and grasped Alice's arm, bringing her to a surprised halt.

'Look . . . over there!' She pointed through the mist. 'There's someone in the church.'

The mist had thinned momentarily. Through a field-gate in the hedge beside the lane, they could see the squat outline of the small, isolated church. Not very far from the cliff edge, it catered for the spiritual needs of those who lived on the Porthluney Estate, and in the adjacent fishing communities.

The light showing through the stained glass windows was so dim, Alice thought at first that Charlotte must have been mistaken. Then it flickered and she realised her friend was right.

'Why would anyone be in the church at this time of night?'

'Well, it is Feast Day. There's always a service held there on Feast Day.'

'There *used* to be,' Alice corrected her friend. 'That was before Parson Kempe fell out with the Bettisons. There'd be no sense his having a Feast Day service now. No one would go to his church. Mr Bettison said they weren't to.'

'Well, I heard tell that Parson Kempe's taken on a young curate. I suppose it could be him. Anyway, *someone's* in the church,' declared Charlotte. In a moment of bravado, she added, 'Let's go and have a look.'

'What for?' Alice tried to sound scornful. 'I don't want to look in no old church. What if it's *not* the parson, or this new curate?'

'Who else would it be?' retorted Charlotte. 'Come on, let's go and find out.'

Without waiting for a reply, she hurried to the lych-gate with its slate slab on which coffins were rested on the way to burial.

The hinges of the lych-gate squeaked noisily as the gate swung open. Once inside the churchyard, where tombstones leaned towards each other at drunken angles, Charlotte's imagination suddenly began to play tricks on her. She even thought for a fearful moment she had seen two of the tombstones move.

She stopped, suddenly uncertain. Perhaps her idea was not such a good one after all . . .

'Have you changed your mind?' asked Alice scornfully, aware that her friend was not the bravest of individuals and was having second thoughts.

'No! Of course I haven't,' Charlotte lied. But she made no move to go on.

It was clear now that there were lights burning inside the small church, but not very many. Nor the number of candles that would normally be lit for a service.

As she neared the building, Alice stepped from the gravel path to the grass of the churchyard, so her footsteps would make no sound. Charlotte remained behind.

Tiptoeing forward, Alice thought of all that had happened within the parish to make it unlikely that there would be a service in progress inside the small and isolated church.

The rector was now an old man. In addition to Porthluney, he held the livings of two other parishes. Both were in wealthy, expanding districts of Cornwall. They contrasted greatly with the living of Porthluney, which traditionally relied heavily upon the generosity and goodwill of the landowning Bettison family for its upkeep and support.

Unfortunately, the present head of the family had neither the money nor the will to give his support to the church. Much of the family wealth had been lost in recent generations through marriage settlements. A large sum also needed to be spent upon the ancient family home if it was to be saved before it decayed beyond repair.

In addition to this, John Bettison was a gambler and a heavy drinker.

In truth, the family was close to ruin. Things were so bad that Bettison had been obliged to increase the rents of his farming tenants. At the same time he reduced the quantity of tithes paid by the estate to the Church. It was this action that had caused the breach between himself and the Reverend Kempe.

The dispute had become particularly bitter when Bettison tried to have Reverend Kempe removed from his living because of his opposition to the landowner's actions. The move had been effectively blocked by the bishop, but had done nothing to heal relations between landowner and rector.

John Bettison might not have succeeded in removing the ageing rector from his living but, such was his influence as the area's principal landowner, he was able to threaten eviction for anyone who attended the church during the dispute. As a result, no one in the parish dared attend services in the small church.

The rector was too old to remain in the front line of the battle between landlord and Church. He removed himself to another of his parishes, St Stephen, some miles away. Here his only problem was the encroachment of the followers of the late John Wesley.

'What can you see?'

Charlotte's loud whisper coming from the mist was more for the reassurance of hearing her own voice than the desire for a reply.

'Shut up!' Alice hissed angrily. 'Whoever's inside will hear you.'

'My gran says she's seen the new curate,' said Charlotte in a hoarse whisper, ignoring Alice's demand. 'She says he goes around with Quakers and is hardly old enough to have learned the Lord's Prayer, let alone look after a parish. Mind you, she's over ninety now. Everyone seems young to her . . . Can't you see anything yet?'

Alice returned to where her friend was standing.

'It would serve you right if I pushed you inside the church to find out for yourself what's happening in there. It was your idea to have a look. Now, come and give me a lift up to that window just beyond the door. There's a clear pane of glass there. I might be able to see through it.'

Reluctantly, Charlotte allowed herself to be dragged to the window. Here, she put her arms about Alice's hips and heaved. She managed to lift her friend no more than a couple of inches from the ground.

It was fortunate it was no higher. She suddenly released her hold and Alice dropped heavily to the ground.

'What's that?' Charlotte sounded suddenly fearful.

The sound was repeated and Alice said scornfully, 'It's only some old owl!'

'Are you sure?'

The long drawn-out, tremulous sound was repeated yet again, and Charlotte said, 'I don't like this place, Alice. Churchyards are spooky. Let's go.'

'Not yet. Now we've come this far I want to see what's going on inside the church.'

An owl hooted once more, this time from the other side of the churchyard.

'You can stay here if you want to,' declared Charlotte hurriedly. 'I'll wait for you out in the lane.' With this she hurried away, her footsteps loud on the gravel path.

Unconsciously, Alice held her breath, believing that whoever was inside the church must be able to hear the noise of her friend's hasty departure.

A few moments later there was the sound of organ music from inside the church and Alice discovered she had been holding her breath. She expelled it gratefully, but was no nearer to seeing inside the church.

She thought she would try one of the windows on the far side, but as she passed by the porch she noticed a thin sliver of light escaping from the doorway. The door was not fully closed.

Slipping quietly inside the porch, Alice pushed the door open a little more, prepared to turn and flee if it creaked.

She could not see the organ from here, so she pushed the door open a little farther.

With a sudden shock, she realised she was being watched – but by no human! On the stone floor of the aisle, beside the front pew, was a rough-haired black and white dog. Head on paws, the animal looked straight at her.

For a moment Alice thought it would bark. Then, as they stared at each other, its tail brushed the floor twice, then ceased.

So too did the music.

A moment later someone passed across her line of vision and walked to the pulpit. It was indeed the young curate. Looking down at the dog, he said, 'Well, Napoleon, there's only you and me here, so it looks as though you're going to have the sole benefit of yet another of my sermons. One thing's certain: if there's a heaven for dogs, you're going to go there.'

The dog responded to the curate's words by wagging its tail far more vigorously than before.

In the doorway, Alice gave a brief but sympathetic smile. The curate was hardly someone of whom to feel afraid.

She remained in the porch, listening to the sermon the curate preached to the patient and loyal dog. It was on the theme of love and forbearance and was a very good sermon – one that would have appealed greatly to the absent parishioners. They had been wont to complain in the past that the ageing rector's sermons lacked the ingredients of 'fire and brimstone' which enlivened proceedings at the nearby Methodist chapel.

Alice was almost equally impressed by the behaviour of the curate's dog. The animal lay with its black and white head resting on its paws. Only the movements of the dark eyes showed her that, unlike its master, it was fully aware of the hidden listener.

'. . . In the name of the Father, the Son, and the Holy Ghost, Amen.'

Bringing his sermon to a close, Toby Lovell looked down from the pulpit to his canine 'congregation' and sighed. 'Well, Napoleon, we've kept to the *letter* of Church law, at least. Now let's put out the candles and go home and I'll see what I can find for us to eat.'

Hurrying from the church porch, Alice found her friend shivering beside the mist-shrouded lych-gate.

'Wh – what kept you so long? Another couple of minutes

and I'd have run home to get someone to come out and look for you.'

'I was listening to a sermon – and it was a very good one.'

'A sermon? *Was* it the curate in there?' Charlotte sounded bewildered. 'But . . . there was no one inside the church to hear it.'

'Yes, there was. The curate's dog was there.'

'His *dog*? The curate was preaching a sermon to a dog? Do you think he's mad?'

'No,' replied Alice, thoughtfully. 'He's certainly not mad. In fact, from what I saw of him, I'd say he's probably a good man. But I do feel sorry for him. I think he must be very lonely.'

Walking along the lane to the rectory, Curate Toby Lovell heard the call of the owl which had so frightened Charlotte and was reminded of the sound of the wind in a ship's rigging – a sound he knew well after three years as a naval chaplain.

He stopped for a moment, and the dog stopped with him. Here, cut off from the world by the mist, Toby could have been the only man in the world. A man alone. It was a far cry from the cramped and crowded surroundings of a frigate of the Royal Navy.

Toby set off once more, his thoughts of ships and battles, and the circumstances that had led to his leaving a sea-going life behind him for ever . . .

Chapter 1

'"A frigate is expected to carry the battle to enemy ships of the line in a battle such as the one which lies ahead . . . "?'

Repeating his superior officer's words, James Tasker, first lieutenant of His Majesty's frigate *Eclipse*, stared open-mouthed at the commanding officer, his expression one of disbelief.

'That's right, James. Those are the orders of our Lord Admiral.'

Commander Henry Kempe shared his first lieutenant's concern, but he did not allow it to show. He even managed a brief, tight smile.

'My Lord Nelson was emphatic. His aim is not the taking of prizes, but complete annihilation of the enemy. We are to follow the ships of the line into battle and make absolute the work carried out by his lordship's men-o'-war.'

Listening from the edge of the quarterdeck, navy chaplain Toby Lovell silently agreed that the first lieutenant's concern was wholly justifiable. A frigate should not be expected to engage vessels possessing more than three times its own firepower. A single broadside from a hundred-gun ship of the line was capable of blowing a frigate into oblivion.

Despite this, Toby knew that every man on board *Eclipse* would raise a cheer when the order was given to engage the enemy's men-o'-war.

He felt a deep sadness within him. There would be much work for a chaplain before the sun sank below the horizon off Cape Trafalgar on this day. Tragic work.

The *Eclipse* was a thirty-eight-gun frigate, with a crew of three hundred men. The vessel was part of a fleet which for months had been seeking a combined French and Spanish force of thirty-three ships. Among the enemy ships were the three most powerful warships in the world.

Yesterday they had finally found them and, today, were closing in to engage them in battle.

Commander Kempe had just returned on board after attending a meeting held on board Admiral Lord Nelson's flagship, *Victory*. The object of the meeting was to make every captain in the fleet aware of the tactics Nelson intended using when they joined battle with the enemy.

That this would be a battle of historic proportions and significance was never in doubt. The ship's officers and the lower deck men could smell it in the very air.

Lord Nelson had pursued the fleet of the French Admiral Villeneuve across the Atlantic Ocean and back again in a desperate game of hide-and-seek. Now the two fleets were on a converging course that was destined to end in a decisive battle. It would be the culmination of a frustrating chase which had led Nelson on a desperate fourteen-thousand-mile pursuit of his elusive enemy. Now the chase was almost at an end, not far from where it had begun, many months before.

Today Nelson intended bringing Admiral Villeneuve to book. The outcome would decide, once and for all, whether naval supremacy would be held by Britain or France for the duration of the war between the two countries.

The date was 21 October, the year 1805. It was a date that would be entered in the annals of British history alongside Crécy and Agincourt.

It was an encounter that Villeneuve would gladly have foregone, even though the ships of France and its Spanish allies under his command had considerable superiority in firepower over the British vessels. He was acutely aware that his men, the Spanish seamen in particular, did not share the British sailors' enthusiasm for a fight.

'You are not relishing the thought of the battle, Padre?'

The frigate's commander had been looking in Toby's direction whilst speaking to his first lieutenant and had observed the expression that passed across Toby's face when the impending battle was mentioned.

'I share Lord Nelson's hope for a decisive victory,'

declared Toby. 'But included in my prayers will be a fervent hope that the price of such a victory might not be a high one.'

'No price can be too high to secure the seas against such a tyrannical enemy,' said Commander Kempe.

'Indeed,' agreed Toby. 'Nevertheless, I would like to hold a brief service. It will do no harm to add the power of prayer to the gunnery of the fleet.'

After only a moment's hesitation, Commander Kempe nodded his agreement. 'Very well. Hold your service, Padre – but keep it brief. My own opinion is that a good meal before battle serves a man better than a prayer. We'll call the men on deck now and they can enjoy a meal afterwards. That should prepare them for whatever the day – and the French admiral – has to offer.'

Half-an-hour later the crew of the *Eclipse* were mustered on the quarterdeck to hear the chaplain's prebattle prayers.

Toby kept the service short – and tactful. He said nothing that might make them dwell upon thoughts of the heavy casualties that must inevitably be suffered during such an engagement as lay ahead. Nor did he mention the joys of the hereafter, that so many seamen would soon know.

His duty was to assure each man that he would be fighting in a just cause. Because this was so, he told them, the angels of the Lord would swell their ranks. This must undoubtedly ensure that at the end of the day, victory would belong to the British navy.

It was a difficult service to conduct. Filled with both excitement and apprehension, there was a restlessness in the men that was not conducive to prayer and contemplation.

Nevertheless, Chaplain Toby Lovell's words were heeded in typical fashion. When representatives from each seamen's mess mustered to collect the daily rum ration, one man, tongue-in-cheek, requested extra tots for: 'Them there angels as is fighting with us.'

As the laughter of his shipmates erupted around him, the seaman added, 'And don't be stinting with it, neither.

If any of them as preaches on the Lord's behalf is anything to go by, they'll be a hard-drinking lot.'

'Then it's lucky we've got Padre Lovell on board *Eclipse*,' retorted the quartermaster. He carefully measured out the rum ration with the aid of a series of copper jugs of differing sizes. 'He's as close to teetotal as you'll find anywhere in His Majesty's fleet. He'll send any drunken angel packing before he has time to get so much as a sniff of your grog. If I'm wrong you can take the angel's name and send him along to see me. I'll give him a double tot – and one extra for you. Now, move along and let me get the rest of this rum issued. If every mess orderly has your chatter we'll be up with the Frenchies before I'm done.'

Below decks, in his small cabin, Toby Lovell pulled off the robes he had worn for the service and dropped to his knees in front of the small crucifix nailed to the wooden bulkhead. He kneeled in silence with bowed head for some minutes before looking up at the symbol of his calling.

Quietly, he said, 'Lord, give me the courage to carry out my duty in the manner expected of me. May I bring comfort to those in pain, and tranquillity to those who are about to pass into Your keeping. Forgive their past transgressions and welcome them as brave men who died fighting for the cause of a Christian country. Amen.'

Crossing himself, he rose to his feet and stowed his cassock inside a sea-chest which occupied a corner of the cabin.

After shrugging on his coat, he looked about the cabin, hoping he would see it again. Closing the door behind him, he made his way to the upper deck. In such a battle as that in prospect for the ships of Nelson's fleet, survival was an outcome upon which few gamblers would risk their money.

Chapter 2

The combined fleet of French and Spanish men-o'-war held a course steadily northwards, past Cape Trafalgar. To the men on the British ships it was a magnificent yet awesome sight.

The British fleet was intercepting the enemy's line on a converging course. Viewing the French and Spanish ships from the deck of the *Eclipse*, Toby Lovell thought that an admiral commanding such a fleet might, with some justification, consider it indomitable.

It should have appeared in a similar light to the crews of the British ships. They headed for a point ahead of the enemy fleet, sailing in two columns, at a tantalisingly slow rate of knots. Yet the British sailors had a sublime faith in their admiral. They were convinced that under his leadership a British battle fleet could outgun, outsail, and outfight any navy in the world.

It seemed the views of Villeneuve were in accord with those of the British sailors. He showed no inclination to turn and fight. Instead, he was driving his ships hard in a bid to reach the relative safety of the Spanish port of Cadiz without doing battle.

Villeneuve's efforts were doomed to failure. His fleet was steering almost due north with little help from the wind. Nelson was intercepting from the west, with what little wind there was behind him.

The signal 'Prepare for Action' had been fluttering from the yardarm of *Victory* for some time. Suddenly, it came down and another signal flag raced to the masthead.

'Engage the enemy more closely,' translated the first lieutenant in an excited voice. The Battle of Trafalgar had begun!

The two lines of British ships turned in upon the enemy immediately. Their intention was to split the French and Spanish fleet into three parts.

Admiral Collingwood, Nelson's second-in-command, was leader of the second of the two British columns. His was the first vessel to go into action, exchanging fire with one of the French ships as soon as they came within range of each other.

It was the opening salvo in what was to be a fierce and unyielding battle, one that grew more bitter with each passing minute. The *Eclipse* was one of four frigates following in the wake of Collingwood's ships of the line. By the time it reached the battle area smoke from cannons and burning ships was rolling across the sea in greeting.

Toby Lovell thought the scene reminiscent of a painting he had once seen that was meant to represent the terrors of Hades.

Two French ships, totally dismasted, drifted clear of the main fleet. Their masts, sails still set, had crashed down on crowded decks, causing many casualties. Canvas, spars, rigging and men were tangled together and had spilled from ship to sea.

Flames had already gained a hold on one of the vessels. Despite this, in the midst of the chaos sailors hacked at the rigging in a bid to clear wreckage from the upper deck and bring more guns into play.

Even as they worked feverishly, a British man-o'-war was closing upon them. Minutes later a broadside was fired from point-blank range.

In every direction the two fleets were locked in fierce and confused battle. Near the *Eclipse*, a British ship had drawn alongside a Spanish vessel and red-coated marines were fighting their way on board.

'Look! Two French ships have struck their colours already, and Nelson and his squadron have only just come within range! Have you ever seen such a glorious sight, Padre?'

The *Eclipse*'s first lieutenant could hardly contain his excitement as the frigate neared the heart of the battle.

Suddenly, the frigate's commander called, 'Take her to

starboard, helmsman. We'll go alongside the large Spanish man-o'-war – the one with only its foremast intact. Her gunners are giving *Conqueror* a desperate fight to starboard. We'll take up position on her port side and give her a broadside. That should provide sufficient distraction and allow *Conqueror*'s boarding party to take her.'

The helmsman heaved on the wheel until the deck tilted and the frigate came around slowly. Catching a little more of the now indifferent breeze, the vessel edged nearer to the furious duel.

Closing in on the far flank of the Spanish ship, the *Conqueror* was taking a severe battering from the heavier guns of its adversary. As soon as the frigate came within range, Captain Kempe brought his ship broadside on to the enemy vessel and fired a salvo.

The cannon balls struck home, raking the upper deck and taking the Spaniards by surprise. All the gunners and seamen had been busily engaged in the fight with *Conqueror*.

The surprise was so complete that *Eclipse* was able to fire off a second broadside before the Spanish ship retaliated. However, when it came, the reply was devastating. Although less than half the Spanish vessel's guns were laid accurately on their target, this number was almost equal to the total armament carried by *Eclipse* – and the guns were of a far larger calibre.

One of the frigate's masts came crashing down, the falling rigging and canvas sweeping a number of sailors into the sea. Many more lay on the deck, having suffered terrible injuries.

'Cut the rigging and heave that mast overboard! Get the wounded men below, First Lieutenant . . . and check the gun deck! I want another salvo fired at the Spaniard – and I want it NOW! Helmsman, bring her broadside on once more . . .'

The *Eclipse*'s captain shouted his orders above the pandemonium on board his ship. The salvo from the Spanish man-o'-war had inflicted many casualties on the smaller vessel and the wounded were being helped below.

Toby helped in this work. It was part of the duty of a chaplain during battle.

The surgeon and his assistants were already working in the dimly lit between-decks area allocated to them as sick bay and operating theatre.

Not noted for his finesse or professional expertise, the surgeon was already carrying out amputations with a speed and efficiency that might have been the envy of a market butcher.

In truth, the sailors of *Eclipse* feared their surgeon far more than they did any Frenchman, or his allies.

While he worked, some of the surgeon's assistants were employed holding down the patients about to be 'operated' on. Others were treating the wounds of those for whom surgery was either unnecessary or inappropriate.

Toby dressed the wounds of a number of men before pausing to offer comfort to a dying sailor. The man was trying desperately, but unsuccessfully, to mouth a last message to be passed on to his family at home.

Meanwhile, the guns were still firing. Shots came not only from the starboard side now, but from both sides of the frigate. Their small ship had reached the heart of the desperate battle.

Suddenly, they shuddered under the weight of yet another enemy broadside.

'There'll be more casualties on deck.' Toby spoke the words to one of the surgeon's assistants. 'Come up top with me and help bring them down.'

He hurried up the ladder to the upper deck, followed by the surgeon's assistant. Here they encountered a scene of carnage. The last enemy broadside had raked the upper deck of the *Eclipse*. Dead and wounded lay everywhere and not one officer remained on his feet.

Commander Kempe was being carried below, barely conscious. Among the dead was the helmsman – and there was no one at the wheel. A mast with spars, rigging and sails hung over the side, causing the small frigate to turn towards the giant bulk of the Spanish vessel. At the same time flapping sails on the broken mast prevented the gunners along most of the starboard side from laying their guns on the enemy vessel.

A quick glance told Toby that the Spanish vessel alongside was in an even worse state. Nevertheless, it carried a huge crew. If the two vessels touched, a swarm of armed men would board the frigate. In its present state the smaller vessel would probably be taken.

Toby leaped to the wheel and hauled it to starboard. At the same time he bawled at the top of his voice for the seamen to cut the mast and rigging free and toss them over the side.

Turning the wheel was desperately hard work, even when a young midshipman came to his aid.

Not until the fallen mast had been chopped free of the ship and was drifting in the sea behind them did the frigate respond to the rudder.

It turned away from the Spanish vessel with seeming reluctance. At the same time the gunners, able to see clearly once more, fired a broadside into the other ship at point-blank range, causing it to shudder from stem to stern.

The decks of the Spanish vessel had been filled with sailors and soldiers, preparing to board the frigate. The broadside caused carnage on board.

Toby winced, but this was war. In battle it was a matter of kill or be killed. Yet it did not prevent him from being deeply saddened by the horrendous waste of human life.

Just then the captain returned to the deck from the cockpit where he had been treated by the surgeon. His wounds not so serious as had at first been feared, he was ready to resume command of his ship.

Commander Kempe took in the situation immediately and inclined his head to Toby. 'Thank you, Padre. You seem to have saved my ship for me. The midshipman can remain at the wheel. Will you take the first lieutenant down below? I fear he's very badly wounded.'

Leaving the wheel, Toby crossed the deck to where the first lieutenant lay in a pool of blood. Beside him only the stump remained of the mast that had been cast into the sea.

Toby dropped to his knees, leaning over the man who lay gasping his life away on the deck.

Suddenly, a solitary cannon on board the Spanish ship,

fired at close range, hit the shattered stump of the mast only feet away from Toby.

Large pieces of hard wood flew in all directions. Some of them hit Toby and he felt a fierce pain in his head. He was aware he was collapsing on top of the mortally wounded first lieutenant but could do nothing to prevent it.

Then the world went black all about him and he knew no more.

Chapter 3

'The senior physician tells me you're lucky to be alive, Padre. He also tells me he'll not be passing you as fit for duty with the navy again. I'm afraid your sea-going days are over.'

Captain Kempe, newly promoted as a result of the *Eclipse*'s role at the Battle of Trafalgar, settled himself on a chair beside Toby's bed. He shook his head disconsolately. 'It's a great pity. You're the first chaplain I've enjoyed having on board my ship. I'd have liked you to come with me to my new command.'

The captain was paying a visit to Toby in the Stonehouse naval hospital in Plymouth, close to the Royal Navy's dockyard.

The hospital was filled to overflowing with the wounded from Trafalgar. The battle had ended in a Pyrrhic victory for Britain, the celebrations marred by the death of Admiral Lord Nelson.

Architect of the great victory, he had been killed at the height of the action and by his death Britain was robbed of the ablest and most daring naval leader the nation had ever known.

Nevertheless, although he had paid for victory with his life, Nelson had succeeded in his aim. Never again would the French navy be sufficiently strong to challenge Britain's supremacy at sea.

It meant that Napoleon's dream of one day conquering England would never be fulfilled.

'Do you have any plans for your future?' Captain Kempe put the question to Toby.

'None. I've been so busy concentrating on survival I haven't dared take life more than one day at a time.'

This was perfectly true. Toby had suffered a fractured skull and broken ribs and the *Eclipse*'s surgeon had been convinced he had also suffered internal injuries.

Unconscious for three days after the battle, Toby had been expected to die. Indeed, Captain Kempe had made advance arrangements to bury his chaplain at sea.

Had he died, he would have joined a quarter of the frigate's crew who had been killed in the action.

However, the young chaplain was still alive when the battle-damaged frigate limped into harbour at Devonport. Here, its crew received a welcome befitting the heroes of such an outstanding victory.

Transferred to Stonehouse hospital, Toby's condition, although remaining critical for many days, gradually began to improve.

'I'll probably look for a quiet curacy somewhere in the country,' he said now. 'But I don't have to worry about it for a while. The physician says I'll be here for some weeks yet.'

'I've recommended to the Admiralty that you be paid a pension for the injuries you sustained on the *Eclipse*,' said Captain Kempe. 'It won't be a huge sum, but there's no doubting that it will be approved. Right now the country is happy to give anything to a man who served at Trafalgar, especially if he was severely wounded as a result. Such euphoria won't last, of course, but once you've been granted a pension it's unlikely to be taken away again. As for the curacy, I think I might be able to help there, too.'

Captain Kempe leaned forward in his chair. 'I have an elderly uncle who lives at St Stephen in Cornwall. He's actually the rector of three parishes, but the work is becoming too much for him. When I met him recently it was mentioned that he was thinking of taking on a curate to look after the smallest of his three parishes. I thought of you at the time. In my opinion you are just the sort of man to take on a parish which includes a small fishing community.'

The captain leaned back in his chair once more. 'At the moment he's having some sort of problem with the landowner in this particular parish. It's probably something to do with my uncle's age. He's getting on a bit and I believe he's finally ready to admit that three parishes are too much for him. You'd enjoy life there, Padre. I visited the place once and thought it delightful. It will be something of a holiday for you. I'll write a letter for you to take to Uncle Harold. You and he will get on very well, I'm quite certain of it. The parish is called Porthluney, by the way. It's on the south Cornish coast, about halfway between Fowey and Falmouth.'

An infection caught in the hospital led to unexpected complications. As a result it was not until the early spring of 1806 that Toby was well enough to make the journey across the River Tamar to Cornwall. He travelled in the hope of taking up the curate's post, although it was by no means certain.

He carried Captain Kempe's letter of introduction in his pocket, but other letters he had written to his elderly uncle had brought no reply.

The coach in which Toby travelled was bound for the busy Cornish port of Falmouth. Many of the passengers were officers of the Royal Navy or the merchant service, on their way to join ships.

Toby had some moments of nostalgia listening to their chatter about ships and places they had known, and of their hopes for future adventures, but such feelings soon passed.

Once the coach had left the River Tamar behind, it plunged into a series of narrow lanes, travelling at an alarming speed. To take his mind off this Toby studied the countryside. He found it fascinating. He had never before visited Cornwall, although he had viewed it from the sea on numerous occasions.

It was a six-hour drive to St Austell where Toby would be leaving the coach, but there was much beautiful countryside to be enjoyed along the way. There was also an occasional busy mine complex to occupy the attention of the passengers.

St Austell was reached in mid-afternoon. As the coach clattered into town, the guard sounded a call on a long brass horn to warn the innkeeper of its imminent arrival.

St Austell was a bustling place, the shops in the narrow streets owing much of their trade to the busy China clay workings and tin mines to the north of the town.

Toby's immediate plans were extremely vague. He had no idea how far his destination, the village of St Stephen, was from St Austell. With this in mind, he took the precaution of booking a room at the inn where the coach stopped.

'Will you be staying with us for very long, Reverend?' The landlord asked the question as he called on one of the servants to take Toby's chest up to a room.

'I hope not, landlord. Much depends upon what happens when I speak with the rector of St Stephen. I'm hoping he will appoint me as his curate at Porthluney.'

'Porthluney, you say?' The landlord looked at Toby with new interest. 'They have need of a curate there, all right, but the devil's had his own way there for far too long for a *curate* to set it to rights. It'll take a bishop or two at least to my way of thinking. Not that we're likely to have any of *them* come all the way here to sort out our Cornish problems. They're far too fond of life's comforts.'

Leaving his enigmatic observation hanging in the air, the landlord turned his attention to an elderly couple who were hoping to find a place on the overcrowded coach. Meanwhile, the other passengers had hurried inside the inn, to bolt down a hasty meal before the coach resumed its journey.

Toby also felt hungry, but he was too excited to eat. He was impatient to settle his future and begin work in what would be his first position as a parish priest.

There were still a few hours of daylight left. Making enquiries from one of the servants, he learned it was some three or four miles to St Stephen. He decided he would walk there straightaway, to meet Captain Kempe's uncle and deliver his letter of introduction.

Chapter 4

The thought of being responsible for the spiritual well-being of the Cornish community of Porthluney thrilled Toby far more than he had believed possible. He hoped he would be acceptable to Reverend Kempe as his curate. Should he be given the curacy he was determined that his responsibility for the parishioners would extend far beyond mere Church duties.

Toby had never before worked in a parish, at any level. It would be a new experience for him, but he looked forward also to becoming involved in the life of the community.

Despite the crowded conditions on board a man-o'-war, his calling had decreed that his should be a lonely life. Indeed, loneliness had been his lot for as long as he could remember.

Both his parents had died when he was still young. His mother's death had occurred soon after giving birth to a stillborn daughter. His father's was brought about by a fever, contracted whilst serving in the West Indies with the Royal Navy.

Toby had been brought up by an elderly and childless uncle and aunt, the uncle running a small private school in Norfolk. Their ambition for Toby had always been that he should enter the Church. As a result, he had been coached hard in order to obtain a place at Oxford.

Eventually, his hard work was rewarded and Toby went to Oxford. After obtaining his degree, he was ordained at the age of twenty-four, three years before the fateful Battle of Trafalgar.

His guardians had expected him to return to Norfolk from Oxford, and settle down to the life of a rural parson, but Toby had had other ideas.

Although quite content to make his future within the framework of the Church, he felt he lacked the experience to take over a parish immediately. Besides, he had always secretly wanted to follow in the footsteps of his sailor father. It was an ambition he had never dared express to his uncle.

When he realised he could combine the Church and a sea-going life by becoming a naval chaplain, Toby had gone to sea. Now, only three years later, his naval service had been brought to an abrupt conclusion.

The thought still saddened him, but he was determined that his new parishioners would gain from his loss. He was a much more worldly man now. He had learned to live with his fellow men; to help them solve the numerous problems that had often been magnified by shipboard life. He hoped he might do the same for the people who lived in the small but scattered parish of Porthluney.

Long before he reached his destination, Toby had realised that although his wounds had healed, he was not yet a fit man. By the time the tower of St Stephen's church came into view, he felt he could hardly walk another step.

Rather than arrive at Reverend Kempe's door in a state of near collapse, Toby turned in at the church. He intended spending a few minutes in quiet prayer before calling at the rectory, and to allow himself some of the rest which his body was craving.

He was on his knees in a front pew, his head resting on his hands, when a gentle voice said, 'Is everything all right, my son?'

Raising his head, Toby found himself looking up at an aged, wispy-haired priest, leaning heavily on a stick.

'Are you . . . Reverend Kempe?'

'I am Harold Kempe.' A puzzled expression crossed the parson's face. 'Should I know you?'

'I'm Toby Lovell. I have a letter of introduction to you from Captain Kempe. I believe he wrote to you about taking me on as your curate at Porthluney? I have written too . . .'

The old man appeared more confused than before.

'Why, yes . . . but that was many months ago. Did young Henry not receive my reply? I felt it best that I write to *him*. I told him the idea was quite impractical. I felt the news would be better coming to you from him.'

Toby could not hide the dismay he felt. 'But . . . I felt certain . . .'

He looked at the frail figure standing before him. Despite the very deep disappointment he felt at the rector's words, he could not bring himself to have an argument with him. Besides, it would serve no purpose. If Reverend Kempe had decided he did not want to take him on as a curate, there was absolutely nothing Toby could do about it.

'I'm sorry, sir. Captain Kempe put to sea soon after he wrote to you. He would not have received your letter. I apologise for wasting your time.'

'Time is of value only to the man or woman who believes this life to be of more importance than the hereafter. I do not. You look tired. Come to the rectory and take some refreshment while we talk. Where have you come from?'

'I travelled from Plymouth by coach this morning and have just walked from St Austell.'

'I see.' The aged parson had eyes of a startling blue and Toby had the uncomfortable feeling that they saw far more than most men would care to reveal. 'You were badly wounded at Trafalgar, I believe?'

'Yes, I came out of hospital only recently.'

The aged rector walked very slowly and with some difficulty, but his infirmity affected neither his mind nor his tongue. By the time they reached his home he had learned a little of Toby's background. Enough to form an initial opinion of his character.

At the rectory, Toby met Rosemary Kempe. Only a year or two younger than her husband, she was a busy, sprightly woman.

'This is Reverend Lovell, my dear,' said the rector, by way of introduction. 'He's the young man Henry wrote and told us about.'

'Oh? I thought you replied to Henry and said there was no place for a curate here?'

'It seems Henry returned to sea before my letter reached

him. This young man has arrived believing I would probably take him on. He's only recently been released from hospital and has travelled from Plymouth today.'

'Then you'll be feeling tired, young man. Take him to the study and pour him a glass of brandy, Harold. I'll tell Cook there will be one more for dinner.'

Toby protested that he did not want to inconvenience the elderly couple, but Rosemary Kempe would not hear of his leaving until he had dined with them.

In truth, Toby would have liked to leave straightaway. He needed to think what he was going to do now the curacy of Porthluney was not available to him. There was always the option of returning to Norfolk, of course, although he realised he would never be entirely his own man there.

As Reverend Kempe was pouring a second drink, Toby asked the question that had been troubling him since their first conversation.

'Can you tell me what led you to believe I would be unsuitable for the curacy at Porthluney, Reverend Kempe?'

'Unsuitable!' The rector paused in his pouring and gave Toby a startled look. 'Oh, no, it's nothing to do with you personally, dear boy. But I wouldn't ask anyone to take on the parish of Porthluney, not while John Bettison remains the main landowner there. The man's a rogue. A profligate. He's no respecter of God or man – and certainly not of woman.'

For a moment Reverend Kempe's quiet, scholarly manner had deserted him. Intrigued, Toby asked, 'What in particular has he done that would make it difficult for a curate to take over the parish?'

At that moment Rosemary Kempe came to the study and called the two men to dinner. It seemed the cook had been able to stretch the meal she had already prepared to cater for their unexpected guest.

When a prayer had been said and they were seated at the dining table, Reverend Kempe repeated to his wife the question Toby had put to him.

'John Bettison is an evil man,' she said, her manner as condemnatory as her husband's had been. 'He already has a third of the tithes that should be paid to the Church by his tenants. He not only tried to take away another third, but declared he would pay no more dues himself. What's more, he swore that unless Harold agreed to the arrangement, he would have him removed from the living of Porthluney. He wasn't able to do such a thing, of course, but he has forbidden all his employees and tenants to attend services at Porthluney church. He has threatened that anyone who fails to heed the warning will be dismissed and left without a home. He owns or controls almost all the land in the parish and there's no doubt he could, and would, carry out his threat. The result was that no one attended any of Harold's services. He eventually made life so difficult for us we decided to leave and come here. That was more than a year ago. There have been no services in Porthluney church since then.'

'Why should he have taken such a stand on tithes in the first place?' Toby was genuinely puzzled. 'Was there an argument between you?'

Reverend Kempe shook his head. 'The truth is, John Bettison is in severe financial difficulty. It's entirely of his own making, of course. He spends too much of his time in London, at the gaming tables. He also has a whole crop of bastard children about the parish. When he's home he's busy begetting more. Unless something entirely unexpected occurs, I think the time will come when he'll be forced to sell Porthluney.'

'Does this mean the parishioners of Porthluney have no one to care for their souls? No one to preach to them – to give them Communion or confirmation? No one to christen, marry, or bury them?' Toby was appalled at such a state of affairs.

'Those who wish to take Communion attend church in the next parish, in Gorran,' replied the rector. 'As for the other rites . . . so far the need has not arisen.'

'But it will. What will you do then?'

Reverend Kempe shrugged unhappily. 'God in His infinite wisdom will provide.'

'Perhaps He already has,' said Toby, trying not to sound

arrogant. 'I admit it isn't an ideal situation for an inexperienced curate to be faced with, but I'm willing to give it a try. With God's help I feel I might succeed.'

Harold Kempe shook his head doubtfully. 'You don't know John Bettison. He's capable of destroying the career of the most experienced parson. He's an evil man – and a powerful one.'

'So is Napoleon,' declared Toby, 'but Nelson defeated him at sea, and one day he'll be defeated on land too. Someone can surely do the same for Bettison?'

Reverend Kempe raised his eyebrows. 'Am I to understand I am entertaining another Nelson in my house, young man?'

'I wouldn't dare be so presumptuous as to suggest I possess a scrap of Nelson's genius,' said Toby with an embarrassed smile. 'But I learned from him that unless you take on the enemy you can never win the battle. I'm quite willing to take on Mr Bettison on behalf of the Church.'

Reverend Kempe looked across the table in silence for some moments and Toby's hopes rose. He thought he might have been able to persuade the older man to change his mind and take him on as a curate. Then, slowly, the rector shook his head. 'I don't think you could achieve anything. But let me sleep on it. I'll give you my decision in the morning. Now, let's talk of something else. Tell me all about the Battle of Trafalgar. My nephew passed it off as though it were no more than some trivial skirmish but I have since been told it was the greatest victory at sea since we defeated the Spanish Armada . . .'

Chapter 5

Toby slept late the following morning, far later than he had intended, but as he listened to the bustle outside in the street, he told himself there was really nothing for which he had to hurry.

He had promised Reverend Kempe he would return to the rectory at St Stephen that morning, but as the decision not to take him on as a curate at Porthluney had been taken many weeks before, Toby doubted it would have been changed overnight.

The walk to St Stephen seemed longer this morning. His legs ached and he was stiff. Consequently, Toby walked fairly slowly, increasingly aware that he had some way to go before he was fully recovered from the wounds he had received at Trafalgar.

The door to the rectory was opened by Rosemary Kempe. Instead of inviting Toby in, she directed him around the side of the building, informing him that her husband was in the garden at the back of the house.

The weather was fine and Toby thought the rector was probably enjoying the spring sunshine. Perhaps this was where he wrote his sermons in good weather?

He was surprised to find that Reverend Kempe was not sitting anywhere. Hoe in hand, he was vigorously attacking the weeds in a bed of spring flowers.

'Hello, young man. I expected you here long before this.'

'I'm sorry, sir. My walk yesterday tired me rather more than I had expected. It seems I'm not yet fully fit.'

'Of course, of course. I re-read my nephew's letter last night. It seems that you are lucky to be alive.' Then, abruptly changing the subject, he asked, 'Are you fond of gardening?'

'I've never had the opportunity to find out. I may give it a try when I have my own home and garden.'

'You must. Rosemary and I had a beautiful garden at St Michael's, Porthluney – that's its full name, did you know?'

When Toby nodded, the aged parson continued: 'I expect the garden is very overgrown now. It's very sad. Very sad indeed.'

Toby waited for him to continue his reminiscences. Instead, Reverend Kempe brought the conversation back to the letter he had received from Captain Kempe.

Leaning on his hoe, he said, 'Henry spoke very highly of you. He says that when he was wounded and his first lieutenant lay dying, you used your initiative to save his ship.'

'I did what I felt needed to be done at the time,' said Toby, modestly.

'Henry also swears he owes his promotion to you.'

'I doubt that. Captain Kempe is a skilful and courageous officer. He'll undoubtedly be an admiral by the time this war is over.'

'It's kind of you to say so. His family are very proud of him. I feel we owe you something too. A curacy, perhaps?'

Toby looked at Reverend Kempe in delighted disbelief. 'You mean . . . you'll take me on as your curate at Porthluney?'

'If it's still what you want, after everything I've told you about the problems of the Church there?'

'It's what I want . . . *very* much.'

'In that case, the curacy is yours.'

Reverend Kempe leaned more heavily on his hoe. 'You can move in to the rectory as soon as you wish. Make a start on restoring the garden. I have already spoken to Mr Fortescue – he is the patron and lives here, in St Stephen. He would have seen you himself but I only just caught him before he set off for London this morning. He sends his good wishes and will no doubt pay you a visit when he returns. In the meantime, I will write to the bishop and inform him. All that remains is for me to wish you well – and to pray for you.'

'Thank you. Thank you, Reverend Kempe. I promise I'll do nothing to let you down.'

The aged rector smiled sadly. 'I don't doubt that, my son. All I wish is that I was presenting you with a parish with no complications. But there are many good people there. They'll no doubt seek you out in time – and you have far more of that on your side than I have.'

Spying another weed, Reverend Kempe attacked it with the hoe before returning his attention to Toby. 'Your new parish is somewhat spread out and some of the hills are extremely steep. Your legs are hardly ready for such country.'

'I'll manage.'

'I've no doubt you will. But I can help you do more than "manage" – if you are not a proud man?'

'I'm sorry . . . I don't understand.'

Reverend Kempe smiled. Putting down the hoe, he retrieved the walking stick which had been leaning against a nearby garden seat. 'Come with me.'

With Toby following, the rector walked to the far end of the garden. Here there was a small paddock, surrounded by a fence constructed from split young trees. Inside the paddock, munching away at a small pile of hay, was a donkey.

'It's a present for you, to celebrate your taking on your first parish.'

'Are you quite certain?' Toby looked from the donkey to the rector.

'I shall never ride this or any other animal again,' explained Reverend Kempe. 'A donkey will prove easier on your leg muscles – but you'll need to protect your knees and shins. His name is Nipper, for reasons which will unfortunately become apparent to you when you come to ride him.'

'It's very generous of you,' said Toby, 'but what has pride to do with it?'

'A donkey is not the most noble of mounts,' replied the rector. 'There are many, especially youngsters and Wesleyans, who find it amusing to see a parson riding an ass.'

'A donkey was good enough for our Lord,' replied Toby. 'It's a blessed animal.'

Reverend Kempe's smile was broader this time. 'You will probably think of a number of additional adjectives to describe Nipper before the day is out. Nevertheless, I have no doubt you will become as fond of him as Rosemary and I are. He does not lack a certain "character". One that is more becoming in an ass than in a human, perhaps, but he's always proved to be a willing enough beast. Now, come inside and have a drink before you go on your way. Rosemary has been baking this morning. She has made bread and a cake or two to tide you over during your first days at Porthluney.'

Early that same afternoon, Toby left St Austell behind. He took the road that would take him to the rectory of St Michael's, Porthluney. The trunk containing his belongings would follow the next day, despatched on a wagon by the landlord of the White Hart inn.

Toby's left arm and right knee were sore, Nipper having lived up to his name and reputation. Nevertheless, he was a very happy man. He was on his way to take up a new way of life in rural Cornwall.

He was the curate of Porthluney.

Chapter 6

Toby's route to Porthluney provided him with an insight into the varied nature of the county in which he was taking up a living and making his home.

First of all he sampled the pleasures of a busy small town. Riding through St Austell's narrow streets was made extremely hazardous by lumbering great wagons drawn by teams of powerful horses. Loaded with blocks of China clay from the workings to the north of the town, they were on their way to the southern harbours of Par, Pentewan and Charlestown.

Once clear of the town, he found himself skirting a mining complex which extended over the nearby hills and valleys. Tall chimneys threw plumes of smoke to the wind while clattering tin stamps beat out an uneven rhythm that shook the earth about them.

A couple of miles farther on the road flirted with the sea before taking an erratic course inland. Toby was now riding between small green fields where cows, sheep and horses grew fat on the rich spring grass.

It was here, in a narrow, high-banked lane, that he came across a cart leaning at an acute angle upon a broken wheel.

A man dressed in sober black serge clothing and a round low-crowned hat with a broad brim, was struggling to raise the cart from the ground. A very heavily pregnant woman, dressed in plain grey, with a poke-bonnet shading her face, was waiting to prop up the axle with a piece of wood apparently cut from the hedgerow.

Nearby, a girl aged about five sat on the ground peeling the bark from a hazel twig in a desultory manner. The horse, freed from the shafts, grazed quite happily nearby.

'Here, let me give you a hand.' Dismounting from the bad-tempered donkey, Toby tied its reins to the low-hanging branch of a nearby tree.

Grasping the bottom edge of the body of the cart, he nodded at the perspiring man. They heaved together and the broken wheel rose clear of the ground. A moment later the support had been put in place. The man straightened his back as though it was giving him pain and breathed a sigh of relief.

'Bless thee for performing a Christian deed, friend. I've been struggling for half-an-hour to no avail.'

It was not the way a countryman would normally address a minister of the Church of England, but Toby did not take offence. He was looking at the woman, who was very pregnant indeed and appeared to be in some discomfort.

'Is there anything more I can do to help?'

The other man shook his head. 'We will be all right now. I won't be able to repair the wheel properly, but by nightfall I should have fixed it well enough to carry us all home.'

'Not before then?' The man's wife sounded anxious. 'Bethany will be concerned for us. The children will want feeding and putting to bed.'

'Thou must go home then. I'll keep Ruth here with me.'

'I want to go with Ma,' said the young girl immediately.

'Why not allow me to escort them home?' suggested Toby. 'Your wife can ride my donkey while Ruth and I walk.'

'It is a kind offer,' said the wife. 'Unfortunately, Ruth cannot walk more than a few yards. She's a cripple.'

As though the words were a signal, Ruth rose awkwardly to her feet. Arms outstretched, and swaying from side to side alarmingly, she covered the short distance to her mother with the gait of a drunken sailor, her legs threatening to buckle beneath her slight body with each step.

Her mother caught her at the end of the brief walk just as she overbalanced and began to fall to the ground.

The grin of triumph on the face of the small girl told

Toby the brief, awkward walk had been staged especially for his benefit.

'I thought you said she couldn't walk very well,' he protested. 'That was a splendid effort.'

Speaking to the man once more, Toby said, 'Your wife can ride my donkey and I'll be Ruth's mount. She can ride on my shoulders.'

Instead of replying directly, the man said, 'Thou art a Protestant minister, but not from these parts?'

'My name is Toby Lovell. I'm on my way to take over the curacy of Porthluney.'

The woman drew in her breath sharply and the man said, 'If thou art bound for Porthluney thee will find problems enough without adding to them by being seen to help us. We belong to the Society of Friends. We are Quakers.'

'Your dress and manner of speech told me that when first we met,' said Toby. He had remembered that Quakers recognised no titles for those with whom they had occasion to speak. Their belief was that all mankind was equal in the eyes of God, be they man or woman, preacher or beggar. 'Now, would you care to help your wife mount the donkey? I'll need to hold his head. He isn't named Nipper for nothing.'

After only a moment's hesitation, the man said, 'Bless thee again, friend. I am Hosking, Jacob Hosking. This is my wife, Muriel. As well as Ruth we have five more children at home. They are being looked after by Muriel's sister. It would be a great relief for everyone were Muriel to be home with them before dark.'

'Then we'd better be on our way.'

Jacob Hosking helped his wife on to the donkey's back. They all laughed when Nipper showed his bad temper by trying to turn his head and bite, and Toby apologised for the animal's behaviour. After handing the reins to Muriel, he swung the squealing young girl on to his shoulders and they set off.

They had not gone far when Toby said, 'I've offered to see you to your home, but I have no idea where you live!'

'We have a cottage close to Boswinger.' The woman's smile was as gentle as her voice. 'It's called Hemmick

Cove. I will guide thee. Jacob works a small fishing boat from there.'

Remembering the problems Rector Kempe had experienced with the Porthluney landowner, Toby asked, 'What do you do about paying tithes to Mr Bettison?'

He was aware that Quakers held strong views against paying tithes to either landlord or the Church of England.

A smile crossed Muriel's face once more. 'Our cottage and the land about it don't belong to the Bettisons. Jacob has come to an arrangement with the owners.'

She looked away for a moment before giving Toby a sidelong glance that made him realise she was still a young woman. In spite of the half-dozen children her husband had mentioned, she was probably younger than he!

'Perhaps thou should ask Jacob to mediate with John Bettison for thee. Though I fear Bettison is not a man who is ready to listen to reason.'

'You've met him?'

She nodded. 'Three times. The first was when he came to try to buy us out. The second time was because he had met my young sister. He expected her to submit to him as do a great many of the estate girls, if rumour is to be believed.'

She was quiet for a few minutes and Toby prompted her, 'What about the third meeting?'

'That was when Bettison came to threaten what he was going to do because neither Jacob nor Bethany would fall in with his wishes.'

'What did you do?'

'We prayed for him. We asked that some of the peace we enjoy might come into his life. What would thou have done?'

Toby knew that, as a minister of the Church, he should have been able to say he would have taken the same line as Jacob Hosking and his Quaker family. Yet he found it difficult to lie to this woman. Neither could he tell her the truth of what was in his mind.

'I don't know.'

'I expect thou wouldst have done the same. Thou art a kind man, or thee would not have stopped to help us. I know of no other minister in these parts who would. Where were thou before coming to Porthluney?'

Toby told her in a few words, but this did not prove sufficient for the Quaker woman. By the time the small party began to descend the path that led to her home, Muriel knew a great deal more about Reverend Toby Lovell than he realised he had told her.

In return, she told him of the lives of her family and much of what went on in and around Porthluney.

There was just the one small cottage in the cove they were now approaching and it was here that Jacob and Muriel had their home.

It was a beautiful and secluded spot. A place where a man or woman might find God, each in his or her own way.

Chapter 7

The first person to see the trio coming slowly and carefully down the wide cliff path was a small girl.

She shielded her eyes with a hand and then hurried inside the house. She was out of sight for only a few minutes before reappearing. Behind her the remainder of the family spilled out through the open door.

There were a number of young children and a dark-haired woman of perhaps twenty-two, with a baby in her arms.

The woman would have stood out in any group. Here, among this small, plainly dressed family of young girls, her long black hair made a striking contrast to the subdued greys of the clothes worn by herself and the others.

She was tall too, taller than either Jacob or Muriel Hosking.

'Is something wrong?'

The young woman called the question to her sister after giving Toby only the briefest of glances. 'Where's Jacob?'

'A wheel broke on the cart. Toby stopped to help and very kindly offered to bring Ruth and me home.'

Remembering her manners, Muriel said, 'Toby, this is Bethany, Bethany Poole, my younger sister. Toby is taking over as the Protestant minister of Porthluney.'

Bethany nodded in his direction and he felt her studying him as he was introduced to the children.

The young girls clustered about their mother as she was helped to the ground by Toby. Then she took the baby from her sister.

As Toby lowered Ruth to the ground carefully, grateful to relieve his aching arm and shoulder muscles, she was promptly picked up by her young aunt.

'Toby hasn't even had a chance to see his church or the rectory yet,' said Muriel. 'He'll be wanting to get on.'

'Thou wilt come in for a drink of water first, at least?' suggested Bethany. 'It isn't every day a Church of England minister pays us a visit. In fact, we've never had one here before.'

'Thank you very much for the offer, but I'm eager to reach Porthluney well before dark. No one has lived in the rectory for more than a year. There will no doubt be one or two things to be done.'

'One or two!' Muriel voiced her disbelief. 'Thou wilt need to light fires in every room, air the bedding . . . there are a hundred and one things to be done. Thou should never have offered to bring Ruth and me home. Thou has far too much to do.'

'I'll go and help him.' The unexpected offer came from Bethany.

Toby saw a disapproving expression cross Muriel's face. Bethany saw it too.

'Biddie can come and help me. She's good at housework, aren't thou, Biddie?'

The eldest of the Hosking girls smiled shyly and inclined her head.

'There's really no need . . .'

Toby's protest was cut short by Bethany. 'There was no need for thou to see Muriel and Ruth safely home – and a great many reasons why thou should not – but thou brought them home just the same. One good turn deserves another. Come on, Biddie. Put on thy Sunday shoes. We're going to help the minister.'

The small party had been travelling for some minutes in silence before Toby said, 'I'm no expert on accents but you and your sister don't speak like any of the Cornish folk I've met so far.'

'That's because we're not Cornish. Muriel and I are from Guernsey.'

'Not many Channel Islands girls find their way to England. What brought you here?'

'Jacob. Some years ago he was on a fishing boat that was

wrecked on the Guernsey coast in a storm. He was hurt and our family nursed him back to health.'

'It was fortunate that he fell in with other Quakers when he was so far from home.'

'Jacob wasn't a Friend when he came to the island but he was by the time he left, and Muriel came to Cornwall with him. I travelled with our parents when they paid them a visit. They returned to Guernsey, I remained here.'

'Do you ever miss Guernsey? It's a very pretty island.'

'Thou hast been there?' Bethany was genuinely surprised that a Church of England minister – and such a *young* minister – should have visited the island.

'Yes, I was with Nelson's fleet when it put in to St Peter Port.'

At Bethany's urging, he told her something of his life in Nelson's navy, glossing over the wounds which had brought his naval service to a premature conclusion.

'So thou have never actually worked in a parish before?'

'No, it's a new beginning for me.'

'Thou could have chosen one where thou would have been given a warmer welcome than will be given thee by the people of Porthluney.'

'So I believe.'

They were passing a small, thatched cottage as they talked. In the doorway a shrivelled old woman was seated on a stool. She peered at them as though she could not believe what she was seeing.

Toby raised his hat and called out a greeting. He received no indication that the old woman had heard.

He smiled briefly at a sudden thought. He and the others made an ill-assorted party. A Church of England curate, a young Quaker woman, and Biddie, who was taking a turn at riding on Nipper.

Still chatting quite happily, they arrived at the rectory. There was a sad, neglected air about the place and they found the same inside when Toby opened the door for them.

It smelled damp. There was also a great deal of black mould around the frames of the windows.

Toby was still wondering where he should make a start when Bethany took charge. She found cleaning materials in a cupboard and handed a duster to Biddie. The young girl's task was to remove the thick layer of dust that had accumulated on much of the furniture.

While Biddie disturbed the dust and sent it rising in the room, Bethany went around opening all the windows. As she did so she told Toby to find wood and kindling and light fires in every grate, upstairs and down.

When all the windows stood wide open, Bethany found a broom and set to work vigorously, adding to the dust Biddie was raising.

Little more than an hour later the place looked much cleaner and Toby was beginning to feel more at home. Fires burned in the grates of every room and bedding was hanging over the backs of chairs placed around the kitchen fire.

Outside, the light was beginning to fail and Bethany said she should be taking Biddie home.

'Of course. You've been a wonderful help. Had you not been here I would still be standing around helplessly, wondering where I should begin.'

'All the linen needs to be washed,' declared Bethany. 'But thou should be all right for tonight. I'll come back in the morning and sort things out a little better. Make certain thou build up the fires before going to bed and try to keep them in all night.'

'I hope Jacob has arrived home safely by the time you get there – and thank you again. Thank you both, and God bless you.'

'He does that every day,' replied Bethany. 'But may He bless thee too.'

Toby watched them walk away. Biddie turned to wave before they both disappeared around a bend in the narrow lane. He knew he should have told Bethany there was no need to come back to the rectory again. That she *ought* not to come. Making friends with a Quaker family on his first day in the parish would not endear him to the community – especially, he suspected, John Bettison.

But he had *not* told Bethany to stay away. He thought

about her now as he went back inside the rectory. It seemed empty and quiet now the others had gone.

Bethany appeared to be a bright and intelligent young woman. Attractive too. She also had an easy way with her that only just fell short of boldness, and he found it strangely disconcerting.

It was probably because the Quakers, or 'Friends' as Bethany insisted upon calling them, regarded their womenfolk as being the equal of men.

This was Toby's first opportunity to experience the result of such a policy at first hand. His initial reaction had been one of shock. It was quickly followed by disapproval, until he faced up to the fact that such feelings stemmed from his own prejudice.

He admitted there was not the slightest hint of impropriety in Bethany's manner towards him, even though she spoke to him as an equal.

He reminded himself that this was one of the reasons Quakers had run into trouble in the past. They accepted only the Lord as superior to those He had made in His own image, whether they be man or woman. They would bow their heads to no one else.

Similarly, they would not concede that any man or woman was *less* than another.

Their views were at odds with the teachings of the Established Church to which Toby belonged. They also clashed head-on with those who enjoyed the privileges to which they had been born and claimed as their unearned right.

Toby knew all this, and yet he knew he wanted to see Bethany again – and intended seeing her. He eventually eased his conscience about allowing her to come to the house again by telling himself he would learn much more about the Society of Friends from her. If there were a number of Quakers living in his parish then he *should* know everything possible about them.

Chapter 8

Bethany did not come to the rectory the next day as she had promised. Nor did she put in an appearance the day after.

Toby was disappointed, but there was much to occupy his mind. The little church of Porthluney had been as neglected as the rectory during Reverend Kempe's absence. Toby set about cleaning it up as best he could.

On the evening of the second day, he answered an unexpected knock at the door of the rectory to find Jacob Hosking standing outside.

Toby had spoken to nobody since Bethany had left the rectory. He was consequently delighted to welcome his visitor and invited him in.

'Come inside, Jacob. It's nice to see you. I hope you succeeded in fixing your cart and reached your home safely?'

'I did, thanks to thee, but I won't come in. I'm here to apologise on behalf of Bethany, for not coming to help thee around the house as she promised.'

'That's all right, she's entitled to change her mind.'

'Oh, she wouldn't have done that. Not after giving her word. But my Muriel went into labour during that same night. It wasn't the easiest of births. In fact, it has been the worst she has ever had. The baby, another girl, did not arrive until the early hours of this morning. Muriel is exhausted. So too is Bethany. She was with Muriel the whole time. However, baby Sophie is well, for which we thank the Lord. But Muriel will need her sister to take care of her for a while yet. Bethany asked me to come and speak to thee. She suggests thou should find someone else to come in and help you out.'

Toby was disappointed that Bethany would not be coming to work at the rectory, but he tried not to allow his feelings to show to her brother-in-law.

'I don't really know anyone yet. I wouldn't know where to begin . . .'

'No doubt thou wilt be paying a call on John Bettison at the manor before too long. Whilst thou art there, have a word with Ada Hambly. She's Bettison's housekeeper and a good and honest woman. She doesn't agree with all that Bettison is doing. I believe she has told him so on more than one occasion. Fortunately for her, she's worked for the family for far too long to be dismissed for expressing her opinions – and is too old to care anyway.'

Toby knew he would need to visit the manor house before very long. There needed to be an understanding, at least, between Bettison and the Church – and as quickly as possible if Toby's curacy was to mean anything.

'Thank you, Jacob. I'll call at the manor tomorrow. My congratulations to you and your wife on the birth of your new daughter. I hope Muriel is soon well again. Thank Bethany, and Biddie too, for their help the other evening. I must admit, I found talking to Bethany a most refreshing experience. She's a very self-assured young woman.'

Jacob smiled. 'Quaker women are equal to the men – and Bethany is more equal than most.'

Toby rode to Porthluney Manor the next morning. It was an imposing but old house, set back from a wide, sandy cove that cut deep into the coastline.

As he approached the front door on Nipper he had a feeling he was being watched. However, no one came out to take the donkey from him.

Finding a hitching-post, he tied Nipper to it and walked the couple of steps to the front door. Here he tugged hard on the bell pull.

He had to repeat the summons twice more before the door opened and a uniformed butler stood before him.

'Can I help you, sir?'

'I'm the new curate at St Michael's. I thought I should come and pay my respects to Mr Bettison.'

The butler seemed embarrassed when he said, 'I'm sorry, sir, but would you mind going to the servants' door, at the rear of the house?'

Toby could not believe he had heard the man correctly. 'I'm here to speak with Mr Bettison.'

'Yes, sir, and I am very sorry . . .' the butler spoke as though his apology was sincere '. . . but neither Mr nor Mrs Bettison is here at present. If Mr Bettison were, I wouldn't dare stand here talking to you like this. He becomes extremely angry if his orders are disobeyed.'

'I see. I'm obliged to you for the warning, but I am a servant of God – not of Mr Bettison. When I call again, and I fully intend doing so, it will be to this door.'

The butler looked unhappy. 'I'd rather you didn't, sir. It will make things very difficult for some of us.'

'That's something you must take up with your master, not with me.'

John Bettison's slight was to the Church, not to himself, and Toby realised it would not be fair to vent his anger on the butler.

'As Mr Bettison is not here, I should like to speak to Mrs Hambly. I understand she is his housekeeper?'

The butler hesitated and Toby thought he was about to repeat the suggestion he should go to the back door. Instead he said, 'You'll find her in the kitchen garden, sir.' He pointed to a high-walled enclosure at the side of the house. 'She's with the head gardener, discussing the needs of the house during the coming year.'

Turning away, Toby made his way to the walled garden. The door stood open and he passed inside to a neat, well-laid out vegetable garden.

Not far away a tall, grey-haired woman was talking to a gnarled old man. When she saw Toby she left her companion and walked to meet the curate, the shadow of a frown on her face.

'Good morning, can I help you?'

'You must be Mrs Hambly? I'm Reverend Lovell. I've been appointed as curate at Porthluney by Reverend Kempe.'

'Well! That's a pleasant surprise, I must say. It's high

time we had someone at the rectory to take care of things in the parish.'

'I understand it's not entirely Reverend Kempe's fault that you've been without anyone for so long.'

'That's as may be, but when a man's too old to fight the Lord's battles it's time he retired and appointed a younger man. Someone like yourself, who's not afraid to stand up to Master John. Take a tip from me, Parson. Fight him, and don't retreat. That was the way to treat him when he was a small boy, and it's the only way to deal with him now.'

Toby was astonished to find this woman so outspoken about her employer.

As though reading his mind, she said, 'I've always told Master John what I thought. I've told everyone else too. He won't get rid of me because I run his house too well. There was a time when he knew he would have to answer to his mother if he tried, and even he wouldn't upset her.'

'Perhaps *she* is the one I should speak to about the problems of the Church, here in Porthluney?'

'She's dead and gone now, and it would have done you no good anyway. She had leanings towards the Quaker faith and would have backed her son on the tithes issue, even if she agreed with him on nothing else.'

Toby thought he was beginning to understand why John Bettison had not been able to find some means of taking over the land occupied by the Hosking family.

'. . . but you haven't come out here to the kitchen garden to discuss the problems of your Church. That's between you and Master John. Was there something else you wanted to speak to *me* about?'

'Yes, I'm in need of someone to come in and clean the rectory. Perhaps to cook for me occasionally, too.'

'What makes you think I can help you?'

'I spoke to Jacob Hosking last night. He suggested I should have a word with you.'

Ada Hambly appeared startled. 'You were talking to a Quaker – and he was helpful to you?'

'That's right.' Toby gave the housekeeper brief details of his earlier meeting with Jacob Hosking. When he stopped talking, she looked at him with an expression that was akin to respect.

'Well! If we now have a curate who is willing to help Quakers and receive their help in return, there's hope for us! We might just see an end to this stupid feud between Master John and the Church!'

'I'd like to think so, but that will depend a great deal upon Mr Bettison's attitude towards me.'

'I think you already know what that will be. I suggest you don't hold your breath waiting for it to change, but I wish you well. In the meantime, I think I know someone who might be willing to come and work for you at the rectory. I'll speak to her and send her to you.'

Riding away from the manor house, Toby realised he had met yet another strong-minded woman. Perhaps there was something in the air of this part of Cornwall that made them so?

He wondered whether all the women in the Porthluney parish were the same.

Chapter 9

The following day was Sunday. There was still a great deal of work to be done in the church, but Toby was determined there should be a service, whether or not any of his parishioners attended.

He would have liked to be able to talk the matter over with the Porthluney churchwardens, but Reverend Kempe had told him the wardens had resigned at the outset of the quarrel between the Church and their landlord, and Toby did not know their names.

Determined the parishioners should be in no doubt that something was happening in their church, Toby spent ten minutes ringing one of the six bells in the tower. It drew no one to the church, but he hoped it might provoke a twinge of conscience in those who heard the sound.

He conducted a full service in the empty church. Although it was a disappointing beginning to his curacy, he was convinced he had gained something from the experience. It somehow brought him closer to the church that was going to be at the centre of his life for the foreseeable future.

He returned again later that day for an evening service. This time he was accompanied by a dog of the type used by farmers to round up sheep and cattle. It had come from the hedgerow along the lane and followed him, even when he entered the church.

Normally, he would have shooed the animal out, but as it settled down in the aisle quite happily, he did not bother. He and the animal would share the church between them.

When Toby ended the unwitnessed service, the dog followed him from the building. Outside, Toby saw a woman waiting in the shadows beside a tree in the churchyard.

He greeted her with surprised delight. 'Are you here for

the service? You're late but that doesn't matter, we can go back inside . . .'

The woman interrupted him hurriedly. 'Oh, no, sir. I'm not here to come to no service. Mind you, it'd be a lot easier on me poor legs than having to walk all the way to Gorran to attend church. But I daren't set foot inside your church, sir, not with me living in a house owned by Mr Bettison. No, I'm Rose Henna, sir. I've been sent here by Mrs Hambly. She said as you were looking for someone to take care of things in the rectory.'

'Oh, yes.'

Toby hoped his disappointment did not show too much. This heavily-built woman had not come to worship in his church. Neither was she as bright or as attractive as the last woman who had worked to clean the rectory . . .

He shook off such thoughts as being unworthy. It would be good to have someone to talk to. Someone able to tell him what he needed to know about his church-shy parishioners.

It was almost dark out here now. He could not see the woman properly. 'You'd better come along to the rectory and we can talk about it.'

'Of course, sir. I thought you might say that, so I've cooked a couple of pasties for you. They'll only need a bit of heating up in the oven. They've got real meat in 'em too. Jack Gilbert killed a pig yesterday and we got a piece of it.'

'That sounds wonderful, Mrs Henna!'

He meant it. The last decent meal he had eaten was at the inn at St Austell. He had never learned the art of cooking. The years spent on board one of His Majesty's men-o'-war had done nothing to teach him culinary skills.

'Shoo! Go on, off with you.'

Rose flapped a hand at the dog which was following them along the lane from the church.

'Do you know whose dog it is, Mrs Henna? It's a friendly animal. It found me earlier and has kept me company all evening.'

'I don't reckon it rightly belongs to anyone now, sir – and I'd be happy if you was to call me Rose, same as everyone else does. It was Tom Stephen's dog, but he was taken to the workhouse a while ago and died there two months since. Tom had a son, but he's not been seen for a couple of years. Not since he went off to Plymouth, or some such far off place. The old dog's been living on scraps and whatever it can catch for itself.'

'Poor old chap. Well, as he seems to be the only friend I've made since coming here, I'll give him a home. Do you happen to know what name he answers to?'

'Well, I used to hear Tom calling him "Nap", but I think that's short for Napoleon.'

'It's a very good name for a dog too. Come on, Nap. I intend doing full justice to Rose's pasty, but I'll make certain there's something left over for you.'

By the time the short distance to the rectory had been covered, Toby knew much of Rose's history – and even more of that pertaining to her neighbours.

Rose had been twice widowed. Wed at eighteen, her first husband, Francis Jane, had been lost at sea when they had been married for five years. He had left her to bring up a young daughter as best she could. This she did, marrying her second husband when the daughter was eight, only to have him die four years later.

'She's eighteen now,' said Rose, 'and it's a troublesome age to be sure, although I suppose she's a good girl really, all things considered.'

'In what way is she troublesome, Rose?'

'It's mixing with the wrong sort, I reckon. Giving her ideas above her station. That's never good for any young girl.'

'What work does she do?' They were entering the rectory now and the dog came in through the doorway behind them.

'Well, she doesn't seem to work anywhere for very long. She painted flowers on vases and bowls and the like for a potter over by Tregony for a while, and met some peculiar folk over there. Every so often the potter would up and go off somewhere. To London or Bristol – somewhere like that. Then she'd be sitting at home with nothing to do for a month or more, until he came back. For the last month or so she's been working for Eli Whitnick over at Portloe, making fishing nets, but I don't know how long it'll last. It's not her sort of work, as she keeps telling me.'

Toby remembered Reverend Kempe telling him about Portloe. The small fishing village was not part of the Porthluney Estate, but its tithes were due to the Porthluney church. However, none had been paid since the dispute had broken out between the Church and the manor.

They were in the kitchen now. Rose looked about the room with a critical eye and shrugged off her coat before continuing her story.

'I've told Charlotte many a time she should settle down with a proper job, like the other girls around here. But she don't want to listen, sir. I suppose eighteen ain't a listening age.'

Crossing to the grate, she attacked the fire vigorously with the poker. 'I'll just put this pasty in the oven for you, then have a little sweep around before I go. I'll make a real start on it tomorrow, when I come in.'

Toby could not recall having told Rose that her employment with him had been confirmed, but it did not really matter. She was his first real contact with the people in his parish, and she obviously enjoyed gossip. He would take full advantage of her loquaciousness to learn all he could about his parishioners. One day they would return to worship in the church. By then he would already know much about each one of them.

He had studied a map that Reverend Kempe had left in the rectory. Porthluney parish was not going to be easy to bring together. Without the church there was no obvious focal point for the community – unless it was Porthluney Manor.

The only place that came close to the designation of 'village' was Portloe. Tucked away on the coast, some miles from the rectory, it had no church of its own and Reverend Kempe had made an intriguing note against it on the map.

His entry, in a neat hand, read simply, 'Fishing – when not engaged in smuggling'.

It was one of the places Toby intended visiting at the earliest possible opportunity.

Chapter 10

'It's such a pity there's all this silliness between you and Mr Bettison.' Rose Henna was standing on a chair cleaning the outside of the study window which stood open.

Inside, Toby was going over the church accounts, trying hard to make sense of them. He looked up in a fleeting moment of irritability. 'It's none of my doing, Rose. I haven't even met the man yet.'

'You know what I mean, sir. Mr Bettison stopping us all from coming to your church. I used to enjoy the services, especially the ones at Christmas and on Feast Day. I shall miss them this year.'

Toby put down his pen. 'Feast Day, Rose?'

'That's right, sir. On Saturday of next week. There's always a fair over at Tregony on that day too. No doubt all the young ones will be there. I used to go there myself when I was a young girl. In fact, I met my first husband there. It's a fine place for finding a husband. It's a hiring fair too, 'though there's not so much of that goes on now as there used to be. Not so far as the Porthluney Estate's concerned anyway.'

Rose reached inside the window to eliminate a smear that had gone unnoticed because the outside of the panes had been so dirty.

'It was the evening Feast Day service I enjoyed especially. The church was always decorated with flowers from the rectory garden and the Reverend Kempe would preach a lovely sermon. It's such a shame the way things are. You'd have had a full church for certain. Everyone would have come along to see what you're like. It's been a long time since we had a new parson here.'

'Well, I shall be putting on a service, Rose, you can be sure of that. Why don't you come along?'

She looked unhappy. 'I can't, sir. It's like I've said before, Mr Bettison would throw me out of my house right away if he was to find out – and there's no doubting that he would. Nothing stays a secret for long hereabouts. It's difficult enough me working for you, but he knows I need to earn a living.'

'Mr Bettison isn't at Porthluney Manor right now,' Toby reminded her.

'That's as may be, sir, but when he comes back there are many who'll be eager to tell him everything that's been going on while he's been away.'

Toby shrugged resignedly. 'If you change your mind, you know I'll be holding a service – whether anyone turns up, or not. In the meantime I'll go around and speak to as many parishioners as I can. They can't all be totally dependent upon the goodwill of Mr Bettison.'

If there were any parishioners willing to defy the orders of the Porthluney landowner, Toby never found them.

He called upon more than a dozen households and farms in the area without success. He would have visited more but he had begun to whitewash the interior of the church and wanted it completed before Feast Day.

He told himself it *should* be finished by then, even though it became increasingly apparent that the church would be quite as empty as it was for his Sunday services.

Wherever Toby called he was greeted politely enough, but he could not obtain any promises from those to whom he spoke that they would attend his Feast Day services.

It was depressing, and became even more so when the day arrived. He had cut many flowers from the overgrown rectory garden in order to add some colour to the newly decorated interior of the small church, and thought it looked exceptionally bright and cheerful

But he could not even ask Rose to come along and take a look at the church, in a bid to persuade her to change her mind. Today was a holiday from work for her, as it was for all who lived in Porthluney parish.

That evening, shortly before he commenced the evening service, a cold, damp mist rolled in from the sea. It made

Toby feel that his church was more isolated than ever from the remainder of the world.

He was determined to hold the service, even if his congregation consisted only of Nap the dog. Nevertheless, there was no sense in wasting candles. He lit only enough to dispel the gloom inside the church before going through the full service. It was an act of defiance, aimed at the yet unseen landowner.

He gave his sermon as he would have delivered it had the church been full. At one stage the dog pricked up its ears, as though it heard something outside. For a moment Toby's heart lifted. Perhaps someone was arriving after all.

The dog lowered its head between its paws once more and Toby continued with his lonely service.

When it was over, he pinched out the candles carefully and said, 'Let's go home, Nap. There'll be no dinner for us tonight, I'm afraid. Rose isn't in and I forgot to get anything. But I'm sure it isn't the only meal you've missed in your sad old life.'

He was carrying a small, candle-lit lantern and by its light saw a small package lying on the churchyard path. Reaching down, he picked it up and opened it. The package contained a folded length of pale blue silk ribbon.

He looked at it thoughtfully. 'So there *was* someone here, Nap. What a pity they did not come inside. Never mind, perhaps my sermon didn't fall entirely upon stony ground.'

When he reached the lych-gate, Toby paused. There was no reason why he should return to the rectory immediately. He had a sudden idea. 'Let's go and pay a call on the Hoskings, Nap. At least there'll be someone to talk to there. They might even find a bone for you.'

With the dog at his heels, Toby set off eastwards along the lane. The pale yellow light from the small lantern he carried was just sufficient to prevent him straying from the lane, and the mist was thinner now.

He must have been no more than half a mile from the Quakers' home when he thought he heard the sound of raised voices in the distance. He paused a moment to listen more closely – and suddenly there was the unmistakable sound of a gunshot!

'Come on, Nap!' Toby broke into a run. It was brought home to him immediately that he was not yet capable of such sustained activity. He settled for a slower jog.

He had not gone very far when he heard the sounds of men's voices. Talking in low tones, they were coming towards him along the lane.

Nap barked and a voice called, 'Who's there?'

'Toby Lovell, the curate at Porthluney. What's going on?'

'Nothing to concern you, Parson.' The reply came in a gruff, rough-voiced Cornish accent. 'The less you know the better it will be for you. Allow us to pass, if you please. We're carrying an injured man.'

'How badly is he injured?'

'We don't know for certain, but he's bleeding a lot.'

'Let me have a look.'

Toby sensed their uncertainty and said quickly, 'I was a naval chaplain. I'm used to dealing with gunshot wounds.'

The men came out of the mist towards him, stepping warily and trying to keep their heavily bearded faces turned from him. They need not have bothered. Toby was far more concerned with the condition of the wounded man.

In the feeble light from his lantern, Toby could see that the blood was on the man's trousers, around a hole that could only have been caused by a musket ball.

'Does someone have a knife? I want to cut his trouser leg away.'

A knife was produced and as the wounded man groaned in pain the trouser was cut clear.

It was an ugly wound. Toby thought the musket ball was probably lodged against the man's thigh bone. It would explain his great pain. However, it was the quantity of blood everywhere that worried Toby.

'Does someone have a belt or a piece of rope? There needs to be a tourniquet tied around this leg if he's not to lose all the blood in his body.'

A belt was quickly produced and Toby tied it around the leg. When this was done he used the knife to cut a piece of wood from the hedgerow. Inserting it beneath the belt, he twisted it until the blood ceased oozing from the wound.

'Get him to a doctor as quickly as you can – and don't keep the tourniquet on too long . . .'

'They're coming!' A hoarse whisper came from one of the unseen men standing in the lane.

'Who's coming?' asked Toby, sharply.

'The navy. They were waiting for us beyond Hemmick and chased us ashore.'

Toby's suspicions were confirmed by the man's words. These men were smugglers. They had quite obviously been surprised by a naval patrol. It was a duty often carried out by naval vessels when they could be spared. He was also interested in their reference to Hemmick, but this was not the moment to pursue the matter.

'Quick! Get behind the hedge and take him with you.' Toby stood away from the injured man.

'Why?'

'Do as you're told. I'll try to keep the search party from finding you.'

The naval party could be heard now, hurrying along the lane towards them.

As suddenly as they had appeared, the smugglers were lost in the thinning mist, taking their wounded colleague with them. Leaving Toby to face the pursuers.

Chapter 11

Minutes after the smugglers had taken refuge behind the hedge Toby found himself surrounded by half-a-dozen men. Someone seized his arm and a voice said, 'Well, we've got one of them, at least.'

'What do you think you're doing? Let go of my arm.' Toby spoke indignantly.

'Not likely! What's your name – and where are the others?'

'I'm the Reverend Lovell, curate of this parish. I don't know who you are or what you're after. Would it have anything to do with the men who just ran past me and went along the lane?'

'Hold that lantern up so we can see if he's telling the truth,' said a voice from the mist.

'It's a parson right enough,' said the man who had taken the lantern from Toby's hand and now held it up close to his face. He sounded disappointed.

'What are you doing out here after dark?' The man who had first spoken now came within the yellow light of the lantern and Toby could see he was dressed as a seaman.

'The hour can hardly be considered unusually late,' retorted Toby. 'I've just completed a Feast Day service. Now I'm on my way to visit some of my parishioners. Who are you?'

It was an unnecessary question. There was no official uniform for sailors, but these men wore the loose trousers and short jackets favoured by most naval men. They were obviously on duty in support of the Revenue Service.

'We're a press-gang from the frigate *Arrow*. We have a warrant to take any man suspected of being engaged in smuggling. We came across a large band who were up to no good. Those who ran past you escaped, but we've got two of their number and their boat. I suppose that will have to do for tonight. We'll go back and pick them up and return on board.'

'I'll come along with you. I have friends who live in a cove a short distance from here.'

In the faint light from the lantern, Toby saw two of the sailors exchange glances. One of them said, 'These friends of yours . . . are they in the smuggling business?'

Toby smiled. 'I doubt it. Jacob Hosking is a fisherman and a staunch Quaker. I doubt if he would break the law if his life was at stake.'

Once again there was an exchange of glances and Toby began to feel uneasy. 'What are the names of the two men you've taken prisoner?'

One of the men shrugged. 'I don't know. We didn't ask them.'

They walked away and Toby went with them.

When they reached Hemmick Cove, they passed two boats, drawn up on the sand. Both were guarded by an armed sailor.

It seemed there were lights in every room in the small cottage. Then Toby heard a voice he recognised as Bethany's, raised in protest.

He hurried ahead of the sailors and went inside the cottage. Bethany was standing in the doorway to the kitchen, arguing with a man whose dress led Toby to believe he was probably a petty officer.

'What's going on?' Toby asked Bethany.

When she saw him, a look of sheer relief appeared on Bethany's face. Hurrying to him, she grasped his arm. 'The Lord must have sent thee here. These men say Jacob is a smuggler. They are going to impress him into service.'

'We're acting within our rights.'

A man wearing the red jacket of a marine and with a sergeant's stripes on his sleeve came from the shadows of the other ground-floor room. 'Any man found smuggling can be immediately impressed for service in the King's navy. We hold an Admiralty warrant on board.'

'I refuse to believe you've caught Jacob Hosking smuggling,' declared Toby scornfully. 'He's a Quaker. He won't have broken the law. If you impress him you'll have a mutinous and innocent man on your hands.'

While he was speaking, the marine sergeant advanced across the room towards him, seemingly far more interested in Toby than in his words.

Suddenly, he stopped and his face lit up in a delighted smile. 'It . . . it's Chaplain Lovell. It *is* Chaplain Lovell! I heard you were dead, sir. Died of the wounds you received at Trafalgar. Don't you recognise me, sir? Charlie Maunder? I was a corporal on board the *Eclipse*. I was on deck when you was wounded. I'm sergeant of marines now, on board the *Arrow*. God bless you, sir, but it's good to see you again.'

The sergeant wrung Toby's hand and seemed reluctant to release it again. To the sailors with him, he said, 'You're in the presence of a hero, lads. Chaplain Lovell saved the *Eclipse* at Trafalgar. Took the wheel himself when the coxwain was killed and the captain and every other officer on deck was either dead or wounded. It was he who ordered the fallen mast and rigging cut away, then he steered the ship clear of a great Spanish man-o'-war. He'd have no doubt brought us back to port too if he hadn't been sorely wounded by another of the Spaniard's shot. We all thought he was a dying man when he was taken ashore at Plymouth.'

Releasing Toby's hand at last, he beamed at him. 'We've got some of the old *Eclipse*'s men on board *Arrow*. They'll be delighted when I tell them I've seen you hale and hearty.'

The sergeant suddenly frowned. 'But what are you doing here, sir?'

'I recovered from my wounds, Sergeant, but they told me I would never be fit enough to go to sea again. I'm now curate at a little church along the road – and what I said about this man is the truth. He's no smuggler. He's . . .'

The marine sergeant held up his hand. 'You need say no more, Chaplain Lovell, sir. Your word's good enough for me.'

Turning to the man who had been arguing with Bethany,

he said, 'Have the Quaker released – and be quick about it.'

Jacob and another man were brought to the kitchen. Toby was angry to see that Jacob had sustained an ugly bruise to his forehead, but he said nothing. He was aware that the sailors were not in agreement with the marine sergeant about releasing one of the men they had impressed.

Both men had been placed in chains. When Jacob was released he stood rubbing his chafed wrists and glaring at his captors.

'How about the other man, sir?'

'I'm no smuggler either,' said the second prisoner plaintively. 'I'm just a poor fisherman who was going about my business when all hell broke loose around me – if you'll pardon the expression, Parson. I still don't know what was happening.'

Toby did not entirely believe the young man, but he was quite obviously very frightened. Toby remembered the many impressed men he had known on board ship. Many soon settled into the life, but some were so desperately unhappy they committed suicide rather than submit to the life into which they had been forced.

'He's telling the truth, Sergeant Maunder. He's a fisherman.'

Toby told himself he was not telling a lie. The man probably *was* a fisherman. Toby did not search his conscience for what else he might have been.

'Release him too,' said the sergeant, and this time the grumbling among the men was louder.

'Is there something you want to say?' asked the marine. 'Are you doubting the word of Chaplain Lovell?'

The murmuring subsided and the newly released man said eagerly, 'Can I go now?'

The sergeant nodded.

'Thank you, sir. Thank you.' The young man inclined his head first to the sergeant and then to Toby. This done, he fled from the room as though fearful the marine sergeant might change his mind.

'I'm afraid you haven't had a very successful night, Sergeant,' said Toby, apologetically.

'Oh, it's not been wasted, sir. Not by a long way. We've got a boatload of smuggled goods and I've learned you're alive. I'd have gone to a whole lot more trouble for such news, sir. Now, I think we've upset Mr Hosking's household quite enough for one night. The best thing we can do is to take our leave and get the smuggled goods back to the *Arrow*. When I next come shoresides at Plymouth I'll pay you a visit, sir – 'though you'll likely be a bishop or somesuch by then.'

'I doubt it very much, but God bless you, Sergeant. Please give my good wishes to all the men who were on *Eclipse*.'

As the sailors filed from the house, Sergeant Maunder was telling them another story of Toby's supposed exploits on board *Eclipse* at Trafalgar.

When they had gone, Bethany turned to him. 'Well! We didn't realise we had a hero in our midst!'

'A hero thou certainly art,' agreed Jacob, fervently. 'It's the second time thou hast come to my aid. This time thou hast done more than I can ever thank thee for. Had thou not happened along it would have meant the breaking up of my family. I would have died under the lash on board ship rather than fight my fellow men.'

'Well, you haven't been impressed,' said Toby, embarrassed at Jacob's gratitude. 'You can forget about it now – but who was the other young man who was taken with you?'

'I think thou knewest, even when thou was speaking up for him,' said Jacob. 'But thou did not lie. He's a smuggler, but he's also a fisherman. He and his friends use this cove quite often. It's none of my business what they do. I could do nothing to stop them, even had I a mind to. I stay here, minding my own business, favouring neither smuggler nor Revenue men.'

'That's no doubt the wisest course,' said Toby. 'But how are Muriel and the baby? Where are they?'

'Tonight's troubles so upset Muriel she fainted away,' said Bethany. 'Some of the sailors helped me to carry her upstairs. She's up there now, with the baby. It's time I went to see how she is. Come with me and see the baby.'

She looked to Jacob for his approval and he nodded vigorously. 'Tell her I'll be up to see her when I've gathered the girls together. If you need me, call.'

Toby was following Bethany from the room when he stopped and turned back to Jacob. 'I helped some of the smugglers with a wounded man on my way here. He was bleeding badly and I applied a tourniquet. I ought to go and see if he's all right.'

'He and the others will be far from here by now. There are many women hereabouts with experience in dealing with men wounded by Revenue men. They will care for him as well as any doctor might.'

At the top of the steep, narrow staircase, Bethany knocked at a door. 'Toby's come to visit thee. Can we come in?'

Without waiting for a reply, she opened the door and Toby saw Muriel struggling to sit up in the bed. She looked desperately weak and unwell.

'Please . . . stay where you are.'

'What's happening downstairs? That was a press-gang. Jacob . . .'

'He's downstairs with the girls. Everything's all right. Toby knew the man in charge of the press-gang – or perhaps I should say, the man knew him. It seems the new curate of Porthluney is one of the heroes of the Battle of Trafalgar. He was able to persuade the press-gang to release Jacob.'

Muriel sank back in the bed. 'Thank God!' Her eyes filled with tears as she said, 'I really couldn't manage without him.'

The tears overflowed as she turned to Toby and held out her hand to him. 'Thou hast been a God-sent blessing to this family, Toby. How can we ever thank thee?'

Embarrassed by her tears, he said, 'You mustn't upset yourself. Rest now. I'll come back and see you when you're feeling better.'

Gazing down at the peacefully sleeping baby, he added, 'I look forward to meeting this little one too. She's going to be the prettiest of them all.'

'Thank thee, Toby. Bethany, wilt thou ask Jacob to come

up and see me. I know thou speaks the truth, but I want to see him . . . to hold him.'

Outside the room, as Toby and Bethany began to descend the stairs, he said, 'Your sister is very much in love with her husband.'

'Of course. Isn't that how it should be for all married couples?'

Toby thought her statement irrefutable but could think of no suitable reply.

Chapter 12

'Thou seemst to have the knack of making others happy, Toby. It must please thee.'

Bethany made the comment as she walked with him from the cottage to the lane. They picked their way carefully, without the aid of a lantern. The mist had rolled away now and Jacob had warned them that if a lantern light was seen from the sea it would be likely to bring the navy, or Revenue men, back to the cove once more.

He had given the warning as he took all the children upstairs to say goodnight to their mother before being put to bed.

'If I possess such a knack it's not one that has shown itself before,' Toby replied to Bethany's comment. 'But I was glad to be on hand to help Jacob this evening. Had he been impressed into service in the navy, his beliefs and the system would have been the death of him. That can't be right. I'm of the opinion that impressing a man is little more than authorised slavery. I am totally opposed to its use as a means of recruitment.'

'To hear thee talk of such matters it would be easy to believe thou were a Friend, Toby. The loudest voice against slavery has always been that of our people.'

'I've never doubted the sincerity of Quakers. If there's one thing I learned in the navy it's that good Christians are not confined to any one particular denomination. Neither are bad ones. I've been proud to serve with Catholics, Methodists, and many others. I've also been thoroughly ashamed of more than one member of my own Church. There are many roads leading to the Lord's house. I'll happily help a man or woman to travel along any one of them – at the same time pointing out why I think my road is the right one, of course.'

Toby stumbled on a large pebble but quickly regained his balance. 'I don't want to destroy the image you have of me by discussing theology. Not tonight. As for slavery . . . I sincerely believe that any civilised man who has ever set foot on a slave ship will campaign against slavery for the rest of his days.'

'Thou hast been on a slave ship?'

'Yes. I and the ship's surgeon went on board one in the West Indies when they had cholera raging among both crew and slaves. Conditions for the slaves were appalling beyond belief. I would add my support to anyone, be they Christian or heathen, who fought to end the trade.'

Bethany was quiet for some time, then she said, 'Thou art an unusual churchman, Toby Lovell. In an ideal world thou would be lauded for expressing such views. As it is, my advice is that thou should be cautious to whom thou speaks of such matters. There are many here in Cornwall who would take thy words and use them against thee.'

'Yet, although they might come as a surprise, they don't offend you?'

'No. They echo many of my own thoughts – and those of some Friends. Even so, there are others, both Friends and members of thy Church, who are not ready to admit there is more than one way to worship the same God. Thou hast troubles enough in Porthluney, Toby. Thou would be wise to keep such thoughts to thyself.'

They had almost reached the lane now and both slowed their pace for no apparent reason.

'Hast thou been able to find someone to do thy cleaning in the rectory?' Bethany put an unexpected question to him.

'Yes. I spoke to the housekeeper at Porthluney Manor, as Jacob suggested. She sent Rose Henna along to see me. She arrived complete with two Cornish pasties for my supper! It wasn't so much a case of my taking her on to work for me as her deciding she was going to clean and cook for me.'

Bethany smiled. 'I know Rose. She's a good woman. But be careful of thy reputation if her daughter comes to the rectory to help her.'

'Oh? Why?'

Again there was an answering smile. 'She's only seventeen or eighteen but rumour has it that she's desperate to find a husband. In fact, *malicious* rumour has it that she has already found one or two husbands, only to have their wives claim them back again!'

'But . . . she wouldn't try to ensnare me. I'm the curate!'

This time his words provoked more than a smile, and Toby discovered Bethany had a very pleasant laugh. 'Hast thou been a curate for so long that thou hast forgotten thou art also a man?'

The silence that followed on her words lasted just a little too long.

'No. Perhaps there was a time at sea when it might have slipped my mind. Just recently I seem to have found much to remind me.'

More seriously now, Bethany said, 'A few minutes ago I told thee there were some things that were best left unsaid because thou hast troubles enough. Take my words to heart, Toby.'

He could have told her that he believed he had taken much more than her words to his heart, but he knew it would be a great mistake to do so after such a brief acquaintanceship. There might *never* be a right moment, but he knew, as Bethany surely must, that right now he was a very lonely man, and loneliness did not walk hand-in-hand with reason.

'I can't remember ever wanting to say what is in my mind so unreservedly to anyone before, Bethany. You're a very easy person to talk to.'

'I hope thou will always think so. But now I must return to the cottage before a scandalised Jacob comes out after me. Goodbye, Toby.'

She had actually moved a few steps from him when she stopped and spoke again.

'I am very grateful to thee for all thou hast done for Muriel and Jacob tonight. I thank thee too for trusting me with thy thoughts. Thou wilt always be a welcome visitor to the Hosking house. I hope thou wilt visit often.'

'Thank you. I look forward to becoming a regular visitor – but I trust that next time there will be rather less excitement than there was tonight.'

'We have never had such a night before! The cove is only occasionally used by smugglers, and the Revenue men sometimes pay us a visit too, but we have never before had the navy, Revenue men and smugglers there at the same time. It will probably never happen again. I think they will find somewhere else to play their games in future.'

The two went their separate ways again, but once more her voice reached him from the darkness.

'Toby!'

'Yes?'

'In all the confusion of tonight, I forgot to tell thee something of importance. Thou wilt no doubt find thy excitement elsewhere very soon. I heard today that John Bettison has returned to Porthluney Manor.'

Chapter 13

It had been Toby's intention to call on John Bettison on the Monday following Feast Day, but the landowner pre-empted him.

Toby was in his church early on Sunday, preparing for the morning service, when the landowner paid him an unannounced visit. He was dressed in riding clothes, and his whole manner exuded arrogance and a contemptuous irreverence.

Toby was in the vestry, and had just put on his surplice when he heard the footsteps on the hard stone floor of the aisle. The heavy, firm tread told him this was no potential worshipper, entering church to take part in a service.

Adjusting his surplice, he emerged from the vestry and the landowner turned to face him.

Toby had been expecting an elderly man, but John Bettison was probably only in his late-thirties or early-forties. Heavily built, he was inclined to flabbiness. This, and the colour of his face, suggested he was a man over-indulged in all that went with good living.

Before Toby could extend a greeting, John Bettison demanded, 'Who are you – and what's all this nonsense?'

The sweep of his arm took in the altar with its lighted candles, the Communion accoutrements, and the flowers that had been placed in the church to celebrate Feast Day.

'All this "nonsense", as you choose to describe it, is the normal preparation for a Sunday service. I'm Toby Lovell, newly appointed curate for Porthluney. You are Mr Bettison, I presume?'

'By your very presence here you are already presuming too much, Curate. Rector Kempe chose to leave Porthluney and take a more remunerative living. The move suited everyone. My tenants now go to church at Gorran and are perfectly content to do so. We don't need a parson at Porthluney.'

'The move might have suited you, Mr Bettison. I've so far found no one else who is happy with the situation. They can attend other churches, it's true, but it causes them considerable inconvenience. You are denying them the right to worship in their own church, in the place where their parents and grandparents worshipped. Where they were christened and married. The place where their ancestors – and yours – are buried. For their sakes I beg you to reconsider your ban on allowing them to worship in this, their own church.'

'Are you willing to renegotiate the tithes claimed from me by the Church?'

Toby shook his head. 'I have no power to do that. Only the bishop can authorise tithe changes – and he would probably need to consult the Church authorities first. Besides, I understand from Reverend Kempe that such a change has already been ruled out.'

'Then I'm damned if I'll reconsider *my* stand on the matter!'

'A church is not the place for profanity, Mr Bettison. Nor can a personal quarrel justify interference with the worship of any man, woman or child. I'm willing to meet you anytime, anywhere, to discuss our differences over tithes. In the meantime, it should not – indeed, it *must* not – be allowed to come between your tenants and God.'

'I wouldn't be dictated to by Rector Kempe and I'm damned if I'll take advice from a whippersnapper of a curate. To hell with you – and with Kempe – and I'll profane as much as I like, wherever I like. I'm the landowner of just about the whole of this parish, Lovell. You'll find life impossible here without my support. Before the year's out you'll be glad to follow Kempe's example and move to another parish – and you'll go without receiving any tithes from me. In the meantime, you and that dog over there can have the church to yourselves.'

'If things are allowed to continue as they are the bishop

will no doubt bring the tithe issue before the appropriate court, Mr Bettison. Should that happen I fear you will lose. I pray that we can reach agreement before then.'

Toby was surprised at his calmness in the face of Bettison's barely controlled rage. He felt it was *he* who was in command of the situation, and not the Porthluney landowner.

'As you're here in the church, won't you at least stay long enough to take Communion?'

John Bettison gave him a look that would have caused one of his tenants to quake in their shoes. Toby fully expected him to utter another oath. Instead, Bettison turned away and stalked heavy-footed from the church. Toby's first meeting with the Porthluney landowner was at an end.

Some time during that night, Toby had a more welcome visitor, albeit one who preferred to remain unseen.

Opening the door early the following morning to allow Nap to go outside, Toby discovered a small wooden keg on his doorstep. It was full. When he brought it inside the house and prised out the bung, he discovered it contained brandy of a very high quality.

There was no message left with the keg, but Toby needed none. He realised it was a present from the smugglers he had met on the evening of Feast Day.

Whether it had come from friends of the wounded man, or from the 'fisherman' whose release he had secured from the press-gang, he did not know.

Neither did it matter.

In Cornwall, smuggling was considered to be more a way of life than a criminal offence. This he knew from conversations he had held with officers during his service with the navy.

It was accepted that whole communities were involved in an occupation that had been carried on in the county for centuries. One that the authorities were finding it well-nigh impossible to stamp out.

The keg of brandy left on his doorstep was more than a way of saying 'thank you'. It was also a declaration of his acceptance by an important section of the community.

Toby's view of the gift was confirmed when Rose came to the rectory that morning.

'I hear you had an exciting time on Feast night, sir.'

'Really, Rose? Where did you hear about it?'

The cleaning woman coloured up and looked mildly embarrassed. 'I can't rightly remember, sir, but I know there's talk going around about it.'

'Is there, now? And what exactly have you heard, Rose?'

She had taken a broom from a cupboard in the corner of the kitchen and began vigorously attacking the seemingly spotless kitchen floor. 'I heard you helped some local men who ran foul of a naval press-gang. Actually persuaded them to give up that Quaker over by Hemmick, and young Billy Kendall from Portloe as well. Least, that's the story one of his aunts gave to me. She says it's a shame that Mr Bettison won't allow folk to come to your church.'

'Does she?' Toby was delighted that his fortunate encounter with the ex-*Eclipse* marine sergeant had given his image such an unexpected boost. But there was more to come.

'Billy's also going around telling everyone that you were at Trafalgar. That you was badly wounded there. Is it true, sir?'

'It's true, Rose. That's why I'm here, in Porthluney. I was a chaplain with the navy, but Trafalgar brought my sea-going career to an end.'

The look Rose gave her employer contained both sympathy and a new respect. 'I'm sorry to hear that, sir. After all you've been through you should have gone to a parish where you could have an easy time of things, instead of coming to Porthluney to face all this trouble with Mr Bettison. Mind you, when word gets around that you've been a sea-going man, and what you did for Billy, you'll be a whole lot more popular than Mr Bettison would like – especially among the fishermen. All *he's* ever done for 'em is to try to increase the tithes they pay out to him.'

'Ah! That reminds me, I need to speak to the fishermen of Portloe about the tithes they owe to the Church.'

The Church claimed a tenth of a fisherman's catch

as its due in the same way as it claimed a tenth of a farmer's produce. Such dues proved difficult to collect and Reverend Kempe and his predecessors had arranged that the fishermen should pay the equivalent in cash when the harvest of pilchards had been caught, salted, pressed and sold.

Toby had gone through the tithe dues and it seemed no money had been paid over for more than twelve months.

'Who should I speak to if I go to Portloe, Rose?'

'You'll need to speak to Eli Whitnick.' Rose shook her head dubiously. 'But he'll not be as helpful as he ought to be, him being a Wesleyan. He's a powerful speaker by all accounts, but a little too fond of the "Thou shalt *nots*" for my liking. Listen to Eli for long and you'll begin to believe that the Lord meant for Moses to bring more than Ten Commandments down from Mount Sinai. According to Eli that was probably all Moses could carry down, them being written on stone. He says that the Lord meant for us to have a few more. Among them would have been commandments saying there should be no singing, no dancing, no swearing, no drinking – and no smuggling, either. He has so many "dont's" that I expect it's why he's never married. He'd have no doubt said "no" instead of "yes" when he was standing with his bride at the altar.'

Toby grinned. 'Thanks for the warning, Rose. I'll bear it in mind when I speak to him. That's no doubt why he's come up with no money. I'm afraid I shall need to convince him that he's not going to get away with not paying, any more than Mr Bettison is.'

Chapter 14

Following directions given to him by Rose, Toby made his way along a narrow bridlepath across the fields. He arrived at Portloe no more than thirty minutes after setting out from the rectory. It was a cold but pleasant ride during which Nipper succeeded in biting him only once, during an unguarded moment.

One of the first people Toby met when he entered the small fishing hamlet was Billy Kendall. Seated on a bench, repairing a net, he rose to his feet and removed his hat the moment he recognised the curate.

'Good morning, Reverend,' Billy greeted him with a broad smile. 'I trust you had something to keep the cold out before your ride?'

'Not yet,' replied Toby, fully aware that Billy was alluding to the brandy left upon his doorstep. 'But I know there'll be some waiting for me when I reach home. Thank you.'

'Thank *you*, Reverend,' said Billy, fervently. 'If it wasn't for you I wouldn't be here mending my nets today. I'm a grateful man, Reverend, and with good cause. If there's ever any way I can help you, you have only to say and it'll be done.'

'I'll remember that, Billy. But I thought you were a fisherman, why aren't you out today?'

'You can see one reason from here, Reverend.' Billy pointed out to sea and for the first time Toby noticed a navy frigate anchored no more than a mile offshore. 'They're out there, daring us to put to sea. Anyone foolish enough to do so will be taken and impressed into the navy.'

'You said the frigate was one reason. Is there another?'

'Yes. There's a storm blowing up from the south-west.

When it arrives, it's not going to be comfortable out in the bay.'

Toby looked out to where the frigate rode gently at anchor. A storm did not appear imminent, but he knew better than to dismiss the forecast of a fisherman.

'Will the frigate be safe out there in a storm?'

Billy shrugged. 'It depends how bad it is. If it gets too bad they'll no doubt weigh anchor and put out to sea.'

The fisherman was probably right. Toby dismissed the frigate from his mind. 'I want to speak to Eli Whitnick, Billy. Do you know where I can find him?'

Billy's expression hardened unexpectedly. 'No. What's more, I don't care. We may be related, but as far as I'm concerned the best thing Eli could do is leave the village and go and live somewhere else. He's not wanted here.'

Toby was startled. People who lived in such places as Portloe usually formed close-knit communities. They tended to shun outsiders and exclude them from all their activities. Despite this they accepted 'frailties' of character among their own.

For it to be suggested that one of their number should leave the community and go and live elsewhere was unthinkable.

It was especially puzzling as Rose had said that Eli was a Wesleyan and a pillar of the Methodist Church. He must have done something particularly bad to stir up such ill-feeling against him.

Toby asked what it was. Billy hesitated a moment before replying.

'When we came in on Feast night it was obvious that the navy was waiting for us to put in to Hemmick Cove. With all the mist around that night they couldn't have seen us coming in. They must have known where we were going to land.'

'We *are* talking of fishing, are we?' asked Toby, sarcastically.

A grim smile crossed Billy's face. 'We all have fishing boats, Reverend – and it's the sea that provides us with a living.'

'Go on. Are you saying that Eli Whitnick informed the authorities you'd be landing at Hemmick that night?'

'There's no doubt about it. He doesn't try to hide his opposition to free-trading.' Billy used the smuggler's own term for his 'trade'. 'There's hardly a Sunday goes by when he doesn't preach against it in his chapel.'

'That doesn't mean to say he'd report you to the Revenue men, or to the navy.'

'He was seen in conversation with a Revenue man along the path above the cliffs, about a week ago. I don't think there's any doubt about it, Reverend. What goes on has never been a secret among the people who live here. There are too few of us to have secrets. He knew of our plans as well as if he'd been part of them. We don't want someone like that living among us. He was left a cottage by his brother, a year or two back, somewhere up on Bodmin Moor. It should suit him well. I don't suppose there's very much free-trading goes on there.'

Toby doubted very much whether any religious leader, whatever his denomination, would risk alienating his followers in such a manner, however strong his personal convictions. But he made no further comment.

'Where can I find him?'

'He'll either be in the chapel, or at the net-making shed, down by the water's edge. He likes to keep an eye on the two girls who work for him there. Making sure they're earning the money he pays them.'

Evading the teeth of Nipper, Toby walked him away towards the water's edge, Nap following at his heels.

Suddenly, Toby stopped and called back to Billy. 'How's the man who had a wounded leg?'

'Dan Rowe? Ask young Alice. She's one of the girls working for Eli. Dan's her uncle.'

Toby made his way towards the beach. He saw Eli's shed immediately. Two girls were seated outside. One looked up as he approached and nudged her companion.

The other girl glanced at him. He thought she seemed mildly embarrassed. Both girls looked down at the nets they were working on as he drew nearer, only pausing in their task when Nap made his way to them, tail wagging.

He put his nose on the lap of the girl who seemed most perturbed at his approach.

'I'm looking for Eli Whitnick. Do you know where I might find him?'

'I expect he's in the chapel,' replied one of the girls, with a bold glance. 'That's where he spends most of his time. More than he does fishing, or helping us make nets, anyway.'

'What's your name?' asked Toby.

'Charlotte . . . Charlotte Jane.' The bold look was there again. 'You'll be Reverend Lovell, the new curate up at Porthluney church. The one my ma works for?'

'That's right.'

Toby nodded an acknowledgement in her direction, but he addressed his next question to the other girl. She had not looked up at him since his arrival.

'You'll be Alice Rowe?'

The girl looked up in surprise. 'How do you know my name?'

Toby smiled without giving her a reply to her question. 'How is your uncle, the one who hurt his leg the other evening?'

'He lost a whole lot of blood and he's still very weak, but he's going to be all right. The doctor says he has you to thank for that.'

'I did what I could, but had he not been doing something he shouldn't, he wouldn't have got himself hurt. The next time, he might not be so fortunate.'

'I thought you were fond of preaching forgiveness and forbearance?' retorted Alice, stung to indiscretion in defence of her uncle.

'I am indeed,' agreed Toby, smiling at her.

Reaching inside his pocket, he brought out the small packet of ribbon. Handing it to Alice, he said, 'I believe this is yours?'

Taking it from him, she exclaimed, 'It's the ribbon I bought at the fair! I must have lost it during the excitement when Uncle Dan was brought home. Where did you find it and how did you know it was mine?'

'I found it outside my church, after the Feast Day

evening service. I thought someone was outside, listening. You just confirmed it when you mentioned the subject of my sermon. You should have come in. You would have been very welcome. Come along some Sunday soon – both of you. It will be nice to have some young people attend a service – and wear the ribbon. The colour will suit you.'

'Young people, indeed!' Charlotte spoke indignantly but quietly as Toby walked away, accompanied by Nipper and Nap. 'He's not very much older himself. As for saying it'd be nice to have *young* people come to church, right now he'd be happy to have *anyone* come there. I think he's got a real cheek!'

'I think he's handsome,' said Alice, gazing after him. 'I thought so when I heard him giving his sermon to an empty church. I'm even more sure now that I've met him. I think he's probably the most handsome person I've ever met.'

'You've not met enough men to know who's handsome, and who isn't! Now, if you come out with me next Saturday night, I'll introduce you to some really interesting men. You'll need to keep your mouth shut about who they are and what we get up to, but you'll find it exciting, I can promise you that . . .'

Alice was not really listening. Charlotte was always boasting about the men she knew and the things she did. Sometimes she tried to persuade Alice to accompany her. On other occasions she was secretive.

Alice believed her friend spent much of her time in a make-believe world, the men of whom she spoke merely a figment of her over-active imagination.

But the new curate at Porthluney church was not. He was also quite unlike the men of whom Charlotte was always talking. Alice wondered how she could persuade him to take an interest in her?

Chapter 15

Eli Whitnick was already on his way to the net-making shed from the chapel and Toby met him halfway.

Before he could introduce himself, Eli demanded, 'What do you think you're doing, disturbing my girls while they're working? A moment's distraction could lead to a loose knot. It only needs to happen once for the reputation I've built up over the years to be ruined.'

'I was asking the girls where I could find you. Nobody else seemed to care about telling me.'

'What's that supposed to mean?'

'It means that Methodist preachers seem to be no more popular in Portloe than do ministers of the Established Church in Porthluney.'

'We're not here to be liked. Our Lord never sought popularity when He was on earth. Neither do I. If it's what you want, you'd do better finding another way to earn a living. Now, is there anything else? I'm a busy man.'

'So busy that you've overlooked the tithe money? Last year's is still outstanding. I believe you collect it and pay on behalf of the whole Portloe community?'

'I collect it when it's there to be collected. We've had a bad year. Come here most other years and my fish cellar would be piled high with salted fish, waiting to be shipped out. Dwellings for miles around would have lanterns filled with oil from my cellar. This year every cellar in the district is empty and the cottages are lit by candlelight, if they're lit at all.'

'There's nothing in the tithe book to say that Rector Kempe demanded extra payments for the good years,' said Toby gently.

'I don't see why Methodists should pay anything to keep a preacher we neither want nor need.'

'It was never John Wesley's intention that his followers should put themselves outside the Established Church, Mr Whitnick. All who sincerely wish to worship are welcome to enter my church. That's their right. The law of the land decrees that tithes must be paid to perpetuate that right. You are aware of this. If you wish to make a complaint against the amount of the tithes you are free to appeal to the bishop.'

'I'll have no truck with the law, nor with any bishop. It would be a waste of time anyway. The courts wouldn't find me right and him wrong.'

'If it really has been a bad year for everyone I'll take it upon myself to collect only half the overdue tithes now. You can pay the remainder when this year's tithe money is due. Mind you, if this proves to be a bad year too it will come hard on everyone.'

'I'll accept no favours from you or your Church, Parson Lovell, and I hope you intend being just as firm with Mr Bettison. He's paid no tradesmen these past six months. I doubt he's been more forthcoming with the Church.'

'He'll be treated the same as anyone else, Mr Whitnick. You have my word on that.'

'Then you'll have your money tomorrow, Parson. Now I'll bid you "good day". I have work to do. It won't get done while I'm standing here talking to you.'

As the Methodist preacher walked away, Toby called after him, 'Are you friendly with the Revenue men, Mr Whitnick?'

Eli stopped and turned to face him. 'What sort of a question is that?'

'One that needs an answer if you're to gain the trust of the Portloe fishermen once more.'

'You're talking nonsense. I've never had anything to do with anyone in the Revenue Service . . .' Eli stopped talking, abruptly, as though suddenly remembering something. 'No . . . that isn't strictly true. I met a Revenue man on the cliff path some days ago and asked what he was doing. He gave me some unlikely story about waiting for a young girl.

It was more likely he was spying on the village. I told him to go on his way. If he wanted to speak to any young girl hereabouts then he should go to her parents' home and ask their permission.'

Eli snorted disapprovingly. 'I got a mouthful of abuse for my pains, but if you regard that as talking to a Revenue man then, yes, I suppose that's what I was doing. If the men of Portloe want to make something of it, then let them.'

Eli glowered at Toby. 'But why am I telling you? What I do is no more your business than it is anyone else's.'

He turned his back and walked away with a stiff gait, his whole being exuding stubbornness and indignation.

On his way out of the village, Toby paused beside Billy once more. He told him of the conversation he had just held with the Methodist preacher.

Billy was sceptical. 'He would say that, wouldn't he? He's hardly likely to admit that he told a Revenue man where to come and look for us.'

'True,' admitted Toby. 'But Eli strikes me as being a man who's likely to tell the truth, whatever the consequences to himself.'

'He's always been a great one for the truth,' admitted Billy. 'But if he didn't tell the Revenue man, then who did?'

'That I wouldn't know,' said Toby. 'I just thought I'd pass on the details of my conversation with Eli, that's all.'

'Why would you want to help a Methodist minister?' queried Billy. 'I doubt if he'd do the same for you.'

'I wouldn't be too sure about that,' declared Toby. 'If it came to bringing a man to God, or letting the devil have him, I think I know which course Eli would take. He'd probably agree with me that it doesn't really matter in the end how a man's soul is saved, just as long as it *is*.'

As Toby rode away on Nipper, Billy thought the new curate of Porthluney was unlike any parson he had ever known. If his father were not employed by Bettison, up at the manor house, he might even have paid a visit to his church, one of these Sundays.

Chapter 16

Toby had intended riding to St Stephen that afternoon, to discuss the matter of outstanding tithes with Reverend Kempe. However, as forecast by Billy, soon after midday the clouds thickened and a severe storm swept in from the English Channel to batter the Cornish coast.

It was as fierce as Billy had prophesied it would be. Heavy rain was preceded by a strong wind that caused trees and bushes to cower away from it. As it grew in severity, Toby hurried to check that all the church windows were closed before returning to the rectory.

The ferocity of the storm came as no surprise to Rose. As she made her way around the rectory, checking windows and doors, she commented, 'We have storms like this every so often. Fierce, they are, but we should give thanks to the Lord that we're on dry land and not out at sea.'

Her words reminded Toby of the frigate he had last seen anchored off Portloe. It would be in acute danger in a storm like this. He doubted whether the captain would have had time to find a safer anchorage.

Had the vessel put to sea in time it would be possible to ride out the storm, but Toby had seen little sign of activity on board before he left Portloe.

As the storm continued unabated, his unease increased. Eventually, he could sit still no longer. Walking from his study to the hall, he put on his cloak and hat.

'Where are you off to in such weather, sir?' Rose sounded appalled that he should contemplate going outside.

'I'm worried about that naval frigate, Rose. I can't just sit here and do nothing when it might well be in danger.'

'Even if there *is* something wrong, there's nothing you

can do about it, sir. You won't even be able to see it in rain like this.'

'I know you're right, Rose, but I can ask whether anyone saw it put out to sea before the storm. If they did, I'll return home with my mind at peace.'

Rose shook her head, doubtfully. 'You just take care, sir. Don't get doing anything foolish like going out along the cliff path. It's a dangerous place to be when it's wet and windy, like today.'

Toby left the house, touched by Rose's concern for him. He decided against taking Nipper. The donkey would be something extra to think about. He did not have to question whether he should take the dog. It followed him from the rectory, as it always did when he dressed to go out of the house.

Nap followed close behind him as he took the footpath across the field, using him as a shield against the gale-force wind.

The rain was being driven in hard by the wind and Toby had his head down, sheltering his face from the stinging downpour, when suddenly Nap growled.

Coming to a halt, Toby thought he heard voices. A moment later he was certain. The sound was coming from the far side of a hedgerow and the voices sounded excited.

There was a gate in the hedgerow and Toby headed towards it. He reached the gate just as a party of about a dozen men and women and a couple of children reached it. They had come from the direction of Portloe.

The party would have passed by without acknowledging his presence. This alone was unusual enough for him to ask, 'What's happening?'

'There's a ship being driven in on the coast by the storm. It should go aground somewhere between here and Dodman Point.'

The speaker glared at Toby belligerently. 'There should be plenty of pickings for all, but if you're coming along don't get greedy, that's all. Remember, we saw it first.'

Having delivered his warning, the man hurried after his companions, who were already some distance ahead of him.

Toby was astounded that anyone should speak to a clergyman in the belief that he would share in an opportunity to loot a stricken ship.

Then he realised his heavy cloak effectively hid the fact that he was a curate. It seemed his fears for the safety of the frigate were justified. Bowing his head against the wind and rain, Toby hurried after the others.

The sea could not be seen from here because of the heavy rain and Toby had difficulty in placing exactly where he was until the path began to drop down a steep hill. Suddenly, the rain eased and he saw Porthluney Manor on his left.

He knew that on his right, not fully visible from here, was a wide sandy cove, with rocky cliffs on either hand. This was probably the only place along the whole of the bay where a ship could run aground without being torn to pieces by rocks.

Toby hoped the frigate commander would see the cove and run his vessel aground without losing any of the men on board.

The greatest danger then would come from people like those he had just met up with. He knew they would loot any vessel that was accessible to them. He took comfort in the thought that the crew of a man-o'-war should be capable of dealing with such a problem.

Suddenly, he heard a roar rise from the throats of a great many more people than were in the party he was following.

He broke into an awkward trot, Nap with him, pausing only when the cove came fully into view.

There was a huge crowd here, and not everyone was from the Porthluney coastal communities. Many wore farmworkers' smocks. A few favoured the hard hats worn by mining men.

It would seem that word of an imminent shipwreck had already spread far and wide. Toby realised grimly that these men and women had not come to the sea's edge with the hope of saving lives. They were here to claim whatever spoils might come their way.

But they were not to take them from this cove. The roar heard by Toby had been caused by the sudden appearance of the frigate out beyond the entrance to the sheltered cove.

It was evident that the frigate had seen the cove too, but the sighting had come about too late. Sailing under a single foresail, the ship was too far offshore to make it to the cove. The ship's bows swung around slowly, but already the vessel had been carried too far eastwards to enter the safe haven.

The commanding officer realised it too. He brought the bow around once more and put the cove astern, in an attempt to steer clear of the coast.

Now a different sound went up from those on shore. This time it was a howl of disappointment as they saw their prize heading away from them.

One of the men in the party Toby had been following shouted, 'She may have missed the cove, but there'll be no clearing Dodman Point. Come on, we'll get it there, for certain.'

There was an immediate stampede from the sandy shore as men and women laboured up the steep lane away from the cove, determined to keep the doomed ship in view.

Toby followed, wishing now he had brought Nipper after all.

It was raining hard once again now. When the first of the crowd reached the brow of the hill there was another howl of disappointment. The ship was nowhere to be seen. At first Toby feared it might have gone aground at the base of the high cliff upon which they stood.

Others thought it might have escaped out to sea.

Then the rain cloud rolled back for an instant once more and the ship could be seen again. It was closer to the shore than before and it was clear there would be no escape for ship or men.

Just then another boat could be seen, much smaller than the frigate, following in the warship's wake.

'It's a Portloe fishing boat,' shouted someone. Toby wondered what a fishing boat was doing out in such appalling weather.

One of the crowd close to him echoed his thoughts as

they continued moving along the cliff top. Meanwhile, the rain contributed to a game of hide-and-seek between the vessels out at sea and those on land.

It soon became apparent that the fishing boat was closing on the frigate, although it was being desperately tossed about by the rough sea. Its oars, sometimes rowlock deep in the water, would at other times futilely flail the air.

Toby realised the crowd was not far from Hemmick beach now and he became concerned for Bethany and the Hosking family. They would not be aware of the approaching mob. If the designs of the would-be looters were thwarted they might turn their wrath upon the Quakers.

The gap between fishing boat and frigate was much narrower now and before long the small boat disappeared behind the larger vessel.

When it reappeared, the fishing boat was pulling ahead of the frigate and a keen-eyed young boy called out that there was now a rope linking the two vessels.

Suddenly there was not one but *two* small boats. The second was the frigate's longboat, manned by sailors. Toby realised the men in the two boats were attempting to turn the bow of the frigate towards the open sea, hoping to steer her clear of Dodman Point. The headland was looming dangerously close now. It was a last desperate, almost foolhardy, attempt to avert disaster.

The crowd onshore was aware the odds were heavily against the sailors. They began running along the cliffs, forging ahead of the drama being played out at sea.

The vessels continued to be forced eastwards, sometimes visible, oft-times not. By now the first of the huge crowd had reached Hemmick beach, where Jacob Hosking had his home.

As the crowd spilled on to the small, shingle beach, Jacob came from the house, looking bemused. Toby hurried towards him as Bethany, Muriel and some of the children crowded the doorway behind him.

'What's happening?' asked the Quaker. 'Why is everybody here?'

There's a ship in trouble,' replied Toby, breathlessly. 'The frigate whose men were here last night. One of its boats and a Portloe fishing boat are trying to pull it out of trouble. I fear their efforts will be in vain.'

As though to emphasise his words, a wave crashed against the rocks to one side of the beach with a boom as loud as a cannon shot, hurling spray halfway up the steep cliffside.

Moments later the squally rain eased yet again and the frigate came into the view of those on the beach. The two small boats still strained valiantly at the end of the taut ropes.

The oarsmen were still attempting to pull the frigate to safety, but it was already too late. Their efforts were doomed to failure.

Wind and a very heavy swell were driving the frigate and the two boats towards the rocks on Dodman Point. The end was only minutes away.

The men crewing the small boats suddenly realised their own danger. The ropes linking them to the ship were hurriedly cast off. But they were even closer to the rocks of Dodman Point than the frigate. Nevertheless, free of the ropes now, the oarsmen set about saving their small craft.

The frigate's longboat successfully turned until it was bows on to the running sea. The fishing boat was not so fortunate.

It was broadside on to the sea when a large wave caught it. For a moment it seemed to be held on the crest of a wave, the oarsmen paddling the air. Then the boat lurched sideways. As Toby looked on in horror, men and oars were spilled into the sea.

Moments later the frigate swept past the upturned boat and was torn open on the rocks beneath the towering cliffs. The watchers on shore had been given the shipwreck they had been so eagerly anticipating.

Chapter 17

When the doomed naval frigate was thrown upon the rocks beside Hemmick beach, the huge crowd that had been following the ship's progress along the shoreline set up a howl of triumph. The ghoulish sound caused the hairs on the back of Toby's neck to rise in horror.

Moments later the first members of the mob were scrambling over spray-washed rocks towards the ship. Above the exultant sounds from the would-be looters, the timbers of the impaled frigate screamed in mortal agony as they were ground and splintered on the rocks.

Toby dearly wished to believe the eagerness of the mob was directed towards the rescue of the shipwrecked sailors, but he knew better. The sole aim of the men – and women too – who scrambled over the rocks was to secure as many spoils as they could from the disintegrating ship.

Jacob was perhaps even more aware of their intentions than was Toby. A Cornishman, he had known a great many shipwrecks along this stretch of coast. He began running towards his own boat, lying keel up on the sand above the water line. At the same time he called for help from the men of the crowd.

'No, Jacob! Thou mustn't go out there! Think of the children . . .'

Muriel's shrill plea followed him to the boat. If he heard, he made no response.

Toby ran in the wake of the Quaker. Much to his surprise, so too did a number of men who had arrived with the loot-seeking mob.

One of the men caught his glance. As though Toby had voiced his thoughts aloud, the man said gruffly, 'That's a Portloe boat that turned over out there, Parson. We're Portloe men.'

'I'll come with you,' declared Toby.

'No,' said Jacob, quickly. 'Thou can do far more by showing thyself among the crowd. There will be some who will help thee pull men and not goods from the sea. It's a difficult sea running out there. It will be safer if I take only men used to handling a fishing boat.'

Toby could see the sense in Jacob's argument. He did not argue, but helped the fishermen to right Jacob's boat and slide it down the shingle beach to the sea.

As the men clambered on board, Toby called, 'Do you know whose boat it was that turned over? In case I need to go and speak to their families.'

The man who had spoken to him before, called back, 'It belonged to Eli Whitnick. I don't know who was crewing for him . . .'

Toby watched apprehensively as Jacob Hosking's diminutive fishing boat, with only four men on board, fought its way through mountainous breakers close to the shore.

One moment it would rise, bows high, on the swell. The next it was lost to view in the deep valley of a trough.

He watched until it was clear of the shallow water breakers. Then he turned away and hurried towards the place where the frigate was being smashed unmercifully against the rocks.

Wreckage from the ship was already spreading over a wide area, some swirling close inshore, much more being carried into deeper water.

In the water among the wreckage were many struggling sailors. Some clung to wreckage and were carried out to sea, crying futilely for help. Others were trying desperately to swim to the comparative safety of the shore.

Ominously, an increasing number were already beyond help. Their bodies floated, half-submerged, among the wreckage.

A few of the crowd *were* trying to reach the men in the water and pull them to safety, but most were callously indifferent to the fate of their fellow men. They were intent only on retrieving something of value from the sea.

Toby threw off his cloak and waded into the sea to help a sailor. He had been clinging to a piece of timber, only to have it wrenched from his grasp by the power of the sea. He now sought to hold on to a rock.

As Toby waded to his assistance the sea pounded the sailor, occasionally washing over him. It was apparent his strength was waning.

Toby tried to ignore the chill of the water, then he was lifted off his feet by a wave and thrown back into shallower water.

He struggled forward once more. Suddenly a voice behind him shouted, 'Toby, here! Take this and tie it around thyself.'

It was Bethany. In her hand she held a length of thin rope. She threw one end to him, but at the first attempt the wind caught it and carried it back to her.

The next throw was more successful. Toby caught the rope and quickly tied a loop about his body. Now he plunged into the water with more confidence. When he was lifted off his feet this time, he struck out against the surging tide.

A moment later he was caught up in a powerful undercurrent and dragged away from the shore.

By swimming as strongly as he could, he reached the rock. He was able to take a grip on the sailor just as exhaustion forced him to relinquish his grasp on the rock.

Another wave roared in and for long moments both men disappeared from the view of those on shore. Fortunately, Toby was able to maintain his grip on the sailor and he felt the rope tighten about his chest. Then he was pulled unceremoniously through the water to the shore.

Spluttering and choking, he fought for breath until he suddenly felt sand beneath his feet. Then he and the sailor were being dragged from the water by a couple of hefty men who had been pulling on the rope with Bethany.

All about him Toby could hear the din from the crowd as men and women squabbled over the spoils now spread far and wide over the surface of the water.

As he sucked in great lungfuls of air, two women nearby came to blows over the ownership of a side of salt pork.

Foolishly, Toby said, 'This is no place for you, Bethany.'

'It's no place for anyone, but there are lives to be saved . . . look!'

She pointed to where a seaman threshed the water desperately, just short of some nearby rocks. On the rocks, a man was kneeling almost within arm's length of the drowning man. He used a piece of timber salvaged from the wrecked frigate in a bid to pull a half-submerged box towards him. He seemed oblivious of the drowning man's struggles, or of the waves which occasionally broke over the rock.

Suddenly angry, Toby scrambled to his feet, the rope still tied about him. Plunging into the sea again, he floundered awkwardly to the rocks.

It was deep enough for a man to stand with his head above water on the landward side of the rocks. Reaching up, Toby grabbed the wrecker's clothing and heaved.

With a startled cry and arms flailing, the man fell backwards into the water, dropping the piece of wood he had been wielding.

Snatching it up, Toby climbed on to the rock and held the wood out to the seaman. Near exhaustion, the man secured a grip on it at his third attempt. Toby pulled him closer until he was able to take a hold of him. Then he slipped from the rock and both were pulled to safety.

More than a hundred men were pulled from the sea that night, but for many more it was too late. Twenty-four bodies were laid out on the cold sand and shingle of Hemmick beach. Among them was that of Eli Whitnick. A number of Portloe men were still missing.

One of the survivors from the Portloe boat was Billy Kendall.

Fires burned in the grates of every room in the small Hosking house and rescuers and survivors crowded inside. When he found himself standing next to Billy, Toby expressed sad satisfaction that Eli and the men of Portloe had managed to resolve their differences and jointly crew the boat. He also praised them for attempting to rescue the very men who had arrested Billy.

'That's thanks largely to you, Parson,' explained Billy. 'I told the others what you'd said about Eli and the Revenue officer. They all agreed with you that 'twas a more likely explanation than the one we'd thought of. Old Eli was more against smuggling than any man I've ever known, but he would never have tipped off the Revenue men about any free-trading that was going on. When he called on us to put to sea today to go to the help of the frigate, I suppose we felt we owed it to him to do it.'

'It's a tragedy that so many men have died,' said Toby, 'but at least Eli's mind would have been at peace at the end.'

While they had been talking, Jacob had entered the house. He now made his way across the room to Toby.

'Some of the men outside are asking whether thou wouldst like to say a prayer for those who died, before they set to and bury them?'

'Bury them where?' asked Toby.

'It's usual for bodies that are washed up on the shore to be buried in shallow graves at the water's edge,' said Jacob. 'Though I'd rather it were elsewhere.'

'They'll be buried in my churchyard,' said Toby, firmly. 'Would you loan me your cart and help take them there? Not Eli or the Portloe men, of course,' he added. 'I know Eli would want to return to his chapel.'

'We'll arrange that for him, Parson,' said Billy. 'I can promise you he'll have as fine a Methodist funeral service as he would have wished.'

Billy hesitated before adding, 'I think Eli would have liked for you to say a prayer at the service for him. I don't know what you think about it?'

'It's an honour to be asked to say a prayer at the funeral of a brave man,' said Toby. 'Let me know when it's to be. I'll be there. Now, let's see if we can find an officer to discuss what's to be done with those sailors who have survived. They'll need food and clothing – and that's the responsibility of the naval authorities.'

Chapter 18

'Thou art indeed an unusual man to be a Church of England curate, Toby Lovell, as I think I have told thee before.'

Bethany was walking to the rectory with him as dusk approached. The storm had passed on as swiftly as it had arrived. Around them birds were singing and nature was returning to normal, unaffected by the scale of the human disaster that had occurred only a short time before.

The survivors of the frigate had already been led away to the grounds of Porthluney Manor. Here they would be accommodated until the naval authorities made arrangements to take them back into the service.

Toby had remained at Hemmick, dressed in some of Jacob's ill-fitting clothing until his own had been dried in front of one of the fires.

Now, both he and Bethany tried to keep the dreadful disaster out of their conversation as much as was possible.

'Why do you think I'm unusual this time, Bethany?'

'Because thou accepts that others might wish to worship in ways of which thy own Church does not approve. Rector Kempe would never have agreed to offer up a prayer for a Wesleyan in a Methodist church, no matter how brave that man had been. Thou behaves very like a Friend, sometimes.'

'Are Quakers quite as tolerant as you make them out to be, Bethany? Is it not equally unusual for a Quaker woman to show such open friendship towards a priest of the Church of England?'

When she made no reply, Toby said, 'Do I take it that someone has already spoken to you about your friendship with me?'

'Jacob mentioned to the Elders that thou had been very kind to all of us. They agreed that such kindness is welcome, but suggested that particularly susceptible members of the family should be discouraged from making close friendships outside the Society.'

'By that they meant you, of course?'

'Yes.'

'What did Jacob say to them?'

'He told them I had been a Friend since the day I was born. I would probably remain one until the day I die. But he also told them I am my own woman. That it is not for him to tell me what I must do. At least, that's what he *said* he told them and I believe him.'

Something in Bethany's voice made Toby say, 'What did he say to *you*?'

'He said he has great admiration for thee, and affection for me. Because of this, and for both our sakes, he suggested I should not allow friendship to become fondness.'

After walking in thoughtful silence for a few more steps, Toby asked, 'What was your reply?'

'I said I thought his warning had come too late.'

The statement was made with such simple and straightforward honesty that its implication did not immediately sink in. When it did, Toby came to an abrupt halt.

'You told him *that*?'

She nodded, but her glance fell away from his when she said, 'Does it trouble thee that I should tell Jacob of my feelings? Am I being immodest by telling thee the truth instead of feigning indifference, as do most girls who are not members of the Friends?'

'I've always preferred truth to hypocrisy, Bethany, but . . . yes, I must confess to being troubled. Very troubled.'

'I see.' She sounded unhappy. 'Then perhaps Jacob is right.'

She turned, as though about to return along the lane to Hemmick. But she hesitated and in that moment Toby said, 'It troubles me because in the short time we've known each other, I've grown very fond of you too.'

'Oh!' She turned back to him and, for a few moments, they stood looking at each other uncertainly.

What might have happened next, they would never know. They both heard the sound of horses and men coming along the lane towards them. Then a number of riders came into view, some dressed in the uniform of Revenue officers.

Riding with them was John Bettison.

When the riders reached Toby and Bethany, John Bettison reined in and the others followed his example.

Looking from Toby to Bethany and back again, Bettison said, 'I heard you were on the beach with the wreckers, Parson. It's a pity you're not still there. It would have left us with an interesting situation had our curate been arrested for looting a shipwrecked vessel.'

Bettison looked at Bethany once more. 'But I can see you have your mind on other activities. I'm disappointed in you, girl. You could do well for yourself, had you a mind. As it is, I doubt very much whether you'll find a Church of England curate any more exciting than one of your Quakers.'

'Your remarks are extremely offensive, Mr Bettison. One expects to hear such talk in a dockside tavern, not from the lips of a gentleman.' A surge of sudden anger temporarily overcame Toby's natural discretion.

'Damn your impertinence, Parson!' Bettison's anger matched Toby's. 'You may have experience of dockyard taverns, but I doubt you're equally familiar with the ways of gentlemen. Stick with your wreckers – and your Quakers. No doubt your bishop will be very interested to hear how you spend your time in Porthluney parish.'

Bettison returned his attention to Bethany once again. 'Now your interest has extended beyond your own narrow religion we should have much more in common when next we meet. I look forward to that occasion.'

Toby was still angry, but as Bettison rode away along the lane, followed by the Revenue officers, Bethany placed a hand upon his arm. 'Don't let him anger thee, Toby. It's what he wants. But I must go now and warn the others of his coming.'

'Why? Men and women who would ignore drowning sailors in order to salvage something worth a few pence deserve no warning. They're as bad as Bettison.'

'Thou hast seen enough of Bettison to guess what he is like, but thou dost not know the half of it. He has been involved in more smuggling, wrecking and looting than anyone for miles around, but he's still an important man. He owns a great deal of land and lives in the manor. The authorities listen to him. There is a sizeable bounty on the head of every man, or woman, turned in to the Revenue men – and Bettison is in sore need of money. He won't stop to enquire which of those on Hemmick beach is a rescuer, and which a looter. Everyone there will be presumed guilty and arrested. They'll receive no more sympathy or justice when they appear in court. They have to be warned.'

Toby would have liked to question her more about Bettison's activities, but she was already hurrying away from him.

'Wait, Bethany! You'll never beat Bettison and the others to Hemmick.'

'Yes, I will.' She paused to slip off her shoes. 'They'll stay with the lane, I'll go across the fields. Don't worry, I know what I'm doing.'

As she climbed nimbly over a gate which led to a field, she called back, 'Goodbye, Toby. I'm glad we were able to say what is in both our minds.'

With this, she was gone. By the time he reached the gate she was halfway across the field. It sloped away from the lane and she was light on her feet and ran surprisingly fast. He did not doubt she would beat Bettison and the Revenue officers to the beach where she lived with her sister and Jacob Hosking.

All the same, he wished she might have stayed. There was so much they needed to talk about now. So much to discover.

Trudging home, Toby thought that in its early days his curacy was turning out to be anything but the sinecure he had been led to believe it would be.

Nobody had been able to tell him that within the first month he would fall in with smugglers, witness an horrific shipwreck and experience the work of looters. He had also promised to speak at the funeral of a Methodist lay preacher and succeeded in antagonising the principal landowner in his new parish.

Yet none of these things was likely to have such a significant impact upon his life as what many of his friends and acquaintances would consider to be the ultimate folly: he had allowed himself to fall in love with a Quaker girl.

Toby thought about the problem all the way home to the rectory. Not until he was letting himself in to the house did he realise that at some time during the day he had lost Nap, his adopted dog. He had last seen him on the beach at Hemmick.

He was in half a mind to return and look for the animal, but decided it would not be wise. If Bethany had succeeded in warning those on the beach, Bettison and the Revenue men would be scouring the countryside, determined to arrest 'looters'. It might be better for him to stay out of their way.

Nap was probably hunting rabbits on the cliffs. He had survived without Toby for a long time before he had come to Porthluney. He would be all right. No doubt he would be waiting outside the kitchen door in the morning.

Toby entered the rectory and closed the door behind him. He decided that his duties as a naval chaplain had been quite straightforward compared with the problems he was having to cope with as the curate of Porthluney parish.

Chapter 19

The day after the shipwreck did not begin well for Toby. His problems started when Rose failed to arrive for work at the rectory. After waiting for some time, he prepared his own breakfast.

He was clearing the plates and dishes away when there came a knock at the kitchen door. When he answered it he found a young girl standing on the doorstep. Her looks were familiar, but it was a few moments before he remembered he had last seen her making nets at Portloe. This was the bolder of the two girls.

She was Charlotte Jane, daughter of Rose. Toby remembered somewhat uncomfortably that this was the girl her own mother had described as being 'a bit wild'.

'My ma won't be coming to work for a day or two,' said the girl. 'She was standing on a chair at home last night, taking something down off a shelf, when she slipped and fell. She's turned her ankle very badly and can't walk on it.'

'Oh! I'm sorry to hear that. Tell her I'll call in and see her sometime today or tomorrow. In the meantime she's not to worry about me, I'll manage.'

'You don't need to do that. She's asked me to come and clean for you, and to cook you a bit of dinner too. I said I wouldn't mind. What with poor Eli being drowned yesterday, I've got nothing else to do at the moment.'

'Yes, of course. It was a dreadful tragedy. I'll be visiting Portloe this morning to speak to the relatives of those who were lost. Would you happen to know their names, and where they live?'

'I knew every single one. Most of 'em as well as if they were me own brothers.'

Charlotte was in the house now, but she seemed more

inclined to chat than get down to work. She also had a tendency to stand much closer to him than was necessary when she was talking. It made Toby feel vaguely ill-at-ease.

'It seems strange having someone so young living here in the rectory. I've never before thought of there being young parsons. All those I've seen have been old, like Rector Kempe.'

Looking up at him, wide-eyed, she asked, 'Don't you get lonely sometimes? I mean, being all alone in this big house with no one to talk to, and no one coming to your church on a Sunday. You must feel you'd like to have someone around sometimes?'

'No.' Toby retreated in the direction of the door leading to the rest of the house. 'Being new here, I need to find out about a great many things, and as there hasn't been a rector at Porthluney for so long, there's a lot to do. If you'd like to take a look around the kitchen I'm sure you'll find cleaning stuff somewhere. I know there's a broom under the stairs.'

He reached the door, turned the handle and opened it. Safely outside in the passageway, he added, 'I must go to the church now. I want to clean the windows before I go to Portloe.'

He left the house with the feeling he had somehow disappointed Charlotte. He hoped it would not be very long before her mother was fit enough to return to work. Toby had not intended cleaning the church windows this morning, it had been a hastily thought up excuse to leave the rectory.

On the way to the church he remembered Nap. The dog had still not returned. Toby was concerned for him. He had felt quite certain the dog would be waiting for him outside the rectory door this morning. After he had been to Portloe he thought he would return to Hemmick beach and ask after him.

The stained glass windows in the church did not appear to have been cleaned for many years and it proved to be hard work. Toby was up a stepladder with a bucket and water when he heard footsteps in the church porch. A moment later the door was pushed open and Jacob entered the church.

In his arms he cradled Nap who looked very sorry for himself. Cloth bandages were wrapped around the dog's body and the thick part of a hind leg.

Toby clambered down the ladder and hurried to meet the Quaker who had stopped to lay Nap gently on the floor of the aisle. Despite the bandage, Nap's tail was wagging vigorously in his pleasure at seeing Toby.

'I was very worried about him when he didn't return with me last night. It seems I was right to be concerned. What's happened to him?'

Tight-lipped, Jacob said, 'I don't know for certain, but young Biddie was watching from the window. She said Bettison struck the dog with a sword.'

Toby looked at Jacob disbelievingly. 'Why would he do such a thing?'

'Biddie said the dog was barking at Bettison and his horse. She tends to exaggerate at times, but I think she is probably right this time. Bettison was angry because there was no one left on the beach for the Revenue men to arrest. I think he was hoping to make some money from the occasion.'

'So Bethany was able to reach you before Bettison and the Revenue men?'

'Yes.'

Jacob seemed ill-at-ease and Toby thought he knew the cause of his discomfiture.

'Bethany has spoken to you about the way we feel about each other?'

'Yes.'

'I gather you don't approve?'

Jacob struggled to find words that would not offend. 'I like thee, Toby. I like thee very much, but thou art not one of us. Thou art not a Friend. Bethany is. She has never been anything else.'

'I've no doubt there will be opposition to Bethany from my own Church, but I am confident I can overcome any objections that are raised. Are you saying that Quakers are less understanding? Will your people stop her from worshipping in her own way?'

'They would not stop her from doing whatever she wishes, but she will no longer be a Friend. They will cast her out of the Society.'

'I am both sorry and disappointed about that, Jacob. I thought that Quakers, perhaps more than any other faith, taught the value of tolerance?'

'We do, Toby, but there are strict rules for those who would belong to the Society of Friends.'

'What does Bethany say about this?'

'We spoke until well into the night. Then, later, Muriel and I prayed for Bethany, and for thee too.'

'Was any decision reached when you were speaking to Bethany?'

'I asked her to do or say nothing until she has discussed the matter with our Elders. I also asked her not to see thee until after then. She eventually promised. I hope thou wilt help her to keep this promise, Toby? It is very, very important to Bethany, to her family, and to the Society too.'

Toby thought about his words for some minutes, then he nodded. 'I won't do anything to make her break such a promise, Jacob, but I'd rather it had not been asked of her. I would like to be able to help her at this time. When she has seen the Elders I want to hear of her decision, and I want to hear it from Bethany. Do I have your word on that?'

Jacob nodded. 'Thou art entitled to that and I am grateful to thee for being so understanding of our ways.' After hesitating for only a moment, Jacob held out his hand, saying, 'I would like us to remain friends, Toby, whatever comes of this.'

'I would like it too, Jacob, but it may not prove easy.'

'Our Lord never said that loving was easy, Toby. Whether it is loving Him, or loving a woman. I had to choose which path to follow when I met Muriel. It has sometimes proved difficult, but I know I chose the only way. I trust Bethany will do the same. Whatever her choice, we will always love her just the same. Now I must return to Hemmick. Three more bodies were washed up there this morning. The fishermen of these coasts will reap a sad harvest in the days ahead.'

Chapter 20

'What you doing with that there dog? My ma didn't tell me nothing about there being a dog in the house. I don't like dogs!'

Charlotte backed away across the room as Toby carried Nap in through the kitchen door.

'He's all right. He won't hurt you. He's been injured. I'll put him in the study. You won't need to clean in there.'

'You sure it's not going to get out while I'm here doing the cleaning?'

'He won't get out, I promise you.'

'All right then.' Charlotte stood back much farther than was necessary while Toby walked through the kitchen to make his way to the study.

He settled the patient animal down on a rug in a corner of the room, then went away to find a bowl in which to leave some water.

Emerging from the study, Toby found Charlotte waiting for him. 'I've got a piece of boiling bacon here that Ma gave to me for you. I'm not a very good cook, but I'll boil it up with a few 'taters and some spring greens.'

'You don't need to do that, Charlotte. I'll manage.'

'Ma said I was to make sure you had some food in your belly, and that's what I'll do,' she said, doggedly. 'I'll never hear the last of it from her if I don't.'

'Very well, but could we have it as soon as possible? I want to pay a visit to Portloe.'

'I'll get on and cook it directly.'

Charlotte's 'directly' would not have satisfied her mother. She needed to peel the potatoes before putting the meal on to cook and proved to be woefully inept at even this simple task.

She then put everything in one pot to cook over the kitchen fire. The result was edible – but only just.

Toby did not have the heart to complain. Charlotte was so pleased to have produced something that bore a reasonably close resemblance to a meal, he felt obliged to eat most of it.

While he was eating, she was never far away and chatted the whole time.

It was with a sense of release that Toby left the rectory early that afternoon.

Behind him, Charlotte watched his departure with some disappointment. She had expected him to flirt with her, at least. She was aware she was not unattractive. True, he was a parson, but he was also a man. No doubt he had the same urges and desires as other men.

She finally decided that Toby must be more successful at hiding his thoughts than most of those she knew. She would need to work on him.

There were also more interesting ways of spending an afternoon than cleaning up the rectory. Anyway, it looked clean enough to her. If *she* thought it was clean, then she believed Curate Lovell would probably think so too.

Toby had hardly disappeared from view before Charlotte put on her coat and slipped out of the house.

Charlotte followed the route taken by Toby, until she reached the footpath which led to the nearby hamlet of Portloe. From here she followed a faint path across the fields, towards the sea.

The path led her to gorse-covered slopes which became steeper before falling away to low, rocky cliffs.

Hastily checking that no one was within sight, Charlotte dropped to her knees and began to crawl through the undergrowth. The dead, dried needles covering the ground beneath the gorse bushes pierced the skin of her knees, but Charlotte gritted her teeth and crawled on.

Somewhere among the bushes, she lost the faint path she was following. For a few minutes she crawled around in an irregular circle, trying to find it again. Eventually, she had to admit to herself that she was hopelessly lost.

She would have to risk standing up in order to get her bearings.

Luck was not on Charlotte's side. She stood up quickly, intending to duck down again once she knew exactly where she was. Unfortunately, there were few landmarks hereabouts. While she was trying to establish exactly where she was, a voice called, 'You there, girl. What are you doing?'

Charlotte turned to see John Bettison sitting his horse on the coastal footpath, no more than forty paces from her.

'Come here.'

Charlotte hesitated for only a moment. One did not defy the Porthluney landowner. There was no need to crawl through the gorse now. She pushed her way between the bushes, holding her arms above her head so they would not be scratched by the gorse needles.

When she reached the footpath, Charlotte dropped Bettison a curtsy. Keeping her gaze on the ground close to her feet, she said, 'Sir?'

'What were you doing in those bushes? Who were you seeking?'

'I . . . I saw a young rabbit go in there, sir. I thought I might catch it.'

'Don't lie to me, girl.' Bettison spoke sharply. 'Look at me. I've seen you before. Who are you?'

'Charlotte Jane, sir.'

'Wasn't your stepfather once the senior stableman at Porthluney?'

'Yes, sir. He died many years ago, sir.'

'You've grown a lot since I last noticed you, girl. You're a young woman now. Why aren't you working?'

'I have no work now. I was employed making nets for Eli Whitnick at Portloe. He was drowned yesterday when he went to the help of the ship out in the bay.'

John Bettison was only half-listening. 'You say you've been working for Eli Whitnick? At Portloe? And now you're here, crawling about in the gorse, giving me some far-fetched story about rabbits . . .'

He suddenly snapped his fingers in jubilation. 'I know what you're up to! You're looking for the Revenue man, aren't you? The one who built a hide out here, so he could watch what was going on in the bay. *You're* the one who gave him the information about the Portloe men landing their free-trade goods at Hemmick. Well, well, well!'

Charlotte opened her mouth to deny the charge, then closed it again without speaking.

'You're out of luck with your young Revenue officer, girl. He's too ambitious for you – and his ambition has been recognised. He's gone to Plymouth on promotion.'

Charlotte's fleeting expression of dismay was sufficient confirmation to the landowner that his surmise was correct.

'I gather he didn't come to tell you he was leaving? Well, it's hardly surprising. He wouldn't have been welcome in Portloe, would he now? But, unless I'm very much mistaken, information isn't all he's been getting from you.'

Dismounting from his horse, Bettison said, 'I think we ought to discuss this, girl.' He gave his horse a sharp slap on the rump and the startled animal took off along the path.

'He'll find his way home easy enough. He's done it before. In the meantime, you can show me where this hide is that your young Revenue man made. When we get there we'll have a little discussion about a few things. The Revenue Service is willing to pay good money to anyone who comes up with information leading to the arrest of a smuggler and his contraband. Did you know that?'

'I didn't tell things to Harry because I wanted to make money from it.'

'Of course you didn't. You don't strike me as a mercenary girl – and that's in your favour too. I think we can come to an arrangement we will both find highly satisfactory, Charlotte. Highly satisfactory. Now, lead the way to this hide before someone comes along and sees us together. I'm quite certain you were the soul of discretion in your relationship with your Revenue man. Let's keep it that way, shall we?'

Chapter 21

Visiting the families of the missing Portloe fishermen was a harrowing experience for Toby. He had little experience of dealing with distraught wives, mothers and daughters. Nevertheless, he was made to feel that his sympathy and solicitude were appreciated, even though two of the families were staunch Methodists and had already been visited by one of their own ministers.

Perhaps the most harrowing aspect of the tragedy was that some of the families were not ready to believe their men had died in the attempt to save the naval frigate. Because all the bodies had not been found, they still nursed a forlorn hope that they might somehow have miraculously survived the previous day's tempest.

Feeling thoroughly depressed, Toby met one of the Portloe fishermen. He reminded Toby of his promise to bury the bodies of the shipwrecked sailors in the Porthluney churchyard.

It posed an immediate problem of a most mundane nature. Due to the total absence of co-operation since arriving at Porthluney, Toby did not even know to whom he could turn to dig a communal grave for the unfortunate seamen.

This difficulty was solved by the fisherman. He declared he and some of his fellows would tackle the task. All they needed was for Toby to mark out an area of sufficient size to cope with the victims of the tragedy.

To add to his despondent mood, Toby received a painful bite on his right hand from Nipper. Bad-tempered as a result of being tethered for far longer than Toby had intended, the donkey caught the preoccupied priest off-guard and succeeded in drawing blood.

The heavy drizzle that was falling as Toby rode home from Portloe was in keeping with his melancholy mood. It lasted until he came within sight of the rectory and saw a wet and bedraggled young woman waiting by the rectory gate.

Believing it to be Bethany, Toby dug his heels hard into the flanks of the cantankerous donkey. The animal was so startled by the sudden, unexpected action, it actually broke into a trot, although the burst of uncharacteristic energy did not last for long.

By the time the gate was reached, the donkey had slowed to its usual lazy gait. Toby did not urge Nipper on again. As they drew closer he had realised that the young girl was not Bethany. It was Alice Rowe, the girl he had last seen making nets with Charlotte for the late Eli Whitnick.

'Hello, what are you doing standing out here in the rain?'

'My mother heard that Rose Henna had been unable to come in to work for you today. She made a pie and asked me to bring it along. She thought you might like it for your supper. It's rabbit. There's too many of them in the warren up by the Forty Acre wood. Pa's been thinning them out for Mr Bettison and he was allowed to keep a couple for the pot.'

'There's nothing I fancy more right at this moment.' It was true. Charlotte's lunchtime cooking had been less than appetising. Toby realised he was hungry. 'Where is it? If you give it to Charlotte she'll put it in the oven for me.'

'Charlotte?' Alice seemed puzzled. 'Why should she cook it for you?'

'She's working in the house today. Rose sent her to work in the rectory in her place.'

'I've just been in the kitchen and I didn't see anyone there. I left the pie on the table for you.' Alice did not add that the kitchen fire had almost gone out and she had made it up.

'I see. Well, I'm much later than I expected to be. No doubt Charlotte thought I wasn't likely to return and went home when she'd finished all her work. It doesn't matter. I'll put the pie in to cook.'

'No, you go and put your donkey away. I'll put the pie in and lay the table for you. It won't take me long.' Alice looked around. 'Where's your dog? It's not usually very far away from you.'

'The poor old chap got himself injured down on the beach yesterday, when the frigate was wrecked on the rocks. He's in my study, bandaged up and feeling very sorry for himself. No doubt a piece of rabbit pie will cheer him almost as much as it will me.'

'Go on then. You put the donkey away while I make things ready. Do you mind eating in the kitchen? That's the only room in the house I know.'

'For a piece of rabbit pie I'd eat on the floor with poor old Nap. Go inside and get yourself dry while you're about it. You look as though you've been standing out in the rain for far too long.'

By the time Toby had put Nipper in his stable, rubbed him down and fed him hay, Alice had laid the table, put the pie in the oven to cook and had also made a cup of tea for him.

'Bless you, Alice.' Toby looked about the kitchen. The fire crackled merrily in the grate and a lamp burned in the window, keeping the miserable night at bay. 'This is the cosiest the kitchen has looked since I came to Porthluney.'

Alice had taken off her hat and cloak and combed her long hair. Only her wet and muddy shoes were evidence that she had been out in the rain.

'You get some dry clothes on, sir. By the time you get back the pie will be almost hot enough for you. It doesn't take long in an oven like the one you've got here. My ma would be green with envy were she to see it.'

'It's very kind of your mother to send me something for supper, Alice, but I don't quite understand . . .'

'There's nothing *to* understand, sir. She'll never be able to thank you enough for what you did for Uncle Dan. She says if it wasn't for you we wouldn't have him with us today. She's right, too. Uncle Dan says so himself.'

'I'm happy to have been able to do something for him,

Alice. We've lost enough good men in the past twenty-four hours, Eli Whitnick among them. His loss is bound to affect you and Charlotte more than anyone. What will you do for work now?'

'I don't know about Charlotte. She's never been really happy making nets for a living. She'll probably find something else to do. Billy Kendall was distantly related to Eli and as there's no one else, he'll be taking over the business when things are sorted out with lawyers and the like. He's asked me to stay on.'

'Well, I'm pleased to know you'll still be in work, at least. From what I've seen there isn't too much of it around the parish.'

'Oh, I haven't said yet that I'll work for him. Billy has a lot of ideas in his head about me. I don't want to seem too eager to go and work for him.'

'He seems a nice enough lad. He'll probably make something of himself if he doesn't get caught smuggling again.'

'He's all right, but I'm not sure whether that's enough.'

Toby was taking off his boots beside the fire when Alice said, 'Haven't you ever thought of getting married?'

'Not seriously. Before coming to Porthluney I was a naval chaplain and spent much of my time at sea. There weren't many opportunities to meet up with young women.'

'Billy was telling us that you were at Trafalgar, with Nelson. He said the man in charge of the press-gang said you were a hero and were badly wounded.'

Toby smiled. 'I was certainly wounded. As for being a hero . . . I was a chaplain, not a fighting man.'

'That isn't what Billy is telling everybody. There's talk in the village that you saved Mr Killigrew from the shipwreck last night too.'

'Who's Mr Killigrew, Alice?'

'He's the brother of Mr Bettison's wife. She's a lot younger than Mr Bettison and I think Mr Killigrew might be her twin. He's a lieutenant in the navy.'

'Is he, indeed?' Toby remembered the men he had rescued from the rock. 'Well, I helped pull a couple of men from the sea last night, but I didn't get around to asking their names.'

'Someone ought to tell him who it was who saved him. Mr Bettison ought to be told, too. Then perhaps he might change his mind about keeping folk from coming to your church. It isn't fair. Everybody says that something ought to be done about it.'

'Well, if enough people say it often enough, I've no doubt we'll be able to change things eventually. You're a wonderful fund of information, Alice. Pour yourself a cup of tea while I go up and change. When I come down there's a few questions I'd like to ask you. I think you might be able to help me.'

Changing out of his wet clothes in his bedroom, Toby discovered that his melancholy mood had quite disappeared. Alice Rowe had acted like a tonic upon him. He decided he liked her company.

Chapter 22

Alice was a very easy girl to talk to. She was also much younger than Toby had at first thought. During the course of her chatter he learned she was only sixteen years old, two years younger than her friend Charlotte. He had presumed them to be about the same age as each other.

Toby decided that his years at sea with the navy had compounded his ignorance of the opposite sex. He had certainly never before conversed with any young women as he had with both Bethany and Alice since his arrival in Porthluney.

He realised that in some ways, the young women were very much alike. In particular, both had a straightforward and honest way of talking that was quite disconcerting at times. It was not the manner he had been led to believe was adopted by women when talking to men. He wondered whether it might be because, as a priest, he was in a privileged position.

It could not be that this was a purely Cornish trait. Bethany was not a Cornishwoman. Besides, he had not felt the same easy familiarity with Charlotte.

His evening with Alice proved to be enlightening. She appeared to be either related to, or friendly with, almost everyone in the parish. She was particularly knowledgeable about the lord of Porthluney Manor and seemed to know every rumour and many of the facts concerning life at the manor house.

He discovered it was common knowledge that John Bettison was in dire financial trouble in spite of the extent of his landholding.

Alice said it was due to both his gambling and his womanising. He was believed to have a mistress in London, who had extremely expensive tastes. There were also regular payments to a number of local women who might otherwise have taken out bastardy orders against him.

A number of these women and their offspring lived in Porthluney parish. Others were dotted among other Cornish parishes.

'You'd never get me working up at the manor,' commented Alice.

She had provided a very satisfying meal for Toby, which he ate seated at the kitchen table. Alice was now busily washing up the plates and dishes.

'I feel sorry for his wife. She's much younger than him, you know. She's also rather kind. I think she knows that her money means more to him than she does. To be honest, I don't know why she married him. Someone said it was because her father thought Mr Bettison was going to get a title. He was heir to an old uncle who's Lord something-or-other. The uncle is rich too, I believe. But, although the uncle is nearly eighty, he's got married to a young girl. Now they've got two sons to take both the title and the money.'

'I am aware that Bettison is short of money,' said Toby. 'But I've never learned the details. It's likely he borrowed money on the strength of his expected inheritance. It must have been a sizeable sum judging by his present desperation. All the same, I'm surprised his wife isn't able to help him out, if only to safeguard the future of any children they might one day have.'

'According to his wife's personal maid, Mrs Bettison would get the money for him if he promised to give up womanising. He told her he would once, but then went and got a friend's governess pregnant. He's just not a good man.'

'I've had very little to do with him,' admitted Toby. 'But from all I've seen and heard so far, I'm not inclined to argue with you.'

'In most other parishes the parson and landowner get along well, don't they?' asked Alice. Apparently not expecting a reply, she continued, 'In St Ewe the Tremayne family spend a lot of money on the church and at Veryan the vicar has a lot of his meals at the manor. One of my aunts is Cook there. She says that more of the food they buy is eaten by the vicar than by the family.'

Toby smiled, amused by her chatter. Looking at him sympathetically, Alice said, 'It must get very lonely here in this house, all by yourself.'

'I haven't really thought about it,' lied Toby, remembering that Charlotte had expressed a similar opinion, but with considerably less honest sympathy. 'If I did, I would probably say how nice it is not being surrounded by people all the time. There were times during my naval service when I longed for peace and privacy.'

Believing Toby was dropping a strong hint that he would rather be on his own, Alice said, 'You're not having much peace with me chatting away. Anyway, I've cleared up everything, I'll go now.'

'I wasn't suggesting that you should leave right away,' protested Toby, then he remembered her age. 'I'll walk home with you.'

'There's no need for you to do that. There's no one around here would hurt me.'

Toby smiled. 'You never know, you might meet up with John Bettison. I'll go to bed happier, knowing I've seen you safely home.'

As they walked along together in the darkness, Alice asked, 'Did you really mean it when you said you don't mind being on your own?'

'I don't mind it for much of the time,' said Toby. 'But you're right, I do get lonely sometimes. It's not really what I expected when I took on the curacy here. It wouldn't be so bad if someone came to my church on Sundays. That's probably the loneliest day of all – even though Nap's a very good listener.'

'It's a shame,' declared Alice. 'You preach a very good sermon.' She suddenly giggled. 'Charlotte was with me that night too, but she got scared when an owl hooted in the trees.'

'It's the closest I've come to having a congregation,' sighed Toby. 'Perhaps you'll both come openly one Sunday? You'll be very welcome.'

'I can't speak for Charlotte,' said Alice, cautiously. 'I'd certainly come if it was at all possible, but it's more than anyone would dare do at the moment. If they were dismissed by Mr Bettison they'd not only lose their work, but their home as well. All his workers live in Estate houses. Even if they found somewhere else to live, there's no one would give them work again around here. They'd have to go right away from Porthluney.'

Toby thought it wrong that one man should have such power over others, but the social system was not peculiar to Porthluney. It existed in every parish throughout the country – and he had witnessed it at its worst in the navy. If a seaman fell foul of a commanding officer, his time on board would be made miserable at the very least. In extreme cases he might suffer the lash until it killed him, or he was driven to take his own life.

'What will you do if people never come to your church?' asked Alice. 'Will you leave Porthluney, like Rector Kempe did?'

'No,' declared Toby, firmly. 'Sooner or later they'll come back, whatever Mr Bettison says or does. People will want to get married, have their children christened, a relative buried, or simply to make their peace with God. I'll stick it out until the tide turns my way – and it will, I assure you.'

Even as he spoke he was thinking of what the next few days would bring. He would be conducting a funeral service for the victims of the frigate tragedy. No doubt the service would be attended by the seamen still camped in the grounds of Porthluney Manor.

Toby agonised over the thought that it should have taken such a disaster to give him the prospect of a full church. It was certainly not the way he had hoped it might be.

'I'm glad you'll not be leaving Porthluney. I can talk to you. I never could to Rector Kempe. I hope things hurry up and work out for you. I think they will soon. I've got an idea . . .'

'Now don't you get involved in the argument between the Church and Mr Bettison,' said Toby, in alarm. 'You've said yourself, he's a very influential man. What he does might affect your family as well as yourself.'

'It's all right. I don't need to become involved. I just need to have a word with someone.'

They had reached a small group of cottages now and Alice stopped. 'Thank you for seeing me home. I'll tell Ma you enjoyed the pie. I expect there'll be another for you later in the week. Goodnight.'

Placing a hand momentarily on his arm, she turned and hurried up the path to her home, pausing in the doorway to wave into the darkness towards Toby.

Chapter 23

The morning after his talk with Alice, Toby received a visit from a young naval officer. Wearing full dress uniform, he rode up to the rectory on a superb horse.

Nipper was tied to the hitching-rail, ready to take Toby out. The naval officer was about to tie his horse beside the donkey and Toby hurried from the rectory to warn him against it.

He was too late. No respecter of humans or well-bred bloodstock, Nipper lunged at the horse, teeth bared. Startled, the horse reared up, but the officer brought it under control quickly. Smiling at the effrontery of the donkey, he tied his mount to the far end of the rail, out of range of Nipper's teeth.

Hurrying from the rectory, Toby said, 'I'm sorry, I should have called out a warning, but I wasn't aware that Nipper's bad habits extended beyond humans.'

'No harm done,' declared the naval officer. 'But the young servant-girl was right. It *is* you who saved my life!'

Removing his hat and tucking it beneath an arm, he extended a hand, and introduced himself. 'Lieutenant Rupert Killigrew. I'm delighted to renew our acquaintance, sir.'

At first, Toby was mystified by the man's words. He was trying to remember on which ship he might have served with this man, when the officer said, 'When we last met you were pulling me from the sea and there was no time for introductions. It wasn't until this morning that one of the servant-girls at the manor told me you were probably the man who rescued me.'

Toby remembered that Alice had told him of Lieutenant Killigrew. She could have wasted no time in taking action to bring him to the attention of the occupants of Porthluney Manor.

Beaming at Toby, the delighted lieutenant said, 'I recognised you the moment I saw you coming from the rectory. Please excuse my formal dress. The clothes I wore when the *Arrow* was wrecked were ruined by water and the rocks. Fortunately, one of the Porthluney Estate workers rescued a trunk from the sea with my name on the outside and brought it to the house. It contained my dress uniform. However, had you not been on hand, I should have had no need for it. I really don't know how to thank you, sir. I'll make a generous donation to your church, of course, but I would like to make a more personal gift to you.'

'There's really no need,' declared Toby, somewhat embarrassed by the effusive gratitude of his visitor. 'It's a welcome change to be saving bodies, instead of souls.'

'If you carry them both out with equal skill, the Lord must be well pleased with you. By the way, the servant-girl told me you had been a naval chaplain. If it's not too impertinent a question, what made you leave the service and come here? You're still a young man.'

'I was rather badly wounded on *Eclipse* at Trafalgar. The surgeons declared me unfit for further sea duties and I was invalided from the service.'

Lieutenant Killigrew snapped his fingers and shook his head in annoyance. 'Of course! I should have known. There are few men in the navy who haven't heard of Chaplain Lovell of the *Eclipse*. You saved the ship when it was caught in the thick of the battle, I recall. I am doubly delighted to know you, sir. Our sergeant of marines never stops singing your praises.'

'I did not see Sergeant Maunder among the survivors. Was he . . . ?'

'I am pleased to say he is safe and billeted with the others at the manor. He was pulled from the sea by our longboat.'

'That's very welcome news. Far less agreeable is the ceremony I must perform tomorrow – the burial of your dead seamen. I thought the afternoon might be a suitable time?'

'Yes,' agreed the lieutenant, his cheerfulness suddenly deserting him. 'It's a tragic business and I've been detailed to help you with the necessary arrangements. We'll have all surviving crew at the service, of course. They are to remain at the manor until a decision about their future has been made by the Admiral at Plymouth. There will be an inquiry into the loss of the *Arrow* and some of the men will be required to give evidence. It was a bad business and I fear someone has to take the blame . . . But to return to the subject of the funeral.

'Our men will provide a guard of honour and all the manor servants will attend. Most estate workers too, I expect. I would also like to extend an invitation to the fishermen who helped rescue some of us. And the family who lived close by the beach and who took my men in, too. I understand they are Quakers, so perhaps they will feel unable to attend. But I would like to invite them.'

'Of course. I'll see they are aware of the time when the funeral is to take place.'

Toby hoped Jacob and Bethany would put in an appearance. He missed Bethany. He also wanted to know if she had spoken to the Elders. And if so, what they had said to her.

Rupert Killigrew was talking once more: '. . . after the service you must come to the manor. Have dinner with us.'

Toby gave the other man a wry smile. 'I'm afraid I am not a welcome visitor there.'

'Not welcome? You are the curate of the parish – and you have just saved my life. The life of John Bettison's brother-in-law. You should be guest of honour at a special dinner!'

'I'm afraid the problems go back much farther than the wreck of the *Arrow* . . .' Toby gave the naval lieutenant a sketchy explanation of the situation between the Church and the landowner. He did his best to avoid speculation on John Bettison's financial state. Nevertheless, Rupert Killigrew seemed well aware of what lay behind the unhappy situation.

'I knew John had a great many problems,' he said,

frowning, 'but Caroline has never said anything about such a serious disagreement with the Church.'

Apparently reluctant to pursue the matter any further, he added, 'However, John is away at the moment. My invitation to you stands. My sister and I will be delighted to have you join us for dinner tomorrow night. Shall we say about seven o'clock?'

It would have been churlish to refuse such an enthusiastic invitation. After only a moment's hesitation, Toby accepted the unexpected offer.

'Good! Now, I am afraid we need to discuss the arrangements for a far less enjoyable occasion . . .'

Chapter 24

The little Porthluney church was filled to overflowing for the funeral of the twenty-nine sailors from *Arrow*. More bodies had been washed ashore that morning to add to the grim total.

All the survivors attended the service. So too did Caroline Bettison, who was introduced to Toby by her brother. She thanked him for his part in rescuing Rupert, but this was not the moment for a long conversation. Caroline Bettison had brought with her servants from the manor.

There were also a surprising number of local men and women, in defiance of their landlord's order. Among these were some whom Toby had last seen pulling more goods than men from the sea at Hemmick beach.

The service in the church was sombre, but accompanied by some excellent music. One of the survivors from the *Arrow*, an impressed seaman, was a talented organist. He took full advantage of the occasion to show off his skills.

Shortly before the service began, one of the congregation came up to Toby. He introduced himself as William Pearson, a Methodist circuit preacher. Pointing out that a number of the dead men had probably worshipped as Methodists, he asked to be allowed to offer a prayer and a brief eulogy on their behalf.

Toby knew that if he granted the Methodist permission to address the congregation from the pulpit, he would call down on his head the wrath of the Established Church. However, he told the minister he had no objection to a brief prayer and eulogy at the graveside.

Outside in the churchyard, while the Methodist preacher was offering a prayer, Toby saw Bethany. She was at the rear of the large gathering. He gained the impression that she had only just arrived for this part of the service.

She was aware he had seen her and acknowledged him with a brief nod of her head. Toby hoped she might remain until the service was over. He felt it would not be breaking his promise to Jacob if he merely asked her whether she had yet met with the Elders of the Quaker community.

Disappointingly, Bethany was nowhere to be seen when the service ended and the local people dispersed without speaking to Toby. By doing this they hoped they might escape the wrath of John Bettison, should he learn the names of those who had attended the funeral service.

Caroline Bettison spoke to him before she left and said she was looking forward to entertaining him at the manor and learning more about him. Rupert and his fellow officers also paused to speak to Toby before marching their men away.

A message had been sent to the Admiral at Plymouth immediately after the disaster and a reply had been received via a mounted messenger that morning.

This would be the last day of the men's brief stay at Porthluney Manor. The following day they were to be marched to Falmouth. Here they would embark on a ship that would carry them to the naval dockyard at Plymouth. After being issued with kit to replace what they had lost, most would be drafted to other ships of the fleet. The *Arrow* had been lost, but the war against Napoleon went on – and the fleet was short of skilled and experienced men.

Toby was tidying up the church when he heard a sound behind him. Turning quickly, he saw Bethany standing inside the doorway. She was looking about her with a great deal of interest.

'It's the first time I've been in here. It's really rather pleasant. It has a nice, quiet atmosphere.'

'Bethany! I saw you in the churchyard and looked for you after the service. I thought you must have returned home.'

'That was my intention. But . . . I find I need to speak to thee, Toby.'

'Does Jacob know you're here?'

'I told him I was coming to the funeral of the sailors. He knows I would not leave without speaking to thee. But what has that to do with anything? He is my sister's husband, not my keeper.'

'Have you spoken to the Elders of your Church yet?'

'They have asked me to go to the Meeting House in St Austell tomorrow. I felt I must speak with thee first.'

Bethany sat down upon one of the front pews and looked up at him. Suddenly she appeared very young and vulnerable.

'It will be a very important meeting for me, Toby. Before I speak to the Elders there are some things I need to have straight in my mind. Wilt thou promise to reply to my questions honestly?'

'Of course, but . . .'

'There can be no "buts", Toby, or "ifs" either. Dost thou promise to say only what is truly in thy heart, even if thou believest I may be hurt by thy words?'

'I still don't . . .'

'Thou hast not promised, Toby.' Bethany was becoming increasingly agitated.

'Of course . . . I promise.'

'I thank thee.'

For a few moments, she played with the cuff of her sleeve, as though trying to marshal her thoughts carefully. Then she said, 'When we were walking back to the rectory after the shipwreck, we spoke . . . of how we feel about each other.'

'That's right. You said you were fond of me. I told you I felt the same about you.'

'Yes, but what exactly does it mean to be "fond" of someone, Toby? Even more important, what does it mean to thee? I mean, thou must be *fond* of this church. *Fond* of Nap – how is he today, by the way?'

'Nap is much improved. He'll be out and about again before very long . . . but you were saying?'

'I was talking of what was said that evening. We haven't known each other for long, Toby. It sometimes frightens me that I am contemplating such a giant step when I really know very little about thee, and thou knowest nothing about me. We are from different backgrounds with differing ways of worship – and religion plays a very important part in both our lives. I . . .'

Bethany made a frustrated gesture with her hands. 'I don't think I'm explaining myself very well. I'm not saying what I want to say to thee. What *must* be said. It is *so* important.'

Toby sat down beside her. After a moment's hesitation, he reached out and took one of her hands in his.

'Now it's my turn to say something that isn't going to come easily because I believe neither of us has said anything quite like it before. It's true we haven't known each other for long. We are also experiencing problems in getting to know each other better, because of our Christian beliefs.'

Toby reached over and took her other hand too. 'If you're asking me whether I want to face these difficulties with you, and accept even more difficult times ahead, then the answer is an emphatic "yes". I have already told you I'm fond of you. That's very much an understatement of how I really feel. My feeling for you is so strong, it both awes and confuses me. I find that when I am troubled, I feel the need to have you with me. When I enjoy a rare moment of pleasure, I wish you were there to share it too. I want you with me all the time, Bethany. I want you to be part of my life – for always.'

Toby released her hands and gave a half-shrug. 'I don't know whether that's what you wanted to hear, or whether it might have dismayed you. I do know that I've broken my word to Jacob. I told him I wouldn't discuss such things until you've had your talk with the Elders of your Church.'

'And I told thee that Jacob does not lead my life for me. I've heard what I wanted to hear, Toby. Thou hast given me the strength I need for tomorrow. Now I can face the Elders knowing that what I feel in my heart is in thy heart too.'

Bethany stood up, an expression of sheer joy on her face. When Toby stood up too, she looked up at him and said, 'Thou may kiss me now, if it would give thee pleasure.'

Toby was still not used to her directness. Startled, he stuttered: 'Here . . . in church?'

'Yes, here in *thy* church. Then I shall know it's all true.'

It took Toby longer than he had anticipated to convince Bethany, but she did not seem to mind.

Chapter 25

Dinner at Porthluney Manor began as a very enjoyable occasion. All the surviving naval officers from the *Arrow* were here, with the exception of the commanding officer who had been called to Plymouth, to prepare a report on the tragedy for the Admiralty.

Also present were two landowners and the vicars of the adjacent parishes of Gorran and Mevagissey. Their wives and daughters were also there, all taking a very keen interest in the background and prospects of the young curate.

For his part, Toby was far too excited at the thought of the new understanding that had been reached between himself and Bethany to pay much attention to the unsubtle questioning of mothers and daughters.

Of all the women at the dinner, he was most impressed by John Bettison's wife, Caroline. She was as charming as first impressions had led him to believe. She was also optimistic about his future relations with her husband.

After apologising for not welcoming him to the manor before today, she said, 'I feel quite certain that when my husband hears what you did for Rupert, the situation will return to normal. He has been through a very difficult time and Parson Kempe was not prepared to contemplate a compromise that would meet with the manor's changing circumstances.'

'I am afraid I won't be able to change things in your husband's favour either, Mrs Bettison. I am only the curate. Reverend Kempe is still the rector.'

'Of course . . . but we will not discuss such matters here, this evening. It is a rare pleasure indeed to have Rupert in the house. Had it not been for you, I would not have him at *all* now. It may be unfeeling to hold a dinner party on the day when so many men of the ship's company were buried, but he and the other surviors march to Falmouth tomorrow. With this war going on, heaven only knows when we'll meet again. Now, come. There are a couple of new arrivals. Let me introduce you . . .'

Toby's respect for Caroline grew as the evening progressed. It was evident to him that all was not as it should be at Porthluney Manor, but there was no hint in her demeanour of anything being wrong.

However, if Toby was impressed with his hostess, he was far less so with his two fellow churchmen.

One had once been a curate in a Portsmouth parish. He persistently dropped names of senior and titled naval officers into the conversation. It came to a halt only when Rupert mentioned that Toby had served with Nelson and had been one of the heroes of the Battle of Trafalgar.

The other clergyman kept up an increasingly virulent attack on non-conformists who practised their deviant forms of worship in his parish.

As the consumption of wine increased, so his voice rose in volume. 'We live in a Protestant Christian country,' boomed the churchman. 'Our Church is the Church of England. It is my considered opinion that all who are dissatisfied with our way of worship should be sent abroad. Other countries take such matters far more seriously than we do here. In no time at all they'd all be clamouring to return home, ready to accept the teachings of the Established Church.'

Turning to Toby, he said, 'Don't you agree with me, sir?'

'I'm afraid I don't,' replied Toby, amiably. 'I liken Christianity to today's navy in many ways, with the devil as the enemy. In order to fight him effectively, we need a wide variety of ships, each performing differing duties when they go into battle. It's true to say they fight far more effectively when they work together. Trying to outmanoeuvre each other in a bid to claim glory is a great waste of time, effort and opportunity.'

'What a refreshing point of view,' said Caroline Bettison, breaking the uncertain silence that greeted Toby's words. 'I look forward with very great pleasure to listening to your sermons. I sincerely hope you will use what you have just said as a basis for one of them.'

Taking their cue from the hostess, many of those at the dinner party registered their approval of Toby's words. The vicar who had expressed opposing views did not join in the general acclaim. He sat staring in Toby's direction, his disapproval clear to see.

Despite the rumoured state of the Bettison finances, the meal put on by Caroline Bettison was impressive by any standards. After soup and fish courses, which included salmon and lobster, there was a choice of at least six meat dishes as well as pheasant and partridge and a confusing array of vegetables.

There was a generous supply of wine too. As the meal progressed, even the disapproving vicar appeared to be mellowing, in common with his fellow guests.

Eventually, the top tablecloth was removed, revealing another of fine linen beneath it. Now a number of hot-house fruits were placed upon the table together with preserves, ginger and confitures. Clean glasses were placed before each guest, and claret, port and madeira began their rounds of the table.

Suddenly, the door to the dining-room opened and John Bettison strode into the room. It had been raining for some time and the landowner was wet and bedraggled. He was also in a mood to match his appearance.

Stopped in his tracks at the sight of the dinner party in his house, he scowled at his wife.

'John! I did not expect you home until tomorrow. You said . . .'

'I completed my business more quickly than I anticipated. What's going on here? We had no dinner party planned for this evening.'

'It is my idea, John. My party. I and my fellow officers must leave for Falmouth tomorrow . . .'

Rupert Killigrew broke off his explanation as an expression of fury appeared on the landowner's face. John Bettison had just observed Toby sitting with the other guests at the table.

'What the . . . ! What's *he* doing here?'

For a few moments everyone stared in the general direction of Toby, without being fully aware exactly who was the object of Bettison's wrath.

'You, Parson. What are you doing in my house?'

Now everyone knew he was referring to Toby. Before he could reply, Rupert said, 'He's here as my guest. In fact, he's the guest of honour. He pulled me from the sea at no little risk to himself. I asked Caroline to arrange a dinner to give me the opportunity to thank him for what he did.'

'I don't give a damn what he's done. He's not welcome in my house – and he knows it. The damned impertinence of the man . . .'

The manner in which John Bettison slurred some of his words made it clear he had not ridden straight home from wherever he had been. He had stopped off somewhere and imbibed a considerable amount of alcoholic drink.

'I said he is my guest, John. I owe him my life.'

As Bettison and his brother-in-law glared at each other across the room, Toby rose to his feet. 'It's quite all right, Rupert. It's been a very enjoyable evening. I thank you and Caroline for your hospitality. I'll leave now.'

'There can be no question of your leaving, Toby. This is my house too.' A pale and drawn Caroline intervened. 'My husband has quite obviously had a very long and uncomfortable ride to get home. He will offer you his apologies. Then, after he has changed his clothes, he will return and join us in the drawing-room.'

'I'll not be told what to do in my own house! I'll be delighted to join you and the others in the drawing-room – but not until Kempe's curate has left.'

'Please, I don't want to be the cause of a family argument. It is time I left. It has really been a very exhausting day.'

'Then I'll ride to the rectory with you,' said Rupert. 'I don't feel like sharing the company of my brother-in-law right now.'

'Thank you for coming,' said Caroline, her face still pale and tight. 'Please accept my sincere apologies for my husband's behaviour. It is quite unforgivable.'

'No one needs to apologise for me . . .' blustered John Bettison.

Ignoring him, Caroline spoke to Toby again. 'I will see you in church on Sunday. I and my servants will be there and I look forward to your sermon.'

'You'll not go to his church,' said John Bettison, angrily.

Turning quickly to face her husband, Caroline said, 'If I don't go it will be because I have left Porthluney – as I may well have done.'

Speaking to Toby once more, she said, 'Good night, Toby. Thank you for all you have done for Rupert and his men. Now, I am afraid my other guests must excuse me. I feel the need to go to my room.'

With this she swept from the dining-room without another glance at her husband, leaving Rupert to escort Toby from the house.

Outside the front entrance of the manor house, Toby said, 'I think it would be prudent for you to stay here and leave me to go on alone, Rupert.'

'Nonsense! It's the least I can do after the unforgivable behaviour of that boorish brother-in-law of mine. I really don't know what my father was thinking of when he allowed Caroline to marry him.'

'It's her welfare for which I'm concerned. Her husband has been drinking – and heavily too, if I'm any judge. Caroline has hurt his pride by having me in the house against his wishes. Rumour has it that he is a violent man.'

'You mean . . . he would strike Caroline? *He wouldn't dare!*'

'You're probably right, but I'll go home happier if I know you're here. Just in case.'

'Very well, but if he lays a hand on her he'll have me to deal with. Once again, I apologise for John's behaviour. You and I will meet again, Toby. You can be certain of that.'

Toby rode home thinking of all that had happened during this momentous day. The scene at Porthluney had been unfortunate, but it did not detract from the one thing that was uppermost in his mind.

That was his meeting with Bethany. For her sake he would pray she might receive understanding from the Elders of her Church when she met them the next day.

Chapter 26

'Art thou quite certain thou wouldst not like me to come to the Meeting House with thee? Or at least walk with thee part of the way?'

Seated in the kitchen of the Hemmick cottage, feeding the baby at her breast, Muriel put the question to her sister.

'It takes all thy time caring for the children,' replied Bethany, as three of them ran into the room, shouting at a fourth who was still some way behind them. 'Besides, thou hast not yet recovered from the birth of Sophie.'

Tying the strings of her bonnet beneath her chin, Bethany looked at her sister affectionately. 'I hope thou art satisfied thy family is complete now? Thou dost not want another birth like the last.'

'I still haven't given Jacob the son he so desperately wants,' replied Muriel, bending to kiss the baby's forehead.

'So thou hast *not* finished having babies!' Bethany sighed. 'Then I hope the next one is a boy so thou canst have done with it.'

'I don't mind having babies,' declared Muriel. 'Each one brings its own love with it, and each in a different way. Thou wilt understand when thou hast babies of thine own.' She looked up at her sister. 'Art thou quite certain of the course thou art taking, Bethany?'

'The only thing of which I am certain is that I love Toby. I am equally certain he loves me too. Even so, it will cause me great unhappiness to be cast out from the Friends. I will need to lean very heavily upon Toby. It would be very much easier for me if he felt able to join the Friends – but that would be asking too much of him.

So, if the Elders decree it should be, the sacrifice must be mine.'

'I will pray that they show understanding,' said Muriel, unhappily. 'But I fear those thou wilt meet at St Austell today are too set in the old ways to show such compassion. I will also pray that Toby proves to be all thou wishest for. He is a very nice man, kind too, but . . .'

'There can be no "buts", Muriel, any more than there were when thee and Jacob met. If he had not become a Friend, would thee not have joined his Church?'

After a few moments of hesitation, Muriel nodded. 'Yes, I would. Even though being a Friend means as much to me as it does to thee.'

'I must leave now,' said Bethany. She looked tense and nervous. 'It's a long walk to St Austell.'

Muriel stood up and the sisters embraced. 'I will be thinking of thee throughout the day,' said Muriel. 'I wish Jacob had been able to go with thee.'

'He has a living to earn,' said Bethany. 'And he would have spent the whole of the journey trying to convince me I should remain a Friend to the end of my days, even if it meant dying a spinster. I need to think my own thoughts along the road today.'

Bethany had plenty of time to think about the likely outcome of the course she was pursuing. From the small house at Hemmick to the Quaker Meeting House in St Austell was a journey of eight miles.

It was futile to hope the Elders would not cast her out of the Society of Friends; nevertheless, she clung to a fragile thread of unreasonable hope. In truth, the Elders had no alternative. Bethany had known it happen to a number of others. Most had been young women like herself, faced with the same dilemma of making a choice between the Society and the man they loved. The Society of Friends was a tightly knit little community. Almost a family group. Because of this, the prospects for marrying within such a family were constantly dwindling.

Bethany and her sister had been a part of this warm-hearted yet strict family for the whole of their lives. Being cast out would be a bewildering and unhappy experience for her.

Despite this, she believed she had made an honest decision. Since her first meeting with Toby she had felt an emotion more powerful than any she had ever known before. Probably stronger than anything she would ever feel again.

If it were possible to keep Toby *and* her membership of the Society she would be supremely happy, but in her heart she realised this was unlikely.

The moment of truth was not far away now. In spite of her resolution she found herself walking more slowly as she entered the market town. She knew her tardiness was no more than a bid to delay the inevitable.

Slowly she made her way up the hill to the small Meeting House, situated on the eastern fringe of the town, and entered the low, thatched building.

There were four Elders waiting for her. Bethany knew each of them by name. She knew their families and had shared in their joys and their sorrows.

But she received no smiles of greeting from the men today. Any remaining hopes she might still have entertained were finally dashed as she looked at each stern face in turn.

These men formed the hard core of old-style Elders. They had always resisted any change in the rigid rules of the Society. Indeed, one of the men had voted to disown not one but both of his daughters for the very reason that had brought Bethany to St Austell to account for her own behaviour.

She could expect little sympathy from such men.

The meeting began with silent prayers and Bethany was surprised to find she was sharing this part of the proceedings with a number of women and older Society children.

They sat in silent contemplation for about an hour. During the course of the meeting Bethany realised the others had been brought here to make her more aware of the close fellowship she would forego by pursuing her relationship with Toby.

When the silent 'service' came to an end, the women and children filed out, each bidding Bethany a solemn farewell.

When the last of them had gone from the building, she was left alone with the four stern men and the questioning began. It progressed much as Bethany had anticipated.

First of all, one of the Elders reminded her of the meeting she had just attended in the company of other Friends. By turning her back on this mode of worship there was a very real danger that she would shut out God from her life.

'I am not turning my back on the way of worship I have always known, and will never forsake God,' protested Bethany. 'I will still enjoy moments of quiet communion with Him. No doubt I will share many of them with Toby Lovell.'

One of the Elders shook his head. 'He will expect thee to share many aspects of *his* life, child. Thou wilt lose thy way in the falsehoods of his Church. There is only one way. That is to be true to the lessons taught to thee by the parents and the family of the Friends.'

Once again Bethany expressed her disagreement with the Elders. The discussion continued for a full two hours. Eventually, it was the man who had disowned his two daughters who brought the proceedings to an end.

'We have been very patient with thee, child, but it seems thou art determined to be intransigent. Thou leavest us with no alternative but to disown thee from the Society of Friends. This is a very sad day for thee and for thy family.'

'A very sad day indeed,' agreed one of the Elders who had taken a slightly softer line than his fellows during the meeting. 'But I think thou shouldst have time to reflect upon what has been said to thee here. Go away and pray, as we shall pray for thee. If thou shouldst change thy mind, as I sincerely hope thou wilt, we will be here at the same time, the day after tomorrow. Come and see us then and we will joyfully receive thee and rejoice in thy decision to remain a member of the Society. If thou dost not change thy mind it will be our very sad duty to remove thy name from the list of Friends.'

Suddenly blinded by tears, Bethany said, 'I have no wish to be disowned by the Friends. It is thou who art showing less understanding than a priest of the Church of England. Toby has not asked me to change anything. I am deeply saddened by thy words, but they do not surprise me. I will pray for thee too – and for the future of the Society. May it one day soon be blessed with members who have the wisdom and the courage to bring it out of the eighteenth century and into the modern world.'

Chapter 27

The route of the survivors from *Arrow* took them past Porthluney church on their way to Falmouth. Toby was waiting for them.

In the narrow lane outside the church the men stood bareheaded as he said a prayer for their future well-being and safety in the service of the King.

The brief service over, the men prepared to march off once more. Sergeant of Marines Charlie Maunder, accompanied by three men who had served on the *Eclipse*, broke ranks and came across to shake Toby by the hand and bid him farewell.

When they had moved off, Lieutenant Rupert Killigrew made his way to Toby.

'Thank you for your concern for Caroline yesterday evening. I very much regret to say it was well-founded.'

'You mean . . . her husband *was* violent towards her?'

'He would have been had I not been present. His bullying manner ceased only when I threatened to take Caroline from Porthluney when I left this morning. Unfortunately, I doubt whether his restraint had anything to do with regard for my sister. It was more likely the realisation that he would suffer a considerable loss of income. My father still makes a generous allowance to Caroline. I have long been aware that most of it is spent on the estate. My father has also paid a number of John's gambling debts in the past. If Caroline were to leave, John would be staring bankruptcy in the face. It's a situation that would bring a stronger man than my brother-in-law to heel.'

'No doubt,' agreed Toby. 'But it's hardly the basis for a sound and happy marriage.'

'I suspect that in John's case it brings more harmony to the marriage than would be there if he had no financial worries. However, I would be very much obliged if you were to take an interest in Caroline on my behalf. I have told her I intend speaking to you on the subject.'

'I would be very glad to,' replied Toby. 'Unfortunately, I doubt very much whether I am likely to meet her again. Certainly not at the manor.'

'You'll see her,' declared Rupert. 'That was one thing, at least, we managed to thrash out late last night. Caroline can be exceedingly stubborn when she sets her mind on something. She told John she will no longer be a part of his foolish feud with you. Attending church will be her way of thanking you for saving my life. She also said she has no intention of coming here alone. Caroline will bring servants from the house and any of the estate workers who choose to come.'

To the casual observer, Toby's delight at Rupert's information might have seemed out of all proportion. But only he knew how much he had wanted this breakthrough to occur.

However, even as he was thinking up a suitable means of conveying his gratitude to the landowner's wife, Rupert sounded a warning: 'Caroline will do as she says, but don't imagine for one moment that your problems with John are at an end. He was not as angry as I felt he should have been at Caroline's decision. He was also drinking heavily enough to be indiscreet. He said it didn't really matter because you weren't likely to be here for very much longer. It might have been no more than a blustering attempt to save face, but I doubt it. He's up to something. Be on your guard, Toby. When I next pay Caroline a visit, I hope you will still be the parson of Porthluney.'

The naval officer extended a hand. After shaking it, Toby watched Rupert Killigrew until he passed from view along the lane. Toby walked back to the rectory pondering over the sailor's words. What could John Bettison have meant by his drunken words?

For some time after the departure of the naval officer, Toby felt very restless and found his thoughts straying constantly to Bethany. He wondered how she had fared in her interview with the Elders of her Church.

He guessed correctly that they would have suggested she go home and think very seriously before making any firm decision about a future that included an Anglican clergyman.

He desperately wanted to see her. To speak to her and assure her everything would be all right. However, this was a decision that would not only decide the course of her future, but would change her whole way of life. It was important she should be quite certain it was the right decision. It had to be made without any undue pressure from him. Otherwise she might one day come to regret what she was doing and blame him for his persuasiveness.

Toby spent the remainder of the morning tidying the church and the overgrown churchyard. He decided he would need to find someone in the parish to take on the task of church cleaner.

He thought momentarily of asking Charlotte, but dismissed the idea immediately. She made heavy work of her duties in the rectory and would not be willing to take on the task of church cleaner.

Charlotte had been late for work once more that morning, but today she had not bothered to offer any explanation or apology.

When he went in to lunch she produced something that was largely inedible. While he was eating she did her best to persuade him to spend the afternoon visiting some of the elderly parishioners. She pointed out that they had not had a visit from a priest for more than a year.

Toby believed Charlotte wanted him out of the way so that she might leave early once more, but today he intended being out of the house for only a short while.

Two more victims from the *Arrow* had been recovered from the sea that morning. They would be interred that afternoon in the churchyard, alongside the mass grave of their shipmates.

Toby performed a brief graveside service for the dead sailors, the only mourners being the two gravediggers. During the service he caught a glimpse of a girl he felt certain was Charlotte. She was running alongside the hedge of a field beyond the rectory.

When he returned to the house after the service, he thought he must have been mistaken. Charlotte was there and showed no sign of having been away from the house. Besides, the girl he saw had not been running in the direction of her home. It *must* have been someone else.

He left the house for little more than an hour later that afternoon to attend Eli Whitnick's funeral at the Portloe chapel. Here he said a prayer for the late Methodist preacher.

Late that evening, Toby received an unexpected visitor at the rectory. He was working in his study when he heard a knock on the door. Believing it might be Bethany with news of what had occurred at the St Austell Meeting House, he hurried to open it.

To his great disappointment, his visitor was a man, standing outside the door, twisting a hat nervously in his hands.

'I'm sorry to trouble you, sir, but would you be Curate Lovell?'

'I am. Have we met before?'

'No, sir, but I've been sent with an urgent message for you from Rector Kempe. He says you're to come and see him tomorrow morning, if you please, sir. As early as you can possibly make it.'

'I see!' Toby frowned. 'Do you have any idea what it's all about?'

'None at all, sir. I only know what I was asked to say to you and I've come here just as quick as I could.'

Toby looked outside for a glimpse of the man's horse. There was not one to be seen.

'Have you walked all the way from St Stephen?'

'That's right, sir – although I ran for part of the way. I thought you might be in bed before I reached here. I'll be going back again now.'

'Nonsense! After coming all that way you'll come in and have a drink and something to eat before you return.'

The man appeared to be uncertain of whether or not he should stay, but Toby insisted. It was a brisk two hours' walk between Porthluney and St Stephen. The man deserved something.

Unfortunately, all he could find in the pantry was some

bread, cheese, and a rather stale piece of salt pork. He hoped Rose would soon return and set about replenishing the larder.

Toby also made the man some tea. Suspecting he was disappointed it was not something stronger, he brought out the keg which had been left on the rectory doorstep for him and gave the man a tumbler of brandy.

This seemed to relax him. As he ate and drank, the messenger told Toby he often helped with Rector Kempe's garden and carried out odd jobs for him.

The peremptory summons from the rector was puzzling Toby more and more. He wondered why Kempe had sent this man and not a written note to tell him what it was all about.

He asked once more if the man had any inkling of the reason for the senior parson's summons.

'Not really, sir – although it might have something to do with a message the parson received from the Bishop of Exeter. The messenger arrived late this afternoon and had ridden hard, or so I heard him say. I suppose he must have done because he said he'd changed horses at half-a-dozen parishes along the way and would be returning them on the way back. Whatever it was he brought stirred up the old parson and no mistake – begging your pardon, sir.'

'And you think whatever the messenger brought has something to do with Reverend Kempe calling for me to go and see him? I wonder what it could be about?'

'I've no idea at all, sir, but you'll find out tomorrow, I dare say.'

Wiping his mouth on a sleeve, the man beamed at Toby. 'Thank you very kindly for that, sir. It'll help keep out the cold very nicely on the way back. It's not often I get to taste brandy the likes of that. I'll be on my way now. What time shall I tell the parson you'll be there to see him?'

'I'll see the girl into the house to begin her cleaning and give her a list of a few supplies I need, then I'll leave right away. Tell Reverend Kempe I hope to be there between ten and ten-thirty.'

Chapter 28

It proved to be one of those mornings when nothing seemed to go right. Toby had risen early, in order to reach St Stephen by the time he had promised. He wanted to see Charlotte before he left, but instead of arriving by eight o'clock, she did not put in an appearance until nine.

She did not seem at all contrite, pointing out that she had work to do at home before coming to the rectory. She was doubtful too whether she would have time to go off and buy provisions for him.

To add to his problems, when Toby hurried to the paddock to fetch Nipper, he discovered the donkey was lame. It meant he would have to walk to St Stephen for his meeting with Reverend Kempe – a prospect that did not appeal to him.

He tried to make up time along the way, but he was not as fit as the messenger of the night before. It was almost eleven-thirty by the time he reached China clay quarrying country and the village of St Stephen.

Toby was not surprised to find the rector working in his garden. What *was* unusual was the lack of warmth in the older man's greeting.

Believing the cause to be his late arrival, Toby apologised. 'I'm sorry I'm late. The rectory cleaner was late arriving, then I found Nipper was lame so I was forced to walk here.'

'You had better come inside,' said Reverend Kempe with no words of sympathy or welcome.

Toby wondered what he might have done to sour the rector's attitude towards him. He could think of nothing. Yet the messenger despatched by Kempe the previous evening had said the rector had sent for him after receiving a letter from the bishop. It must have contained something that pertained to him.

In the house, the rector led the way to his study. A letter lay open on the desk. Toby deduced it was the one of which the messenger had spoken.

His deduction was correct. Dropping heavily into the chair behind the desk, Harold Kempe picked up the letter and shook it in Toby's direction. 'I received this last night. It's from the bishop – and it's about you.'

'I should be flattered to have come to the bishop's attention,' said Toby. 'But I have a feeling he's not singing my praises.'

'Your feeling is correct,' said Kempe, grimly. 'Listen to this . . .'

Picking up the letter he began to read: '"A number of very serious complaints have been levelled against Curate Lovell of Porthluney. It is alleged he has preached in the chapel of non-conformists, namely Methodists, and allowed a Methodist preacher to take a service in his own church. He is also said to have formed close friendships with members of the non-conformist sect known as 'Quakers'. Further, there is said to be proof that he associates with smugglers and wreckers and was personally involved with wreckers who carried off articles from His Majesty's ship *Arrow* when that vessel was tragically wrecked on the coast in his parish."'

Lowering the letter, Reverend Kempe said, 'Finally – and we both know the truth of this – it says that since coming to Porthluney you and your church have been boycotted by the parishioners and not one has attended a single service in your church.'

The rector dropped the letter to the desk. 'There are other accusations of a rather more trivial nature, such as being unfeeling in your attitude towards landowners, tenants and fishermen who are suffering hard times and having difficulty in raising their tithes.'

'Does the bishop say who has made this catalogue of complaints to him?'

'No, but does he need to? I would hazard only one guess. No doubt you would too. But let's go through the letter and take the complaints one by one. I think we can dismiss immediately the accusation that no one is attending Porthluney church . . .'

'That problem has been resolved,' declared Toby. 'We have a congregation once more. It came about as a result of my being on the beach when the frigate *Arrow* was wrecked. Far from being involved with these so-called "wreckers", I was helping to save lives. One of those I saved was Rupert Killigrew, brother of John Bettison's wife. As a result I was invited to dinner at the manor during Bettison's absence. Unfortunately, Bettison returned while I was still there. He'd most likely just been to see the bishop, in Exeter. There was an ugly scene and I left. I saw Lieutenant Killigrew again the following day, when he was leaving the area with his men . . .'

Toby told the rector what had been said and of Caroline Bettison's intention of attending church, with the house servants. He added, 'So I am confident the boycott of the church imposed by Bettison is at an end. At least, it is so far as his wife and servants are concerned.'

'Well! You've achieved more in a few weeks than I in more than a year. That's also dealt with another of the more serious allegations, but there are the others . . .'

'Let's deal with the matter of the Methodist preacher and preaching in each other's churches. It was pointed out to me that some of the ship's company I buried in Porthluney churchyard were probably Methodists. The local Methodist preacher asked permission to offer a eulogy from the pulpit of the church. I would not allow this, but I did agree he could say a prayer at the graveside of the men buried that day. I also said a prayer at the Methodist chapel at Portloe yesterday for Eli Whitnick. You too knew him, I believe? Bettison would not have known of this when he listed his complaints, and I certainly would not apologise for it. Eli died trying to rescue some of the sailors. He was a brave and good man. I have no regrets in letting it be seen that I was praying for his soul.'

Reverend Kempe frowned thoughtfully before saying, 'I am perhaps less tolerant of non-conformists than you are. They would not find me quite so accommodating. However, I have never had to bury men from one of His

Majesty's men-o'-war. What you did is not without precedent and our bishop is a very tolerant man. He will probably approve of your allowing a Methodist to say a few words.'

The rector glanced at the letter once more. 'It also mentions Quakers here. I presume that would be Jacob Hosking and his wife and young family who live at Hemmick beach?'

'I have met Jacob on a number of occasions, yes, and I feel I can call him a friend, but it's more likely to refer to the sister of Jacob's wife. I have become very fond of the girl. Very fond indeed, and she of me. Because of our association she has already been interviewed by the Elders of her Church. It's most likely she will be cast out of the Society of Friends as a result. If this happens it's my intention to ask her to marry me.'

Rector Kempe looked at Toby open-mouthed for a few moments. When he had regained some of his composure, he said, 'You have confounded me, Toby. When I took you on as my curate I felt you would become so bored that within a matter of weeks you would consider leaving. Instead, you seem to have stirred up a hornet's nest, thrown a great deal of Ecclesiastical law to the four winds – yet achieved commendable ends. It seems almost a crime to have to suspend you.'

'Suspend me?' Toby looked at the rector in disbelief. 'Why should you do that?'

'Because I have been instructed to do so by the bishop.'

'But . . . he can't do that! I've just succeeded in sorting out the problem of attendance at the church and Mrs Bettison has taken the lead in bringing the congregation back. Everything is beginning to fall into place at Porthluney. It doesn't make sense!'

'I agree. However, let's now go through all the points mentioned in the letter once more and make written replies to each one. Then I will write a letter on your behalf and you can take it with you.'

'Take it where?'

'Oh, haven't I mentioned it? The bishop wants you to travel to Exeter immediately. When you meet him he will decide whether or not it will be necessary to convene a Church court to try you.'

Chapter 29

Toby walked back to the Porthluney rectory in a very unhappy frame of mind later that evening, having spent the whole day at St Stephen.

He had believed things were beginning to go right for his curacy. He had been accepted by the fishing community, and the shipwreck had put an end to the spiteful boycott of the Church ordered by John Bettison.

Had this malicious complaint not been made to the bishop, Toby believed he would be well on the way to bringing Porthluney back within the orbit of the Church as a normal rural parish.

There was still the matter of disputed tithes to be settled with the lord of the manor, of course, but with a modicum of goodwill from all concerned, this too would have been resolved in due course.

Toby was also deeply concerned lest this latest setback affect the plans he had in mind for Bethany and himself.

He was fully aware of the sacrifice she was ready to make for him. She had always been a Quaker, having been born into a Quaker family. To be cast out of the Society would be a very upsetting experience for her – and he had no doubt she *would* be expelled. If she married him – and this was what he intended – he hoped to be able to show her the many advantages to be gained from living life in an orderly, loving parish.

Much of the tradition and ceremonial of the Church of England would be alien to her, yet he felt confident she would come to understand it was part of the tradition that was at the heart of his own religion. He wanted her to learn to love the Church as he did.

He hoped she might also find there was room for many of her own beliefs within his Church.

With all this in mind, he returned to the Porthluney rectory via Hemmick Cove, hoping to be able to speak to Bethany and tell her of his thoughts and acquaint her with what was happening.

The small cottage was in darkness. The Quaker family tended to rise with the sun and to go to bed with it too.

Reverend Kempe had insisted that he and Toby should go through the bishop's letter time and time again until he was finally satisfied they had found the answers to all the allegations that had been made against him. As a result, he had left St Stephen much later than he intended.

Toby would not run the risk of waking the children tonight. Instead he would leave a few minutes earlier in the morning and call on Bethany before catching the coach to Exeter.

Toby rose at dawn the next morning. He viewed the thought of the next few days with a great deal of trepidation. It would not be exaggerating the situation to say the whole of his future depended upon the bishop's decision.

It had been his intention to leave a note for Charlotte, in the hope that she could read. Much to his relief and surprise, she arrived as he was preparing to leave the house, shortly before eight o'clock.

He had already decided not to inform her of his reason for going to Exeter – or even to tell her where he was going. All he said was that he would be absent from the rectory for a few days. He requested that she should come to the house daily to clean through and feed Napoleon and Nipper. When he was quite certain she understood her duties, Toby set off.

He would be walking to St Austell to catch the coach that connected the port of Falmouth with London. But first, he intended calling once more at the cottage on Hemmick beach.

He was surprised when he reached the Quaker home to find no one there.

However, a quick check was all that was needed to

ascertain that Jacob's horse and cart were gone too. The Quaker fisherman had probably made a good catch the day before and taken it to market very early. His family, and Bethany, must have gone with him.

Toby would look out for them in St Austell.

The walk took rather longer than he had anticipated and he was unable to search for Bethany. He arrived in the small town with barely enough time to catch the coach. The vehicle was very full. Toby found himself wedged between a heavily-built woman who smelled strongly of stale perspiration, and a pert young girl of perhaps eight or nine years of age.

The girl was travelling with her mother and a grandfather who, like Toby, was a cleric.

The older man nodded a brief greeting in Toby's direction when he entered the coach, but further conversation became impossible as the passengers were made to move up somewhat grudgingly to make room for a late arrival.

For some minutes, during the time it was at the inn, there was frenzied activity on and about the coach. Once the passengers joining at St Austell had taken their places and each passenger's right to a seat was established, a number of the travellers decided they needed to take advantage of the inn's facilities.

Meanwhile, a great deal of luggage and freight was loaded and unloaded, with refreshments on offer for those passengers who wanted them. Despite the early hour most accepted alcoholic drinks. The large lady beside Toby downed a quart of ale which was quickly followed by a very large brandy, 'To ward off the chill'.

She gave the explanation to no one in particular, even as she wiped excess perspiration from her forehead with a large square of towelling cloth, produced from the basket balanced on her ample lap.

The horses were changed, luggage secured and the passengers squeezed into their places. A defiant blast on a long posthorn signalled their departure and the driver whipped up the horses. A moment later the coach clattered from the yard.

In the narrow streets of the small market town there

was a brief altercation between the coach guard and the driver of a large, slow-moving wagon, loaded with blocks of chalk-white China clay. It was settled only when a town constable ordered the heavy wagon to move over and make way for the coach.

Eventually, after labouring up a steep hill to the east of the town, St Austell was left behind. Now the driver shook out the reins and the coach began its long journey through the narrow lanes of Cornwall.

Only then did the elderly parson break his silence to speak to Toby.

'Good morning. I don't think we've met before? I am Jeremiah Trist, Vicar of Veryan.'

Toby nodded his head in acknowledgement of the information. 'Toby Lovell, sir. Curate of Porthluney.'

'Are you indeed? I heard old Harold Kempe had brought a younger man in to tackle his problems! So you're the one, eh? I've been meaning to call on you as we're in charge of adjacent parishes, but life's been somewhat busy of late.'

He glanced across the coach to where the woman and girl were seated alongside Toby. 'My daughter's husband, Commander Jarvis, died at the Battle of Trafalgar, leaving his affairs in something of a muddle. We seem to have got things sorted out at last and are on our way to Plymouth to put signatures to the final documents. In the meantime, my daughter Sally, and my granddaughter Anna, are living at the vicarage, although Sally has bought a house close to the vicarage, in Veryan.'

Toby smiled at the young girl and inclined his head in the direction of her sad-eyed mother. When he spoke, it was to the mother.

'You have my deepest sympathy on the loss of your husband, ma'am. On what ship was he serving with Nelson's fleet?'

'Thank you for your kind commiseration, sir. My husband was the commander of the *Belleisle*.'

'The *Belleisle*!' Toby repeated the name of the ship with an almost reverent respect. 'I trust you will one day allow pride to ease the pain you are feeling right now, ma'am. The *Belleisle* fought a magnificent battle. To watch her follow Admiral Collingwood into action, taking on and defeating ship after ship, was sheer joy. It gave added incentive to every sailor in Nelson's fleet to fight just that little bit harder than the enemy. It's such examples that win battles – and ultimately the war too, I hope.'

'You were at Trafalgar, Curate Lovell?' Reverend Trist voiced his surprise.

'Yes, sir. I was chaplain on a frigate. The wounds I received there forced me to leave the service and take the post of curate at Porthluney.'

Sally Jarvis murmured sympathetically before asking, eagerly, 'You actually saw the *Belleisle* go into action, Mr Lovell?'

'I did. We were at the end of the line and saw every detail of the battle before we too engaged the enemy. When we saw her run aboard the *Fougueux* there was a cheer from our crew such as I had never heard before. There was no ship in the fleet fought more bravely, you have my word for it.'

'Thank you, Mr Lovell, thank you very much. I will try to comfort myself with those words when I am feeling particularly sorry for myself and for Anna.'

Toby was disturbed to see tears trembling in the young woman's eyes. Her daughter was upset too, but others had seen and heard the exchange. A man who must have been in his early-thirties leaned forward from the seat opposite Anna's. Reaching out an apparently empty hand towards her, he said, 'You're the daughter of a hero, young lady – but what are you doing hiding eggs in your ears?'

Anna was about to recoil from him, thinking him to be mad, when his hand brushed against her right ear and apparently produced a hen's egg from it. A second swift movement produced another from the young girl's left ear.

Anna looked startled for a moment. Then she giggled.

Lifting her bonnet, the man apparently placed the eggs there. A moment later he retrieved them from her grandfather's neckcloth.

'How did you do that? Show me?' The young girl had forgotten her earlier unhappiness and her mother too was smiling.

For the remainder of the journey to the River Tamar the magician kept the coach entertained and showed Anna how to carry out a few simple tricks.

The Reverend Trist was initially uncertain of encouraging the magician, but he too gradually relaxed. He even allowed his watch to be used in a trick, although he was disconcerted when the magician wrapped it in a kerchief and appeared to stamp on it on the coach floor.

This trick was brought to a conclusion when the magician told the heavily-built, perspiring woman to remove the cloth from the top of her basket and she found the watch there.

'Well, I never! I'm sure I never put it there! I don't want no one thinking I did for a minute. Who'd have believed it?' It was a theme she repeated time after time with many variations for the remainder of the journey.

When the coach and horses were loaded separately on the ferry which linked Cornwall with Plymouth, the passengers disembarked from the coach to stretch their legs.

Reverend Trist and his daughter stood at the rail as the ferry set off across the wide river. On the far bank was Plymouth, destination for the Vicar of Veryan and the two members of his family.

'Are you leaving the coach here too?' Sally asked Toby.

'No, I'm going on to Exeter for a meeting with the bishop.'

Jeremiah Trist looked at Toby shrewdly. 'Is it to be a pleasurable meeting?'

'I fear not,' he admitted. 'It seems the principal landowner in Porthluney has laid a number of complaints against me. I've been summoned to Exeter to answer to them.'

'The complainant will no doubt be John Bettison,' declared the Vicar of Veryan. 'It's unbelievable that he has the gall to lay a complaint against anyone – especially a priest. Are you confident of countering his charges?'

'I think so, and I have Reverend Kempe's support.'

'Good! When you meet Bishop Fisher tell him you have met me. I know very little about you, Curate Lovell, but I *do* know a great deal about Mr Bettison. Tell the bishop

I will send him a letter informing him of what I know of your landowner.'

'That's very kind of you . . .' Toby spoke hesitantly and Jeremiah Trist guessed the reason.

'You're wondering whether it's likely to make any difference?' He smiled. 'I think it might help. Bishop Fisher and I joined the Church together. We shared lodgings during our student days at Oxford. We have a great many friends and interests in common too. The only difference between us is that John has always possessed ambition. I have none. That's probably the reason we have remained friends.'

'Perhaps Curate Lovell can come to Veryan and have dinner with us when he returns?' suggested Sally.

'I would like that, thank you.' Looking over to where Anna was laughing happily with her new-found friend, Toby added, 'Perhaps I should bring the magician with me?'

'He has been wonderful for Anna,' said Sally. 'It's the first time since her father died that I've seen her look really happy.'

'Yes indeed,' murmured Reverend Trist. Reaching inside a pocket, he pulled out a purse. 'I must reward him for entertaining her so well.'

Shortly afterwards the coachman called for his passengers to rejoin the coach. As Toby stood back to allow Sally to precede him on board, she said, 'You *will* visit us at Veryan, Mr Lovell?'

'It's a promise, but please call me Toby.'

'Thank you, I would like that. I'm afraid all the visitors at Veryan have been of Father's age and I wouldn't dare even ask their first names. It will be so good when I have a place of my own once more and have made new friends for Anna and myself.'

'She's a delightful little girl,' said Toby, looking over to where Anna was following her grandfather's example and gravely shaking hands with the magician from the coach. 'I'm quite certain neither of you will have any difficulty at all in making friends in your new home.'

Chapter 30

Sally and Anna Jarvis waved vigorously after the coach as it pulled out of the Plymouth inn yard. Reverend Jeremiah Trist was inside the hostelry, arranging for a carriage to take the three of them on to their eventual destination.

Toby and the magician, who had just introduced himself as Matthew Vivian, waved in return until the coach left the yard and turned into the busy Plymouth street.

'You've made one little girl very happy today,' said Toby to his travelling companion. 'It should be very pleasing for you. I'd say there is room for a little happiness in her life.'

'Yes, and I was paid for doing it. Her grandfather rather generously gave me two shillings for entertaining her during the journey.'

Something in his voice made Toby ask, 'Aren't you usually paid for performing your magic?'

'No. I learned my earliest tricks from an ex-fairground magician. He was a pickpocket too, I suspect. He worked for my father. I was always getting into trouble for wasting my time with him. My father was fond of telling me I would make no money from performing tricks. Would that he were alive now for me to tell him he was wrong.'

'Did he have another career in mind for you?'

'Yes. He intended I should take over the family shipping business with my brother, as indeed I have.'

'You own a ship?' Toby was surprised. He had always imagined shipowners to be wealthy men. This man showed no outward signs of wealth. Indeed, he fitted the role of fairground magician more than he did that of a shipowner.

Matthew's next words came as even more of a surprise. 'We have half-a-dozen ships, actually. Whenever possible I leave my brother to run things in the Falmouth office while I involve myself in more interesting work. I much prefer to be at sea. Right now I'm on my way to a small shipyard on the River Exe, below Exeter, in which my brother and I have an interest. It's been carrying out work on a rather special ship we've purchased.'

'What's so special about this one?'

'She's Baltimore-built and can outsail any ship afloat, even with a dozen twelve-pounder guns on board. She was taken as a prize when the navy raided a French port.'

'A fast ship with guns? You mean you're purchasing . . . a privateer?'

A privateer was a ship that roamed the oceans of the world, seeking merchantmen flying the flag of an enemy country. Had a privateer not carried authorisation from its home government it would have been hunted down as a pirate vessel.

Matthew Vivian smiled at Toby's surprise. 'That's what she was when sailed by an American crew, and that's what she'll be for me. I already have letters of marque from the Admiralty.'

Others in the coach were taking a great deal of interest in the conversation and Matthew Vivian changed the subject abruptly. 'When do you hope to conclude your business with the bishop?'

'I don't know. It shouldn't take more than a day or two at the most. I'm hoping to return to Porthluney the day after tomorrow.'

'That's the day when I intend sailing the *Potomac* to Falmouth. Before we part company I'll give you the name of the yard where she's lying. Come back to Cornwall on her with me. As an ex-naval chaplain you'll no doubt appreciate what a fine ship she is.'

Toby thought it would be a novel experience. However, the talk of meeting the bishop had reminded him of the reason for his visit to Exeter. He spent much of the remainder of the journey thinking of what he would say in his own defence when he met the bishop.

Toby called at the bishop's palace early the following

morning, only to be kept waiting in an ante-room for half-an-hour. When he was eventually escorted to the bishop's office and shown inside, he found the prelate seated at a huge desk, flanked by his chaplain and an archdeacon.

The bishop seemed affable enough. 'Hello, Curate Lovell. I am Bishop Fisher.' Indicating the grey-haired, sallow-complexioned man on his right, he said, 'This is Archdeacon Scantlebury. We also have my chaplain David Ball present. He is here to take notes for us.'

Bishop Fisher waved Toby to a chair placed on the far side of the desk, opposite the senior churchmen.

As Toby seated himself, the bishop said, 'Please don't feel over-awed by our numbers, Curate. Such an inquiry would normally be carried out by Archdeacon Scantlebury alone. However, as he has occupied the office for less than a month and the letter was delivered to me in person, I felt I should sit in on the interview.'

Toby wondered whether this was the reason the archdeacon appeared disgruntled. Speaking to the bishop, he said, 'May I be permitted to give you a letter from Reverend Kempe, written on my behalf?'

When it appeared the archdeacon was about to protest, Toby added hastily, 'It's addressed to you personally, my lord, but I'm quite certain Reverend Kempe would have no objection should you wish to show it to Archdeacon Scantlebury. I believe you will also be receiving a message from the Reverend Trist of Veryan in the near future.'

'You know Jeremiah?' The bishop's delight was evident.

'We met for the first time yesterday when we travelled to Plymouth together. He knows very little about me, as I am quite certain he will inform you, but he appears to know a great deal about Mr Bettison.'

'I also know Mr Bettison,' snapped the irascible archdeacon. 'At least, I know his family. Now, shall we proceed?'

'Would any of the Scantleburys buried in Porthluney churchyard be your ancestors?' asked Toby, trying to appear unruffled.

'All of them. I spent part of my childhood in the area. As

I recall, the Bettisons are an old family and highly respected landlords. Now, shall we proceed? I presume you are aware of the complaints made against you, Curate?'

'I am.' Toby had an uncomfortable feeling that this man had already pre-judged the issue.

'Can you give me your initial reaction to them?' The question came from the bishop.

'They have been made by a spiteful and vindictive man, my lord. One who seeks to discredit me and the Church for his own ends. For the archdeacon's information I would like to add that I have the support of Bettison's wife and her family. From all I have heard, it would seem John Bettison possesses few of the qualities of his forebears.'

'Are you saying there is no truth whatsoever in these allegations?' The archdeacon's question contained a thinly veiled scepticism.

'The allegations are a deliberate distortion of the truth,' replied Toby. 'Reverend Kempe's letter gives some of the reasons why the accusations have been made.'

'I will decide whether Reverend Kempe's letter is pertinent to this matter,' snapped the archdeacon.

'Then I trust my lord bishop will allow you to read it,' replied Toby, trying very hard not to allow the archdeacon's manner to rattle him.

'It is a most interesting letter,' declared the bishop who had been reading during the exchange between Toby and the archdeacon. 'It would seem to indicate you walked into a situation that was already difficult when you took up your curacy. Come to think of it, I seem to recall a problem being brought to my attention a year or two ago. I think you should read it, Archdeacon Scantlebury.'

'Thank you, my lord.' The archdeacon took the letter and placed it face downwards on the desk in front of him. Returning his attention to Toby, he said, 'Now, let us go through the complaints, one by one . . .'

Toby was in the bishop's office for almost two hours. He felt he had been able to give satisfactory explanations to all except two of the complaints made against him.

The two complaints which were made much of by the archdeacon were those touching upon his dealings with the Methodist Church in Cornwall, and his relations with Bethany and her Quaker family.

Time and time again the archdeacon returned to these two subjects. On more than one occasion Toby considered his questioning concerning Bethany to be offensive, but he managed to maintain a tight grip on his temper.

Eventually, when the questioning had become repetitious, the bishop said gently, 'I feel that Curate Lovell has already answered your questions adequately, Archdeacon. There seems little point in pursuing the matter any further.'

'Nevertheless, I am not entirely satisfied, my lord. However, I agree we are not likely to arrive at a satisfactory conclusion today. I would therefore like to bring the interview to an end, review all that has been said, and continue enquiries in my own way.'

Bishop Fisher stared at the archdeacon for some moments before inclining his head in reluctant agreement. 'As you wish, Archdeacon Scantlebury. You are in charge of the inquiry. It would be rather more satisfactory for all concerned were it to be brought to a swift conclusion . . . but it is in your hands.'

Toby was uncertain what was to happen next. Speaking to the archdeacon, he asked, 'Does this mean I must remain in Exeter until your enquiries have been completed?'

'No. They may take some time.'

'Am I to remain suspended, or may I return to my duties as curate of Porthluney?'

'You will remain suspended – and may I suggest you reside outside the parish until this matter has been brought to a conclusion? I feel it would be in the best interests of all concerned.'

Toby wanted to argue with the archdeacon. The suspension served only the interests of John Bettison. For a moment he felt the bishop might also intercede on his behalf. Instead, both he and his chaplain kept silent.

It was a very despondent Toby who returned to the inn that evening. He no longer held a curacy – and he also had to leave his home in the rectory at Porthluney.

Chapter 31

The longer Toby thought about his meeting with the senior churchmen in the bishop's palace, the more convinced he became that the findings of the archdeacon, when they came, would not be in his favour.

Had the meeting been with the bishop only, he was convinced John Bettison's complaints would have been dismissed before he left the office. As it was, the matter was likely to drag on for weeks – months, even.

Toby was aware that matters of this nature fell almost entirely within an archdeacon's jurisdiction. It was he who was responsible for the discipline of the clergy within a diocese.

It was Toby's misfortune that he should find an archdeacon who was not only new in his post, but who had been brought up in Porthluney parish. Furthermore, it seemed he was steeped in the respect traditionally accorded to the local landowner.

Toby's melancholy was apparent to Matthew Vivian the following morning, when he arrived at the shipyard where the conjuring shipowner's vessel was being fitted out.

'Did the interview with your bishop not go well?' The question was put to Toby sympathetically.

'I'd say that sums up the situation well enough,' he replied. 'I'm suspended until various complaints against me have been investigated. Until then I'm supposed to live outside my parish.'

Matthew Vivian whistled through his teeth. 'What have you done to deserve that? I don't suppose there's a woman involved? Another clergyman's wife, perhaps?'

Toby smiled, despite his despondency. 'Nothing quite as dramatic as that, I'm afraid. I inherited a feud carried on by the local landowner against my predecessor. He's raked up many of the old complaints, found one or two new ones, and submitted them to the bishop.'

Toby gave the other man a brief summary of his problems before adding, 'I thought I'd take advantage of your kind offer and sail to Falmouth in your new ship. Perhaps the sea air will help me think more clearly about everything.'

'It's the best cure I know for life's difficulties,' agreed Matthew. 'When we get to sea I'll put the *Potomac* through her paces. She'll soon outsail all your problems. Come below and have a drink before I show you over the ship. She's even more of a beauty than I remembered . . .'

The *Potomac* was certainly impressive. Long before the inspection was over, Toby had conceded it was the finest ship he had ever seen. It had been designed on the lines of a fast merchantman and could undoubtedly outsail any man-o'-war. Yet the vessel carried sufficient armament to put up a spirited defence should it be surprised by an enemy warship.

The crew's efficiency matched that of their craft. They had spent a couple of weeks on board, familiarising themselves with their new vessel and training for the role they would be required to carry out at sea.

When the *Potomac* left the mouth of the Exe behind and reached the choppy waters of the English Channel, Matthew ordered all available sail to be put on. The ship responded immediately. Heeling over, the vessel sliced through the water at a thrilling speed.

To Toby's surprise, the *Potomac* did not immediately set a course for Falmouth. Instead, they headed southwards, on a bearing that at their present speed would bring them close to the French coast in a matter of hours.

When he commented upon this, Matthew merely smiled. 'For the *Potomac*, one part of the sea is as safe as any other. Neither of us has any reason to rush home to Cornwall so I thought we'd take advantage of the good weather and put the ship through its paces.'

Toby kept to himself the reservations he had about

Matthew's statement. He was anxious to return to Porthluney to learn what had happened in Bethany's meeting with the Elders of the Society of Friends. The outcome would have a considerable impact on his life and, in view of the archdeacon's inquiry, his future within the Church of England.

He was also missing Bethany. He wanted to be with her again.

Five hours after leaving the mouth of the Exe, a lookout called to say he could see land ahead.

'That will be the Cherbourg peninsula,' said Matthew. Pulling out his watch, he added: 'We've made good time. There are no ships in the French navy capable of keeping up with us.'

Calling to the helmsman, he said, 'Right, Sam, bring her round to starboard and steer west-nor'-west. We'll go home now.'

No more than an hour after the change of course, there came another shout from the lookout. This time it was to report he had sighted the sails of a ship, almost dead ahead of the *Potomac*.

It aroused only minimal interest on board, until the ships drew closer to each other. There were many British naval vessels patrolling these waters. But after peering at it through a telescope for some time, Matthew frowned and called up to the lookout.

'What flag is she flying?'

There was a brief pause before the lookout replied, 'She isn't. There's not a flag to be seen.'

'This could be promising,' mused Matthew. 'The only ships reluctant to identify themselves in these seas are usually French. She's a sizeable merchantman too, and I can't imagine an English merchantman sailing so close to the French coast.'

After a brief conversation with one of the seamen, a signal flag was run up to the mast. Its message read: 'Identify yourself'.

The signal brought no reaction and by now the two vessels were closing quite rapidly.

'Bring her around, Coxwain,' commanded Matthew. 'We'll travel with her for a while and take a closer look.'

The merchantman was larger than the *Potomac* and had half-a-dozen gunports on each side, but the ports were closed.

'Fire a shot across their bows,' ordered Matthew. 'And prepare to follow it with a salvo. I'm pretty certain it's a French merchantman and they probably have no experienced gunners on board, but it could be a trick to draw us in closer.'

The shot from the *Potomac* splashed harmlessly into the sea ahead of the merchantman – but it produced an immediate reaction. The gun ports on the side closest to *Potomac* were flung open, guns were run out and suddenly a tricolour was run up to the masthead.

'Fire a salvo!' shouted Matthew. 'And make it count!'

Despite the advantage held by the French merchantman, the salvo from the *Potomac* struck home before a gun was fired from the other vessel.

Every shot struck home and one of them brought down the vessel's foremast. The sailors on *Potomac* prepared for swift retaliation – but none came. While the privateer's gunners were hurriedly reloading their cannons, the French flag fluttered down from the masthead, the guns were run inboard, and now the sails were furled, one by one.

The French merchantman had surrendered to the *Potomac*, without firing a single shot!

In spite of this, Matthew brought his ship alongside the other vessel cautiously.

Such caution proved unnecessary. As the *Potomac* eased alongside, the French captain called to them from the guard rail.

'I will not fight you. There are women and children on board, and also a number of sick crew and passengers. We have been at sea for a long time and are desperately short of food. All I ask is that you will spare the women and children and arrange for them to complete their voyage to France.'

'I'll do all I can for them,' replied Matthew. 'I am sending an armed boarding party on board. Tell your men not to do anything foolish.'

As the *Potomac* went alongside and the two vessels bumped together in the swell, twenty heavily armed men scrambled on board the merchantman. Others remained on the deck of the privateer, their guns aimed at the French seamen as they were gathered on the forecastle of their ship.

The *Potomac*'s seamen, led by the ship's mate, made a thorough search of the merchantman before the mate scrambled back on board the privateer to report his findings to Matthew.

Grinning widely, he said, 'I think having a clergyman on board has brought us luck. Perhaps we should sign him on. The Frenchman is homeward bound from the West Indies carrying a cargo of sugar and rum. The captain has taken a roundabout route across the Atlantic and thought he was safely home. Our appearance came as a nasty shock to him.'

'It's a good start to the career of the *Potomac*,' agreed a jubilant Matthew. 'You and your men sail the ship to Guernsey. It's only a couple of hours from here. I'll follow you. It will be dark by the time we get to St Peter Port so we'll anchor outside and you can enter port in the morning. Once you're safely in harbour I'll sail on to Falmouth and file a report on the capture for the Admiralty.'

'There are also half-a-dozen slaves on board. They've asked if you'll take them on the *Potomac*. They don't want to remain on board the French boat for a minute more than they have to.'

'Send them over. You'd better stow the French crew in one of the holds overnight – and set a strong guard over them.'

When the mate had returned to the French vessel, Toby asked, 'What will you do with the slaves when you get them back to Cornwall?'

'There are a number of societies dealing with freed slaves. One has a branch in Falmouth. They'll take care of them.'

Some minutes later, with the French seamen watching sullenly, the slaves clambered on board the *Potomac*. Suddenly, there was a commotion around one of the companionways on the merchantman and the *Potomac*'s mate emerged, accompanied by a very attractive young woman. Not until she came close to the guard rail did her dark skin give her away as a mulatto.

Behind the woman an elderly man was being restrained by some of *Potomac*'s boarding party. It did not prevent him from shouting and gesticulating in her direction.

The mate helped the woman to step over the guard rail to the British ship. When Matthew hurried to her aid, the mate explained, 'This lady claims that she too is a slave. She asks for asylum. The gentleman back there is not too happy about it. He says he paid a high price for her.'

'Then she *must* be a slave!' Matthew looked at the girl in disbelief. 'Who would have believed it?' Still looking at the woman, he added, 'I doubt if that's the real reason he's so upset. Nevertheless, no one, man, woman or child, should be bought or sold as though they were a chattel.'

It was immediately apparent that the woman was no ordinary slave. Four men carried two heavy chests from the French ship and placed them on the deck of the *Potomac*, explaining that they contained the mulatto woman's clothes.

An hour later, as dusk fell, the *Potomac* was following the merchantman. Toby and Matthew were standing on deck, close to the wheel. The two men had been talking about the 'slave' girl, whose name they had learned was Grace.

Suddenly Toby said to the shipowner, 'Here she comes now. I get the distinct impression she puts a somewhat higher value on herself than your average slave. The clothes she's wearing wouldn't be out of place in the great houses of England.'

Grace had been allocated the cabin of the *Potomac*'s mate who was sailing the captured French ship to Guernsey and she had changed her clothes since coming on board.

Nodding to the two men, she said, '*Bon soir, messieurs* . . . I am sorry, it should be "Good evening", should it not?'

'Your English is excellent, Mademoiselle,' Matthew complimented her.

'My name is Grace – and my English was once very much better.'

She spoke English with a French accent that Toby admitted to himself was very appealing. He was aware that Matthew thought so too.

'My mother was a slave on a plantation owned by an Englishman. He was also my father, I believe. We had to speak English, even though it was on an island that belonged to France. Then, when I was about thirteen years of age, France and England went to war with each other. The owner fled and the plantation was taken over by the French. So, you see, if that man *was* my father, as my mother always claimed, then I am more English than French! If he was not . . .' She shrugged. 'At least I learned to speak English.'

As she spoke, Toby had been making some rapid calculations. War between France and England had begun in 1793. This made Grace about twenty-five now.

'Was that man on the French ship the new plantation owner?'

'Him? Oh, no. He won me, playing cards. The man who owned me lost a great deal of money. More than he had. Monsieur Flaubert took me in place of the money. He was fond of telling me it was a considerable sum.'

She smiled at Matthew. 'Now you have taken me from him. It is, I believe, "*Droit de guerre*"?'

'So Rabelais said,' agreed Toby, who had recognised the quotation. '"The right of war. Let him take who take can." I believe that's the full quotation. But you've been freed, not taken.'

She gave the same dazzling smile to Toby. 'Of course! Thank you.'

Returning her glance to Matthew, she said, 'England will be very strange for me, I think. I do not know what I will do there.'

'I've no doubt we can work something out,' said Matthew, hastily. 'In the meantime, I have an old aunt in Falmouth who will be delighted to have you in her house.'

Toby thought of reminding Matthew of the anti-slavery society he had mentioned, but he remained silent. As Grace herself had said, it was '*Droit de guerre*'.

Potomac followed the French vessel through the gathering darkness until they were within sight of the lights of St Peter Port. Here they anchored for the night.

At first light a small naval brig came out of the harbour to check upon the two vessels. When explanations had been given, it escorted the captured French merchantman into harbour and the *Potomac* set sail for Falmouth.

The male slaves who had seemed bewildered by their new freedom felt more at home when Matthew allowed them to help with the various shipboard tasks.

Grace, on the other hand, behaved with a bearing and assurance that belied her station in life. Toby watched her as she stood with Matthew at the guard rail. Laughing, she touched his arm in a warm and intimate gesture, as though she had known him for years and not hours.

He was of the opinion that her earlier statement about being unsure of her future in England fell far short of the truth. Toby believed she knew exactly what she would do.

He sincerely hoped that Matthew was equally certain.

Looking back to St Peter Port, he watched the naval brig leading the captured French vessel inside the harbour. Behind the two vessels a diminutive fishing boat steered the same course, bobbing up and down as it encountered the wake of the larger vessels.

Toby thought Bethany would be surprised if she knew how close he was to her birthplace right now.

He would have been far more surprised than Bethany had he known that at this very minute she was closer to her childhood home than he.

The small fishing boat sailing into St Peter Port belonged to Jacob Hosking. Bethany was a passenger on board. Had she stood up, Toby would have seen her.

Chapter 32

Bethany's second meeting with the Elders of the St Austell Society of Friends proved very upsetting for her. It was due, in part, to her own naivety.

She had been a Quaker for the whole of her life and had gone to the meeting nursing the forlorn hope that they might allow her to retain her membership of the Society. At least, until there was some formal understanding between herself and Toby. By then, she believed it might have been possible to arrive at some form of compromise.

She argued this point with the Elders, while acknowledging that it was a difficult situation for everyone involved.

The Elders refused to contemplate compromise. They told Bethany quite bluntly that she must promise to end her association with the Church of England curate, or she would be disowned forthwith.

Before the meeting, Jacob pleaded on her behalf against immediate dismissal, as did Muriel. Each of them pointed out that Bethany could claim to be descended from many generations of Quakers. They argued that she deserved to be given sufficient time to think about the consequences of her actions. Time, perhaps, for her family to talk to her and change her mind.

The Elders remained unmoved by the pleas. Bethany had been given forty-eight hours to think over what she was doing. She had returned to them with her mind unchanged.

The Elders agreed that a girl of her age should find a husband. However, they were adamant she should seek him within the Society of Friends.

'It was a harsh decision,' complained Muriel to her sister,

as they left the Meeting House, together with Jacob and the children. 'They made no attempt to understand.'

'They could do nothing else,' admitted Jacob, grudgingly. 'Had Toby not been a Church of England curate it might have been different. As it is. . . ?' He shrugged resignedly.

'What dost thou want to do now?' asked Muriel of her sister, sympathetically.

'I think I'll go home.'

'The girls and I will come with thee,' said Muriel.

'No. I would rather be on my own. So much is happening in my life. I need to be able to think about everything.'

'All right.' Muriel gave her sister a hug. 'I hope Toby is worth all the heartache he is causing thee, Bethany.'

'I still have much to learn about him,' the unhappy girl replied. 'But I believe in my heart he will be. He is a fine man.'

Walking home from St Austell, Bethany thought of what Muriel had said, and of her reply.

It was true. She knew very little about the real Toby. They had met and she had fallen in love with him. She believed it had happened the first time she saw him. Her instincts told her he was a good man. All she wanted in a husband – and yet . . . ?

She was still thinking along those lines when she came to a fork in the narrow country lane. There was no signpost, but she knew the road to the left led to Hemmick. The one on the right, to Porthluney.

Acting upon a sudden impulse, she took the road to the right.

Walking alone through the quiet countryside gave her time to relate all that had been said to her today by the Elders, to her own future.

Life would be different, certainly. She would miss the silent, emotional meetings of the Friends. It was a very personal form of worship. Yet at times it was possible to feel the very essence of the Lord spreading among the silent congregation.

But Toby too was a man of God. He had taken a different

route to find Him, but that did not matter. Toby was a good man. She would learn his ways.

If there were things she did not understand, he would explain them to her. She would like that.

There was no doubt she would miss Muriel – and the children too, especially the crippled Ruth. But she would have left their house no matter whom she married.

She had a moment's unease when it occurred to her that she and Toby had never actually discussed *marriage*.

The moment passed as quickly as it had been conjured up. Marriage had been implicit in all they had said to each other at their last meeting. Toby knew she was prepared to give up her membership of the Society to marry him.

Bethany was drawing closer to the rectory now and she found herself walking faster. Her doubts allayed, she was excited at the thought of seeing Toby and telling him all that had happened. Informing him that religion no longer stood between them.

She turned a bend in the lane and the rectory came into view. She could see Nipper in the paddock and the small plot where Toby had made a start on tidying the overgrown gardens.

She decided happily that it was something she would help him with. She enjoyed gardening.

When Bethany reached the front door of the rectory, she knocked and tried the handle. Much to her surprise, she discovered it was locked. It was almost unheard of for a house door to be locked in this part of Cornwall.

She stepped back and looked up at the front of the house. A curtain was twitching in an upstairs window. Someone had just looked out from a bedroom.

It seemed Toby was in – but why should the door be locked, especially at this time of day?

She tried the door once more, in case she had been mistaken. It was certainly locked. Perhaps it had been locked for some time and had been forgotten.

Still puzzled, Bethany made her way to the rear of the house, to the kitchen door. This too was locked.

As she wondered what she should do next, she heard a sound in the kitchen. She knocked loudly on the door and a few moments later the bolt was drawn and the door opened.

A girl stood before her. Had Bethany not seen the movement of the upstairs curtain she would still have suspected that this girl had just left a bed – and left it in a great hurry. Her dress was awry, two buttons fastened in wrong buttonholes and her hair was straggly and untidy.

'What do you want?' The girl was as surly as she was untidy.

'I'm looking for Mr Lovell. Who are thee?'

'I'm Charlotte, I work here. The curate's not home. Nobody's here but me. Anyway, what do you want him for? You're one of they Quakers from down at Hemmick, ain't you?'

'Who I am is none of thy business . . .'

Anger was not a familiar emotion for Bethany, but she felt it rising in her now. It was accompanied by a sense of deepening dismay. Who was this slatternly girl? What was she doing in the rectory? And why should she be lying about Toby not being at home? Nipper was in his paddock and there was the movement of the curtain . . . in a bedroom.

' . . . And don't lie to me. I know he's in the house, upstairs.'

She moved to brush past the girl, but Charlotte barred her way. She was heavily built and Bethany only slight.

'You're not coming in here. You've no right.'

Faced with the inevitable, Bethany knew that what this girl said was correct. She had no right to force her way into the rectory. No right to go upstairs to the bedroom and accuse Toby of betraying both her and the principles of his own Church.

Neither did she any longer possess the right to run from the house and find solace among the Society of Friends, as she had on occasions in the past.

She no longer belonged there. She belonged nowhere.

Turning, she ran from the house. At the gate to the lane she looked back. Any doubts she might have entertained about what she had just witnessed were immediately dispelled.

The girl, Charlotte, was standing on the path outside

the house, fumbling with the buttons of her dress. At the upstairs window, Bethany caught a glimpse of a face peering around a curtain. Then it was gone.

Lifting the hem of her dress, Bethany ran from the rectory, hardly able to see where she was going for the tears that burned her eyes and blurred her vision.

Chapter 33

When Charlotte returned upstairs to the front bedroom, John Bettison was seated on the edge of the bed, wearing only his shirt.

'Was that the Quaker girl I saw leaving? What did she want?'

'She was looking for the curate. You shouldn't have gone to the window, she might have seen you. I think she must have noticed me at the window when I got up to see who was at the door. She realised there was someone up here. What if she tells the curate?'

'You'll say she was mistaken. That you were merely cleaning the room. Isn't that what you're paid for? Anyway, I don't think you have anything to worry about. I doubt if Curate Lovell will be here for very much longer. A report of his goings on has been given to the bishop. He's most likely in Exeter trying to explain them away right now.'

'What's going on? He's not been up to anything – and I should know. Either Ma or me's been working here for him ever since he arrived in Porthluney. He don't even drink very much!'

'Come now! A single young man as often as not alone in a big house like this with a lusty young girl like yourself – and nothing has gone on? But it doesn't matter, his misdemeanours extend beyond the carnal. He might not even return to Porthluney.'

Charlotte looked dismayed. 'Where does that leave Ma and me? He owes us both money. If he goes, what are we going to live on? There's no work for me down at Portloe now Eli's been drowned.'

'You'll find something,' replied John Bettison, unfeelingly.

'And if you continue to please me there'll be an occasional few shillings for you.'

'A few shillings ain't going to go far when there's two mouths to feed,' pouted Charlotte. 'And the way you've been going at me there's likely to be another one by this time next year.'

'You're beginning to sound mercenary,' snapped Bettison. 'I don't like women who have money on their mind when they ought to be thinking of other things. Now, are you coming back into this bed, or shall I ride away and forget all about you?'

Charlotte realised she had pushed the landowner far enough. She had made her point, it was time to pander to him now. 'I don't know where you get your energy from, I'm sure. Another half-hour in bed with you and I'm hardly going to have the strength to stand on my feet, let alone tend to my chores.'

'There's more to life than work, girl. Come on, let me show you . . .'

'Art thou quite certain this is what thou wants to do, Bethany?' Muriel put the question for at least the fourth time that morning. 'Won't thou tell me what this is all about? After all, I am thy sister. Thou canst surely trust me?'

'Right now I feel I can trust nobody,' declared Bethany bitterly. 'And, no, it's not what I *want*, but it's the only thing I can do.'

The two young women stood on the beach at Hemmick. At the water's edge a silent Jacob prepared his small fishing boat for the long voyage across the English Channel to Guernsey.

'Won't thou even tell me what it is that's so upset thee? I know the decision of the Elders was a harsh one and difficult for thee to accept. But thou seemed so certain of Toby and of the life thou wouldst share with him. What has happened to turn thy whole world upside down?'

'I don't want to talk about it, Muriel. Especially now. It's hard enough to leave thee and the children like this.'

'What do I tell Toby if he comes here asking of thee?'

'Tell him nothing. But I doubt if he'll even come calling.'

'Thou knowest well that Quakers do not lie, Bethany. Not even for a sister who is as loved as thee and who is so desperately unhappy.'

'There is no need for lies. Just tell him that thou hast promised to say nothing of where I am.'

'I wish I understood what this is all about,' said Muriel, unhappily. 'I am sure Jacob and I could do something about it for thee.'

'I have already brought thee both into conflict with the Elders on my behalf,' said Bethany. 'They were right and I wrong – but Jacob is ready for me now. Goodbye, Muriel. Take care of everyone. When we shall meet again I do not know, but I shall think of thee and the children often.'

Fearing she would break down and cry if she remained any longer, Bethany ran to the boat riding gently at the edge of the water. She clambered on board and Jacob pushed the boat clear. Minutes later he raised the sail and the boat heeled over and headed southwards, away from Hemmick, from Muriel – and from Toby.

Chapter 34

The first voyage of the *Potomac* under the command of its new owner had been an exciting one. Matthew and his crew were elated at their success in capturing the French West Indian merchantman.

The presence of Grace was an additional fillip for the men, although it was Matthew who was the main recipient of her close attention. She was with him for every minute he was on deck.

Toby suspected they spent much of the below decks time together too during the thirty-six hours it took them to reach Falmouth. He decided he could not sit in moral judgement on them. Besides, he would have found it difficult to decide who was taking advantage of whom.

In view of the ship's earlier performance, Toby knew it could have reached the Cornish harbour in half the time, but it was Matthew's ship. He could do with it whatever he wished.

It was early in the morning when the *Potomac* berthed in Falmouth. At the top of the gangway leading to the shore, Toby said his farewells to the crew, to Grace and to Matthew.

The freed slave girl sent him on his way with a kiss that would have put an end to his career in the Church once and for all had it been witnessed by Archdeacon Scantlebury.

Grinning at Toby's obvious embarrassment, Matthew promised to pay him a visit as soon as he was able, adding, 'Let me know when you return to the parish. I'll bring Grace along with me . . . if she's still around.'

Toby's eyes followed Grace's progress as she went below to complete her own packing. 'I have an idea you're going to have that young lady around for quite a while – as long as it suits her to stay. Slave or not, she's used to having her own way. I wish I were as confident of my own future.'

'You'll come through all right,' said Matthew, cheerfully. 'As for Grace . . . I hope she remains in Falmouth for a while.'

Toby had refused Matthew's offer of the loan of a horse for the ride to Porthluney. He did not know where he would be staying while the complaints about him were being investigated. It might prove difficult to return the animal.

However, he did accept Matthew's suggestion that he send a boat from *Potomac* to take Toby across the Carrick Roads to the village of St Mawes. By landing here the journey to Porthluney would be cut considerably.

Here Toby's luck was in. Toiling up the steep hill, past the sixteenth-century castle guarding the entrance to the popular harbour, he was overtaken by a farm wagon and offered a ride as far as Veryan. It would take him more than halfway to the Porthluney rectory and he was pleased to accept.

The ancient driver was more garrulous than Toby would have wished, but as he was also extremely deaf, it did not matter too much. Toby was not expected to reply, or make conversation himself.

On the few occasions when he tried, the wagon driver interrupted with yet another long tale. Eventually, Toby gave up trying to make it a two-sided conversation. It was a fine day and he abandoned himself to the leisurely pace of the wagon and the songs of birds in the hedgerows along the way.

At Veryan, the wagoner stopped to allow Toby to alight, before turning off the lane to a muddy farm track. Shouldering his bundle, Toby paid little attention to a horseman coming along the lane towards him.

Suddenly the horse was reined in. 'Mr Lovell! What are you doing in my parish, my dear sir?'

It was the Reverend Jeremiah Trist, who had been a passenger to Plymouth on the Exeter-bound coach.

'I'm on my way back from Exeter. I was offered a passage to Falmouth . . .'

Toby was about to explain that it had been in a ship owned by the conjuror who had entertained them in the coach. Then he remembered that Jeremiah Trist had paid Matthew for his services as a conjurer. He had no wish to embarrass the Vicar of Veryan.

'. . . and it proved to be an eventful voyage.'

'Your meeting with Bishop Fisher went well, I trust?'

'Not exactly. Archdeacon Scantlebury was present too. He's decided he wants to carry out a full inquiry into the complaints against me. Until it's completed my suspension will not only continue, but I have been ordered to reside outside the parish.'

Reverend Trist was genuinely shocked. 'My dear boy! What utter nonsense. I am both surprised and disappointed that John Fisher allowed the matter to go so far. He will have received my letter by now. He must surely realise you are entirely blameless.'

The vicar frowned. 'Of course, Grenville Scantlebury is our archdeacon now, isn't he? His father was butler to John Bettison's grandfather. The old man paid for Scantlebury's education, I believe. The trouble is, a respect for the Bettison family has been instilled in him that is not justified so far as the present generation is concerned. But don't worry yourself too much, dear boy. You'll have the support of every priest in this part of the diocese, I can assure you of that. But that'll be small comfort to you for the moment and no doubt Scantlebury will take his time sorting matters out. Where will you be staying in the meantime?'

'I've made no arrangements yet. Plymouth, probably.' Toby had not yet given the question of accommodation any serious thought. There were a number of more important issues to be settled first.

'Nonsense, dear boy! You must come and stay with me, here in Veryan. My daughter Sally will be taking Anna to their new home in a few days' time. When they've gone I'll rattle around in the vicarage like a lone pea in a colander. There'll only be me and my old housekeeper in a house that's far too large.'

Aware he had not completely won Toby over, the vicar added, 'Besides, you could help me out too, if you'd care to. Some mornings my rheumatism is so bad I can hardly put my feet to the ground. If you were to take the occasional service, or make a sick visit for me, you'd more than earn your keep, dear boy.'

After only a moment's hesitation, Toby nodded. 'It's extremely kind of you, sir. I'll be delighted to stay with you.'

'Splendid! Splendid! I can't wait to get home and tell young Anna. She hasn't stopped talking about you and that conjuring chap since we returned from Plymouth.'

Toby suspected that Anna had talked far more of Matthew Vivian than of himself. Once again he wondered what the vicar's reaction would be if he knew the truth about Matthew and the way of life he was leading.

'You'll come to the vicarage now, of course,' said Reverend Trist. 'Take some refreshments with Sally and me, then borrow a horse for the remainder of the journey?'

'Thank you, but no, sir. I have one or two things to settle and I possess a rather bad-tempered donkey that wouldn't tolerate a stable companion.'

'Will you have your affairs settled by tomorrow? After all, your absence from the Porthluney rectory will be no more than a temporary thing. You can leave many of your things there.'

Toby nodded. His future as the Porthluney curate may have been in doubt, but he hoped that by tomorrow a number of other matters would have been resolved. 'Yes, I should have most things settled by then.'

'Splendid! I'll have my housekeeper prepare a room for you.'

'I'm extremely grateful to you, sir. It's taken a load off my mind.'

'Good! We parsons need to help each other these days, dear boy, especially when we come up against landlords like John Bettison. Unfortunately, there are others like him.'

Toby went on his way more relieved than he had anticipated, knowing he had somewhere to stay. He was also happy that he would still be close to Hemmick. One of the day's priorities was to call on Bethany.

They would have a great deal to tell each other.

Chapter 35

When Toby reached Porthluney rectory, he was surprised to find Alice Rowe there, feeding Nipper. She was scolding the donkey for taking more interest in her backside than in the hay she was forking into a hayrack for him.

When she saw Toby coming along the path to the paddock, Alice stopped what she was doing. Nimbly avoiding Nipper's final attempt to bite her, she hurried to meet him.

'Hello, I didn't know you were back. I came to the rectory to feed the donkey and Nap.'

'That's very kind of you. I have only just arrived home. But where's Charlotte?'

He thought Alice seemed somewhat ill-at-ease when she replied: 'She's not feeling very well and her mother's leg isn't healing the way it should. I said I'd come here to see to whatever needed doing.'

'I am obliged to you, Alice, but don't you have work of your own to attend to, making nets for Billy Kendall in Portloe?'

'Not yet. The lawyers still haven't sorted everything out, so Billy hasn't been able to take over the business. I expect he will though, eventually.'

Toby's bag was still on the path where he had left it when he saw her tending to Nipper. Alice moved to pick it up and carry it inside, but he beat her to it.

'Have you had to walk far to get home?' she asked as she held the door open for him.

'From St Mawes, but I had a ride in a wagon for much of the way.'

'You must be tired out – and hungry too. I'll make you a cup of tea and find something for you to eat while you put your things away.'

'I won't be putting them away, Alice. In fact, I need to

pack. Tomorrow I'll be leaving the parish for a while.'

'Why?' They were in the hallway now and Alice swung around to face him. 'Has it something to do with Mr Bettison?'

He nodded. 'How did you know?'

'There's very little that goes on in Cornwall that remains a secret for long. I expect the servants at the big house heard something and passed it on.'

This was no more truthful than was the story of Charlotte's illness. In fact, Charlotte had told Alice that she had no intention of spending any more time working at the rectory, declaring it would be a waste of everybody's time. She had hinted very strongly to Alice that the Porthluney curate would not be returning to the parish.

Alice had not believed her statement about Toby, but her immediate concern had been for his animals. When she'd asked about them, Charlotte had shrugged indifferently. 'His animals are not my problem.'

This was the reason Toby had found Alice feeding Nipper when he arrived.

'Will you be taking Nap and the donkey with you?'

'I'll be taking Nipper, but I don't think I'll be able to take Nap. Do you think you could take on the responsibility of looking after him for me until my return?'

Alice smiled. 'So you really do think you're coming back?'

'I'm certain of it, Alice, but I don't know exactly when.'

'That's all right then.' Embarrassed she might have sounded too pleased, she said quickly, 'Nap's a lot better now. I've had him outside for a while and moved his basket to the kitchen. It's warmer there.'

Toby followed Alice to the kitchen. On the way he noticed that the house was tidier than he had seen it for a long time, and realised this must be the result of Alice's attentions. Charlotte had never done any more than was absolutely essential.

When they reached the kitchen, Nap was delighted to see Toby and would not remain in his basket. He insisted upon coming out and giving his master a greeting and seemed to be recovering well from his wound.

Nap followed Toby upstairs while he sorted out some clothes and Alice cooked a meal. It did not take long to pack. Toby's belongings fitted quite comfortably into a couple of bags.

Alice realised the two bags contained the sum of his worldly possessions and felt a great deal of sympathy for him.

As she cooked eggs and ham in a frying pan, over the kitchen fire, she said, 'Everyone's going to be pleased you're not leaving Porthluney for good.'

'I'm very happy about that.'

Colouring up once more, she added, 'You've made a very good impression upon the people of Porthluney.'

'That's good news, at least. I must admit, I never expected parish work to be quite as difficult as it has proved to be.'

'Would you like me to look after the rectory for you while you're away? Clean around as well as taking care of Nap? At least until Rose is well enough to come back again?'

'That would be wonderful, Alice.' She was sliding the food she had cooked on to a plate now and he said, 'You're an absolute treasure, Alice, you really are.'

Pleased with his praise, she put the food on the kitchen table in front of him. As he ate she told him all the local gossip, as though he was a long-established resident who had been absent for many months.

It seemed the residents of Porthluney had lately seen much more of John Bettison than was usual. Most would rather have foregone the experience. He had visited at least one tenant farmer and demanded he produce more during the coming year. Bettison left with the threat that if the farmer failed, he would end the tenancy and bring in a more efficient farmer from outside the parish. It was a hitherto unheard of ultimatum.

It was generally accepted that every farmer worked the land to the best of his ability, spurred on by the knowledge that the tenancy of the farm would eventually pass on to his sons. Toby thought it sounded as though John Bettison was becoming ever more desperate for money. He wondered what was going on at the manor.

When he had finished the meal Toby pushed back his plate with a sigh of satisfaction. 'That should set me up beautifully for all I have to do this evening,' he said, cheerfully. 'First I must saddle up Nipper. I doubt very much whether he's going to approve.'

'You're not going out again? You've only just returned from a long journey,' Alice expressed her concern, before adding, 'but I suppose you're used to travelling a lot, being in the navy and all. I've never been farther than St Austell in all my life.'

'It's sometimes very exciting to see new places,' replied Toby. 'But it's even more pleasant to have a permanent home with loved ones around you. To live in a place where everyone and everything is familiar.'

'Don't you have any family?'

'No close family, Alice. I was brought up by an uncle and aunt.'

Toby was embarrassed to see tears well up in her eyes.

'That's *very* sad,' she said. 'I can't imagine what it would be like if I didn't have my family around me most of the time.'

'You're far too soft-hearted, Alice,' said Toby, kindly. 'But your parents must be happy to know how much you appreciate them. Now, I really must go. I'd like to take Nap with me, but I don't think he's quite up to it yet.'

'You don't need to worry about Nap. I'll take him for a walk around the garden before I go. Would you like me to stay here until you come back, in case you want something to eat?'

'No, thank you, Alice, but I do appreciate all that you're doing for me. I really do.'

'That's all right. I'll be here early in the morning to cook you breakfast. You haven't got much in the larder but I'll bring a thing or two from home.'

Alice gave him a shy smile. 'At least you'll start whatever you have to do tomorrow with a good breakfast inside you.'

Chapter 36

As Toby had anticipated, Nipper was not at all happy at being called upon to work, especially as he had not yet eaten all the hay given to him by Alice. He managed to give Toby a painful nip before he was finally saddled up and ready to set out for Hemmick.

Today, Toby was prepared to forgive the bad-tempered animal. Happier than he had been for many days, he was fully aware it was because he was going to see Bethany once more.

As he rode down the narrow lane that led to the small cove he could see the cottage and the beach, but Jacob's boat was not there. It was hardly surprising; the weather was fine and Jacob was a fisherman. He would be out earning a living.

Some of the Hosking children were playing on the sand. Ruth was among them and was the first to see him. Calling the news of his arrival in at the front door of the cottage, she limped as quickly as she could to meet him.

He dismounted as she reached him. Holding the reins in one hand, he swung her up on to Nipper's back.

'I swear you're walking better than when I last saw you, Ruth. How are you?'

'I'm all right, but the new baby cries a lot and keeps us awake sometimes.'

Toby smiled. 'I understand babies are like that – but you should be used to them by now.'

'Hast thou come to see Pa? He's not here.'

'I've already noticed the boat's gone. I hope he returns with a large catch. But I'm actually here to see your Aunt Bethany.'

'She's not here either. She went off with Pa.'

'Oh!' Toby found it difficult to hide his disappointment, but Ruth had not noticed.

'Ma's here, though.'

Even as Ruth spoke, Muriel Hosking came from the house carrying the latest baby in her arms.

Unlike Ruth, Muriel did not seem at all pleased to see him. Toby thought it probably had something to do with the meeting Bethany had held with the Elders.

'Hello, Muriel. My word, that baby of yours has grown already!'

Toby's smile brought no response from Muriel. He tried again. 'I really came to see Bethany, but Ruth tells me she's off fishing with Jacob.'

'They're not fishing.'

Toby frowned. Something was definitely wrong here. 'I'm sorry, I don't understand. I thought Ruth said they were.'

'I doubt it, although Ruth might have said she had gone with Jacob. He's taken her to Guernsey.'

'Why? Are your parents ill? Has something happened there? When do you expect her to return?'

Toby was taken aback by the unexpected news. He also found Muriel's cold, almost hostile, attitude difficult to understand.

Bethany's sister was no more forthcoming now. 'So far as I'm aware, our parents are well. As for something happening . . . I thought thou might have the answer to that?'

'Me? How . . . Has she said when she'll be returning?'

'She won't be returning,' came the cold reply. 'She's returned to Guernsey to live. When she left here she was very, very upset. As for the reason . . . perhaps thou shouldst have words with Jacob when he returns. Bethany might have told him something during the voyage. She certainly said nothing at all to me before leaving.'

Toby was absolutely stunned by Muriel's news. He could hardly think straight. All he could say now was, 'I can hardly believe it, Muriel. Why should she go? We had so many plans to make . . .'

Pulling himself together, he asked, 'When are you expecting Jacob to return?'

Muriel glanced up towards the sky before replying, 'It will depend upon God and the weather. Perhaps tonight, but most probably not until tomorrow. Now, thou needst to forgive me, I must go inside . . .'

For the past couple of minutes there had been the sound of an unhappy child complaining inside the house. 'I fear young Susan is sickening for something. Good day, Toby.'

Muriel left him standing at the entrance to the cottage in a state of utter bewilderment. He was brought down to earth by Nipper who took advantage of his bemusement by biting him on the upper arm.

The bite was painful but did not draw blood, and it amused the Hosking children. Toby rode away with their delighted laughter ringing in his ears. He did not share their happy mood. It was incomprehensible that Bethany should have gone off so suddenly, without leaving any message for him. He had known that a decision by the Elders to exclude her from the Society would upset her, but it could not have been entirely unexpected. Something else must have occurred to make her flee to her parents' home in Guernsey and throw away their future together.

Toby did not feel like returning to the rectory immediately. Alice would still be there. She was kind and understanding, but she was also a very happy young girl. Toby did not think he could take too much of someone else's happiness right now.

He decided he would ride to St Stephen, and tell Reverend Kempe all that had taken place at Exeter. Perhaps the rector could analyse his meeting with the bishop and archdeacon.

Along the way, Toby went over once again all that had been said between himself and Bethany when they last met. All had seemed well then. Bethany was happy. He was quite certain he had said or done nothing since that could possibly have made her leave Cornwall in such a hurry.

On the contrary, he believed he had persuaded her that they both had a future together in the county. Perhaps he should have made much more of his feelings for her. Had he done so she would surely not have gone away in this fashion.

Toby felt more despondent than he could ever remember. With all that was happening in his own Church, to his own life, it had been the thought of Bethany and their future together that had sustained him. Now this too had been taken from him. He felt as though he were sliding into a deep abyss of despondency with no way out.

Toby had hoped that speaking to Reverend Kempe might help his morbid mood, but here too he was frustrated.

He was met at the door of the St Stephen rectory by Rosemary Kempe. Before Toby could say a word she put a finger to her lips. Taking his arm, she led him to the study where he and the rector had last met.

When the door closed behind them, Toby asked, 'What's the matter?' He discovered he was whispering.

'It's Harold.' Rosemary Kempe's voice was equally low. 'He's had a heart attack. It wasn't too severe, but he won't be able to carry out his duties for a while and has been ordered to keep quiet. He must hear nothing to excite him in any way.'

'I am very sorry. Very sorry indeed. Is there anything I can do?'

Toby then explained the outcome of his interview with the bishop and archdeacon, adding, 'Perhaps I could take on some of his duties here?'

Rosemary shook her head. 'I think it wiser if he does not meet you. I'll tell him you called and say that things will soon be back to normal at Porthluney – as I am quite certain they will be. If you were here, or he were to see you, he would get the truth from you and want to become involved. That would not be good for him. As it is, his services can be conducted by his friends from adjacent parishes. I know you will understand, Toby, and I am most grateful for your offer. But I have no doubt you'll find plenty to occupy you in Porthluney once you are fully reinstated.'

He understood Rosemary Kempe's concern for her husband, but when he left the St Stephen rectory he felt more alone than ever.

Chapter 37

Toby had an uneventful ride back to Porthluney from St Stephen, but he hardly noticed the beauty of a full moon riding high in a star-sprinkled sky. Even a near collision with a silent-winged barn owl failed to excite him as it might have done on any other night.

At the rectory paddock, he discovered that Alice had put out new hay for Nipper. He turned the animal loose and hung up the saddle and tack in the room beside the stable.

In the kitchen, he received an enthusiastic and affectionate welcome from Nap. Alice had carefully made up the fire and placed the dog's basket beside it. She had also left a note for Toby, informing him there was a pasty in the pantry that only needed heating.

Although fully appreciative of the young girl's kindness and thoughtfulness, he did not feel hungry. Neither was he yet ready for bed.

'Come on, Nap, let's take a walk. We won't go too far for you.'

In fact, they went only so far as the small church, standing silent and reassuringly solid in the light of the moon.

Going inside, Toby lit a couple of candles on the altar and kneeled down before the altar rail to pray for a few minutes. Here was a peace that he hoped might help him to understand all that was happening in his life.

He was not left in peace for very long. He had kneeled in prayer for no longer than fifteen minutes when Nap raised his head from his paws and growled deep in his throat.

It was a moment or two before the sound got through to Toby. He looked up as the door opened. Caroline Bettison was standing in the doorway.

As he rose to his feet, she said, 'I am very sorry to disturb you, Toby. I wouldn't have come in had I realised you were praying. I was passing in my carriage when I saw the lights in here. I ordered my coachman to stop so I might come in and speak to you.'

'It's all right. I haven't been home for a few days. As I shall be leaving again for a while I thought I'd take the opportunity of spending a short time in here.'

'You are going away? Is there a special reason? Surely you are not considering moving to another parish so soon?'

'No, I'm not taking over another parish.' Toby found it difficult to tell the wife of John Bettison that he was suspended as a result of complaints made to the bishop by her husband.

He made a dismissive gesture. 'I've been suspended. I'm to reside outside the parish until a number of complaints made against me have been investigated.'

Caroline Bettison looked aghast. 'Why, that's a *dreadful* thing to happen! What are the nature of the complaints? Who has made them?'

'There are a number. Most are trifling. They'll all be sorted out in due course. It's really more of a nuisance than anything else.'

Hesitantly, Caroline said, 'These complaints . . . they were made by John, were they not?'

'It doesn't really matter who made them. As I said, they will be resolved soon.'

There was an uneasy silence between them which was eventually broken by John Bettison's wife. She apologised on behalf of her husband.

'I'm very sorry, Toby. Try not to blame him too much. He has a great many problems at the moment, but I think they too will be resolved very soon.'

'I am very pleased to hear it.'

Caroline appeared to be trying to make up her mind about saying more to him. Eventually, she blurted out, 'Toby, can you keep a secret?'

'I can, but please don't tell me anything you might regret later.'

'I trust I will never have any cause to regret what I

am about to tell you. John and I are expecting a baby. I am on my way back from Truro right now after having it confirmed by a doctor.'

'Congratulations, Caroline – but surely this will only add to your husband's problems?'

She shook her head. 'No, it will be my father's first grandchild. If it's a son he'll settle an estate he has in Devon on him right away. It brings in a considerable income. Father has also promised John that if we give him a grandson he'll settle all his debts – just the once. I really do think that is all John needs, Toby. I know he's been foolish in the past, but I believe he has learned by his mistakes.'

'That's all very well, but what if it's a daughter?'

She smiled. 'My father loves children. He will be very generous, whether it's a boy or a girl. Once he has held the child in his arms, it won't matter to him what it is – but it *is* going to be a boy, I just know it.'

Toby smiled. 'I sincerely hope you're right. I would be very happy to see things going well for you.'

'The baby will be christened here in your church, of course. Just as his father and many generations of Bettisons have been.'

'That will give me a great deal of pleasure, Caroline. When that happy day comes I shall feel I really do belong to Porthluney.'

'You already belong here, Toby. The people have taken you to their hearts. You're going to be a memorable parson, loved by everyone, believe me.'

Toby wondered for a moment why he was having to leave the parish if he was so popular with everyone. But he kept silent. Nothing should mar the joy Caroline Bettison was feeling today. She did not have the easiest of lives and there would have been few days when she felt as happy as this.

Chapter 38

Alice was visibly upset when Toby left the Porthluney rectory the following morning. She had arrived at the house very early. After cooking him a substantial breakfast, she assured him she would take good care of Nap and the rectory in his absence.

As he rode off, Toby was content to leave everything in her care. He would not have had an easy mind had her friend Charlotte been left in charge.

He did not ride to Veryan immediately. Indeed, he rode in the opposite direction, to Hemmick.

He did not remain in the vicinity of the Quaker cottage for very long and spoke to no one. He did not feel he would be very welcome after Muriel's attitude towards him on the previous day.

He could see no boat pulled up on the small beach which meant Jacob was not at home. He had probably not yet returned from Guernsey, although Toby thought the Quaker fisherman was unlikely to spend more time away from his wife and young family than was absolutely necessary.

Toby received a warm welcome at the Veryan vicarage. Jeremiah Trist was out of the house, but Sally and Anna Jarvis were delighted to see him.

With Mrs Abbott, the rather dour housekeeper, leading the way, they walked with him through the spacious vicarage to a room on the first floor that had been prepared for his occupation.

It was a huge room combining bedroom and sitting-room. There was a large window giving a panoramic view over open countryside. A cosy fire burning in the grate completed the feeling of comfort and welcome.

Toby was quick to express his appreciation, but before Sally could reply, Anna said, 'Mother chose it for you. Grandfather was going to give you a smaller room at the other end of the house, but she said you needed space in which to think. This room has a much nicer view.'

'I'm very grateful, I really am.' Toby nodded his appreciation to Sally.

'It's the same view Mother has from the room next to yours. I'm just across the passageway, so I'll be able to come here and visit you sometimes,' Anna chattered on happily. 'Until we move, that is. Then you'll have to come and visit us.'

'That's not going to be for a while yet,' said Sally. She explained to Toby: 'We had been expecting to move in this week, but we've now decided to have a couple more alterations carried out. It will put things back for a while.'

'Oh! Then your father could probably do with not having me here . . .'

'Nonsense! You've seen the size of the house. We could all be here for a week or more without ever seeing each other.'

'Is there anything more you think you might be needing, sir?' the housekeeper broke in on their conversation. 'If not I'll go to the kitchen and have the maid make a pot of tea for you.'

'Everything is fine, Mrs Abbott. I'm absolutely delighted with the room. I know you must have worked very hard to have it ready for me. Thank you.'

When the housekeeper had gone about her business, Sally smiled at Toby. 'You said exactly the right thing. Mrs Abbott's always saying that no one appreciates what she does for them and that most of her efforts go unnoticed.'

'I spoke no more than the truth. This room is an absolute delight.'

'Mother put the flowers in the room – and had the big picture put over the fireplace. It came from her room. She said you would like it,' said Anna.

The picture was an oil painting showing men-o'-war battling against rough seas.

'That was very kind of your mother,' said Toby.

'I thought you might like it.' Sally was embarrassed by

her daughter's disclosure. 'It was really far too large for my room.'

'Shall I show you my trick?' Without awaiting a reply, Anna pulled a thimble from her pocket and proceeded to make it 'disappear'.

At the first attempt the thimble fell from her sleeve to the floor. Behaving as though the secret of the vanishing thimble had not been revealed, she made a successful second attempt.

Toby applauded loudly. It seemed Anna had forgotten he had been present when Matthew Vivian taught her how it should be performed.

When Anna ran off, Sally said, 'She hasn't stopped practising "magic" since our coach trip. The conjuror turned a tedious journey into a happy one.'

'Ah, yes! May I let you into a secret?'

Toby proceeded to reveal the identity and true profession of the 'conjuror', adding that he had travelled from Exeter to Falmouth on his ship. He said nothing about the capture of the French merchantman, or the 'freeing' of Grace.

Much to Toby's relief, Sally was highly amused by the whole incident.

'How very amusing . . . and to think my father gave him two shillings!' Her laughter was a very pleasant sound.

'I'd rather you didn't tell him,' said Toby. 'It would make him feel foolish.'

The subject of the conjuror was broached once more during lunch, when Anna told her grandfather of the trick she had demonstrated for Toby's benefit.

He and Sally exchanged glances across the table and her mouth twitched briefly in amusement, but nothing was said.

It was a pleasant family meal, something Toby had never known before. He had no memory at all of either of his own parents, and his aunt and uncle had strict ideas of behaviour at the meal table.

Jeremiah Trist suggested he should take Toby to look at his church after lunch and Toby agreed. As the two men walked along the lane together, the Veryan vicar said, 'Your coming to stay at the vicarage has acted as a tonic for Sally and Anna. They both need someone more lively than me and my aged friends in their lives, especially since the loss of dear Tom. They hadn't seen much of him lately, with this ghastly war going on, but they always lived in the hope he might turn up unexpectedly next month, next week, or even the next day. It gave meaning and a certain excitement to the rather lonely life they both led. At that time, of course, they were living in a naval town. It was always filled with rumours, what with ships coming and going and news being received from despatches. With Tom gone they have nothing but a rather dull life in a quiet little village, with the parson as father and grandfather. It's hardly the life for a young woman, eh, dear boy?'

They turned off the road and Jeremiah Trist said, 'Here we are at my church. It needs to have some work done on it, but I'm very fond of the place. My father was vicar here too, you know. Having grown up here I feel I'm almost a part of the fabric of the place.'

Toby spent an hour in the church with his host. Eventually, Jeremiah said he was going to call on one of his parishioners who was in her nineties and determined to live to a hundred. He suggested Toby might care to accompany him.

'Thank you, but not today. There are one or two people I would like to visit in Porthluney. I have been told I am not to live there, but the archdeacon said nothing about visiting.'

'Of course, you come and go as you wish, dear boy. We dine at eight and shall expect you back by then. Mrs Abbott has bought some lamb in especially for you. We must put on a grand dinner soon. Invite some of the people you should meet, who might be of use to you once you've returned to the rectory at Porthluney.'

Chapter 39

Toby made his way back to the vicarage but did not go inside the house. He located Nipper in a stable that was palatial in comparison with the single loose-box that was his home at Porthluney.

The donkey made no attempt to bite when he was saddled. Toby hoped Nipper had finally accepted him as his master, but it was more probable the bad-tempered animal was overawed by his new surroundings.

Toby rode through the lanes, passing the Porthluney rectory. He resisted an urge to go inside and say 'hello' to Alice and Nap. He was on his way to Hemmick again, this time determined to learn more of Bethany's whereabouts.

There was still no sign of a boat on the tiny beach, but on this occasion he was not prepared to ride away without speaking to Muriel.

Tethering Nipper, Toby went up the path to the cottage. Muriel must have seen him approaching. Before he had time to knock she came to the door, surrounded by her children.

'I've come hoping I might have a word with Jacob,' he said. 'But I see his boat isn't here.'

Muriel's earlier coldness seemed to have thawed a little and she said, 'He still hasn't returned from Guernsey. I am very worried about him. He should have been back long before now.'

'If you tell me where he was going on Guernsey, I might be able to get a message to him. To find out what's happening.'

Toby was thinking of Matthew. He would probably need to send *Potomac* to Guernsey to bring back the members of his crew who had been left there with the merchantman. It might also be necessary to bring the French vessel back to the mainland.

'I can't do that, Toby. I gave my word to Bethany. She said she would write if she needed to contact thee.'

Trying hard not to allow his impatience to show, Toby said, 'You've just said yourself that Jacob should be back. He isn't. You're worried about him and I'm worried about Bethany. Are we both going to stay here and do nothing, or shall I try to learn what's happened to both of them? For all we know they might not have reached Guernsey . . .'

Toby broke off. He did not want to pursue this line of thought.

For a moment, Muriel hesitated and he thought he had got through to her. Then she repeated, 'I'm sorry, Toby. I can't tell thee anything.'

The next moment, the door was shut in his face and Muriel had gone.

Toby knocked on the door, but he knew it was a futile gesture and was not surprised when no one answered him.

As he walked away from the cottage he was left with a picture in his mind of the expression of distress on Ruth's face. She had been limping towards the door from inside the house. It had shut before she had an opportunity to say 'hello' to him.

Toby wished he had been invited inside the house, to sit down and talk things over with Muriel. That way he thought he could at least have extracted some sense from her. He was certain he could have convinced her he had done nothing to upset Bethany. He was desperate to learn the reason she had left Cornwall so abruptly.

There was also Jacob's failure to return to his cottage. It was worrying, to say the least. What if something *had* happened before he and Bethany reached the Channel Islands?

But what could Toby do? He could not force his way into the cottage and insist that Muriel speak with him.

For the next ten days Toby was kept far busier at Veryan than he could have anticipated. Jeremiah Trist caught a bad cold and Toby took on many of the older man's duties. He conducted Sunday services, visited the old and sick, and conducted his first christening.

The christening was particularly pleasing to him. Ironically, it was for a baby from Portloe, in his own parish.

The baby's mother shyly told Toby afterwards that she was very pleased he was the officiating priest. It was what she had wanted, especially as both Toby and her husband were involved in the rescue of sailors from the frigate *Arrow* on the very night the baby was born!

During this busy spell, Sally was a great help and support and Toby felt increasingly close to her and young Anna.

As time went by he grew concerned about this. His feelings for Sally were those he thought he might have felt for a sister. He was not altogether certain this was the way she believed it to be.

Then the Veryan vicarage received unexpected visitors. Matthew Vivian arrived with his brother – and Grace.

It was a fine afternoon and Jeremiah Trist was feeling better. He, Toby, Sally and Anna were having tea on the vicarage lawn when the trio rode up the drive to the house.

Mounted on a magnificent thoroughbred horse, Grace sat astride in the manner of a man.

When they drew level with the party on the lawn, she leaped from the horse, threw the reins to Matthew and ran to Toby. To his consternation, and to the surprise of the company, she threw her arms about him and gave him a warm hug.

When she drew back she beamed at him. 'Toby, how wonderful to see you again! We have just been to your dear little church and the house there. A charming young girl told us you were here, so we came to find you.'

Recovering from his initial shock, Jeremiah Trist was staring at Matthew perplexed, when Anna gave a squeak of delight.

'It's the conjuror. The one who taught me my trick!'

Matthew smiled at her and at Sally, then held out his hand to the Veryan vicar. 'I am delighted to make your acquaintance once more, sir. I don't think I introduced myself on that occasion. Matthew Vivian, at your service – and this is my brother, Charles. The effervescent young lady is Grace. She hails from Martinique.'

He smiled again. 'As you can see, she is a very uninhibited young lady.'

Grace grimaced at him. 'I am just happy to meet Toby once more.'

Turning to Jeremiah, she offered an explanation that served only to confuse him even more. 'Toby was one of the men who rescued me and gave me my freedom. I will *always* be delighted to see him. He is my very good friend.'

Not knowing quite what to say to her, Jeremiah turned his attention to Charles. 'Would you be *Sir* Charles Vivian, the ship owner?'

Charles Vivian nodded. 'The same.'

Jeremiah was suddenly flustered. 'And I gave your brother two shillings for entertaining my young granddaughter on the coach to Plymouth!'

Sir Charles possessed the same degree of charm as his brother. 'He told me about it and I was delighted. It's probably the first honest money he has earned for many years.'

Looking to where Sally sat with Anna, he said, 'This will be your daughter and granddaughter? I have heard all about them from Matthew.'

'I am sorry, this is Sally – Sally Jarvis – and the young lady is Anna, my granddaughter.'

Sir Charles took Sally's hand. 'I am delighted to meet you. May I offer my commiserations on the sad loss of your husband? Matthew told me about him. He was a brave man, ma'am.'

'Thank you.' A cloud passed over her face at the mention of her late husband, but it was soon dispelled by Anna's intervention.

'Mr Vivian says he'll teach me a new trick. Can I use a pack of your cards, Grandfather?'

'Surely . . . but I shall have to come with you to find them. They are in one of the drawers in my study. I can't remember which one. While I am in the house I will ask

Mrs Abbott to bring more tea. In the meantime, madam . . . gentlemen . . . please take a seat. I will only be a few minutes.'

When he and Anna had gone and the others were seating themselves, Sally said to Toby, 'I am afraid Father feels extremly foolish at learning Mr Vivian is no mere conjuror. Poor Father!'

'You must assure him he has the sympathy of Matthew's family,' said Sir Charles. 'Matthew has been embarrassing *us* for as long as I can remember. Do you know how he learned these tricks of his? When he was fifteen he ran away with a troupe of travelling actors and conjurors. He was finally located working at a fair in Plymouth . . .'

While he was relating the tale of Matthew's adventures to Sally and Grace, the subject of his story, who was seated on the other side of the garden table, said quietly to Toby, 'I have some very good news for you. It concerns the French merchantman. The sale has not yet taken place, but a valuer has been on board. The ship and its cargo should fetch a very good price indeed. Rather more than was anticipated.'

'I'm delighted for you . . . and for the crew of *Potomac*.'

'It's good news for you too. You were one of us. The men have all agreed you should have an equal share. They are convinced it was you who brought us our good luck.'

Toby began to protest, but Matthew cut his words short. 'It's the decision of the officers and crew. I will let you know when all is settled.'

The Vivians and Grace spent a pleasant couple of hours on the vicarage lawn. Matthew taught Anna a couple of simple card tricks which delighted her, while Grace flirted outrageously with Toby, and Jeremiah too.

Meanwhile, Sir Charles and Sally seemed so at ease in each other's company that Toby felt a twinge of totally unreasonable jealousy for a moment. He decided it was more for the fact that they were happy with each other than because someone else was claiming Sally's attention.

'Is there any more news of the end of your suspension?' asked Matthew.

'No. The archdeacon has not paid his visit to Porthluney yet.'

Toby was already restless because of the archdeacon's apparent tardiness. He had visited the St Stephen rectory two days before, but no messages had been received there.

Reverend Kempe was improving slowly from his heart attack, but his ever-vigilant wife still refused to allow Toby to speak to him.

On his way back to Veryan, Toby had called in at Porthluney, as he had on two other occasions, just in case a message had arrived for him there.

Alice had heard nothing either, but she seemed to be coping very well about the house and Nap was now fully recovered from his wound.

It was of Alice that Grace now spoke to Toby. 'The little girl who takes care of your home . . . she is very pretty, no?'

'Yes, I suppose she is,' said Toby. 'She is certainly a very pleasant and willing young girl.'

'Ah! She is your mistress?'

Her words caused Matthew to splutter on the cup of tea he was drinking.

'No, she is not my mistress,' replied Toby, with all the dignity he could muster. 'Apart from any other consideration, she is barely sixteen years of age.'

Toby believed Grace had asked the question for effect, possibly because she was not receiving the attention she thought she was due. Her next words tended to confirm his view.

'So? By the time I was sixteen I had been the mistress of three men and . . .'

'Behave yourself, Grace.' The admonition came from Matthew. 'You're in England now. Such matters are not discussed in polite company.'

'I find so many things difficult in your country. How do I know when I am in polite company and when I am not?'

'The answer is, when in doubt – don't! You're at the home of a man of God right now. Would you have discussed such matters in the company of your Catholic priest in Martinique?'

'But of course! We all knew him well. He would visit the plantations and take his pick of the slave girls. If one was especially nice to him she would become his mistress. He never kept one for very long. I remember . . .'

'That's quite enough, Grace. I think we have probably already outstayed our welcome.'

Matthew rose to his feet and spoke to Jeremiah Trist. 'I thank you for your hospitality, sir. I trust you and your charming family will pay a visit to Falmouth in order that I might repay your hospitality. I will think of some new tricks to teach Anna in readiness for your visit.'

Anna clapped her hands and Sir Charles Vivian said, 'I would like you to pay a visit to me too, sir. In fact, I will send you a formal invitation to a dinner I am putting on next week. I sincerely hope you and Mrs Jarvis will be able to attend.'

He spoke to the Veryan vicar, but his eyes were on Sally. Her pleasure at his promised invitation was plain for all to see. Toby had a feeling she would not remain a widow for too long.

Toby walked with the party to the gateway at the end of the drive. As they rode off, he waved to them until they disappeared from view.

He had turned back to return to the house when a figure emerged from some nearby bushes. It was Billy Kendall, from Portloe. He looked hot and out of breath.

'Hello, Billy. What are you doing hiding in the bushes?'

'I came looking for you, Curate. I would have come in but I saw you on the lawn with your friends. As it seemed they was about to leave, I waited here until they'd gone. I've got some news for you. Important news. About Jacob Hosking the Quaker.'

Suddenly fearful, Toby asked, 'What is it? Is he alive and well?'

'He's alive. As for being well . . . he's a prisoner of the French. They took him and his boat.'

'Was Bethany taken with him? Where did you hear this? From Muriel . . . Jacob's wife?'

'No, she knew nothing about it until I told her an hour or so ago. The news came to me second- or third-hand. One of the Portloe fishermen had a rendezvous with a free-trader last night. A French seaman on board has been ashore at Hemmick and met Jacob more than once. He told the Portloe man he'd seen Jacob at Roscoff a couple of days ago. He was on his way to a prison near Morlaix.'

'But what of Bethany? Was she taken prisoner with him, or was Jacob captured when he was returning to Cornwall?'

Billy shook his head. 'Jacob's wife asked me the same question, but there was nothing said about Bethany or when Jacob was taken. All I know is what I've already told you and her. She said I should come and tell you right away. She said if you went to see her, she'd give you the address of her parents in Guernsey.'

Chapter 40

Toby's decision to ride to Hemmick immediately brought perplexed protests from Jeremiah Trist and his family. Anna wanted to practise her latest card trick on him and Sally was keen to question him on how much he knew of Sir Charles Vivian.

The Veryan vicar had so many questions he wished to ask he would have found it difficult to know where to begin.

Toby did not tell them where he was going, or why he was leaving in such a hurry. He said no more than that a messenger had come from his parish and he was required there urgently.

Only Sally guessed the reason for his urgency.

'Does this have something to do with the young girl who is looking after the rectory in your absence?'

She had walked to the stables with Toby and asked the question as he saddled Nipper.

'No.' He did not want to amplify his reply, but Sally was persistent.

'Is there another girl?'

'Yes.'

'I thought there must be. Will you be coming back to the vicarage tonight?'

'I hope so.'

'I'll wait up for you and you can tell me what is happening. You never know, I may be able to help. I would like that.'

She reached out and gripped his arm for a moment. 'Good luck, Toby. I hope things work out the way you wish them too.'

'Thank you, Sally.' He was touched by her genuine concern. Thinking of the rapport that had been apparent between her and Sir Charles Vivian, he added: 'I hope they will for you too.'

As he rode away from the vicarage, he thought it was just the sort of affectionate exchange there might have been between a brother and sister.

The thought was no more than a fleeting one. He was already casting his mind ahead: to what he was likely to learn from Muriel.

Muriel Hosking was more agitated than Toby had ever seen her before. Her mood had affected the children. Two were sitting outside the cottage, crying. The baby could be heard somewhere inside, following the example of her elder sisters.

Muriel must have been watching for him through a window. As he arrived, she hurried out of the house to meet him.

'Toby! Thou hast heard what has happened? Jacob is a prisoner of the French.'

'At least we know he's alive,' replied Toby. 'But Billy brought no news of Bethany. We need to know if Jacob was taken prisoner before reaching Guernsey, or on his way back.'

'Thou wilt try to find out, Toby?'

'Will you tell me where your parents live?'

With no discernible hesitation, Muriel nodded. 'They live in a small cottage at Fermain Bay, no more than a couple of miles from St Peter Port.'

'I'll go to Guernsey and find out all I can.'

Muriel was startled. 'You'll *go* there? When?'

'As soon as I can. I have no parish duties here to hold me back.'

Toby was confident that Jeremiah Trist was now well enough to resume his full duties. 'I'll set off tomorrow if I can make the necessary arrangements.'

'That will put my mind at rest about Bethany, but it won't help poor Jacob.'

'We'll see about that. First we need to find out exactly what happened.'

'Come into the house for a while. I'll write a letter for

thee to take to my parents. I am sorry for the way I have behaved recently, but I was upset about Bethany's leaving. Now this has happened . . . I am glad to have thee as a friend, Toby. Truly.'

Toby called in at the Porthluney rectory on his way back to Veryan. He was relieved that none of those present at the vicarage for afternoon tea were there to see the expression on Alice's face when she saw him.

Billy the young Portloe fisherman was seated in the kitchen when Toby arrived. Alice apologised for his presence, explaining, 'He came to speak to me about net-making. As I've almost finished here, I said he could wait and walk me home so we might discuss it along the way.'

'It's all right, Alice, you have no need to apologise. I don't mind Billy being here. Indeed, I am grateful to him for passing on the message to me today.'

'He told me about poor Jacob Hosking. I don't know how his wife's going to manage. She's got all those little girls to look after and no man about the house to provide her with the means of feeding them.'

'Is there anything you can do for Jacob?' Billy put the question to Toby.

'I don't know, but I'm certainly going to try. I shall go to Falmouth tomorrow to speak to someone I know who owns a ship. I'm hoping he will take me to Guernsey. When I've learned a bit more of what happened, I may even go on to France.'

'But . . . we're at war with France. You won't be safe there!' Alice was genuinely concerned.

'Not all the French are out to kill every Englishman they come across. Billy will tell you that's so.'

Ignoring Toby's oblique reference to his smuggling activities, Billy asked, 'How will you get to Falmouth tomorrow?'

'On Nipper, I expect. He's not the speediest of mounts, but he'll get me there.'

'I'll take you in my boat,' said Billy, unexpectedly. 'It's the quickest way to Falmouth. With the wind set in the direction it is now it'll take no more than an hour-and-a-half. That's a lot quicker than you'd make it by road – especially on a donkey.'

'That's very kind of you, Billy. You're right, it will be a lot quicker.'

The young fisherman shrugged. 'I can do a bit of fishing on the way back. The trip won't be wasted. Besides, I *like* Jacob. He's always been a good friend to me . . . and to those like me. We'll do all we can to help his family while he's a prisoner. Likely drop some fish and a few vegetables down to Hemmick. Perhaps eggs too. If you get to see him, you say we'll make certain they don't starve.'

'Bless you, Billy. Even if I don't manage to reach Jacob, I'll get a letter to him somehow and tell him what you're doing for his family. It will ease the torment he must be going through. Now, will you be ready if I'm at Portloe by eight o'clock in the morning?'

Chapter 41

When Toby returned to the Veryan vicarage and made his admittedly vague plans known, Jeremiah Trist was dismayed by what he intended doing. He tried very hard to dissuade Toby from undertaking what he referred to as 'this misguided adventure'.

'The man is not even a member of our Church,' he argued. 'There will be many eyebrows raised if word gets around that a Church of England priest has gone off and risked his own life and freedom for the sake of a Quaker. Think of the inference Archdeacon Scantlebury will draw from such an escapade!'

'Jacob and his family were the first friends I made in Porthluney. I couldn't live with my conscience if I did nothing when there's even a slight chance I might be able to help him. There *are* other considerations too, but I am not prepared to discuss them right now. I am barred from my duties as curate of Porthluney at the moment – and it was the archdeacon himself who ordered me to leave the parish. Whatever I do need not concern him further.'

Later that night Toby was in his room, placing clothes in the bag he would take with him the following day. He was determined to get to Guernsey by some means. If Matthew was unable to take him, he would find another boat going there.

He had almost completed his packing when there was a soft knock at the door. He opened it to find Sally standing outside.

Before he could say anything, she put a finger to her lips and slipped past him through the doorway.

When he closed the door and turned back into the room she was standing beside his bag.

'I didn't want to disturb Anna – or my father. If he knew I had come to your room at this time of night he would be scandalised.'

She looked down at the bag. 'I can see that nothing Father said has changed your mind about trying to rescue your friends?'

'No.'

'You have no idea how long you'll be gone, I suppose?'

He shook his head and Sally moved closer to him. 'Who is she, Toby? I know there has to be a girl involved in this somehow. She must also be someone very special if you're prepared to risk your career – and your freedom – for her.'

'She is.' He told her briefly of Bethany and her family and what had happened.

When he had finished his explanation, Sally said rather wistfully, 'She's a very lucky woman, Toby. I hope she will realise that one day.'

'Even if she doesn't, I've got to find her. She left so suddenly . . . It flew in the face of all we'd talked about.'

'A woman is entitled to change her mind, you know?'

'Not about something as important as this. At least, not without having a very good reason – and that's what I find completely baffling. Bethany's not the sort of woman who would go away in such a manner without giving a reason.'

Sally gave him a wan smile. 'Well, hurry back. Anna is bursting to show you her latest card trick.'

'Matthew finds her delightful. I noticed his brother was paying *you* a great deal of attention too.'

'He's very gentlemanly. Actually, both brothers are. But I am glad I'm not competing with Grace. I don't think I have ever met such an attractive woman. She was very well named.'

After a few moments of silence between them Sally said, 'I must go now, or we'll both end up losing our reputations.'

She gave him a brief kiss and before she broke away from him, rested her head against his chest and whispered, 'Take care of yourself, Toby, and don't try any heroics, please.'

* * *

Toby left the vicarage very early the next morning to walk to Portloe. The house was quiet, with only a couple of servants at work.

He reached Portloe earlier than had been arranged, but Billy already had his boat in the water and was ready to set off for Falmouth.

The young fisherman seemed very quiet when they set out, but Toby put it down to the early hour.

In an attempt to make conversation, he said, 'Did you sort out your net-making venture with Alice last night?'

'No. She says that taking care of you and the rectory must come first.'

There was a trace of bitterness in Billy's voice and in a moment of intuition Toby realised this was the source of the young fisherman's reserve.

'By the time I get back Rose Henna will most probably have returned to work. Alice will be free to work with you then.'

'Alice is going to be unhappy when that happens. She enjoys working for you. She believes you're a lonely man who needs someone to look after you. She said as much last night.'

'I think Alice might be confusing being alone with being lonely, Billy. I'm very often on my own, but not necessarily lonely. Mind you, I do enjoy having Alice working at the rectory. She does her work well and is a happy person to have around. Yet I don't think that's where her future lies, do you?'

'You know I've asked her to marry me?'

'No, I didn't know. What has she said?'

'She says she's too young at the moment to think about it seriously.'

'That's a very sensible attitude to take, Billy. Too many young girls rush into marriage without thinking properly about its responsibilities. Don't worry, she'll accept you eventually. I'm convinced there's no one else in her life.'

The young fisherman grinned sheepishly. 'I'm pleased to hear you say that, Curate. I thought . . . I thought you might be sweet on her yourself. If you were I'd stand no chance, no chance at all, me being just a fisherman, although I've got plans for the future. As it is . . . well, as you say, Rose might be back working at the rectory by the time you return. If she is, then Alice will be working with me, at Portloe.'

When they reached Falmouth, Billy offered to remain with Toby until he knew exactly what he was doing. He refused the offer. He intended making his way to Guernsey by any means possible and would remain at Falmouth until he found a boat to take him there.

Shouldering his bag, he asked directions from a Revenue officer on duty on the quayside and was soon heading towards the Vivian shipping office.

Before he arrived he espied the *Potomac* berthed alongside the quay and made for the ship instead.

As he reached the gangway, one of the seamen on deck recognised him and waved.

Responding to the greeting, Toby called, 'Is Mr Vivian on board?'

'You'll find him in his cabin.' Grinning knowingly, the seaman added, 'Grace is there with him. Would you like me to go below and tell him he's got a visitor?'

'I'll do it myself,' called Toby, as he stepped to the gangway from the quay.

'You'd better make it quick,' said the seaman when Toby was on deck. 'We'll be putting to sea within the hour. Mind you, I doubt if we'll have the luck we had when you were sailing with us.'

'You never know,' replied Toby. 'It's possible you'll have me with you again for this trip.'

He knew which was Matthew's cabin and when he knocked at the door, the ship's owner called for him to come in.

Matthew had a chart spread out on the desk before him. Grace was seated on a bunk, dressed only in a petticoat, sewing a button on a dress. When she saw Toby she jumped up with a squeal of delight and he hurriedly put the desk between them.

Shaking him by the hand, Matthew said, 'I hardly expected to see you again quite so soon, although it's always a pleasure.'

He nodded his head in the direction of the bag Toby had placed upon the floor. 'It looks as though you're travelling somewhere?'

'One of your seamen just told me you're sailing within the hour. Are you going anywhere near Guernsey?'

'I shall be working along the French coast, so I won't be far away from the island. Why?'

'A friend of mine, a fisherman, has been taken prisoner by the French. He left Cornwall to take a young woman to Guernsey. I want to find out whether he was captured on the way back, or whether the young woman is a prisoner too. I'd like to try to secure the release of both of them, if I can.'

Matthew drew in his breath. 'I'd say that might be easier said than done. Do you have any particular plan in mind?'

'Nothing specific,' admitted Toby. 'But if the crew and passengers of the French merchantman have already been returned to France, I'll ask the French authorities to reciprocate by releasing Jacob and Bethany. If the French prisoners are still at St Peter Port it might be possible to arrange some form of exchange.'

'I doubt if the French will bother very much about a few nationals from Martinique,' said Matthew. 'They'll probably be quite happy for us to keep them and feed them until this war is over.'

'I don't think so,' said Grace, joining in the conversation for the first time. 'There was one passenger on board they will be very anxious to get back.'

Putting her sewing to one side, she said, 'Monsieur Flaubert – the man who claimed to own me – was very fond of boasting that his sister is the wife of Monsieur Fouché, Minister of Police for the whole of France. I think perhaps they might be anxious to have him returned safely to France, although, of course, he might already have returned there.'

'There's only one way to find out,' said Matthew, rolling up his charts and inserting them in a leather tube. 'We'll set sail for Guernsey right away.'

Toby was following him from the cabin when Grace called him back. 'Toby! Wait.'

He stopped in the doorway and turned to see her slipping the dress over her head. 'I wish to go on deck too, but I need someone to help me to fasten my dress.'

She had wriggled herself inside it now. Turning around she revealed a triangular expanse of bare, dark skin. It seemed it would be an impossibility to draw together the already tight-fitting dress and button it, but Grace assured him it could be done.

As Toby secured button after button through increasingly distant buttonholes, she said, 'The woman who might be a prisoner of the French . . . she is the one who is your mistress?'

'I don't have a mistress, Grace, but she is the one I hope will one day be my wife.'

'Ah! So there *is* a woman in your life. I am very happy for you, Toby. You must not worry. Matthew will help you to get her back. I will too.'

As she spoke, he realised that she must have been deliberately breathing in to make his task more difficult and keep him talking.

'I would have thought you'd never want to see this Monsieur Flaubert ever again.'

'I do not care if I see him or if I do not. I am a free woman now. But it would make me very happy if I could help arrange for a price to be paid for him, as though he too was a slave. Especially if it means freedom for others. Yes, that would make me very happy.'

Adjusting the neckline of her dress, she said, 'Come, Toby. We will go on deck now. I think it is very exciting to be on the deck of a ship when it is entering or leaving harbour.'

Chapter 42

Toby felt more apprehension than excitement when the *Potomac* entered the harbour of St Peter Port, guided in by a brightly painted pilot gig. The wind had not been sufficient to enable the ship to complete its journey before dark and they had been forced to spend a frustrating night anchored outside the harbour.

The captured French merchantman was still here, tied up alongside the quay, and the *Potomac* was edged towards a berth only a short distance away.

There appeared to be no one on board the French vessel. When Toby commented on this, the *Potomac*'s mate explained: 'They were all taken off when we brought the ship into harbour. The crew were lodged in gaol, the passengers accommodated at an inn – at their own expense, of course.'

'I hope they're still there,' said Toby, fervently. 'We need them.'

He was feeling extremely tense. So many unanswered questions were hanging in the air. 'I think we must check on that before we do anything else.'

Matthew agreed with him. As soon as the *Potomac* was safely moored, the two men went ashore. They were accompanied by Grace. This was a British island, but French was the mother tongue for many of its inhabitants.

Much to their relief they discovered the crew and passengers of the merchantman were still held on the island – but they would not be here for long. The harbourmaster informed them that a French vessel was expected to reach the island the following day, to convey them to the mainland.

'We need to stop them,' said Toby. 'One of the passengers from the French ship is a man of some importance. We hope to exchange him for some English prisoners.'

The man shrugged his shoulders, expressing indifference. 'I am simply the harbourmaster. My duties are to arrange a berth for the French ship and collect the harbour dues from its master. Who it takes, or doesn't take, is nothing to do with me. You'll need to speak to the Constable.'

It was the beginning of a frustrating succession of meetings held by Toby and his companions. The Constable, in common with the harbourmaster, said the matter was outside his jurisdiction. He referred them to the office of the Procureur. The official felt this was a matter that would require a decision from the Bailiff, ruler of the Bailiwick of Guernsey.

By this time it was late-afternoon, and when they reached the Bailiff's office they were told he would not be available until the following morning.

'By the time we have things sorted out, the French boat will have come and gone,' said Toby, trying very hard not to allow his frustration to boil over into anger.

'I don't think so,' said Matthew. Demanding paper and a pen from the clerk in the Bailiff's office, he wrote a quick note. Sealing it with the Bailiff's own sealing-wax, he imprinted it with his signet ring.

Handing the note to the clerk, he said, 'Please have this delivered to the Bailiff . . . today. If it reaches him tomorrow it will be too late and you will find you no longer have a position here.'

Such was the authority of Matthew's manner that the startled clerk promised he would personally deliver it to the Bailiff's home, within the hour.

'Is there anything else you need to do?' asked Matthew, as they left the building.

'Yes. I suggest you return to the ship in case there's a reply to your note. I'll be back there later,' suggested Toby. 'I am going to find a family of Quakers and see if they can tell me anything of Bethany and Jacob.'

Matthew realised this was something Toby wished to do

on his own. He and Grace went off to have a brief look at the old town of St Peter Port before returning to the *Potomac*.

Toby found the cottage home of Bethany's parents with very little difficulty. The location was not dissimilar to Jacob's home in Hemmick Cove. He paused to look at it for a while, hoping that in some mysterious way he might will Bethany to come from the cottage and greet him. He desperately hoped she would be here.

No one appeared from the house and he made his way to the door aware that he would soon know the worst.

He knew immediately the door was opened that he had come to the right place. The woman standing in the doorway was dressed in a plain grey dress with no baubles of any description. It was the traditional dress of a Quaker woman.

'Can I help thee?' The woman's voice was soft, like Bethany's.

'My name is Toby Lovell and I carry a letter from Muriel. I'm seeking Bethany and need to talk to you also. May I come in?'

'Thou art the Church of England minister from Cornwall?'

'That's right.' There was no invitation to enter the house, but Toby's hopes soared. The fact they knew of him probably meant that Bethany *had* been here. Of course, there was also a possibility she had written to tell them of him, but he doubted it . . .

'Who is it?' a man's voice called from inside the house.

'It's . . . it's the Church of England minister from Cornwall. The one Bethany told us about.'

There was the sound of a chair scraping on a stone floor, then a man appeared behind the woman. As she moved out of his way apprehensively, Toby could see the man's face more clearly. He appeared to be struggling to control his anger.

Thrusting his head forward as he spoke, he said to Toby, 'Thou art the man who is the cause of Bethany's being expelled from the Society? Who persuaded her to forsake the ways of her parents, grandparents, yes, and great-grandparents too? Thou hast the gall to come here, to my house?'

Now Toby knew for certain Bethany *had* reached this cottage from Cornwall. It meant that Jacob had been captured by the French *after* delivering her.

'It's my intention to marry Bethany, just as soon as I find her again, sir. I'm sorry we won't have your blessing . . .'

'Thou won't have Bethany, either. She has put thee and thy ways behind her. She will marry within the Society of Friends.'

Not wishing to have a fierce argument with her father, Toby said, 'I'm sorry we can't agree, sir, but may I speak to her, please?'

'The answer would still be no, even were it possible, but Bethany is not here.'

'Where is she? Did she leave with Jacob when he sailed for Cornwall?'

'I do not know where she is, or what she is doing. I told her she was welcome to remain in this house only if she would return to our ways and apply for readmission to the Society. She refused and left.'

'Please . . . did she set out to return to Cornwall with Jacob?'

The urgency in Toby's voice finally broke through the other man's prejudice against him.

'Bethany herself declared she intended having nothing more to do with thee. Why should it matter?'

'Jacob was captured by the French on his way back to Cornwall. I'm trying to discover whether Bethany was with him.'

Bethany's mother put a hand to her throat in a gesture of dismay. 'Jacob taken? What of Muriel and her family?'

'They're being taken care of by fishermen who know and respect Jacob. I'm trying to find Bethany. Have you heard nothing from her since she left your house? Is there anyone she might be staying with?'

Bethany's mother shook her head, very close to tears. 'I can think of no one. If she were still on the island we would have heard. I think she must have decided to return to Cornwall with Jacob . . . He had already left the house when Bethany said she could not stay. He had been anxious to return to his family. What will become of her if she has been taken too?'

'We will pray for her,' said Bethany's father, less belligerent now, although he was not inclined to converse with Toby. 'Come.'

The last word was spoken to his wife before he turned and walked back inside the house.

Toby realised he would learn nothing more here. Then, as he turned to walk away, Bethany's mother hurried after him, still clutching the letter he had given her, and took his arm. 'Don't think too harshly of him. He knows he behaved badly towards Bethany. He will blame himself if anything has happened to her.'

When Toby made no reply, she asked plaintively, 'What will thou do now?'

'I intend going to France to secure their release.'

Her hand dropped from his arm and she said, 'God go with thee. Thou wilt be in my prayers – and his too when he learns what thou art doing, although he will never admit it to anyone.'

She turned and scurried back to the house without looking at Toby again.

Chapter 43

Toby was in Matthew's cabin on board the *Potomac* that evening, sipping a glass of wine, when a messenger arrived from the Bailiff of Guernsey.

The messenger waited while Matthew read the letter he had delivered. When he came to the end, Matthew nodded. 'Thank you. Please tell the Bailiff we will be there.'

As the messenger was escorted from the cabin by a seaman, both Toby and Grace waited for the shipowner to disclose the contents of the letter.

Matthew smiled at their expressions. 'We've been invited to take dinner with the Bailiff tonight, to discuss our requirements with him.'

'How did you manage that?' Toby had difficulty hiding his astonishment.

'Vivian ships have traded with Guernsey for very many years. Besides, my father and the Bailiff were fellow privateers in their younger days.'

'You said nothing of this when we set off,' said Toby, accusingly.

'One takes advantage of friendships only when it is really necessary and when all else has failed,' replied Matthew. 'Come, we'd better ready ourselves and set off.'

'What about me?' asked Grace, uncertainly.

'You'll come too, of course. We have a story to tell the Bailiff – and you're the one who knows all about M'sieur Flaubert.'

The Bailiff's house was an impressive building on the hillside of St Peter Port. When they were shown into the room where he was drinking with a number of his guests, he gave Matthew a very warm welcome. If he was surprised that he had brought Toby and Grace with him, he did not allow it to show.

After introducing the newcomers to his guests, he took them off to a study, to listen to their problem.

Toby explained the purpose of their visit to the island, and his proposal for how it might be possible to obtain the release of Jacob and Bethany.

Thoughtfully, the Bailiff said, 'Do you think the capture of this Cornish fisherman and the young lady – if indeed she has been taken – took place within Guernsey's territorial waters?'

'I couldn't say that with any certainty,' said Toby, hesitantly.

'Then I think we need to make the assumption that it *did*,' declared the Bailiff. 'It will give me justification for delaying the repatriation of the French prisoners until these people for whom you are so concerned, are returned.'

'You'll do that?' asked Toby, eagerly.

'Of course. I won't allow such goings on within the area of my jurisdiction. We'll send word that the French vessel and its crew and passengers are to be held in St Peter Port until we decide what's to be done. Do you have any ideas?'

'I think it might be a conciliatory gesture if we were to return the women and children and keep the men here,' said Matthew.

'Yes, that would be a civilised act,' conceded the Bailiff. 'Then what?'

'I'll travel to France with the French vessel,' said Toby, instantly. 'Once there I'll journey on to Morlaix and arrange for an exchange of the prisoners.'

While the two men were still thinking about this, Grace said unexpectedly, 'I will come with you, Toby.'

Of the three men in the room, only Matthew was not shocked by her words.

When Toby protested, she countered, 'Do you speak French?'

'No, but . . .'

'Then how do you expect to learn what you need to know, make your way to Morlaix – and arrange for the exchange of the French prisoners for Bethany and Jacob? Are you forgetting that England and France are at war? You will be in the country of an enemy. Every hand will be against you.'

'I realise that, and I could do with some help, but you're . . .'

'A woman? Would it be safer for a French-speaking man to travel with you? I think not. Besides, I am your friend. I will be there to take care of you, and of your interests. That will be important, I think.'

When Toby still hesitated, Grace said, 'Or is it something else? Do you not trust yourself with me? Are your feelings for this Bethany not strong enough for you to resist temptation?'

Aware of Matthew's amusement, Toby said, 'All right, what you say makes sense – but I hope we can convince Bethany there was no other way of helping her. What do you think, Matthew?'

Smiling enigmatically, he said, 'Grace is a free woman now. She makes her own decisions – but, for what it's worth, I think her idea is a sound one. *I* couldn't possibly come with you, that's a certainty, and I doubt if you would find anyone else you could trust with your life.'

'Thank you, Matthew.'

The smile Grace gave to the shipowner caused the Bailiff to look sharply and questioningly from one to the other. However, when he spoke again, it was to say, 'Madam . . . gentlemen. Now we have decided on our course of action, shall we join the others for dinner? I have some interesting guests tonight and am quite certain they are going to find you fascinating. One or two of them knew your father, Matthew. They will be absolutely delighted to meet you . . .'

Chapter 44

Toby watched with mixed feelings as the French vessel entered the harbour of St Peter Port. It was closely followed by a brig of the British navy. The small man-o'-war had intercepted the other vessel on the seas between France and Guernsey.

The master of the French ship had been able to produce a letter from the British Admiralty, authorising him to proceed to Guernsey, pick up French prisoners who had been on a captured merchantman, and convey them to a French port.

The document appeared genuine, but the commander of the brig chose to escort the other vessel to its destination anyway.

When the French ship berthed, the harbourmaster went on board, accompanied by a number of officials. Toby went with them.

Arrogantly, the Frenchman waved the Admiralty letter in front of the harbourmaster's face. 'I have come to take home the men, women and children who were taken when their ship was attacked and captured by an English pirate. You will bring them here, please.'

'I'm afraid there's been a change of plan,' said the harbourmaster. 'They won't be coming with you. At least the men won't, although you may embark the women and children tomorrow morning, when all the formalities have been completed.'

'But . . . this is outrageous!' protested the master. 'These men are not combatants. They have not, and will not, become involved in the war against your country. They must be allowed to go free.'

'I am pleased to hear you express an opinion that

non-combatants should not be held in prison,' said Toby. 'I trust your government is of the same mind. We will hold these men until the release of a fisherman who is in a Morlaix gaol. We also need to find the young woman we believe was with him when he was taken prisoner by the crew of a French ship.'

'It is utterly outrageous!' repeated the French ship's master. 'I insist . . .'

'You have been informed of the new arrangements,' said the harbourmaster, brusquely. 'The women and children will be ready to embark at an early hour tomorrow morning. You will also be taking the Reverend Lovell and Miss Grace. They are coming with you to France to make the arrangements for an exchange of prisoners.'

'I wish to make a protest . . .'

'You can make whatever you like,' retorted the harbourmaster. 'Your passengers come on board tomorrow. When they have embarked you will leave immediately. In the meantime, you and your crew must remain on board your ship. Anyone who attempts to set foot on shore will be arrested – or shot.'

To prove he was making no idle threat, he pointed to a company of soldiers marching along the quay towards the ship.

'I don't think we're going to be made very welcome on board,' Toby said to Grace as they returned to the *Potomac*.

'We cannot expect to be treated as honoured guests,' agreed Grace. 'But much of what the master said would have been for the benefit of his crew and those to whom they will speak in France. They will be aware he was meant to embark the brother-in-law of the Minister of Police. He wants it to be absolutely clear to the authorities in France that he did his best to make us change our minds.'

As the Frenchwomen and children boarded the boat the following morning, Toby remained on the quayside with Grace. They were both aware that the women recognised Grace, but all except one averted their eyes as they passed her by.

The exception was the widow of a French army sergeant who had died of a tropical disease whilst serving in Martinique. The woman was of peasant gipsy stock from the French Basque region. Her easy life on the West Indian island had been very different from the one she had known before, and would soon know again. She was bitter with the whole world for taking such a way of life from her.

When she passed Grace, the woman spat at her feet and mouthed the word, '*Esclave*!' 'Slave!'

When Grace translated the word for him, Toby said, 'You shouldn't be coming to France with me, Grace. That woman could make trouble for you.'

'I don't think so.' Grace sounded far more nonchalant than she felt. 'Bonaparte has banned slavery in France.'

'Are you sure of this?'

Grace nodded, hoping she was right. She remembered that slavery had been banned in Martinique too, for a while, but none of the French plantation owners took any notice of the directive. After a minor riot on the island, it had been officially annulled but fortunately the only man who could lay claim to her was in prison here, on Guernsey.

When the last of the women and children had made their way on board, Grace and Toby said their farewells to Matthew and embarked on the French ship.

It was not a large vessel, and the only available cabin was given to a woman who was heavily pregnant. The other passengers remained on the upper deck.

Grace and Toby were here too, but once at sea were ignored by the others.

The ship's master also seemed reluctant to speak to them, but after they had been at sea for about an hour, Toby asked him where they were heading.

'Paimpol,' replied the master. 'We shall arrive there late this afternoon.'

Toby tried to recall the charts he had studied of the French coast. He thought he remembered Paimpol. It was farther west than he had expected the ship to take them. He had believed they would head for a port more convenient for Paris.

When he voiced his thoughts, the Frenchman shrugged.

'I am only the master of my ship, M'sieur, not its owner. I go where I am ordered to go. But I was told that one of the men I should be bringing back from Guernsey is a man of importance. Paimpol is nearer to his home than any other port, and I was ordered to take the ship there.'

It meant they would be much closer to Morlaix than Toby had anticipated. However, it might pose a problem if he were forced to go to Paris to arrange the release of Jacob and Bethany – and he was determined he *would* secure their freedom.

While Toby was thinking of his plan of action when they reached Paimpol, the master said, 'A list of those who are being held in Guernsey was sent to France. Many friends and relatives will be waiting at Paimpol. They will be both disappointed and angry. It is probable they will turn their anger upon you, I think. It will be better for you to remain on board until officials arrive to speak to you.'

'You're probably right,' said Toby, thoughtfully. 'Thank you.'

He looked at Grace. She would be the main target for the anger of the relatives, especially if the Frenchwoman who had spat at her stayed around to incite the crowd.

He would ask the ship's master to allow her to go below if it seemed there might be violence. But, as Grace had already pointed out, Britain and France were at war. Enemies of France could not expect to be made welcome.

Chapter 45

Paimpol was a small fishing port on the north coast of Brittany. As the French ship carrying Toby and Grace entered harbour, Toby thought there must be a celebration taking place. Flags and bunting decorated buildings about the harbour and a great many people were milling around the quayside.

Not until their ship approached the quay and a band began playing, did Toby realise the celebrations were to welcome the arrival of the ship – and, no doubt, the important passenger it was believed to be carrying.

'I think it would be better for us to go below deck for a while,' said Toby to Grace. 'There are going to be some angry people on shore when they learn M'sieur Flaubert isn't on board after all.'

Grace agreed. 'I'll speak to the master.'

This was easier said than done. The Frenchman was engaged in bringing the ship alongside the harbour wall. By the time he was free to hold a conversation, a gangway was being pushed across to the ship.

The French passengers gathered excitedly around the head of the gangway with their baggage, anxious to go ashore.

Standing close to a hatchway that led to the small cabin area, Toby could see a number of happy faces as those on shore recognised friends or relatives.

There were also a number of perplexed expressions among the waiting Frenchmen and women.

To one side of the crowd, a tall and elegant man sat on a horse at the centre of a small uniformed guard. Toby thought they must be soldiers. He was soon to learn they were uniformed police.

The women and children swarmed down the gangway to the shore, and there were many noisy and emotional reunions. When it became evident there were no more French passengers disembarking, the man on the horse spoke to an officer of the guard. The uniformed man immediately hurried up the gangway to the ship.

The officer made his way to the master and they began talking in French, the conversation accompanied by much gesticulating, some of it in Toby's and Grace's direction.

'What are they saying?' asked Toby.

'The officer is asking for M'sieur Flaubert,' explained Grace. 'The master is telling him what happened in Guernsey.'

As the master pointed to where they stood, Toby saw the woman who had spat at Grace. She was talking excitedly to the man on the horse and pointing in the same direction as the master of the French vessel.

Two uniformed men hurried up the gangway. After speaking to the officer, the three men approached Toby and Grace. The officer held a terse conversation with Grace, in French.

'They want us to go with them,' she said.

'I don't see that we have any alternative,' said Toby. 'Did he say anything else?'

'Yes. The man on the horse is Minister Fouché, Chief of Police for Napoleon Bonaparte and Monsieur Flaubert's brother-in-law. He has been told I am his slave, but that I abandoned him and changed sides when the ship was taken.'

'Don't worry, we'll soon put things right, Grace. This is the biggest stroke of luck we could possibly have. M'sieur Fouché has the power – and a very good reason – to be of help to us.'

Toby was left with the impression that he had failed to convince Grace, but now the French officer was hurrying them down the gangway towards the minister.

When they reached the quay they were met by the hostility of the crowd, who realised they had something to do with the non-appearance of the men they were expecting.

The uniformed escort pushed their countrymen and women roughly aside and soon Toby and Grace stood looking up at the French minister. The angry mob crowded around them, kept at bay only by the guns of the police.

Ignoring Toby, the Chief of Police spoke to Grace. Toby was unable to follow the conversation, but at one stage he heard the angry voice of the French sergeant's widow shouting from the crowd.

As Grace became visibly agitated, Toby broke in on the conversation. 'What's going on?'

'M'sieur Fouché is referring to me as a slave whore who revealed the identity of his brother-in-law to the English authorities. He said I am a traitor, and he will see that I go on my knees before the guillotine.'

'M'sieur Fouché is talking nonsense. Tell him *I* am the one who stopped the prisoners from being returned, and it is only a temporary measure. When Bethany and Jacob are released, M'sieur Flaubert and the others will be returned too. As for your so-called "treason" . . . you are not French but English, through your father. What's more, slavery does not exist in England – or in any other civilised country. You are a free woman.'

Hesitantly, Grace began to translate Toby's words, but the French minister waved her to silence.

'I do not need anyone to interpret English for me.'

Studying Toby for the first time, he asked, 'Who are you? And what are you doing in France?'

'My name is Toby Lovell, I am a priest of the Church of England. I am here to arrange the release of two prisoners taken by your countrymen from a fishing boat, somewhere between Guernsey and England. At least one of them is being held in gaol in Morlaix. They are non-combatants – the same as your brother-in-law and his companions. I carry a letter from the Bailiff of Guernsey.'

He took the letter from his pocket and passed it to the horseman.

'He promises to release his prisoners when you return those taken by you. I am here to make the necessary arrangements, and have brought Grace as my interpreter.'

The Minister of Police tucked the letter in a pocket

without opening it and looked from Toby to Grace, and back again. 'You have an admirable taste in interpreters, M'sieur Lovell. I too was trained for the priesthood, but it would appear you have little to learn from French clerics. However, she will need to be questioned about her nationality and status.'

'I would like to point out to you, sir, that Grace is accompanying me on a mission sanctioned by the Bailiff of Guernsey. Should the need arise, it will be endorsed by the British government.'

'Surely I do not need to remind you, M'sieur Lovell, that Britain and France are at war? The protection of your government means nothing here. You have not received the approval of *my* government for your mission, therefore I do not accept it as official. I would be justified in having you shot for a spy.'

At that moment someone from the crowd threw a stone, aimed at Toby. It missed and hit the minister's horse.

The Frenchman gave an order and the police surrounding them began beating back the crowd with their muskets.

When he had brought his horse under control, Minister Fouché spoke to Toby once more. 'You will be held in custody while I decide what is to be done with you. This woman will be held for questioning too. It could be that you will find your friends at Morlaix, and be able to enjoy their company once more, as a guest of my government.'

'That would be a very foolish thing to do, M'sieur Fouché. I am a comparatively young man and have my God to comfort me, wherever I may be. I fear that M'sieur Flaubert has neither time nor the Lord on his side. Until both Grace and I return safely to Guernsey, he too must languish in prison. In such conditions, I fear this war might well outlast your brother-in-law. He did not impress me as a very fit man.'

For a few moments the French Minister of Police appeared to be thinking about what Toby had said. Then he issued an order in French and Toby was led away, berated by the crowd through which he was led.

Behind him he could hear Grace protesting volubly to

Minister Fouché at his actions. Toby was worried what might happen to her if they decided she *was* a slave and a French subject.

He was not overly worried about his own future. He felt quite certain that when Minister Fouché had thought about it he would realise Toby had spoken the truth. It needed little more than a stroke of the pen to have Jacob and Bethany released, and his own brother-in-law returned to France.

Chapter 46

Toby was placed in a tiny, two-cell gaol in the heart of the small fishing town. There was nothing in either cell except for a deep layer of straw on the flagstoned floor.

There were no other occupants and when Toby was locked away, he felt very much alone. When it became dark and no one had paid him a visit, he felt as though he had been forgotten by those who had put him there.

He spent a long time on his knees, praying, before settling down to sleep.

He was awoken by a rustling in the straw, somewhere close at hand. It was pitch dark and he could see nothing at all. At first, he thought another prisoner must have been brought to the gaol while he slept, although he could not understand why he had not woken up. Then he heard a high-pitched squeaking. The sound that had disturbed him was being made by rats!

The squeaking came from various parts of the small gaol. There must have been a great many of the rodents.

He had very little sleep for the remainder of the night. The rats were extremely bold. However, he soon learned that if he kicked out at them when they came too close, they would scurry away – for a while.

The rats did not disappear until the grey dawn filled the small barred aperture high in the wall that served as a window.

It must have been midday when he heard a key rattling in the lock of the outside door. When the door swung noisily open on unoiled hinges, an old man entered the gaol. His spine was so seriously deformed that he walked with his head permanently at waist level. In his hands he carried a tray on which were a bowl of soup, a chunk of coarse, dark bread, and a jug of wine.

The simple meal was passed to Toby through a hinged hatch that formed a section of the bars.

The crippled gaoler spoke in guttural French that Toby found quite unintelligible.

'Do you speak English?' he asked, hopefully.

His question brought forth more of the French patois. When this provoked no response from Toby, the man shrugged. Slamming the barred hatch shut he left the gaol, locking the outside door behind him.

Although he was disappointed he had been unable to communicate with the gaoler, the sight of the food reminded Toby that he was very hungry.

The bread was hard and quite obviously not fresh. However, he found that by soaking it in the soup, it was reasonably edible.

The wine was quite palatable, but there was no drinking vessel. Toby drank it straight from the jug. He decided he would save half for that evening as he was not at all certain there would be anything more to eat that day.

He wished he had a bible with him to read in the cell. He had brought one from England, but it was in his bag. There was no way of knowing whether he would ever see it again.

As he settled down in the straw after his frugal meal, Toby's concern centred on Grace once more. He wondered what form her 'questioning' would take. Since the revolution, only a few years before, some horrific stories had circulated in England about the methods used by the revolutionary courts and their agents.

He was also still distraught at the thought of Bethany being held in France. Was this the way she had been treated after her capture?

In spite of his present situation, Toby was not too concerned for himself. He knew he held the key to the release of Monsieur Flaubert. He had no doubt at all the Minister of Police would see reason before too long. When he did, Toby's lonely ordeal would be brought to an end.

* * *

Somewhat to his surprise, Toby was brought another meal that evening. This time it consisted of cold, fatty pork cut in thick slices. With it were a few boiled potatoes and a vegetable that looked somewhat like turnip. It had a distinctive taste that Toby failed to recognise. There was more wine, too.

Tonight, the old gaoler brought another man with him, who must have been at least twenty years his junior. This man smiled at Toby as he began to eat. Pointing to the food, he said, 'Good, eh?'

Toby looked at the man in undisguised delight. 'You speak English?'

The other man nodded his head and repeated, 'Good.'

It was the only English word he knew. He used it in reply to every question put to him before Toby realised this was the full extent of the man's English vocabulary.

Disappointed, Toby nodded, 'Yes, it's good.'

Both Frenchmen smiled their delight and the conversation came to an end. Smiling and bobbing their heads, they left the small gaol and the door was once more locked behind them.

The bread proved to be inedible without soup in which it might be soaked. Toby tried dipping it in wine, but it did nothing for its taste. He left a little of his fatty pork too . . . and then he remembered the rats.

He ate the pork, even though he did not want it. The bread was a different matter, but he eventually hit upon the simple solution of lobbing it through the bars into the other cell.

When the pewter plate was empty, he put it through the bars to the stone floor beyond.

He heard the rats once more, while he was praying. They seemed to be fighting amongst themselves for the bread he had thrown into the other cell. Later, in the darkness, he drank the last of the wine and dozed off in a fitful sleep.

Once, he woke with a sudden start and realised that a rat had run across his legs. After this he was reluctant to fall asleep again.

The next day was very much like the previous one. When the crippled gaoler, accompanied by his friend, brought him his midday meal Toby asked him to empty the slop bucket that had been placed in a corner of the cell and bring some water for him in order that he might wash.

The gaoler made no effort to understand him and Toby demanded to speak to Monsieur Fouché. The name brought recognition and a great deal of nodding of heads by both men. It also brought a flood of 'Good! Good!' from the gaoler's linguistic friend, but Toby realised he had been unable to get the message across that he wanted to speak to the Minister of Police.

Toby's third night in the small gaol was even worse than the two that had gone before. The bread that accompanied the evening meal followed the same course as the night before, but tonight the rats were bolder than ever.

At one stage, Toby retrieved his plate and threw it into the next cell at them, but to little avail. Tonight they were intent upon spending more time in his cell.

Then, at some time around midnight, there was the sound of a key rattling in the lock of the outside door. A lantern lit up the inside of the gaol and two watchmen entered, supporting a shackled man between them.

He seemed to have difficulty in standing but they dragged him to the other cell, unlocked the door and threw him inside. They left without saying a word to Toby.

There was now the strong smell of stale wine in the air and the man in the other cell began complaining bitterly in French to the world at large, about being locked up.

When it finally sank into his befuddled mind that there would be no response to his protests, he began to cry.

Although it was obvious the man was very drunk indeed, Toby felt sorry for him and eventually called out. His intention was to let the drunken man know he was not alone in the darkness, in the hope that it might calm him.

Unfortunately, Toby's efforts produced quite the opposite effect. Only for a few moments did the Frenchman cease his abject pleading to ask who was there.

When the voice from the darkness replied in an unintelligible tongue, the Frenchman's drunken imagination conjured up a vision of demons, sent from another world to torment him.

In spite of the disparate languages, it was possibly the most rapid conversion Toby had ever made. The Frenchman fell upon his knees in the straw, pleading with God to forgive him all his misdemeanours and protect him in his hour of need.

This stage of his drunkenness lasted until the wine he had imbibed finally produced a soporific effect. His prayers became more and more incoherent until he eventually lay down and went to sleep.

Grateful now for the silence, Toby did the same.

He was awakened by screams of pain. It was the drunken man once more, but this time Toby heard another sound: the squeaking of rats.

The Frenchman began crying once more, but he had a genuine reason for his tears this time. Guiltily, Toby remembered the bread he had thrown into the other cell.

He shouted and clapped his hands in a bid to frighten off the rats, but only succeeded in terrifying the other man more than before.

Eventually, Toby resorted to prayer once more, his devotions frequently disturbed by the sobs and pleadings of the man in the other cell. It was a night about which he would have nightmares for many months to come.

Chapter 47

Dawn was slow in reaching the interior of the high-windowed gaol-house. A dull, grey light had filled the small aperture for some time before Toby was able to see the man in the other cell.

He was squatting on the floor, legs drawn up, his head resting upon his knees.

When Toby called to him, the man looked up. It was immediately apparent where the rat had bitten him. There was a wound on the cheekbone beneath his right eye and the whole of the cheek was bloody. He was much younger than Toby had realised and even this morning looked as though he was still in a drunken stupor.

Toby would have liked to be able to communicate with the man, but neither spoke the other's language, and Toby was not to be held in the gaol for very much longer.

Soon afterwards, the door opened and the aged, crippled gaoler entered. He was accompanied by a uniformed policeman who appeared to be an officer.

The uniformed man gave Toby a brief semblance of a bow then looked at his condition with some distaste.

'You will come with me, please. Minister Fouché wishes to speak with you.'

Correctly interpreting the Frenchman's look, Toby wished he had been given an opportunity to clean up before meeting with the elegant Minister of Police, but he did not want to delay leaving the gaol. If he put off his departure now, he feared there might be a change of heart by the minister.

Before going through the door he pointed out the man in the other cell, saying, 'I think he should receive medical attention. He was bitten on the face by a rat during the night.'

The officer called out something in French to the prisoner. The man looked up, his face dirty, tear-streaked and bloody.

The officer shrugged unsympathetically, saying to Toby, 'I do not think it is too serious for him. But for the rat, perhaps.'

As he and the officer walked through the streets of the small fishing port, Toby found he was attracting a great deal of interest and more than one hostile shout.

The officer smiled. 'I do not think you are the most popular of men, M'sieur. It is as well you have the protection of Minister Fouché.'

'Do you know what he intends doing with me?'

'You will be able to ask him for yourself. We are here now.'

The officer turned off the street to an inn yard and Toby followed. Inside the building the Frenchman led the way to a small private room which seemed overcrowded with servants.

Minister Fouché sat at a table, taking breakfast.

Grace was seated at the table too, but when she saw Toby she leaped to her feet and hurried across the room to embrace him.

Stepping back a pace she looked at him, dismayed at his unkempt state. 'Toby! What have they done to you?'

'I'm all right . . . but you?'

It was an unnecessary question. Grace looked as elegant and attractive as when he had left her in the company of the man with whom she was now taking breakfast.

'I am well, but sit down here. Have they been feeding you? Please, you must take some breakfast.'

She touched his arm in a gesture of sympathy. 'Poor Toby. They would not tell me where you were or I would have found some way to come and find you.'

Minister Fouché dabbed delicately at the corners of his mouth with a napkin before saying, 'I think M'sieur Lovell would prefer to bathe and change his clothes before he sits down to eat.'

He raised his hand and the inn's landlord hurried to the table. The autocratic Minister of Police said only a few words, but they were effective. The landlord scurried away, calling out orders as he went and sending servants hurrying away to carry out his bidding.

Minister Fouché now spoke to Toby for the first time. 'A bath will be prepared for you, M'sieur Lovell. I understand you will find your luggage in a room that has been put at your disposal. When you are bathed and are wearing clean clothes you will feel refreshed. We can then discuss the arrangements I have made for you to find your friends. I look forward to talking to you. It seems you are more than a simple priest. Grace tells me you were at Trafalgar and made a name for yourself as a hero?'

Toby looked at her accusingly. She must have spent a great deal of time talking to Minister Fouché and he doubted whether their discussions had all taken place over the meal table.

Fouché called for the landlord again and when he hurried to the table, the minister directed him to take Toby off with him.

'I will go too,' said Grace suddenly.

Her decision caused the minister to raise his eyebrows, but he said only, 'As you wish. You can tell your friend what has been decided. It will save me wasting more of my time on this unfortunate matter.'

The minister resumed his breakfast and Grace led Toby from the room.

When the door closed behind them, she put her hand on Toby's arm once more. 'Have you had a dreadful time?'

'I've stayed in better places,' he admitted. 'But how about you? When Minister Fouché said you were to be questioned I feared the worst. In England we've heard a great many stories of the interrogation methods used by French revolutionaries. I was very concerned for you.'

'Poor Toby.' Grace leaned against him affectionately. 'You were shut in a horrible filthy dungeon and yet you were worried about me? I am deeply touched.'

'*Did* they question you?'

'Of course! But it was a game, no more. M'sieur Fouché accepted my story that I was the mistress of his brother-in-law and not a slave. Once that had been settled I was able to persuade him to allow you to go to Morlaix to seek Bethany and the Quaker fisherman.'

'I'm impressed, Grace, but how did you manage it?

Minister Fouché does not impress me as a man who is easily "persuaded".'

'That is because you are a man, Toby. He is a man too – but I am a woman. It was not too difficult.'

Toby looked at her sharply, but she smiled up at him disarmingly. 'I know you must be very tired, but M'sieur Fouché has agreed to allow us to leave today. Indeed, I believe he is anxious that we should. He has received news that his wife is on her way from Paris. She is expecting to meet her brother here. He would prefer her not to meet me, I think.'

She giggled. 'It might almost be worth staying here until she arrives – but come, this is the room where you will bathe and change.'

They entered a room where servants were bustling to and fro, carrying buckets of hot water which they poured into a large bath, placed on towels in the centre of the room.

Toby's bag, which he had feared he would never see again, stood in a corner.

Leading him towards it, Grace said, 'Choose the clothes you wish to wear. I will see to it they are pressed and made ready for you while you bathe. You really need the clothes you are wearing to be washed, but that would take too long. We will have it done when we reach Morlaix. It is not too far, I believe.'

Releasing his arm, she said, 'I have had many discussions with M'sieur Fouché about what we will do when we reach Morlaix. Would you like me to stay while you bathe and tell you about it?'

'No, Grace. I would find that too much of an embarrassment.' He looked for a suggestion of mischief on her face, but could see none.

'As you wish.' She smiled at him. 'We will have much time to talk when we are on our journey. M'sieur Fouché is supplying a carriage and escort to take us all the way to Morlaix. I think you will soon find your Bethany.'

Now there was undisguised amusement in her expression as she added, 'Perhaps it is better that when we meet her you do not have to explain that we planned our journey while you were enjoying a bath.'

Chapter 48

Toby and Grace set off for Morlaix that afternoon in a coach provided by Minister Fouché. Their escort consisted of Inspector Bernard, the officer who had fetched Toby from gaol, and six uniformed policemen. All were mounted and it was expected they would make good time along the roads they had in this area.

The inspector carried authorisation from Minister Fouché to free the English prisoners sought by Toby.

Travelling at high speed, the journey took just seven hours. It involved two changes of horses and a dangerous estuary crossing with the tide sweeping in across the sand and around the wheels of the coach.

Eventually, when it was too dark to see the well-wooded countryside about them, the road began to descend a hill. Grace leaned out through a window and reported that she could see the lights of a town in the valley ahead of them.

Reining in beside the open window, Inspector Bernard informed them they were about to enter Morlaix. 'We will stay in a hotel in the centre of the town,' he added. 'Tomorrow we will go to the prison.'

'No,' said Toby, unexpectedly. 'We lost three days in Paimpol. Too much time has passed already since they were taken prisoner. I want to go there tonight.'

'I don't think that will be possible, M'sieur Lovell . . .'

Toby cut the other man's excuses short. 'You don't have to come if you prefer not to. Grace and I will go. We'll get in somehow.'

'I have been ordered by the Minister to remain with you at all times,' said the inspector, frostily. 'I think you will be wasting your time, but if you insist, I will accompany you.'

'Good! The sooner we reach the hotel, the sooner we can do something about having Bethany and Jacob released.'

Some forty minutes later, with the inspector still protesting it was a waste of time, they were on their way to the fortress-like building that housed the British prisoners-of-war.

At first, it seemed Inspector Bernard's assessment of the situation was likely to prove right. The guard performing gate duty was slow to put in an appearance. When he did, he slid open a small hatch through which they could just observe the outline of his face.

'Who are you?' he asked, in French. 'What are you doing here at this time of the night?'

Both Grace and the police inspector explained their mission to him, but the gaoler seemed determined not to be helpful.

Fortunately, his attitude offended the pride of Inspector Bernard. He demanded that the chief gaoler be brought to the gate immediately.

Eventually, muttering darkly about officials from Paris who thought that gaolers at the country's prisons had no more to do than escort visitors at any time of the day or night, the gaoler slid the hatch shut and went off inside the prison.

They waited for so long the inspector became impatient and tugged on the bell once more. Then they heard voices from inside the prison and the hatch was slid open yet again.

The chief gaoler was even grumpier than the first man had been. Then he realised that one of those standing outside the prison gates was a personal emissary of the Minister of Police.

The door swung open heavily and the trio entered. A few minutes later they were in the senior gaoler's office and the duty gaoler was lifting a heavy leatherbound book from a shelf.

He spoke no English, but Grace interpreted what he was saying. 'No,' he said in reply to her first question. 'There were a number of English prisoners, but no Englishwoman.'

'Tell him to look under her name,' said Toby. 'She is from Guernsey and will undoubtedly speak French. She might be passing as a Frenchwoman.'

The gaoler ran his finger down the names in his book. 'No, there is no Bethany Poole,' translated Grace. 'No Bethany anybody.'

Toby was concerned, but there was someone who could solve the mystery. 'Tell him to check the men for the name of Jacob Hosking.'

The gaoler recognised the name and did not need to consult his book. He spoke to Grace and she translated.

'Yes, Jacob is here. He will take us to see him, if we wish.'

Without waiting for Toby's reply, the inspector told the gaoler that of course they wished to speak to him. The Paris police inspector was hungry. He wanted to conclude their business and return to the hotel for dinner.

Carrying a lantern and accompanied by the man to whom they had first spoken, the gaoler led them along a stone-floored corridor and down a curving flight of stone steps. At the bottom was a barred door. Unlocking this, he stood aside while they filed into another, narrower corridor. Locking the door behind them, the gaoler led the way forward once more.

It felt damp down here, damp and cold, and Grace shivered.

Soon they heard the sound of voices – and the men were speaking in English! The sound came from behind a door made of stout iron bars. The voices came from the darkness on the other side.

'M'sieur Hosking! Jacob Hosking!' The shouts from the gaoler made Toby jump.

Other voices inside what was apparently a communal cell took up the shout. There was much rustling of straw and Toby realised that the prisoners in here enjoyed the same primitive facilities accorded to him in the small gaol at Paimpol.

'Who wants me?' A voice that Toby recognised came to him from the darkness.

'It's Toby, Jacob. Toby Lovell from Porthluney.'

There was an excited scrabbling in the straw inside the cell, then in the yellow light from the gaoler's lantern, Toby saw Jacob.

'Toby! What are thee doing here? Thou hasn't been taken prisoner?'

'No, Jacob. I've come to get you out and take you back to Cornwall. You and Bethany – but no one seems to know where she is. Can you help us? Do you have any idea where she might be?'

'Bethany? Is she a prisoner? Where was she taken?'

Now Toby's bewilderment matched that of Jacob. 'But . . . I thought . . . Wasn't she with you when you were captured by the French?'

'No. I left her with her parents. Bethany is probably still with them. I was on my way back to Cornwall when I was taken.'

'She isn't on Guernsey, Jacob. Her father turned her out of the house soon after you left. I felt certain she must have decided to return with you and been captured too. Do you have any idea where she might be?'

'None at all.' Jacob clutched the bars of the prison cage with both hands. 'This doesn't mean I will have to stay here? Thou will still have me released?'

Toby was utterly bewildered by the unexpected turn of events, but was still able to recognise the desperation in Jacob's voice.

'Yes, Jacob, you'll be released just as soon as Inspector Bernard here can make the arrangements with the prison governor. I'd like to take you out of here with us tonight, but there are a number of formalities to be completed first.'

'How about me, Parson?' said a voice from behind Jacob. 'The Quaker's not the only Cornish fisherman in here. There's eight of us, Mevagissey and Gorran men, taken off Dodman Point nigh on a year ago.'

A chorus of Cornish voices backed up the man's claim.

'Are you all fishermen in there?' asked Toby.

'No, only the eight men thee were just told about – and myself,' said Jacob. 'The rest are navy men and marines. They were captured when a frigate was driven ashore in a storm.'

Toby looked over to where the police inspector stood, a little way from them. Impatient to be away now the prisoner they had come to release had been found, he was talking to the gaoler about calling on the prison governor the next day.

'I doubt very much if I'll be able to help the sailors and marines, but I'll speak to the inspector about the fishermen.'

'No, Toby, leave this to me. For tonight at least,' said Grace, speaking for the first time since they had found Jacob. 'He might be more inclined to listen to me than to you. If I do not succeed, you may try your own means of persuasion in the morning. We must go now. The inspector's patience is running out. We need to keep him happy if we are to get what we want from him.'

Chapter 49

Toby was deeply puzzled and concerned about the disappearance of Bethany. The fact that she was not, after all, a prisoner of the French had come as a great relief – but where could she be? What had been her state of mind when she left home, having been turned out by her father? And why had she run away from Cornwall in the first place?

He hoped Jacob might be able to provide at least some of the answers when he was released from prison the following day.

There was also the question of the other Cornish prisoners being held in Morlaix. As non-combatants, there was no reason at all why they should be detained as prisoners-of-war. They posed no threat to France.

Despite Grace's suggestion that he should leave the matter to her for tonight, Toby put the question of their release to Inspector Bernard that evening, over dinner. The police inspector was less than enthusiastic.

'I am able only to authorise the release of your particular friend. Had the girl been held, she would have been freed too. The others are of no concern to me or to Minister Fouché. Forget them.'

'I can't forget them,' said Toby. 'They are from adjacent parishes to my own. Besides, when the Bailiff of Guernsey hears you are holding non-combatants in prison, he may feel he is obliged to release only M'sieur Flaubert. The others will remain as prisoners-of-war, following the precedent set by France.'

'That is a matter of indifference to me,' said Inspector Bernard, callously. 'My orders were to arrange the release of your two friends in order that M'sieur Flaubert might be released. When your captive friend is set free tomorrow, I will have carried out my orders. I expect you to keep your word in respect of M'sieur Flaubert. What you do with the others is nothing to me.'

Inspector Bernard placed his knife and fork on an empty plate and pushed back his chair. He had dined well. 'I shall go to my room now. Tomorrow morning we will return to the prison and your friend will be released. Then I will try to arrange for a boat to take you from Morlaix to Guernsey. When you have gone I can return to Paris and my regular duties. I find them far more congenial than a task such as this. Good night to you both.'

He bowed awkwardly and made his way from the room, walking with some care as he passed other tables.

'I don't think I was able to persuade Inspector Bernard with my arguments,' said Toby, ruefully. 'But it's difficult to see what else I could have said to make him change his mind. Just so long as M'sieur Flaubert is set free, he really doesn't care what happens to the other Frenchmen held on Guernsey.'

'You must not despair,' said Grace. 'He might have changed his mind by the morning. He has had a tiring day, as have you and I – you in particular. I think we too should go to our rooms now.'

'You're right, Grace.'

Throughout the meal Toby had found himself desperately fighting the need to sleep. The past few days and nights had hardly been restful. It seemed a very long time since he had enjoyed the comfort of a real bed. It was time to heed the aches and pains of his body and catch up on lost sleep.

When they rose from the table and were making their way upstairs to their rooms, Toby said, 'The trouble is, whenever I stop worrying about other things, my thoughts return to Bethany. I wish I knew where she was.'

'Poor Toby.'

Grace took his arm and squeezed it affectionately. 'If you were not an *English* clergyman I could help you to forget your problems, for one night at least. But you are a priest and your thoughts are of Bethany.'

She made a small, rather sad gesture. 'We can none of

us change what we are, or how we think. Try to remember only the good things that have happened today, Toby. We do not know where Bethany is, it is true, but at least we have learned she is not a prisoner of the French. For that you should be very grateful. Your friend Jacob will be freed tomorrow and – who knows? – the inspector might change his mind about the others by the time it is morning.'

Toby felt Grace was being unduly optimistic about the inspector having a change of mind, but he was so tired he could not think clearly about anything right now and what she said was true. He *did* have a great deal for which to be thankful.

Despite his worries, Toby had no sooner laid his head on the pillow than he fell asleep.

He slept all night without interruption. When he awoke, the sounds of people going about their business reached him through the open window.

Washing and dressing hurriedly, he made his way downstairs. Grace and Inspector Bernard had already finished breakfast and were waiting at the table for him to put in an appearance.

He apologised for being late and suggested they should leave immediately for the Morlaix prison to arrange Jacob's release.

'There is no great urgency,' replied Grace. 'It is doubtful whether the prison governor will be there yet. Order your breakfast. While you eat, Inspector Bernard has something to say to you.'

'Yes, of course.'

Toby thought the police inspector seemed somewhat ill-at-ease.

'I . . . I have been thinking of your suggestion that the fishermen captured off the Cornish coast should be released. It will require the authorisation of Minister Fouché, of course, but it is my recommendation that they be freed. It will be subject to each man declaring he will not take up arms against France at any time while our countries are at war.'

'You will certainly receive such an assurance,' declared Toby, joyfully. 'They are fishermen, not fighting-men. I thank you on behalf of the men and their families, sir. I thank you from the bottom of my heart.'

Even as he was expressing his gratitude, Toby was wondering what could have persuaded the police inspector to change his mind overnight . . .

He looked across the table to where Grace sat. She was sipping from a cup, apparently absorbed with tracing the pattern on the tablecloth with a finger.

Toby decided he would not delve too deeply into her involvement in the matter at this stage. Perhaps when they returned to England . . . He knew that if she were one of his parishioners, he would feel obliged to have a very serious talk with her. She was a free woman now, it was true, yet he could not help thinking that she was taking her freedom just a little too far, albeit in the best of causes.

'Will the men be released today?' Toby returned his attention to Inspector Bernard.

'No. It will require written authorisation from Minister Fouché. I despatched a messenger this morning. He will be able to commandeer horses along the way and should return tonight. Your friend will be released today, the fishermen tomorrow.'

The news of their imminent release was greeted with great jubilation by the Cornish fishermen. A couple of them immediately dropped to their knees, hands clasped in silent prayer, as tears of joy ran down their faces.

Behind them the captured Royal Navy men remained silent. They knew there would be no freedom for them until the war came to an end.

As Jacob was let out of the cell and led away to freedom, the fishermen clamoured about the bars of the communal cell, begging Toby not to forget them or leave them behind.

'You won't be forgotten,' he promised. 'You'll be released tomorrow. In a couple of days' time you'll be home in Cornwall, celebrating with your families.'

Chapter 50

Eager to return home, Jacob was greatly relieved by Toby's assurance that Muriel and the children were being taken care of by the fishermen of Porthluney.

'Poor Muriel,' he said with deep feeling. 'It must have been very hard for her when I failed to return. I have spent much time praying for her and the children. I knew she would be doing the same for me. The Lord heard us and sent thee to win my freedom.'

Toby wondered whether Jacob had considered the irony of his statement. If true, it meant the Lord had chosen a Church of England curate and a freed slave girl as His emissaries. They had achieved His aims by negotiating with a man who had been educated for the Roman Catholic priesthood. All to secure the freedom of a Quaker!

He said nothing of his thoughts and asked what Jacob could tell him about Bethany.

'I know only what I have already told thee,' declared Jacob. 'I took her to Guernsey and left her at her parents' home. Then I set off to return to Cornwall.'

'Does she have any friends she could have turned to in Guernsey?'

'Undoubtedly,' replied Jacob. 'She spent most of her life on the island, but I don't know who they are. Muriel will probably know.'

The two men were walking in Morlaix town, not far from the hotel. There was a light drizzle, but Jacob had spent weeks in gaol. He wanted to breathe fresh air and get the stench of prison from his nostrils.

'What puzzles me is why Bethany left Cornwall in the first place – and in such a hurry. Did she give any reason to you? Was it because of something the Elders had said to her?'

'She was upset because the Elders put her out of the Society, yes, but their decision wasn't entirely unexpected. It's the usual thing when someone wishes to marry outside the Society – and she planned to marry a Church of England curate!'

Jacob shook his head. 'But I don't think it was anything to do with the interview she had with the Elders. She seemed all right when she left St Austell and called on thee at Porthluney. How was she when thou sawest her there?'

'I wasn't at the rectory,' said Toby. He gave Jacob brief details of his suspension and of his visit to Exeter.

'I am truly sorry,' said Jacob. 'Thou hast enough problems in thy own life without being led on a wild goose chase to Guernsey, then coming to France to rescue Cornish fishermen foolish enough to get themselves captured.'

He looked perplexed. 'I was convinced Bethany's decision had something to do with thee and her visit to Porthluney that day. She was not in such a state when she left St Austell. But if thou weren't there . . .'

He shook his head. 'Whatever it was happened between leaving St Austell and the time she arrived home, I am convinced of it. If thou wert not at home, it must have been something else. But *what*?'

Toby could offer no explanation. The drizzle had become rain now and he said, 'I think it's time we returned to the hotel. I don't want you taking a chill after all the trouble Grace and I have taken having you set free.'

The two men turned and retraced their footsteps, discussing Grace and her background. Along the way they had been so engrossed in their talk and thoughts they had not noticed the hostile glances thrown at them by many of the Frenchmen they passed. There were whispered asides too for the benefit of those who were not aware of the Englishmen in their midst.

When they were only a short distance from the hotel they found their way blocked by a line of silent Frenchmen.

Toby sidestepped to pass them by, but the Frenchmen also moved, preventing them from passing once more.

'I would be obliged if you would let us pass, please,' said Toby.

One of the men made a reply, in French. When neither Toby nor Jacob responded, the man spat out one word: 'English!'

While they were talking, Toby looked about him for a means of escape but a number of men had moved up behind them. There *was* none.

'We're in trouble, Jacob. We may have to force our way through them . . .'

'Quakers do not use violence, Toby. I will pray, and suggest thou does the same.'

Toby was a great believer in prayer, but his years at sea had brought him face-to-face with reality on many occasions. There was a time for prayer – and a time when it was necessary for a man to render the Lord a little physical assistance.

'There is no violence involved in running, Jacob. If I manage to break through the line, run to the hotel with me.'

Toby advanced to the line of men between himself and the hotel. 'Excuse me.' He put his arms between two of the men and tried to pass between them. One of the men pushed him back.

Toby advanced once more and it looked as though he was going to repeat his attempt. Instead, he lowered his shoulder and charged – at the same time shouting for Jacob to follow him.

His actions took the Frenchmen by surprise. One of them went flying and Toby was through them. He took to his heels, but made the mistake of looking back.

Jacob was on his knees in the cobbled street, head bowed, hands clasped together in prayer. As Toby watched, one of the Frenchmen moved in and aimed a vicious kick at him.

Toby groaned, but he had not come to France to rescue Jacob only to see him kicked to death by these men. He turned and dived into the violent crowd of Frenchmen, fighting his way back towards Jacob.

Grace and Inspector Bernard were in the hotel talking to a member of Fouché's uniformed police. Bespattered with mud from the long journey he had just completed, he had joined them in the private dining-room allocated to the party. Suddenly, one of the hotel's servants burst into the room to tell them what was going on outside. He declared the two Englishmen were being murdered!

Grace was the first out through the hotel door. The servant had hurried inside the hotel at the first sign of trouble and she was in time to see Toby dive back into the hostile crowd, to be beaten to the ground immediately by the fists and feet of the mob.

Screaming at the top of her voice, she lifted her skirts, ran to the scene and began pummelling all and sundry with her fists.

There was not a great deal of strength in her blows, but she succeeded in creating a diversion. Toby had Jacob by the collar and was dragging him clear of the mob when Bernard and the policeman ran from the hotel.

The crowd had been eager to attack the two men from a country with whom France was at war. Now they decided it was not a cause for which they were prepared to go to prison.

They took to their heels and ran.

Toby's body felt bruised and his face was grazed, but he was otherwise unhurt. Jacob winced when he rose to his feet and clutched at a bruised rib, but he had kept his hands up to protect his face. He did not appear to be seriously injured.

When Toby reproached him for not running when he had the opportunity, the Quaker spread his hands wide. 'Why? I told thee the Lord would take care of me. He did.'

Toby wondered what would have happened had not he and Grace given the Lord a little help yet again.

'Are you all right, Grace?' Toby smiled at her dishevelled appearance. 'You were magnificent! Without you, Jacob and I would have been in serious trouble.'

'You were foolish to walk around Morlaix flaunting yourselves, M'sieur Lovell,' the police inspector pointed out. 'You and this man are enemies of France. What were you thinking of?'

'I was thinking what a pleasant little town this is and

how sad that our countries should be at war. But we will be gone tomorrow and our presence will no longer anger the men of Morlaix.'

'Your friends will be gone, M'sieur, Mademoiselle Grace too, but I regret you will not. My messenger has just returned from Minister Fouché. He has granted your countrymen their freedom, but he wishes me to escort you to him – to Paris if he has left Paimpol by the time we arrive. We will leave once the others have been put on board a boat and sent on their way to freedom.'

Chapter 51

Toby protested vehemently that night and the next morning about being forced to remain behind in France. When the other Cornishmen were leaving he made his feelings known yet again, but it was to no avail.

On this occasion all Grace's wiles failed too. As she and the Cornish fishermen sailed out of Morlaix en route to Guernsey, Toby was leaving the small French town in a coach, bound for Paimpol.

The destination of Inspector Bernard and the police escort, with Toby, was the château owned by Monsieur Flaubert, a few miles from Paimpol.

When he stepped from the coach at the château, Toby was still angry at not being allowed to return to Guernsey with the others. However, he realised immediately why the Minister had insisted that Grace leave with them. His wife had arrived from Paris and was here in the château with him.

A tall, sharp-featured woman, she greeted Toby with open hostility and spat out a torrent of French at him. She had a high-pitched unpleasant voice and Toby had no need for a translation to catch the gist of what she was saying. It would have been abusive in any language.

This was confirmed by Inspector Bernard. 'It seems Madame Fouché has an intense dislike of Englishmen, M'sieur Lovell. She is also of the opinion that you are probably the most despicable example of your race she has ever seen. I should not allow it to trouble you. To my knowledge you are the first Englishman to whom she has spoken.'

Toby detected a hint of unexpected humour in the inspector's eyes when he added, 'I think it might have something to do with the capture and detention of her brother.'

'Please tell Madame Fouché that when I left her brother, only a few days ago, he was in excellent health. He will probably be returning home tomorrow. I trust my own future is equally certain.'

They were standing in the high portico of the impressive château and Toby was concerned that the Minister of Police was nowhere to be seen.

If he had returned to Paris and Toby was taken there, it might be weeks before he returned to England.

Madame Fouché spat out a reply before entering the house ahead of them.

As they followed, the inspector said, 'Madame Fouché has little interest in your future welfare, M'sieur Lovell. She is of the opinion that you should be lodged in the stables with the animals and not be treated as a guest in her brother's house.'

'I've slept in worse places than a stable since arriving in France,' retorted Toby. 'But where is Minister Fouché? Has he returned to Paris yet?'

'No. It seems he intends remaining here until his brother-in-law is returned home safely. He is out of the house at the moment, watching Madame Guillotine at work. The Bretons are an independent people, M'sieur Lovell. It is sometimes necessary to remind them that they too are subject to the laws of Mother France.'

Toby was appalled the inspector could be so matter-of-fact when talking about men, and possibly women too, suffering execution. But he remembered the inspector had exhibited such callousness before today.

The two men were left in a vast study while they waited, but a manservant ensured they were kept well supplied with drink.

It was almost two hours before Minister Fouché put in an appearance. He was in a jovial mood.

'Ah! There you are. Thank you for coming, M'sieur Lovell.' He spoke as though Toby had been given a choice. 'I trust you were satisfied with the results of your visit to Morlaix and that you have not been too inconvenienced by coming here before returning home yourself?'

'It was unexpected,' admitted Toby. 'I had other things planned.'

'You will be able to do as you wish soon enough,' declared Minister Fouché. 'I am offering you an opportunity that should delight any priest: the chance to help your fellow men – both English and French. Each of our countries holds many captives who are not involved in the war. I am offering you an opportunity to negotiate the release of some of them. Does this appeal to you?'

Before Toby could reply, Fouché turned his attention to his fellow countryman. 'You have performed your duties well, Inspector Bernard. You and your men may return to Paris now.'

The inspector bowed to his minister and inclined his head briefly in Toby's direction before making his way from the room.

When he had gone, Minister Fouché ordered the servant to fill the glasses held by Toby and himself, then waved the man from the room.

Seating himself in a comfortable armchair facing Toby, he raised the glass to his lips and gazed at Toby while he drank. When the glass was lowered, he said, 'Your friends and the admirable Grace will no doubt be close to Guernsey now.'

'They should be,' agreed Toby. He kept his reply short, waiting for the other man to come to the point of what he really wanted to say.

'You spent some time on a British man-o'-war I believe, M'sieur Lovell.'

It was not a question, but a statement.

'Three years. It would have been much longer but for the battle at Trafalgar.'

'Ah, yes! It was a comprehensive defeat for Admiral Villeneuve. Did you know he recently committed suicide?'

'No. I am sorry to hear it. He was a gallant commander.'

'He was a loser. I do not admire losers, M'sieur Lovell. It would have been better for him had he died in action, as did your brilliant Admiral Nelson. Do you think the British navy will survive his death?'

'It's still far and away the finest navy in the world,' replied Toby. 'With many excellent officers.' He wondered where this conversation was leading.

Minister Fouché made no comment upon the patriotic reply. Instead, he asked another question. 'What of your army? It has seen little action so far in this war.'

'It will fight when the time is right,' said Toby. 'When it does, it will face an army that is spread so thinly around the world it won't be in sufficient strength anywhere to offer effective resistance.'

'It would be as foolish for the British to underestimate the generalship of Emperor Napoleon as it would for the Emperor to misjudge the fighting qualities of the British soldier. Nobody is invincible.'

'I don't think you have kept me in France to discuss the relative merits of our armies and navies, Minister Fouché. Perhaps we can discuss your ideas on the exchange of prisoners? I would like to return to England as quickly as possible.'

'And so you shall. Do not be so impatient. You impress me as an honest man, M'sieur Lovell. A man to be trusted. You also now have experience of negotiating for the freedom of prisoners. I will give you a letter to take to England for me, to M'sieur Fox, your Foreign Secretary. It must go to no one else. Indeed, no one must even be aware of its existence, you understand?'

Toby nodded, but his mind was racing ahead of this conversation. The Minister of Police had been talking to him of plans for the exchange of prisoners, but Toby believed he had something of far more importance in mind. *Now* he thought he understood why he had been kept behind. He felt a great excitement rise within him.

'It is probable that at some time in the future you will be required to return to France, to speak to me about the exchange of prisoners. You will not return until you have a reply for me from Secretary Fox – and it will not be in writing. I want nothing from England in writing. You will memorise Fox's reply and carry it here.' He tapped his forehead. 'You understand me?'

'I do,' said Toby. 'I'll deliver your letter and return as many times as the Foreign Secretary feels is required.'

'Good! I did not think I had underestimated you. Now I will write the letter. I will give it to you with another which will guarantee you safe conduct in France whenever you return.'

Minister Fouché rose to his feet and smiled down at Toby. 'Remain here and help yourself to the Cognac. I will return with the letter in an hour. In two you will be on your way to Paimpol. From there you will take passage on a boat to England. Once there, make your way to London as quickly as you can.'

Minister Fouché paused before passing from the room. 'You served your country well at Trafalgar, M'sieur Lovell. It may be that you will perform an even more important duty in the future.'

Chapter 52

The small French merchantman carrying Toby to England was intercepted by a brig of the British navy in mid-Channel. The officer in command was a young lieutenant. Initially disappointed that the enemy vessel was not to be his prize, he was enthralled when he heard details of Toby's mission to France and the official version of its consequences.

Acting upon his own initiative, the lieutenant took Toby to Portsmouth harbour and put him ashore early the next morning. From here he would continue his journey to London by fast post-carriage.

The meeting with Charles Fox, the minister responsible for Foreign Affairs, came as an anti-climax to all Toby had experienced in France.

He was kept waiting in an outside office for over an hour before finally being shown into the presence of the Foreign Secretary.

After a brief formal introduction Toby told the government minister of his journey from Cornwall to Guernsey and France. He then went into the details of his meeting with Minister of Police Fouché.

As Toby was talking, the English minister was reading Fouché's letter. 'Yes, yes, a very interesting story,' he said. 'Very interesting indeed. Thank you, Parson Lovell. Thank you very much. Perhaps you will leave your name and address with my secretary on your way out?'

'Do you have any idea when you might need me to return to France, sir? I do have a great many matters to attend to at the moment.'

'Oh, I don't think it will be necessary for you to return. We have a number of men skilled in such matters. Besides,

I have a man in France at the moment who has been in discussion with Bonaparte's government for some weeks. In my opinion Minister Fouché is trying to provide some sort of bolt hole for himself should things go wrong in France – as well they might. He has been responsible for some of the worst excesses of the Revolution. These things have a nasty habit of catching up with a man, sooner or later.'

'But isn't it worth pursuing, if only to obtain the freedom of some of the many British prisoners held in France?'

'I'm afraid as Foreign Secretary I need to view the wider picture, Lovell. It would be good to have all our prisoners released, of course. Unfortunately, the innocent must suffer as well as the guilty in times of war. Leave your address. If we need you, we will know where we can find you.'

The interview was over. Toby left the building with the feeling that he might as well have thrown away the letter and made his way straight to Guernsey to search for Bethany.

Toby's despondent mood remained with him all the way to Cornwall. The British Foreign Secretary's response to Fouché's letter was as unexpected as it was disappointing. The French Minister of Police had led him to believe it might well change the course of the war, and would certainly be instrumental in having many prisoners freed.

Toby left the coach at Tregony to walk to the vicarage at Veryan. Along the way he wondered about Jacob and the other freed fishermen. They should have arrived home by now. He would visit Hemmick Cove on the following day and catch up on all that had happened to them.

As he walked along the driveway to the vicarage he could see Anna playing in the stable yard. It seemed she and her mother had not yet moved to their new house.

Anna saw him at the same time and let out a shout of delight as she ran to meet him. When she reached him Toby swung her up in his arms. She hugged him and gave him a kiss on the cheek.

'You *have* come home safely. Grandfather told everyone you would. He said you knew how to look after yourself.'

'Did he now? And just who was everyone?'

'The fishermen who called, Mr Vivian, that lovely lady – and the archdeacon from Exeter. The one who always looks as though he's cross with everyone.'

'Archdeacon Scantlebury! He's here?' Toby set Anna on the ground once more.

'He was.' She took his hand and led him towards the vicarage. 'He came when some of the fishermen were here looking for you. They got angry with him. Grandfather was amused. He said afterwards the archdeacon had left with a sizeable flea in his ear. Did you know that fleas went into ears?'

'I have heard it said.' Toby grinned at her. Meeting Anna had lifted his mood of depression.

At that moment, Sally hurried from the house, having seen them from a window. She too gave Toby a much warmer welcome than he had anticipated. When Reverend Trist came out to greet him in a similar fashion, Toby thought it felt more like a homecoming than the return of a guest to the vicar's home.

Toby spent the remainder of that afternoon and evening telling Jeremiah and Sally as much as he was able of his adventures in France. In return he was brought up to date on local news.

It seemed Archdeacon Scantlebury had arrived in Porthluney parish a couple of days after Toby had left for Guernsey. He had been somewhat put out to learn that the curate was not available to assist in his inquiries.

'He has spoken to a great many parishioners,' said the Veryan vicar. 'But if he was hoping to have Bettison's complaints confirmed, I'm afraid he's been out of luck. All the reports that have come back to me tell of your parishioners demanding to have you back with them as quickly as possible. Bettison himself is in London at the moment, I believe, but I am told the archdeacon received a similar request from Mrs Bettison.'

'Do you know where Scantlebury is staying?' asked Toby.

'Yes, at the Porthluney rectory. He told me he had intended putting up in a hostelry, but when he found the rectory was empty and you away, he thought it far more convenient to stay there. Young Alice Rowe has been looking after him and I've no doubt she's been singing your praises at every opportunity. That girl cares for you, Toby. You must be careful upon your return to the rectory, or there will be talk.'

'It's all right. I've already spoken to young Billy Kendall from Portloe about Alice. He's asked her once to marry him, and intends asking her again. If she accepts him they will be married at the earliest opportunity. That should quell any gossip.'

'Talking of gossip . . .' said Sally. 'That young woman who was once a slave came here looking for you yesterday. She was riding alone and seemed very upset that you hadn't returned from France. Now *there's* someone who could set tongues wagging in Porthluney – or any other parish for that matter.'

'I think it's something she enjoys doing, Sally, yet it would be difficult to find a more courageous companion. If I hadn't met Bethany first, it's possible the tongues would have wagged with good cause.'

'Talking of such things,' said Jeremiah, 'we've seen a great deal of Sir Charles Vivian since you left. His excuse has been that he sought news of his brother and his ship. Yet they were home when he last called and spent most of his time with Sally.'

'He has become a very dear friend.' She coloured when she met Toby's glance. 'And he *was* very concerned for Toby, as we all were.'

'Yes indeed,' agreed Jeremiah. He added, 'I think we should take out the carriage tomorrow, Sally. Make a journey to Falmouth and inform Sir Charles that Toby has returned safely.'

Toby would have liked to say he would accompany them to Falmouth, but he had a far less congenial meeting in view. Before he went anywhere else he knew he would need to go to Porthluney to face Archdeacon Scantlebury.

Chapter 53

As Toby walked along the short driveway to the Porthluney rectory, the door opened and Alice ran from the house. She gave him a welcome that was almost as enthusiastic as the one he had received from young Anna.

Clutching his arm, she cried, 'You've come back, safe and sound! Me and Billy was talking about you only last night. We've both been worried sick for you, especially since the Mevagissey fishermen came back and told of leaving you behind in France.'

Suddenly aware she was still clinging to his arm, she blushed and released it, saying, 'Billy's going to be delighted. He thinks a lot of you.'

'I'm very pleased to be back, Alice,' said Toby. 'I've been deeply touched to hear of all the people who've been concerned for me. Thank you – and I thank them too.'

Suddenly serious she said, 'Archdeacon Scantlebury's in the study. I think he's writing up some report about you. At least, that's what he said he was going to do.'

'I heard he was staying here. I suppose I'd better see him, hadn't I?'

'I was upset when he said he'd come here because there'd been a complaint against you. I told him that Mr Bettison had stopped us from going to church for a whole year before you came to Porthluney. That we were just getting used to going to church again when you were told you mustn't take services for us.'

'What did he say to that?'

'He said he'd have things sorted out one way or the other before very long and he'd see we had a new curate quickly, if need be. I told him there was only one way we wanted things sorted out, and that was to have you back with us again.'

'You're a good girl, Alice. I haven't been at Porthluney for very long, but I seem to have made some very special friends in that short time.'

Pink with pleasure at his praise, she said, 'Shall I go and tell Archdeacon Scantlebury you're here?'

'No. I'll go straight in myself. Take him by surprise. That way I might find out what he intends recommending for me.'

When Toby knocked and entered the study, Archdeacon Scantlebury looked up – and promptly dropped the pen he was holding.

'Lovell! You're back!'

'That's right. I returned late yesterday. Reverend Trist told me you were here.'

'I've been here some time. What on earth were you doing dashing off to the Channel Islands – and to France!'

'You told me to move out of the parish. There was no reason to stay around here.'

'Had you remained in Cornwall I might have been able to satisfy the various delegations who've come here looking for you. Have you been to see Reverend Kempe?'

'Not yet.'

'He's a dying man and has been asking for you.'

'I'll go and see him right away.'

'That's a good idea. By the time you return I should have finished this report. Bishop Fisher wants to see it as soon as I return to Exeter, but there are one or two things I need to discuss with you – and with John Bettison.'

Toby wanted to ask the archdeacon whether the report would be favourable to him, but felt it better to remain silent until the report was completed.

He would have liked to go to Hemmick too, to speak with Muriel and Jacob, in case they had heard something of Bethany. But in view of the news about Reverend Kempe, that would need to wait.

When he left the study he was given an enthusiastic greeting by Nap, now fully recovered from his injury. Alice told him the archdeacon would not have the dog in the house, so she had made him up a bed in the stable.

'I'll take him with me to St Stephen,' said Toby. 'He'll enjoy the exercise.'

Riding Nipper, and with Nap walking happily beside the donkey, Toby arrived at St Stephen.

Rosemary Kempe was relieved to see him. 'I'm so glad to know you've returned safely from France. I should think the whole of the county has been wondering about you. Harold certainly has. He's so proud of all you've done. You'd think he'd done it all himself!'

'How is he? Archdeacon Scantlebury said he was, well . . . rather seriously ill.'

'He's dying, Toby. He knows it, and so do I.'

Toby began to protest, but Rosemary Kempe said, 'It's all right, I am aware of the truth, and so is Harold. There's a time for everything, Toby. He has had a wonderful life, and so have I. All we both wish is that things might be settled at Porthluney before he dies.'

'I haven't really helped much there, have I?'

'Nonsense, you've worked wonders. Before Bettison made his malicious complaints against you things had taken a turn for the better. You resolved a great many problems that had been plaguing Harold for years. The trouble is that Archdeacon Scantlebury is a vain man and you've upstaged the arrival of an archdeacon in Porthluney. He also remembers the Bettisons as they were when he was a boy. He doesn't know John Bettison as we do.'

After they had chatted for a while longer, Toby went in to see the rector and found him in a very weak state.

Grasping his hand warmly, Harold Kempe said, 'I understand you've been to France and have had a number of Mevagissey fishermen released from captivity. It was a master stroke, dear boy. A master stroke. The Mevagissey fishermen have long memories. They won't forget what you've done for them. Not only that – what the Mevagissey fishermen say and do influences every fisherman on Cornwall's south coast. Even men like Archdeacon Scantlebury can't ignore their views. Have you seen him since your return?'

'I spoke to him before coming here. I think he's in

the middle of writing up a report, to submit to Bishop Fisher.'

'I can't see what he can possibly say against you. Everyone he's spoken to in Porthluney has said you're the man they want as their parish priest.'

'He didn't seem happy that I wasn't around when he arrived in Porthluney.'

Rector Kempe tried to make a contemptuous sound in his throat, but it ended as a distressing cough. When he had recovered his breath, he said, 'Grenville Scantlebury has never been a particularly happy man, and there's no reason at all why you should be at his beck and call.'

Their conversation seemed to tire Rector Kempe and it was not long before Toby said, 'I mustn't stay too long. There are a great many people I need to see at Porthluney. Is there anything I can do for you while I am here?'

'Yes, Toby. There are two sisters up at Greensplatt. When I was up and about I used to visit them regularly to give them Communion. With all that's been happening throughout the parish, they've been rather neglected. If you could visit them, it would make me very happy. Borrow whatever vestments you need from my church, but be heavy on the ceremonial. They both enjoy that.'

When Toby left the sick rector's bedroom, he spoke to Rosemary Kempe and told her what he was going to do.

'Thank you, Toby,' she said. 'He's fading away, but his thoughts are still with his parishioners. The thing he would most dearly like is for all to be as it should at Porthluney before he dies.'

'I hope he's not in imminent danger of dying, but I'll do what I can to put his mind at rest. Unfortunately, I can't hurry Scantlebury. He tends to work at his own pace.'

'He's probably hoping Bettison will return soon. He can hardly return to Exeter without speaking to him. But don't worry. I'll tell Harold that things will soon return to normal. If I'm honest, I think they will. That was probably what particularly aggrieved Bettison.'

Rosemary Kempe looked at Toby and shook her head sadly. 'It's a pity Archdeacon Scantlebury can't see John Bettison as we have for all these years.'

Chapter 54

Archdeacon Scantlebury's idealised image of the lords of Porthluney as benevolent landlords was about to be dispelled for ever.

Alice had stayed on at the rectory, awaiting Toby's return with the dog. She would then give Nap his food and lock him in the stable for the night, before returning to her own home.

Toby was much later than either of them could have anticipated. His visit to the elderly sisters in the clay country had taken far longer than expected. The more active of the two women had fallen a few days earlier and hurt her leg. As a result, there were a number of tasks about the house that needed to be tackled. When Toby had completed them he arranged for a great-niece to call in on the two spinsters and give them some help about the house.

When Toby had not returned to Porthluney by the time darkness had fallen, Alice took a lantern and made her way to the stables. She would check there was enough straw for the dog's bed.

After adding some straw she turned to make her way back to the house. Suddenly, she became aware of a horse and rider standing motionless between her and the rectory.

She was about to call out, thinking it was Toby, when she realised the mount was far too tall to be Nipper. This was a man mounted on a large, dark-coloured horse.

'Who's that? Who's there?'

'Is that Charlotte? Come closer, girl.'

Startled, Alice recognised the voice even though the speaker was slurring his words as though he had been drinking. It was John Bettison. She wondered how he knew Charlotte, and why he should be looking for her here after dark.

'I'm not Charlotte.'

'Not Charlotte? Who are you, then? What's your name?'

'It's Alice, sir. I'm helping out at the rectory.'

'Hold the lamp up to your face, girl, so I can see you when you're talking.'

Alice did as she was told. At the same time she tried to think of a way she could get past the Porthluney landowner and reach the house.

Peering down at her, Bettison said, 'Well, you're a pretty little thing, and no mistake. Do you know who I am, girl?'

'Yes, sir.'

'Good, then we don't have to beat about the bush, do we? I came here looking for Charlotte, for a little bit of fun. But you'll do just as well.'

Alice's heart was racing as she said, 'I . . . I don't know what you mean, sir.'

Bettison had dismounted from his horse and said, 'Nonsense! You're a country girl, aren't you? You see it going on around you all the time. I've no doubt the minute you leave here you'll be scurrying off to the dunes down by the beach with some young village lad. You'll learn more from me than from some boy. Where is it to be, eh? Upstairs in the bedroom? The one overlooking the front door? Or would you prefer the stable, among the hay?'

John Bettison had looped the rein of his horse around the branch of a tree and was advancing upon her. She could smell the brandy on his breath even though he was more than an arm's length away.

'I . . . I need to go to the house, sir. I'm cooking something for the master's supper.'

'Don't lie to me, girl. Your young curate isn't living here now. You'll be lucky if you ever see him again, so there'd be no sense saving it for him, even if you were telling the truth.'

'I . . .' Before she could say any more, Bettison lurched towards her, grabbing the arm that held the lamp. It crashed to the ground and then she was struggling with him in the darkness.

Bettison was powerfully built. She was unable to free herself from the arm he had about her. But when he reached down inside the front of her dress, squeezing her painfully, she kicked him.

It made little difference because he was wearing heavy riding boots. Then he tried to pull her face around to kiss her and she bit him on the thumb.

'You vicious little slut!' He hit her with the flat of his hand on the side of her face and she saw coloured lights before her eyes. He was dragging her towards the stables when she thought she heard a sound from somewhere close to the house and began screaming.

It provoked another blow from Bettison. Thoroughly aroused now, he did not release his grip on her.

Then she heard voices from the direction of the house, and from the driveway. Suddenly, she felt something brush past her legs and crash into Bettison. There was the angry snarling of a dog and Bettison cursed but did not release his hold on Alice.

Then he began kicking out at Nap and shouting for someone to 'Call the brute off'.

She heard Toby's voice calling off Nap and Archdeacon Scantlebury came from the house, carrying another lantern.

Toby had heard Alice's cries from the rectory lane. Unable to make the donkey hurry, he had leaped from the animal's back and run towards the house.

In the light of the lantern held by Scantlebury, Toby saw Alice struggling with a man. He ran to her rescue but Scantlebury reached the couple first.

'Leave that girl alone, you rogue. Leave her this minute.'

'Go away and mind your own business. This is nothing to do with you.'

'It's *everything* to do with me.' Scantlebury had been taken aback by the assailant's refined speech. He had thought the man to be a vagabond. Instead, his voice was that of an educated man. Nevertheless, he was molesting the rectory servant. 'You're on Church property, sir. Leave her alone this instant or I'll have you before the constable. Who are you?'

Toby had recognised the man's voice and as he hurried towards them, called to Scantlebury, 'This is the man you've been wanting to interview about the complaint he made against me, Archdeacon. You have just met Mr Bettison of Porthluney Manor.'

Bettison released Alice and turned to face the two men. 'Lovell . . . *Archdeacon*?'

Toby pushed past the landowner and put an arm about Alice. 'Archdeacon, will you bring the lamp over here, please?'

'Things are not quite as they seem,' said Bettison. 'The girl led me on . . .'

In the light from the lantern held by Archdeacon Scantlebury it could be seen that one half of Alice's face was red and angry. It was already beginning to swell close to her left eye.

'She led you on . . . so you hit her?' said Toby, scornfully. 'You may consider yourself a gentleman, Bettison. In my book you're an oaf and a drunken bully. If you're on your way home, I suggest you think again. Go and find a local inn. Take a room and sleep it off. Your wife can do without you at home in your present state.'

'Who the hell do you think you're talking to, Lovell? No one talks to me in that manner . . .'

Toby turned his back on the landowner. With his arm still about Alice, he said to her, 'Are you all right, Alice? He didn't do anything?'

'No . . . but he would have done if it hadn't been for you and Nap.'

She was trying hard to control her voice. The incident had shaken her more than she wanted to acknowledge, even to herself.

'Come into the rectory. We'll have a look at that face of yours and give you something to calm your nerves.'

'But . . . I've got to put Nap to bed.'

'I'll do that later. We'll leave him out here for a while. It might persuade Mr Bettison to leave the premises more promptly than he might otherwise do.'

Leading Alice away, Toby paused to call back to his colleague: 'You told me you needed to speak to John Bettison before you could complete your report, Archdeacon Scantlebury. Well, now you have your opportunity – and in circumstances that illustrate his character far better than any words of mine. I trust your report will reflect your enlightenment.'

Chapter 55

When Toby took Alice to her home that evening, to explain to her parents what had happened, Billy Kendall was waiting for her. When he saw her injuries he was so angry, he wanted to go straight to Porthluney Manor and confront John Bettison about his actions.

It took a great deal of persuasive talking from Toby to convince him it would be in no one's interest to tackle the landowner. Bettison would simply dismiss Alice's father and make things difficult for Billy too.

'Why can't we bring him before the courts for what he's done? You were there, you can give evidence on Alice's behalf.'

'I saw them struggling, yes. But Bettison would have clever lawyers in court speaking for him. They would probably be able to convince a Grand Jury of gentlemen that Alice agreed to what went on – until she heard someone coming.'

Toby saw the angry flush come to Billy's face. He said hurriedly, 'We all know it isn't true, but we're talking of the need to convince a panel of landowners. Men like Bettison himself. Can you see them sending him to prison for what he's done?'

Billy was torn between the reality of the situation and wanting to do something about Bettison, and Toby said gently, 'No, Billy. We'd only put Alice through a lot of unnecessary anguish. At the end of the day she'd wind up with her name blackened, her father thrown out of work, and no roof over their heads.'

'So John Bettison will get away with what he's done to her?' Billy spoke bitterly, knowing that what Toby had said was the truth of the matter. 'If you'd not come along he'd have done what he wanted with her and no one could do anything about it, is that what you're saying?'

His voice broke and he whispered fiercely, 'If he had done it I'd have killed him, Parson. I swear I would.'

'He may seem to be getting away with what he's done, Billy, but God will punish him in His own way. You ask Curate Lovell if I'm not right. He'll tell you.' Alice's mother spoke with complete conviction.

A plump, warm woman, Mrs Rowe had an arm about her daughter's shoulders and now gave her a comforting squeeze. 'Let's take you to the scullery and see what we can find to put on that eye of yours. I should be able to find something to take the swelling down, at least.'

When they had left the room, Alice's father said, despondently, 'You're right in what you've just said to Billy, Parson. All the same, it's hard for a father to have his daughter attacked in such a manner and not be able to do anything about it.'

'Share your wife's faith, Mr Rowe. Bettison *will* be punished in God's own time and way. I can't help feeling sorry for his wife. She's expecting a baby. I had hoped that would be sufficient reason for him to give up his ways, but it seems it's going to take something more to curb his lechery.'

Leaving the two men, Toby went to the scullery to speak to Alice.

'I must go now. After what John Bettison said to you about Charlotte I need to speak to her, but I feel it should be at a time when her mother is not with her. I want to find out what's been going on at the rectory between her and Bettison.'

'I'll do it for you. She'll say more to me than she will to you. She can be very stubborn when she wants to be.'

Putting a hand gingerly to her face, Alice said, 'It'll be better if she doesn't learn the truth of who did this. I'll say I fell and hit my face on something.'

'All right. I'm very sorry this has happened to you, Alice. Don't think of coming back to work until you're feeling much better.'

Leaving the cottage, Toby made his way back to Veryan, wondering what *had* gone on in the rectory between Charlotte and the landowner.

* * *

Archdeacon Scantlebury left Porthluney early the next morning to ride back to Exeter.

He left a letter for Toby. It came close to an apology for all the trouble he had caused by giving credence to the complaints made by Bettison. He regretted suspending Toby before he had inquired further into the matter.

He concluded by stating that he had found nothing at all to substantiate the landowner's allegations. Indeed, all he had learned during his time in the parish had served thoroughly to discredit John Bettison's complaint.

It would be necessary for the bishop to endorse his findings, but he assured Toby this would be no more than a formality. He closed by urging the curate to return to the rectory and resume the excellent work he had begun in serving the needs of the Porthluney parishioners.

Despite her injured face, Alice had come in to work. Her delight was evident when Toby read the archdeacon's letter to her.

'There! I knew things would turn out all right for you. I told you so. Everyone's going to be very happy when they hear the news. You'll have more people in church this Sunday than have ever been there during Reverend Kempe's time at Porthluney.'

'He'll be delighted too, Alice. I must get news to him quickly. He's a very sick man and could do with some good news to cheer him up.'

Reaching down to stroke Nap, who seemed to have caught the happiness of the moment, Toby said, 'I shall return to Veryan now and collect my things. The sooner I move back here the better. Just in case John Bettison decides to pay another call, I'll leave Nap here to guard you. We'll not take any chances with the man.'

Pausing in the doorway, he said, 'I only regret that you had to take a beating before Archdeacon Scantlebury saw John Bettison for what he really is.'

Alice watched Toby ride away on his irascible old donkey and touched her face. It hurt, especially around the injured eye, but she did not mind about it now. It had brought Curate Lovell back to Porthluney rectory. She would have suffered much more in such a cause.

Chapter 56

Knowing Toby would soon be returning to live in the rectory, Alice gave everything an extra clean. As she worked, Nap followed her around the house. He seemed to be aware he had been left to guard her against another visit from the Porthluney landowner.

He was with Alice in the kitchen when he suddenly growled, turning to face the door. For a moment, Alice paled, thinking it might be Bettison, but it was another unexpected visitor.

Without bothering to knock, Charlotte opened the kitchen door and walked in, shooing Nap outside before Alice had time to stop her.

'That damned dog is a nuisance,' were her first words. 'I don't know why you have it in the house. It would have been better if it had been left to die when it was hurt down at Hemmick. It's a bloody nuisance, leaving hairs all over the place.'

'Hello to you too,' said Alice sarcastically. 'Have you come visiting just so you can carry on about a dog, or was there something else?'

Alice had been cleaning out the kitchen ashes. Now, as she turned, Charlotte peered more closely at her face. 'What have you been up to? Did you get that from Billy Kendall?'

'No, of course I didn't. Billy would never hit me. I wouldn't stay around for very long if he did! I tripped over on my way home in the dark last night and hit my face on something. It must have been a stone, I suppose.'

'Are you quite sure you hadn't drunk too much of Curate Lovell's smuggled brandy? It's strong stuff. I know, it had me staggering home from work one night.'

'Charlotte! I'm surprised you have the nerve to show your

face here again. Why *are* you here, anyway? Are you after your old job back?'

'There's no fear of that! I've got better things planned for my life than clearing up after some lifeless young curate. He wouldn't know what to do with a girl if she climbed in bed next to him.'

'You shouldn't talk about Curate Lovell that way, just because he hasn't tried anything on with you,' said Alice, indignantly. 'I think he's a good man. Anyway, you're going to have to find work for yourself, especially with your ma not being able to do anything at the moment.'

'She'll be well enough to come back here soon, but it won't be for very long if I have my way. In another few months, with any luck, we'll both be able to give up work for good.'

Alice was puzzled. 'What do you mean? Is your ma getting married again?'

'At her age? Even if she was, I doubt if a new husband would want to keep me. No, it's going to be the other way around. *I'll* be keeping *her*.'

Alice still could not understand what Charlotte was trying to tell her. 'How are you going to do that if you're not working?'

'The way you'd do it if you had more sense than to waste yourself on Billy Kendall. I'm pregnant, Alice. Carrying a bastard for a man who's rich enough to look after the both of us for the rest of our lives.'

'I don't believe it! Anyway, who do you know who's that rich?'

Alice asked the question, even though she was quite certain she already knew what the answer would be. She wanted to hear it from Charlotte. 'Who are you trying to blame for making you pregnant?'

'I'm not trying to blame anyone. I *know* who it is.' Giving Alice a sly look of triumph, she said, 'It's him up at the manor.'

'John Bettison! Where would you and him do anything like that without being seen by someone?'

'Trust an innocent girl like you to ask such a question, Alice Rowe! We've done it in all sorts of places. Down on the cliffs. In the churchyard, one night. We've even done it right here, in the rectory.'

'I don't believe you. Curate Lovell was living in the rectory all the time you were working here. There'd have been big trouble if he'd walked in on the pair of you.'

Alice had promised Toby she would find out all that had been going on. It was not hard to persuade Charlotte to boast of her affair with Bettison.

'There was never any danger of that. He was away when we did it. Gone to Exeter. We had the house to ourselves for days. Mind you, I thought we'd be found out when that Quaker woman of his came calling. I left John upstairs in the bedroom when I came down to answer the door. I felt sure she'd suspected what was going on and would tell the curate. She couldn't have done, though, or he'd have said something about it, wouldn't he?'

'He could still say something. He's moving back to the rectory this morning. That's why I'm having a special clean up of everything. You can stay and help me, if you'd like to.'

Charlotte showed alarm. 'John said Curate Lovell would never be coming back to Porthluney.'

'Well, it just goes to show he can't be relied upon. You remember that, Charlotte.'

The other girl shrugged. 'It doesn't matter very much now. All the same, I'd rather not stay here just to get a lecture from some holier-than-thou curate. Call on me at home sometime, Alice. I miss having you around to talk to.'

Alice walked with Charlotte as far as the gate. As her friend was about to walk away, she asked, 'Does Bettison know about your condition yet?'

'No. Neither does anyone else. So if anyone says anything to me about it, I'll know where it's come from. If John is going to pay me to look after his bastard he'll want me to keep the name of its father to myself.'

Anna Jarvis, in particular, was upset to learn that Toby was to leave Veryan. Sally too was sorry to see him go, but a great many other things were happening in her life. The new cottage was finally ready and they would be moving to their new home within the next few days.

Sally was also excited about her increasingly close relationship with Sir Charles Vivian. She expressed pleasure for Toby that he was to return to his parish. She would have been even happier had Porthluney been closer to Veryan, so she might be able to discuss things with him, as they progressed.

'You don't really need me around,' said Toby, when she expressed her views. 'I'm confident things will work out in the best possible way for both you and Anna. All I ask is that when you marry Sir Charles, as I feel quite certain you will, you'll allow me to assist your father at the wedding.'

'Should it come about, you have my promise,' said Sally. 'Thank you for the support you've given to both Anna and myself. You have helped us come through a very difficult and unhappy time. We will both always be very grateful to you for that.'

Jeremiah was also sorry that Toby was leaving the vicarage, but for a different reason.

'I had hoped you might stay on here and take some of the weight from my shoulders,' he explained. 'I am no longer a young man and Veryan is a large parish. I suppose you wouldn't consider staying on – at the same salary that is being paid to you by Harold Kempe?'

'I'm deeply flattered by your offer,' replied Toby, sincerely. 'But Reverend Kempe is a sick man. A *dying* man. I couldn't let him down at this time.'

'No. No . . . of course not.'

Jeremiah shook Toby's hand warmly as he settled in the saddle of the donkey. 'You'll always be a welcome visitor to Veryan, Toby. I hope you'll come to see us often. Take a service or two for me occasionally.'

Toby gave the assurance he sought and turned at the gateway to wave to his three friends and to the aged housekeeper who leaned from an upstairs window to see him off.

He left the vicarage with very real regret. The three people of the house had come closer to being a family to him than anyone he had ever known.

He wondered whether he was ever going to find Bethany again and have a *real* family. Perhaps one like Jacob and Muriel Hosking's . . .

Chapter 57

By the time Toby reached the Porthluney rectory, Charlotte had been gone for more than an hour, but he found Alice highly agitated.

'Thank goodness you've arrived,' she said. 'I was thinking I was going to have to come to Veryan to find you. A man came here all the way from St Stephen. Poor Reverend Kempe has taken a turn for the worse. He's dying, so the man said. Mrs Kempe wants you to go there as soon as you can.'

'Then I must go there right away, Alice. If I leave my bags here, will you unpack them and put the things in my room?'

'Of course. I know you're likely to be there for some time, but I'll stay on here and have something to eat waiting for you when you get back.'

Toby protested there was no need for her to stay on after dark, but she insisted.

'I want to. It'll be my way of doing something for Reverend Kempe. I was always fond of him when he was here. He wasn't like you, of course, but he was a kindly man. He meant well.'

'You're a good girl, Alice. Thank you. I'll try not to be too late returning.'

It was only after Toby had left that Alice realised she had said nothing to him about the visit of Charlotte to the rectory. She decided the information her friend had given her would keep until another time.

When Toby reached St Stephen and turned Nipper in at the rectory drive, he knew he had arrived too late. The blinds were drawn at every window and two carriages were standing outside the door.

The death of Reverend Harold Kempe was confirmed by the tearful servant-girl who opened the door to his knock.

'Oh, sir! I'm so glad you're here. Poor Reverend Kempe is dead, sir. Passed away no more than an hour ago. The mistress found him when she went to his room to see how he was. She was that upset, though it didn't come as a surprise to any of us. He'd been going down fast these past few days.'

When Toby was shown into a room where Reverend Kempe's widow was being comforted by some of her late husband's close friends, she was in control of herself.

After offering his sincere commiserations, Toby told her of the letter left for him by Archdeacon Scantlebury, adding, 'It's a very great pity he didn't arrive at his decision twenty-four hours earlier. Reverend Kempe would have been delighted.'

'He always knew in his heart that Scantlebury would find in your favour,' said Rosemary Kempe. 'He died at peace with himself.'

After Toby had spent some time with her and the others, she suggested he should return to Porthluney, adding that she was aware he would have a great many things to do. 'Harold and I were very happy for a great many years at Porthluney,' she said. 'I would like him to be buried in the churchyard there.'

'Of course,' said Toby. 'I will write to Scantlebury right away and tell him of your sad loss. I shall remain in the rectory, at least until a new rector is appointed.'

Rosemary said, 'Is there any reason why you should not stay on there after that?'

'No doubt a new rector will want to move into the Porthluney rectory. If he is a youngish man it's doubtful he will need a curate. But today isn't the time to talk about such things. Please call on me if I can help in any way possible. You have only to ask.'

Toby made the journey back to Porthluney with a heavy heart. It seemed every time he made some progress in the Porthluney parish, something happened to set him back. Once again, his future was in doubt.

He returned via St Austell. There were a few things he

needed to buy and it would probably be some time before he passed through a town again.

Toby spent longer in the town than he had intended. As a result, it was dark before he reached Porthluney. He was still some distance from the rectory when he heard the sound of cannons firing in the darkness, just off the coast to westward. It seemed to be in the vicinity of Portloe.

He was concerned. It was possible that a French warship, or privateer, had sneaked unnoticed across the Channel and was attacking a ship off the coast. More likely, it was a Revenue vessel taking action against a smuggling ship.

This latter view seemed to be confirmed when Toby was putting Nipper in the stable. He heard the rattle of small-arms fire. It was much closer this time. It sounded as though it was just off the coast. He thought of setting off to find out what was happening, but decided against it.

He had become involved in a fight between smugglers and the authorities once before. If it happened too often he would have more difficulty explaining his position to Archdeacon Scantlebury.

To his surprise, Alice was not in the house as she had promised to be. However, he had returned later than expected. She had probably decided he would not return to the rectory at all that night.

She could not have been gone long, though. The fire was burning cheerfully and the kettle did not take long to bring to the boil.

Nap was in the kitchen too and gave Toby an enthusiastic greeting.

There was cold meat, cheese and bread in the larder and Toby sat down to a good meal before preparing for bed.

He had almost finished eating when a growl from Nap warned him the dog had heard some unfamiliar sound outside.

A few moments later, Toby heard voices from outside the house. He rose to his feet as the door burst open and Alice stumbled inside the rectory, almost falling over in her haste.

'What is it?'

Alice looked at him wild-eyed and it was a moment or two before she was able to speak coherently.

When she did, she gripped his arm. 'It's Billy . . . he's been shot. I . . . I think he's dying. We've brought him here. You must help him . . . please!'

Chapter 58

'How did this happen?'

Toby asked the question of Alice as he used a piece of torn-up sheet as a pad to try to staunch the bleeding from a serious wound high on Billy's chest. The young fisherman was breathing heavily and in great pain. At times he lapsed into unconsciousness.

'There was a fight between the Revenue men and some free-traders,' Alice replied, trying hard to control the fear she felt for Billy.

They were in one of the rectory's bedrooms with the wounded man. He had been carried inside the house by fellow 'free-traders' who had immediately left again, without saying a word.

'Why was he brought here? Why didn't they take him home so his mother might look after him?'

'Billy doesn't have a mother. She died some years ago.'

Alice's statement brought home to Toby how little he knew about Billy. How little he knew about *any* of his parishioners. This was something he would have been aware of had he been the parish priest for any length of time.

'Besides . . .' Alice spoke hesitantly. 'It wouldn't be safe for Billy to be there at the moment. The Revenue men are making a search of Portloe.'

'Why?' The men of the Revenue Service were known to be diligent, but it was rare for them to search all the houses in a whole community.

'One of the Revenue men was shot and killed.'

Toby drew in his breath sharply. Hiding and caring for a wounded smuggler was one thing. Harbouring a man implicated in murder was something quite different.

'Shot by one of the smugglers?'

Alice shook her head. 'None of them carries a gun. They never have. One of Billy's friends said there was an ambush and the Revenue men started shooting at them. He believes they must have shot their own man.'

'They would never admit to that,' said Toby. 'The smugglers will be held responsible. If Billy's caught he'll be hung – if he survives. He's in urgent need of a surgeon. There's a musket ball inside him somewhere. Unless it's taken out he'll die.'

Looking from the distraught young girl to the wounded fisherman, Toby asked, 'Who treated your uncle's leg when he was wounded? Can we get the same person to come here and take out the musket ball?'

'No . . .' Alice's voice faltered. 'It was one of the women from Portloe. She's good at healing wounds and things, but couldn't operate to take out a bullet.'

'It must be removed, and quickly,' insisted Toby. 'Where is the nearest doctor?'

'I don't think there's one nearer than St Austell. If we called him in he'd have to report Billy to the Revenue men. Then he'd be arrested.'

'If he isn't operated on very quickly he's going to die anyway, Alice.'

Tears sprang to her eyes as she said, 'I don't want him to die! Please do *something*. You helped my uncle when he'd been shot. Please . . .'

'That was very different, Alice. I was able to stop him bleeding, that's all. It couldn't compare with trying to remove a musket ball from a man's chest.'

Even as he was denying his ability to help Billy, Toby was remembering the many times he had helped the surgeon on board the *Eclipse*.

'The wound needs to be probed to find the musket ball. Even if I managed to do that – and it's doubtful – I don't know enough about the human body to enable me to prise it out. I'd probably do more harm than good. I could kill him.'

'What's going to happen to him if nothing is done?'

'He's unlikely to live.' Toby was aware he was backing

himself into a corner. 'It's likely the musket ball is pressing on something important.'

In tears now, Alice said, 'Please don't let him die. You must do something for him.'

Billy's breathing was harsh in the silence that followed her words.

'Does Billy have a father? Can we get him here quickly, to see what he would want done?'

'He's at Portloe. Will there be time for me to go there, find him, and bring him back here?'

Toby looked once again at Billy. He had already lost a great deal of blood. His condition had deteriorated noticeably during the short time he had been in the rectory. Toby had not exaggerated the seriousness of his condition to Alice. Without urgent surgical attention, Billy would not survive the night.

'No. No, it would probably be too late.'

'I don't want Billy to die,' Alice pleaded. 'All the time I've known him, I've never been certain how I felt about him. Now, when it could be too late, I *am* certain. Don't let him die, Curate Lovell. Please don't let him die.'

'I'm a priest, not a surgeon, Alice.' Toby tried to put off the inevitable. On the *Eclipse* his duties had included assisting the surgeon whenever the ship went into action. He had watched him at work. Had held down patients as the none-too-skilful surgical practitioner probed for a musket ball. When the ball had been removed Toby had dressed the wound.

He had also been forced to watch helplessly as men died as a result of such operations.

He tried not to dwell upon this aspect of primitive shipboard surgery. Without the surgeon's intervention most men would have died anyway. With it, the odds shifted in their favour, albeit only slightly.

He weighed up the situation with which he was faced. Without surgery, Billy was going to die – and there was no surgeon available to carry out an operation to remove the musket ball. If one were found and his life saved, Billy would be handed over to the authorities and hanged.

Bearing all this in mind, Toby knew there was only one

chance of saving Billy's life, albeit a slim one.

'He's likely to die if I try to remove the musket ball, Alice. On the other hand, he *will* die if nothing at all is done. That doesn't give me any option, does it?'

'You'll do it? You'll operate on Billy?' Alice looked at him wide-eyed. Whether her expression was registering wonderment or fear, Toby did not pause to consider. Now his mind had been made up he acted swiftly.

'You'll have to help me, Alice. We'll need something to probe the wound. Is there a skewer in the kitchen? The thinner it is the better.'

Alice nodded.

'And I'll need stout tweezers – and a sharp knife. Fetch my dressing-box from my room. It contains a razor and tweezers. I'll need brandy too, to clean off the instruments and apply to the wound – I'll fetch that. Hurry, Alice. Bring the skewer first, please.'

Toby found the brandy, ironically brought to the rectory by Billy. Carrying the decanter and a tumbler, he hurried with them to the bedroom.

He filled the tumbler with brandy, hastily swallowing a mouthful to calm his nerves. Had Billy been conscious, he would have been given some too. Mercifully, the young fisherman had slipped into unconsciousness.

When Alice brought the metal skewer, Toby stirred it around in the brandy. Frowning as he tried to remember details of the probes he had seen on board ship, he bent the skewer in a gentle curve. Then he rinsed it in the brandy once more.

After a moment's hesitation, he uncovered Billy's wound and splashed some brandy in it.

By the time Alice hurried back to the room with his dressing-box he was very gingerly probing the wound. It would have to be a very hit-or-miss affair. Knowing little of the anatomy of the human body, he proceeded with great caution.

He had been at work for some eight or nine minutes when he felt the probe touch something solid. At first he thought he had struck a rib – then the object moved slightly beneath the skewer.

'The tweezers, Alice – soak them in brandy first, please.'

Alice did as she was told and passed them to him. It was not easy to get a grip on the object inside Billy's chest. To add to Toby's problems, his efforts caused Billy to bleed more profusely than before.

When he obtained a firm grip, he gingerly withdrew the tweezers. Held in them was a fragment of rib.

'That certainly needed to come out,' said Toby, disappointed. 'But it isn't what I'm looking for.'

He was afraid the musket ball might have lodged somewhere in one of Billy's lungs. If this was so, there was no chance at all of removing it and Billy would not survive.

Re-inserting the makeshift probe inside the wound, he bent low over Billy once more and discovered he was perspiring heavily. Droplets were falling from his forehead on to his mercifully unconscious patient.

Further gentle exploration seemed to indicate the musket ball had been deflected by the rib towards Billy's shoulder. This worried Toby even more. He remembered the *Eclipse*'s surgeon telling him there was a major artery in this region.

Suddenly, the probe touched something solid once more. Toby believed the end of the probe was now just beneath one of the upper ribs – and whatever he had found moved beneath the probe.

'I think I've found it, Alice.' Toby's voice shook. Whether it was from excitement or fear was uncertain.

He removed the probe carefully, measuring the distance and direction where he believed the musket ball to be. It seemed he would need to cut sideways across Billy's chest for a couple of inches, away from the wound.

'The razor, Alice.'

He did not have to tell her again about the brandy. Once it was thoroughly doused, she handed the razor to him. Before he could make the incision Toby needed to pause, to control his trembling hands. When he was satisfied, he laid his fingers against two of Billy's ribs and cut between them.

In a sudden moment of panic he realised he had not cut deeply enough. Blood was welling out of the wound, making his task more difficult. He made another cut. This time the razor exposed a rib bone.

He believed he was exactly where he wanted to be now – and the probe proved his calculations to be accurate. Another cut, large enough for him to insert the tweezers. A few moments later he gave a shout of triumph and was holding a musket ball in the palm of his bloody hand.

He turned to show it to Alice and was in time to see her slide to the floor.

She had fainted.

Chapter 59

'I'm sorry. I've never fainted before.'

Looking pale and wan, Alice sat on a chair in the rectory study. In her trembling hand she held a glass of the same brandy used by Toby during his operation. But this had been drawn direct from the barrel left at the rectory by the smugglers.

'You don't have to apologise, Alice. You did very well. I've seen strong, tough sailors on a man-o'-war faint at the sight of less blood than Billy lost in the bedroom.'

Alice held the brandy to her lips then lowered the glass immediately. Placing it upon the small table beside her, she said, 'I can't drink it. I don't think I'll ever be able to smell brandy again without thinking of what went on upstairs tonight.'

Billy had been left in the room where the operation had taken place. He was still unconscious. Toby had helped Alice downstairs when she recovered from her faint and had done his best to return her to normality.

'Is Billy going to be all right now?' she asked, anxiously.

'I wish I could tell you the answer to that, Alice. I just don't know. He appeared to be breathing more easily when we left him, but I'm not a medical man. I doubt whether the most skilful surgeon could tell you exactly what damage the musket ball might have caused inside him. I've done my best. Later tonight I'll pray for him.'

Toby smiled reassuringly. 'I'm better at praying than I am at playing the surgeon. I promise you I'll give of my very best.'

Suddenly, Nap rose to his feet facing the door and growled. At the same time, Toby caught the sound of a horse's harness from somewhere outside.

Thinking fast, he said to Alice, 'Quick! Upstairs to Billy's room. Stay there with him until I call you.'

As Alice hurried from the room Toby heard the sounds of footsteps and men's voices outside. Alice had left her brandy glass on the table. Toby snatched it up and hid it inside a cupboard as heavy knocking sounded on the door.

Nap barked loudly and persistently. Making a great show of telling him to be quiet, Toby answered the door. Outside was a man dressed in a uniform very similar in style to that worn by naval officers.

'Good evening, Parson, may I come in, please?' Beyond the man, Toby could see a number of horses and riders.

'Of course, but what can I do for you?'

The man entered the house and Toby shut the door. Standing beside him, Nap looked at the Revenue officer and growled deep in his throat.

'You have a good guard dog there, Parson. Has he been at all edgy this evening?'

'Only when he heard you and your men arrive. But I haven't been in for much more than an hour or so myself.'

'Oh?' The Revenue officer expressed considerable interest. 'Would you mind telling me where you've been, sir?'

'I moved back to the rectory only this morning, and was then called to St Stephen. The rector in charge of both parishes died there earlier today.'

'Harold Kempe? I am very sorry indeed to hear that. I used to call in to see him quite frequently when he was here. He was a good man. I must pay my condolences to his widow.'

It seemed that much of the Revenue man's suspicion had been allayed. Suddenly, to Toby's horror, he saw a bloodstain, barely dried, on the stone floor of the kitchen.

Taking a pace to one side, he stood squarely upon the incriminating stain, justifying the sudden movement by reaching down and patting Nap.

'I suppose you saw nothing suspicious on your way home, Parson?'

Toby shook his head. 'No, although I thought I heard cannon fire out at sea – and what might have been musketry some time later.'

The Revenue officer nodded confirmation. 'We have had

a desperate fight with smugglers. One of my men has been killed. I'm convinced we shot one of the smugglers too. We found a great deal of blood at Portloe. Unfortunately, the man's friends carried him away and we haven't been able to find him. But we will.'

Toby frowned, uncomfortably aware of the bloodstain hidden by his foot. 'Surely your search should be in the vicinity of Portloe? A sorely wounded man would scarcely have been carried this far.'

The Revenue officer seemed vaguely ill-at-ease. 'Not usually, sir, but I hope you won't think me impertinent when I say that you have achieved a certain popularity among men who are known to be smugglers. It was thought they might have come to you for help. I trust you won't take it amiss when I also tell you I instructed my men to search your stables on our arrival.'

'I *do* take it amiss,' replied Toby, indignantly. 'The men of whom you talk are fishermen, as you well know. I'm the curate of this parish. As such it's my *duty* to offer whatever help is needed to any one of my parishioners, whether they be fishermen, farmers – or Revenue men.'

'That's what I mean, sir. They turn to you for help when in need. I trust you will understand that I too was only carrying out my duty by coming here tonight.'

'I will view your duties with more understanding if you come to me and ask permission before searching my stables and outbuildings again, sir. You have no need to tell me the results of their search. They will have found nothing.'

The Revenue officer inclined his head. 'I have no doubt you are right. By the way, I saw a lamp in a bedroom as we arrived. Is anyone else in the house with you?'

Meeting the Revenue officer's eyes, Toby said, 'Yes, my servant. She has been working late because she was aware of the sad nature of my visit to St Stephen and waited to give me a meal. She could have heard nothing, or else she would have told me when I came in.'

'Of course, sir. I am sorry to have disturbed you, but you will appreciate I have a duty to perform. In view of what Mr Bettison has told us . . .'

'Ah! I thought Bettison might have something to do

with your visit. Perhaps you may also know that he has a long-running feud with the Church in Porthluney. You are welcome to return to the rectory anytime you wish – but not if you come here as Mr Bettison's lackey. I wish you goodnight, sir.'

When the man had gone and he heard the Revenue party ride away, Toby breathed a huge sigh of relief. It had been a difficult few minutes.

He called Alice down from Billy's room. After checking that there was no change in the condition of the young fisherman, he pointed out the bloodstain and asked the frightened young girl to check there were no more.

'When you've done that, you must go to Portloe and find Billy's father,' Toby said. 'Tell him what's happened. He's welcome to come here and visit Billy – but he's to travel cautiously and make absolutely certain he's not being followed. Then you must go straight home, Alice. You've had enough distress for one day.'

She did as she was told. It was not until she was well on the way to Portloe that she remembered the other drama of the day: the visit from Charlotte and her revelation about the child she was expecting.

She had meant to tell Curate Lovell what had been going on in the rectory during his absence. In her concern for Billy she had forgotten all about it.

She would tell him in the morning, when she went in to work. Convinced she would not sleep because she was so worried about Billy, she decided to go in early. In the meantime she would follow Curate Lovell's example and pray that Billy was a little better when she next saw him.

Unwanted tears welled up in her eyes once more. He *had* to be better. He had to get fully well, as quickly as possible. Billy had asked her many times to marry him and she had declined to give him her answer.

The events of the night and the wound he had received changed everything. It had made her realise how much she cared for him.

As well as praying for Billy, Alice made a solemn vow. If Billy made a full recovery and still wanted her, she would marry him – just as soon as it could be arranged.

Chapter 60

Alice arrived for work almost an hour early the next morning, such was her anxiety for Billy.

Toby was already in the church and Alice went up to the room where Billy was lying.

Tom Kendall, the young fisherman's father, had arrived at the rectory after midnight and stayed in the room with his son all night. He was coming from the bedroom when Alice arrived there.

'How is he?' She asked the question in a whisper, fearful of what the reply might be.

'There doesn't appear to be any change,' replied Tom Kendall, his voice lowered to match Alice's. 'He's either asleep or unconscious. The curate came up to see him earlier. He said the bleeding seems to have stopped.'

Pessimistically, he added, 'Mind you, judging by the colour of Billy's face, he can't have a lot of blood left in him.'

Brushing past him, Alice entered the bedroom and looked down at Billy. His father was right. In the morning light his face appeared bloodless. Furthermore, he did not appear to have moved since she had last seen him.

She was very upset, but took a tight grip on her feelings before she turned back to Tom Kendall. 'What are you going to do now?'

'Go back to Portloe. I've got a living to earn. Mind you, if the Revenue boat's still lying offshore there'll be no fishing done by anyone today. Nobody will dare put to sea for fear of being arrested. They'll be pressed into naval service, whether they were out with the free-traders last night or not. A Revenue man's been killed. They won't leave us alone until someone's been made to pay for it.'

'Well, it's not going to be Billy,' said Alice fiercely. 'I'll make certain he's well cared for today. Tonight too, if need be. When you get back to Portloe make sure Billy's name isn't mentioned to any of the Revenue men who come snooping around.'

'You're a great one for giving orders, young lady. I can see now why Billy's so taken with you. You're just the way his mother was.' Inclining his head to her, Tom Kendall said, 'You're none the worse for that, mind. She was a good woman.'

Taking a last look into the bedroom, he said, 'Take good care of him, Alice. He's not a bad lad.'

The strain of the previous evening was telling on Toby. He felt tired and drained of energy. The day had been a particularly exhausting and dramatic one, even before he had been called upon to operate on Billy.

He had looked in on the patient this morning before coming to the church. There had been little sign of improvement, although he was certainly breathing easier. However, Toby grasped at the fact that he was no worse as being a very good sign. The surgeon on the *Eclipse* would say that if a man survived an operation for twenty-four hours he would most likely recover.

One in four failed to meet this criterion, but Billy was already halfway there. After dropping to his knees and saying a fervent prayer for his recovery, and for the soul of the unfortunate Revenue officer, Toby returned to the rectory.

Later that morning he sat down to work in his study trying to make sense of the parish tithe books. The details would need to be passed on to Reverend Kempe's successor.

Looking up from the desk, he saw through the window Jacob approaching the rectory.

Toby jumped up and hurried to meet him. When the two men met, they embraced warmly.

'I heard only this morning that thou wert back from France,' said Jacob. 'One of the servants from the manor came to buy fish from me and gave me the glad news.

Muriel and I have been concerned about thee. Why did M'sieur Fouché keep thee behind in France instead of allowing thee to return with the rest of us?'

'There was talk of an exchange of prisoners. He gave me a letter for our Foreign Secretary. I went to London with it. But I might just as well have come straight home. Our government doesn't seem to be interested in having our men returned.'

'A visit to a French prison would change that,' declared Jacob, grimly.

'Have you heard anything of Bethany?'

Before the Quaker fisherman could reply there was the sound of someone running down the stairs to the hall. A few moments later Alice burst into the study, hardly able to contain her excitement. 'Curate Lovell! It's Billy. He's come round. He's asking for a drink . . .'

For the first time she noticed Jacob sitting in a chair that had been partly hidden by the open door. 'Oh! I didn't know Mr Hosking was here . . .'

'It's all right, Alice. Jacob already knows all about Billy's activities in the past. He'll say nothing to anyone. Here.'

Toby handed the brandy decanter to the excited girl. 'Mix up a drink of brandy, warm water and sugar – but don't make it too strong. I'll come upstairs and see him in a few minutes.'

When Alice had hurried away to the kitchen, Toby explained to Jacob what had happened the previous evening, including his part in it.

'Thou must be careful, Toby. If the Revenue men ever find out it will make no difference that thou art a curate. The courts will make an example of thee. A Revenue man has been killed. They'll want to make someone pay for it. As for Billy . . . it's time he gave up free-trading. If he survives this he will have had two clear warnings from the Lord. It is more than most men are given.'

'That's true. But let's go and see him.'

Both men went upstairs. In the bedroom Alice had lifted Billy's head gently and was spooning brandy into his mouth, taking it from a small bowl.

He drank almost half before turning his head away as a signal that he had taken enough.

When Alice laid his head gently down on the pillow, Toby said, 'I'm greatly relieved to see the improvement in you, Billy. You had us all worried last night. Jacob has just been suggesting it's time you gave up free-trading.'

Billy gave a wan smile, and in a weak voice said, 'He's right. The Revenue men seem to turn up from nowhere these nights.'

Pausing for breath, he asked, 'Were any of the others hurt?'

'No. At least, no *local* man. But one of the Revenue men was killed.'

Billy looked horrified and Toby added, 'That's why you've been brought here. The Revenue men are out for revenge. They know one of the smugglers was wounded and they searched Portloe for you. But don't worry yourself about it. We'll not let them take you and they don't have a name. Just lie here, let Alice care for you, and get well as quickly as you can.'

Turning to Alice, Toby said, 'He needs to get his strength back. Meat broth would be just the thing. I brought a small piece of beef with me from Veryan. Use that.'

He smiled cheerfully at Billy. 'We'll leave you now. We mustn't tire you out. Alice will take good care of you and let me know if there's anything you need. You just rest. You're lucky to be alive.'

As the two men made their way downstairs once more, Toby said, 'You've heard of the death of Reverend Kempe?'

Jacob nodded. 'What will it mean to thee?'

'We won't know the answer to that until a new rector is appointed. He may want me to stay on as his curate, he may not. But we need to have Billy fit enough to be moved by then. Another rector might not be sympathetic to smugglers, whether or not they are local men.'

'These are uncertain times for thee, Toby . . . but what am I thinking of! You asked me if I had news of Bethany and I have come here especially to give it thee. Yet here I am talking about everything except that which I came for! When we left Morlaix we were taken to Guernsey before being brought back to Cornwall in Matthew Vivian's ship. In Guernsey I visited Bethany's home and spoke to her parents. They have heard that she was seen in St Peter Port helping a woman take care of four young children. The woman's husband is believed to be a soldier. She and her children are known to have left Guernsey shortly afterwards, although I was not able to learn for where. It is believed Bethany left with them, although no one seems to know where any of them has gone.'

Chapter 61

When Bethany was turned away from her family home by her father, she made her way back to St Peter Port, thoroughly confused about her future. There could be no question of returning with Jacob to Cornwall. She felt she could not face a meeting with Toby. She was far too hurt and confused.

On the outskirts of the Guernsey port, she passed the Meeting House she had attended as a young girl with Muriel and their parents. Bethany was no longer a Society member, but she felt a need for the peace it had always provided in happier days.

She went inside and found a woman scrubbing the floor of the small hall inside the door. The woman stood up to allow her to pass.

Looking at the woman as she moved past her, Bethany suddenly paused. 'Are thou not Mrs Briard, mother of Esther?'

The woman peered at Bethany short-sightedly for some moments, then her face broke into a smile. 'Yes, and thou art Bethany Poole – or dost thou have a married name now?'

'No.' Bethany shook her head. 'Is Esther still at home with thee?'

The pleasure left the woman's face, and was replaced with an expression of sadness. 'She left the island two years ago to marry outside the Society. She and her husband now live on Jersey. Her father died a year after she went away. I am alone now. But what of thee?'

Eyeing the baggage Bethany was carrying, she asked, 'Hast thou just returned home? I heard thou had gone to England with thy sister.'

'I returned to Guernsey today . . . but no, I will not be going home. I too am no longer a member of the Society. I was to have married a non-Friend. It . . . it did not work out as I had hoped.'

Mrs Briard knew the heartache it had caused everyone when her daughter had wanted to marry outside the Society of Friends. She believed it had contributed to her own husband's death.

She had no doubt Bethany was going through the same anguish suffered by Esther, and it would be worse if she had lost the man responsible for her expulsion from the Society. It was well known that Bethany's father was one of the strictest of Guernsey's dwindling Society members. He would be making life very difficult for his daughter. That was probably the reason she had sought the peacefulness of the Meeting House today.

'Where art thou staying, Bethany?'

Mrs Briard was not surprised when Bethany shrugged her shoulders. 'I don't know. I'm not really certain quite what I *am* doing at the moment, Mrs Briard. Life has become so . . . confused.' Suddenly, she felt very close to tears.

'Then thou must bring thy things to my house. Stay with me for a few days and think about what it is thou wants to do. I will enjoy thy company. It will be like having a daughter in the house again.'

Bethany's brief stay in the Briard house did all that the kindly Quaker woman had hoped it might. It gave her time to gather her scattered thoughts together and come to terms with all that had happened. She was still uncertain of her future, but she regained the faith that this too would be decided for her, as had her present.

She was walking by the harbour on the third day of her stay with Mrs Briard when she saw a well-dressed woman walking along the quayside. Three young children walked with her and she carried a baby in her arms.

As the woman and her family drew near, one of the children, a lively young boy, suddenly pointed towards the harbour entrance and cried, 'There's a ship coming in . . .'

He ran towards the edge of the quay, ignoring his mother's shout for him to: 'Come back!'

At the edge of the quay his foot caught on an iron ring secured in the ground and he stumbled towards the quayside. There were no railings here, only a sheer drop to the water, at least twelve feet below.

Bethany had seen the danger to the child the moment his mother had shouted and was already running towards him. As he fought to recover his balance, screaming because of the danger he was able to see for himself, she reached him. Grabbing his coat, she pulled him back to safety.

'William! You foolish boy. You foolish, foolish boy!'

The child's mother took him from Bethany's grasp and, using her free arm, hugged him to her. She was breathing heavily and, fearing she might faint, Bethany said, 'Here, let me take the baby from thee.'

She took the baby from the woman's grasp without awaiting a reply and the woman hugged the thoroughly terrified small boy who clung to her, shaking with fright.

In the meantime, Bethany was shepherding the two little girls safely away from the edge of the quay.

After a few minutes, the woman led her small boy by the hand to where Bethany stood with the baby and the two girls. She was pointing to some of the houses up the hill and telling them of people who lived there. The characters she was describing were imaginary, but it held the interest of the young girls.

'How can I ever thank you?' Speaking in a cultured voice, the woman took the baby from Bethany. 'You saved William's life.'

'I would not say that,' replied Bethany. 'But I probably saved him from a ducking.'

The two girls were tugging at the woman's skirts now, both trying to pass on the information Bethany had given to them about the houses on the hillside.

Smiling in their direction, she said, 'Thou hast thy hands full with four such lively children. I know how difficult it is to keep them all under control. My sister has a family of seven little ones. Until recently I helped her with them. It is a full-time task for a woman.'

'I have come to realise the truth of that,' said the woman, ruefully. 'I was travelling with a nursemaid but she was terrified of boarding the ship at Portsmouth and ran off, leaving me without anyone.'

Even as they were speaking, Bethany ran after one of the girls who had wandered into the path of a passing horse and cart.

'I think I had better take them back to the inn where we are staying,' said the woman. 'The task of controlling them seems to be beyond me.'

'It's too nice a day for children to be shut inside,' said Bethany. 'I'll walk with thee, if thou wouldst like me to?'

'I would be delighted,' replied the woman. 'Perhaps we should introduce ourselves? I am Jennifer Cecil. The children are William – whom you saved from falling in the sea – Daphne, the child you just pulled from the path of the horse, Mary, who is clinging to my skirts, and this is baby Marian.'

'I'm Bethany Poole.'

'You are a Quaker, Bethany?'

'Yes.' Bethany realised her dress and speech would have given her away.

'How fascinating. My mother flirted with it as a way of worship for many years, but never joined the Society of Friends. I presume you are a member?'

'Not any more.' Bethany tried to pass it off as though it was of no importance. 'I was expelled because I intended marrying out of the Society. In the event, I did not marry.'

'I see.' Jennifer Cecil sensed the deep unhappiness in Bethany and guessed correctly that the events of which she spoke were very recent.

The two women and the children walked around St Peter Port for some time, during the course of which each of the women learned something of the other, while the two young girls vied with each other to hold hands with Bethany.

Jennifer Cecil was the wife of a serving army officer who had been posted for duty to the Channel Islands. Uncertain of what his duties were to be, he had travelled on ahead, making arrangements for Jennifer to follow with the children, promising to meet her here, in St Peter Port. He had not contacted her yet, but she had no doubt he would do so before very long.

'Are you staying here with your parents?' asked Jennifer, as they walked back to the inn where she and the children were staying.

'No. They aren't too pleased about my reasons for leaving the Society. My father feels I have let the family down. I'm staying at the house of a friend at the moment, while I decide what I shall do.'

At that moment, Mary slipped and fell to her knees. As she pushed out her lower lip and decided whether or not to cry, Bethany lifted her to her feet, brushed off her knee and told her what a brave girl she was for *not* crying.

'You will have had considerable experience with young children if you helped your sister with seven of them, Bethany?'

She smiled. 'Yes, there isn't a great deal that a child can do I haven't come across at one time or another.'

'Do you . . . Would you consider coming to work for me as a children's nurse? I can offer you a good salary and you will be free to worship in whichever way suits you best.'

Bethany thought about it for only a few moments. It would suit her very well indeed. She enjoyed taking care of children and it would give her both employment and accommodation.

'Yes . . . Yes, Mrs Cecil. I think I would enjoy that very much.'

Chapter 62

It was a week before the soldier husband of Jennifer Cecil came to St Peter Port to find his wife, by which time she was frantic with worry. She had expected him long before this. Indeed, she had expected him to be at the harbour to greet her when her ship arrived a week before.

It did not help that the military authorities in Guernsey could give her no information about her husband. Communications between London and the Channel Islands left a great deal to be desired and it was not much better from one island to another. Each of the islands resented the slightest hint of what they termed 'interference' from any of the others.

During this week Bethany gradually took charge of the children, but it had been a difficult time. As Jennifer frequently said, she did not know how she would have coped had she not had Bethany to help her.

Bethany had moved to the inn on the first day of her employment, telling Mrs Briard only that she had taken employment as a children's nurse with the wife of a British army officer.

Then, one morning, as Bethany was about to take the three oldest Cecil children out for a walk about the town, they met an army officer coming in through the inn door.

With shrieks of delight, the children launched themselves at him.

It was Major George Cecil. As the children clung to him, Bethany studied him closely. He was somewhat older than she had expected him to be, probably in his early-forties, but he was quite obviously very, very close to his children.

After allowing them some minutes in which to show

their delight at being reunited with their father, Bethany gathered them together once more.

'Mrs Cecil will be very pleased to see thee,' she said. 'She has been concerned for thee.'

Major Cecil frowned. 'I don't think we've met before. You are . . . ?'

'Bethany. I am the children's nursemaid.'

'Oh! What happened to Nancy, the nursemaid they had when I left them in England?'

'She was frightened of coming with us on the ship,' said William. 'She ran away and left us. Bethany saved me from falling in the sea!'

'Did she now? I can see I have to catch up on a whole lot of news. Off you go with Bethany. When you return I'll tell you all about our new home. I think you're going to like it. It's on an island, but it's a much smaller island than this one.'

The children wanted to hear all about it there and then and protested when Bethany insisted that they take their walk.

Eventually, she managed to usher them from the inn, after promising they would take a shorter walk than the one they usually took. When they returned she would take them to their room and they would all hear about their new home.

During their absence from the hotel, George Cecil and his wife enjoyed a peaceful reunion, with only the baby for company. It gave them an opportunity to talk about events since they had parted, and George was able to tell his wife what he would be doing on the Channel Islands.

Bethany managed to keep the children away from the inn for almost an hour. When they returned they found Jennifer Cecil busily putting their clothes into the trunks they had brought to the inn with them.

Bethany immediately began to help by packing the clothes belonging to the children. As they worked, Major George Cecil told his children what the future held for them.

He had been posted as officer in charge of the garrison on the Channel Island of Alderney. Although it ranked in size as the third largest of the islands, it was no bigger than a good English estate. It was also closer to the French mainland than any of the other Channel Islands.

France, a constant menacing presence, was visible for most of the time, no more than nine miles away to the south and east.

'When will we be going there?' asked William, eagerly. 'I want to see France!'

'We'll be leaving this afternoon,' replied their father. 'A Royal Navy frigate is waiting in the harbour to take us there. It's no more than three or four hours' sailing, so we should be in our new house long before nightfall. In fact, it's not really a house at all, but a fort.'

All the children were very excited at the prospect of moving into a fort on a tiny island. They needed very little persuasion to hurry off and gather up their toys in order that they might be ready to leave the inn as quickly as possible.

'My wife has told me how you saved William from falling off the quay into the sea,' said George Cecil to Bethany, while the children were busy. 'I am very grateful to you. Very grateful indeed. I would also like to thank you for taking on the task of children's nursemaid at such short notice. Are you willing to come to Alderney with us?'

'Of course. I enjoy looking after the children, and I think they are happy with me.'

'Good! There will not be a great deal on Alderney for you to do outside the house. I doubt whether you will find a Meeting House there, but I do hope you'll enjoy life with us. We're a close and happy family.'

'I already know that,' said Bethany. 'I don't doubt that the children are going to have a very happy time on Alderney. A time they will remember for the remainder of their lives.'

'Thank you. Unfortunately, I am told that Alderney is a very isolated place when the weather is too rough for ships to call there. Would you like half-an-hour or so to yourself, to write to those close to you and tell them where you will be? You can tell them that any letters sent care of me will find you.'

Bethany hesitated for only a few moments before replying.

'No, I'll leave my writing until we are on the island.' A picture of Toby came into her mind but she tried to put it away.

'There is no urgency. My whereabouts is of no great importance to anyone.'

Chapter 63

The voyage to Alderney took four hours. Accompanying the Cecils and Bethany on the frigate were a hundred men of the Major's regiment.

The threat of a French attack on the island was being taken very seriously.

The home allocated to the military commander reflected the importance of his position. It was an impressive fortress, situated close to the ancient south-facing harbour at Longis Bay. The harbour was no longer used, a newer one having been built on the north coast. However, it was felt the beaches around the older harbour might well be chosen as a landing place for French forces.

The fort itself had never been completed by its sixteenth-century builders, although work had recently been carried out on the living quarters for Major Cecil and his family. The garrison was to be quartered in temporary accommodation nearby.

From the fort there were wonderful views of the island, the sea – and the French coast.

Major Cecil had a powerful telescope in the living quarters. By using it, Bethany and the children were occasionally able to see men and women working in the fields of France, or travelling along a piece of road close to the sea.

They could also see patrols of mounted soldiers. The French authorities were as nervous of an attack from the Channel Islands as the islanders were of a sortie from the mainland.

Major and Mrs Cecil intended to enjoy a great deal of entertaining during their stay and held frequent dinner parties for the island dignitaries. On such occasions Bethany would sit down to eat with the family and their guests. As a result, she was paid a great deal of attention by the younger officers of the regiment.

Unused to such a style of living, she was not entirely at her ease in such company. Her mode of speech also tended to set her apart from those who frequented the Cecils' house.

But this was not the main reason Bethany began making a conscious attempt to eliminate 'thee', 'thy' and 'thou' from her everyday speech.

She would always retain much that she had been brought up to believe was right, especially in her way of worship, but she was very conscious of no longer being a member of the Society of Friends.

She was also aware that her employers would prefer her to adopt the modern mode of speech. Neither had said anything about it to her, but she had overheard George Cecil trying to explain to William why the young boy should not refer to his father as 'thou'.

Bethany and the Cecils had been on Alderney for only a fortnight when one morning Major Cecil returned home in a great hurry from his headquarters in the island's small capital town of St Anne.

'I have been ordered to take a company of men to Guernsey immediately,' he explained. 'They are being mustered at this very moment. A Royal Navy brig is waiting at Braye harbour to embark them.'

'What has happened?' Jennifer sounded alarmed. 'How long are you likely to be away?'

'It should only be for a few days,' said her husband. 'And there is no cause for concern. A French ship is due to arrive at Guernsey today, expecting to take off a number of French civilians. They were captured when a privateer took a French merchantman. There is to be a change of plans that neither the ship's captain nor the prisoners will like. There might be trouble.'

'Why should the plans be changed? Surely we have no reason to detain innocent civilians? They cannot be regarded as bona fide prisoners-of-war.'

'Not normally, I agree,' said her husband, 'but one of

the men is related to an important French government official. A Cornish parson has approached the Bailiff of Guernsey and suggested that the prisoners be exchanged for a Cornish fisherman and a woman who have been taken by the French.'

Bethany had been listening to the conversation. Her interest quickening, she asked, 'Do you know the name of the Cornish parson?'

George Cecil was slightly taken aback by the question, but only for a moment. 'Of course! I forgot that you spent many years in Cornwall. No, I don't know his name, but I'll try to find out for you. All I know is that he is a friend of a shipowner from Falmouth – a privateer – who also knows the Bailiff.'

Bethany asked no more questions. Toby had not been in Cornwall very long. It was doubtful whether he would know an influential shipowner.

As she helped Jennifer Cecil to pack clothes for her husband to take with him to Guernsey, Bethany was angry with herself for the emotion that had swept over her when she had thought the Cornish clergyman might be Toby.

She had hoped she was getting over the love she had for him, but now realised she was not. She was also aware that the wound she had suffered as a result of his behaviour was still raw.

Bethany and Jennifer took the children across the island to Braye harbour as soon as Major Cecil left the house. They watched the soldiers board the small warship, and then waved to them until the ship sailed out of the harbour and was lost to sight.

There would still be a strong garrison left on the island, but it meant there would be none camped in the fort at Longis Bay.

'It's going to feel strange not having the men around for a few days,' said Bethany, as they reached the fort and made their way to the living quarters.

'It will certainly seem very quiet,' agreed Jennifer. 'I suppose we could invite some of the women from the town to the fort. We could discuss the entertainments I would like to put on throughout the summer for the soldiers and the islanders.'

The idea did not appeal very much to Bethany. She was happy when Jennifer changed her mind almost immediately.

'No, we won't, Bethany. We'll take the opportunity of enjoying a few days to ourselves with the children. We'll do nothing but savour the peace and tranquillity of Alderney without an army about us.'

Chapter 64

Major George Cecil was away from Alderney for longer than he had anticipated and sent a note to his wife informing her that his troops would be remaining in Guernsey for a while.

He told her that although the women and children from the captured French merchantman had been repatriated, the men were being detained pending the release of the Cornish prisoners. The Frenchmen were resentful. It was felt they might create a disturbance. Major Cecil's company would remain in the vicinity of the prison.

He was not to remain with them while they maintained their vigil. Something of an expert on fortifications, he had been asked to carry out a survey of the island's defences during his time on Guernsey.

After a few days, Jennifer Cecil's resolution to have a 'restful time' during her husband's absence faltered. She was becoming bored. As a consequence, when she received an invitation to dine with the commander of the Alderney militia and his wife, she accepted.

The dinner was in St Anne and Jennifer told Bethany she would not be returning until late. 'Put the children to bed at their usual time, and don't wait up for me. I shall be escorted home by some of Captain Andros's militiamen, so I will be quite safe.'

Bethany did not mind. Only a couple of servants actually lived in the fort. The others came in each day from an inland hamlet near by. Once she had put the children to bed it would feel almost as though she had the fort to herself. That was something to look forward to.

After the baby had been laid in her cot, Bethany allowed the other three children to look through Major Cecil's telescope at a French warship, cruising not far off the coast.

They had watched the same ship twice during the day; each time it was closer to the coast. It was almost as though it was testing the reaction of the Alderney forces. Tempting them to send a ship out after it.

Bethany and Jennifer had discussed the vessel and the army officer's wife had said she would report its presence to the island's militia commander that evening.

When Bethany and the children looked out to sea on this occasion the ship was so close they could pick out the uniforms worn by those on board. William became very excited when he reported seeing a blue-uniformed man on board studying the fort through a telescope.

'Do you think he can see me?' he asked Bethany, excitedly.

'I expect so,' said Bethany. 'Wave to him and see if he waves back.'

'But . . . he's a Frenchman,' said William, uncertainly. 'We're at war with them.'

'True,' agreed Bethany. 'All the same, he might have a small boy at home just like you. I expect he'd be pleased to have another little boy wave to him.'

William looked out at the ship uncertainly for a while. Then he straightened up and waved, just once – a quick, embarrassed wave – before he returned his eye to the telescope.

Suddenly he stood upright, startled. '*He waved back*,' he said incredulously. 'He saw me and waved!'

'There you are,' said Bethany. 'I told you he might. Thou . . . *You* have probably made him very happy. Now, that's enough excitement for today. Off we all go to bed.'

There were protests from all the children, but Bethany insisted.

When they were all in bed and had settled down, she returned to the telescope. The French ship was still off the coast. She found its presence disturbing. Contrary to her earlier thoughts on the subject, she would have felt more reassured had the garrison of the fort not been elsewhere.

The French ship was carrying hardly any sail now.

Although the light was fading too much for Bethany to observe all that was going on in any detail, there seemed to be a great deal of activity taking place on the upper deck of the vessel.

So uneasy was Bethany that once the children were asleep, she decided to go outside and listen for any unusual sounds. Asking one of the maidservants to attend to them, should any of the children wake, she left the house and went down to the beach.

There was quite a lot of high cloud about tonight and the moon made only fleeting appearances. Bethany looked out to sea, but could see no lights.

She waited until she began to feel cold. Eventually, she decided her imagination had probably got the better of her. The French ship was probably merely curious about what might be happening on the British island so close to their own country. It was probably heading back for a French port right now.

Then she thought she heard the sound of a voice coming from somewhere out in the bay. About to return to the fort, she paused. There was another sound, as though a careless sailor had allowed his oar to slap the water.

At that moment the moon put in a fleeting appearance between two clouds. Bethany had imagined nothing. There, much closer to the shore than before, was the French ship, riding at anchor.

Between the ship and shore, alarmingly close, were two boats. Both appeared to be packed with blue-uniformed men.

Gathering up her skirts, Bethany ran for the fort, not slowing her pace until she reached the living quarters.

A servant-girl had been sitting at the foot of the stairs, listening out for the children. Startled, she sprang to her feet as Bethany careered in through the front door.

'Quick! Find the other servant. Tell her to run to the houses and warn them. A French raiding party is about to land. When you've done that come back and help me take the children to safety. We'll make for St Anne. Hurry!'

The young servant was close to panic, but she did as she was told, running towards the kitchen.

Bethany hurried upstairs and snatched up the baby. Then she ran to the children's rooms, shaking them into protesting wakefulness.

She told them to put on only shoes and coats and come with her.

She needed to help the youngest of the girls to dress. By this time the young servant-girl, still shaking with fright, had come upstairs to help her.

'Good girl!' said Bethany. 'We'll take the road to St Anne.' In the excitement of the moment she reverted to her familiar mode of speech. 'Thou takest care of the two girls. Don't let go of their hands, even for a moment. Should we lose touch with each other in the darkness, go to St Anne and the house of Captain Andros. We will all meet there.'

They left the house together, Bethany doing her best to stop the baby complaining and trying to prevent the two girls from becoming too frightened. She also had to cope with William's questions.

'Who's coming, Bethany? Is it the man who waved to me from the French ship? You said he had children like me. Why should he want to hurt us?'

'I doubt if he's coming ashore, William, and the men who are may not be so kind. But try not to speak now. See if you can remain silent until we are well away from the fort. Sounds carry for a great distance on a night like this.'

'I want to go back to bed.' The complaint came from Mary, the younger of the two girls.

'And so you shall, but let's see if we can find your mother first. She will want to have you all safely in bed at Captain Andros's house.'

Not until the small party reached St Anne did they meet up with anyone else. Then Bethany could have repeated her story a dozen times to curious islanders who wanted to know what she and the servant were doing out at night with three children and a baby, dressed in their nightclothes.

Instead, she said nothing and ordered the servant-girl to hold her tongue. She wanted nothing to delay them reaching the house of the militia commander. Neither did she intend causing unnecessary panic.

While two boatloads of soldiers or sailors from a French ship might carry out a damaging raid, on a small scale, it hardly constituted an invasion.

There was a guard on duty at the doorway to Captain Andros's house, placed there mainly to impress the militiaman's guests.

Although curious, he made no attempt to prevent Bethany from entering the house when she said she needed to speak to Captain Andros and Mrs Cecil on an urgent matter.

Bethany pushed aside the butler who wanted to keep them out of the dining-room while he tried to ascertain the reason for their dramatic arrival at the house. The unexpected appearance of the little group caused a sensation when they entered the dining-room.

Jennifer Cecil stood up hurriedly, spilling the drink she was about to carry to her mouth.

'Bethany! Children! What's the matter?'

'Yes, what's the meaning of this?' Captain Andros rose to his feet, finding it unbelievable that two women, three children and a baby should burst in upon his dinner in such a manner.

'There is a French ship anchored in Longis Bay,' said Bethany, breathlessly. 'They have sent two boatloads of men ashore. When I saw them they were heading for the beach close to the fort. I brought the children to safety and sent a servant to warn those who live in the nearby houses.'

For a moment it seemed everyone in the room had been struck dumb by the news.

It was Bethany who broke the silence. 'The children are very, very tired. Is there somewhere they might be put to bed?'

Chapter 65

Within minutes of Bethany's arrival, the Andros household was in turmoil. Those women who lived in St Anne had hurried off to their homes. Others who lived in more remote parts of the island were being allocated rooms in the house. Here they would spend a sleepless night.

Meanwhile, Captain Andros had ordered the militia to muster immediately. The men among his guests had either hurried off to fetch guns and swords, or accepted what was available in the Andros house.

The servant from the fort had taken the children to a room where they would all spend the night together. Downstairs, Bethany passed on every scrap of information she possessed to one of the militia officers.

When Captain Andros returned to the room, resplendent in the uniform of the Dragoons regiment to which he had once belonged, Bethany had to repeat her story yet again.

'The chances are that the Frenchmen will already have taken the fort,' said Captain Andros. 'But I don't think they will try to hold it. If only a couple of boatloads of men were landed, this will be a nuisance raid. They will try to cause as much damage as possible in the quickest possible time, then return to their ship and sail away. What we will do is head for the beach first of all. If we can capture or sink the boats, their men will be trapped on the island. It won't take us long to deal with them then.'

'I think it would be a good idea to send some men to the fort right away as well,' suggested the young officer to whom Bethany had been telling her story when Captain Andros arrived. 'We might be able to keep them busy enough to prevent their causing too much damage.'

'A good idea.' Captain Andros nodded his approval. 'But

we'll need to find out the lay-out of the fort. I know nothing at all about it. Do you?'

The young officer shook his head. 'No.'

'I think I had better come with you,' said Jennifer Cecil, unexpectedly. 'George has a great many confidential documents in his office. He would not want the French to get their hands on them and if they were destroyed it might cause some embarrassment.'

Captain Andros protested that he could not allow her to accompany his men on what was likely to prove to be a very dangerous expedition.

Bethany agreed. 'The children need you, Mrs Cecil. So does your husband. I know the fort as well as anyone. I will gather up all the documents in Major Cecil's office and put them somewhere safe.'

'The girl's right,' said Captain Andros. 'We'll take her with us – and don't be concerned for her. I'll only allow her inside the fort if there is no danger. On the way she can describe the lay-out of the place to me. If the French are inside, we'll have them out in no time. No time at all.'

When the party set off from St Anne there were about twenty mounted men. Some wore the uniform of the militia, others had learned what was happening and hurried to join battle with the French landing party without donning uniform. Bethany too had been provided with a horse, although she was a very inexperienced rider.

There were also some thirty militiamen accompanying the party on foot. It was less than a third of Captain Andros's total force, but he was too impatient to await the arrival of others.

They were joined by more men along the way, some running all the way from St Anne to catch up with their colleagues, rather than miss the anticipated battle.

There was no question of travelling secretly. It was impossible to maintain silence. The jingling of the trappings of the horses, together with the rattle of accoutrements and metal scabbards, travelled ahead of them. Added to this was the sound of marching feet and the excited chatter of the men. The talking would die down when Captain Andros barked an order for them to keep silent but would break out again within a few minutes.

There were also shouts and the sound of running feet from the latecomers.

There were two companies of regular soldiers on the island, one at the harbour of Braye, the other on the southern tip of Alderney. It had been suggested that the professional soldiers be called in, but Captain Andros was reluctant to ask for their assistance. Determined to achieve maximum glory for himself and his militia, he declared the regular army would be called upon 'in due course'. He was fully confident his own men could deal with two boatloads of Frenchmen.

When they were a little distance from the fort, Bethany pointed out a path, barely discernible in the darkness, which led directly to the beach where the French boats would probably have been run ashore.

Captain Andros decided he would split his force in two here. He would head the party going to the beach to deal with the boats. His second-in-command would lead the remainder to the fort.

The younger officer showed a sound knowledge of tactics. 'I'll not attack the fort immediately,' he said. 'We'll take up positions outside the entrance and wait until we hear you attacking the men guarding the boats. The sound is bound to bring the Frenchmen from the fort in some disarray. They will realise that if their boats are destroyed or captured they will be marooned on Alderney.'

It was a good plan and deserved to succeed. However, unknown to the militiamen, the French landing party had divided into not two, but three, each of some twenty men.

One party had been left to guard the boats, a second had gone directly to the fort, while a third made for the group of houses where many of the Cecils' servants lived.

The Frenchman on the ship had used his telescope to good effect. He knew there were no soldiers at the fort and had counted the houses in the small hamlet. Furthermore, to ensure maximum surprise, the landing party had been ordered to rely upon the sword unless they met with determined resistance from an organised force.

Had it not been for Bethany's concern at the presence of the French ship so close off the coast, their plan might have been entirely successful.

Insisting that she should remain clear of the entrance to the fort, the young officer sent her some distance away with a resentful militiaman to guard her, while the others were positioned about the entrance.

He had not completed his deployment when there was an outbreak of musket fire from the beach. Captain Andros and his militiamen had located the boats.

It was not certain who commenced firing first, but it was a fierce fight from the beginning. The boats were being guarded by the French sailors who had manned them on the way to the shore. This had left the soldiers to make their way inland.

The sailors put up a brave but brief fight. When it became increasingly clear they were outnumbered, a number of them pushed one of the boats into deeper water and climbed on board. They were helped by the darkness which kept the Alderney men from knowing what was taking place.

The sound of firing was heard at the fort and produced the anticipated result. The French soldiers had been looting. Now, suddenly aware of their predicament, they ceased their activities and fled.

Outside they were met by the fire of the militiamen. Had the accuracy of the militiamen's musketry matched their enthusiasm, the battle would have been brought to a swift conclusion. As it was, few of the musket balls found their target and within minutes the French force sent to attack the nearby hamlet had returned to join in the battle. They too had heard the initial firing from the beach.

In the darkness, the battle soon became chaotic. There was not even the distinction of language to separate Frenchman from militiaman. Most Alderney men spoke French as their everyday language.

Bethany was some distance from the fort, yet before long men were running past her in the darkness and her militiaman guard had disappeared. She decided she would carry out the task for which she had come to the fort.

Much of the fighting seemed to have moved away and she was able to slip inside without attracting attention.

There were a number of lights burning within the living quarters. Finding the fort deserted, the Frenchmen had lit lamps in order to locate items worthy of looting.

Much had been left behind when fighting erupted on the beach. Silver cutlery was scattered around the floor. Vases, statuettes and clocks lay on sheets and tablecloths, ready to be bundled up and carried off.

Fortunately, not every room had received the attention of the French soldiers. Since work on the fort had begun in the sixteenth century, various additions and modifications had been made. The result was that the fort had become a maze of rooms, passageways and narrow staircases.

The room chosen by Major Cecil for his office was at the top of one of these narrow stairways. It had not been immediately evident to men whose prime interest was to obtain loot.

Taking one of the lamps, Bethany made her way up the stone stairs. As she had hoped, the door was locked and she located the key where it was usually kept, in a small recess in the shadows above the door.

She let herself into the room and was able to confirm that no one had been in there.

In view of what was going on outside, she decided it would be safer to leave all Major Cecil's papers where they were.

She was about to leave the room and lock the door behind her when she heard a noise on the stairs, accompanied by the sound of shouting.

A few moments later a young, hatless but uniformed Frenchman, scarcely more than a boy, scrambled up the stairs.

He stumbled into the room and Bethany saw he was bleeding from a severe gash on his hand. He also had an ugly cut on his cheek.

There was a look of sheer terror on his face. Seeing Bethany in the lamplight, he pleaded, 'Help me . . . please!'

He was being pursued by two Alderney militiamen. As the young Frenchman crouched on the floor behind Bethany, one of the men pushed past her. Before she could stop him he placed the muzzle of his musket against the young soldier's temple and pulled the trigger.

Nothing happened.

Cursing loudly, the militiaman drew a long bayonet from a scabbard carried at his belt. Ignoring Bethany's scream for him to stop, he drew back his arm with the intention of plunging the bayonet into the young Frenchman's body.

Bethany charged him, her shoulder knocking him off balance.

'Stop him!' she appealed to the second militiaman, who had paused at the top of the stairs and seemed less excited than his colleague.

'He's an enemy soldier,' cried the first militiaman, rising to his feet, still clutching the bayonet.

'He's wounded – and he's unarmed.' Bethany placed herself between the militiaman and his intended victim. 'If thou killest him I will see thou art charged with his murder.'

For a moment it seemed the half-crazed militiaman might ignore the threat. Then his companion said, 'She's right, John. He's no threat to anyone.'

For a moment, the first militiaman glared from one occupant of the room to the other. Then he lowered his bayonet and said to his companion, 'Stay here and guard him. I'm going down to rejoin the fight.'

Pushing past the other militiaman, he clattered down the stairs.

'I thank thee,' said Bethany to the remaining militiaman. She was aware that her body was shaking and she had unconsciously reverted to her Quaker mode of speech.

The Alderney militiaman looked at the terrified Frenchman. 'He can't be much older than my sixteen-year-old daughter,' he said pityingly. 'Whoever sent him to fight ought to be ordered to take his place.'

'Please . . . do you live here?' The young Frenchman spoke to Bethany.

'Yes.'

'Then I must warn you. One of our men has started a fire in the wood store.'

The wood store was a lean-to building against the kitchen wall. If a blaze got going there it would quickly spread to the whole of the fort.

'It must be put out quickly,' said Bethany. 'We'll need as much help as we can get.'

'I will come too,' said the young Frenchman.

'Thou shouldst have thy hand treated,' she said.

'Later. Come.' The Frenchman made his way down the stairs with the militiaman following close behind and Bethany bringing up the rear.

The blaze in the store was not yet out of control, but it was fortunate there was a well nearby in the kitchen yard.

Two more militiamen came to help and the fire was extinguished before it had taken a firm hold. As an added precaution, the charred logs were pulled clear of the store and strewn clear of the yard.

By the time all had been made safe, the battle between the invasion party and militia was over and the young Frenchman allowed Bethany to dress his wounds before he was handed over to the custody of the militiamen.

One of the boats had escaped, but the other had been captured, together with its crew. Those French soldiers who had survived the battle had also been taken prisoner.

By the time a company of regular soldiers from Braye harbour arrived, the Frenchmen were under guard in the grounds of the fort and Bethany was treating the wounded men of both sides, in the kitchen.

The 'Battle of Longis Bay' was over. It had ended in a decisive and satisfactory victory for the Alderney militiamen.

Chapter 66

By the time Major Cecil and the company he had taken to Guernsey returned to Alderney, the servants at the fort had cleared up after the chaos caused by the French raid.

Had the commander of the island's forces not received a detailed and self-glorifying report of the events of the night from Captain Andros, he would have found it difficult to believe a raid had taken place at all.

Speaking in the sitting-room of the fort's living quarters on the evening of his return, he commented upon this fact, adding, 'One thing not in doubt is the courage and highly responsible action taken by you, Bethany.'

The children were in bed and Bethany had been asked to join Major Cecil and his wife.

'Your prompt action ensured the safety of the children and undoubtedly saved many lives in the houses of the servants. It also meant the French raid failed in its aim of causing terror and destruction on the island.'

'Thank you, but how many men were killed in the fight? Far too many, I suspect.'

'Fewer than would have died had the French soldiers had a free hand with no one to oppose them. Your actions saved lives, Bethany. *Innocent* lives. I am told you personally saved the life of a young French soldier. He has insisted upon telling everyone who would listen.'

When Bethany made no reply, George Cecil said, 'I am proud of you. So too are the soldiers of my regiment. I am very pleased and greatly relieved that Jennifer employed you to take care of the children. We both owe you more than can ever be repaid.'

Bethany was not used to receiving such glowing praise. It embarrassed her. 'I have had plenty of practice, taking care of my sister's children, in Cornwall. Living so close to the sea, there was always something going on. Muriel was either carrying or taking care of a new baby for much of the time, so I was left to cope with the others.'

'Ah, yes! I keep forgetting you have lived for many years in Cornwall. Is your sister's home close to Mevagissey?'

'Yes, very close. My brother-in-law is a fisherman so I knew many of the Mevagissey fishermen.'

'They all have much to celebrate. The clergyman from Cornwall had a very successful visit to France. With a young woman acting as interpreter he went there seeking only two people. In the event, he was able to arrange for the release of a great many fishermen whose homes are along the coast around Mevagissey. I understand that while in France he met with Minister Fouché, the French Minister of Police – a man with much blood on his hands. I spoke to the interpreter who accompanied him.'

Major Cecil smiled at the memory of his meeting with Grace. 'She is a quite remarkable young woman – and strikingly attractive. It is rumoured she was a slave, held in French hands until she was freed by a Falmouth privateer. The same ship returned to St Peter Port and conveyed the freed fishermen back to Cornwall. The lady is a most unusual young woman. Not at all the sort of company you would expect a Church of England parson to take with him on a jaunt to France. Mind you, offhand I can't think of a parson of my acquaintance who would undertake such a mission. But, from what I understand, he is not a run-of-the-mill parson. Someone told me he used to be a naval chaplain . . .'

'Bethany, are you all right?'

Jennifer had been watching Bethany's expression while her husband was talking. She had seen the blood suddenly leave her face.

Instead of replying, Bethany spoke urgently to Major Cecil.

'This . . . parson. Did you speak with him? What is his name?'

'I would very much have liked to have a chat to him. He would appear to be a very interesting man. Unfortunately, he did not return with the fishermen. According to the young woman – his interpreter – he was taken off to meet Minister Fouché once more. She was quite upset about it. I don't doubt she would have led a rescue force herself, had we provided one.'

Suddenly, Major Cecil realised, as his wife had earlier, that what he was saying seemed to be important to Bethany.

'Do you think you might know this parson? Now I come to think of it, it's highly probable, your being a Quaker. His reason for going to France in the first place was to arrange for the release of two Quakers, a man and a woman. It caused a great deal of comment among the Guernsey authorities. There was certainly a Quaker among the freed men but, apart from the interpreter, there was no woman in the party. Perhaps that is the reason he failed to return with the others. I don't know. Maybe you can throw some light on the matter . . .'

Jennifer, who was still watching Bethany closely, said, 'Do you think you know this parson, Bethany?'

'Yes . . . Yes, I am certain I do. He is Toby Lovell, the man I was going to marry before I left Cornwall. Not only that, I believe I am the woman he was seeking, although I don't know what led him to believe I might be in France. Unless something happened to my brother-in-law before he returned to Cornwall and Toby thought I was with him . . . Yes, that could be it.'

Visibly upset now, she said, 'It's possible my mother knows something of what is going on. If Toby came to Guernsey he would have gone to my home before trying anywhere else. He would also have told her if something had happened to Jacob – that's my brother-in-law. Please, I would like to go to Guernsey to speak to her.'

Appealing to Jennifer, she said, 'If I left first thing tomorrow morning, I could be back in Alderney by nightfall.'

'Of course, Bethany.'

Jennifer put an arm about her shoulders and with a meaningful glance at her husband, said, 'We'll go to the kitchen now and make something for us all to drink. While we are there I think you should tell me something about this Cornish parson and the reason why you left Cornwall without marrying him. You obviously still care a great deal for each other. Perhaps George or I might be able to help . . .'

Chapter 67

'The money should enable you to buy a few more luxuries than a curate's salary will allow.'

Matthew Vivian was speaking in the study of Porthluney rectory. He had just brought Toby a banker's draft for his share of the prize money received for the French merchant ship captured by the *Potomac*. It was a substantial sum, being well in excess of two thousand pounds.

'It's an incredible amount!'

Toby had at first not wanted to accept the money, but Matthew insisted. He declared it was the wish of the officers and crew of the privateer, adding that after Toby's exploits in France they would have been quite happy to double the amount!

'It's very generous of you,' added Toby. 'In fact, it's more money than I've ever possessed at one time in the whole of my life.'

This was the truth. It represented more than ten years of his curate's stipend, had he been able to look forward to receiving it for so long.

His situation was, at the very least, precarious at present. The sum of money given to him by Matthew Vivian gave him some much needed security.

'The *Potomac* will be putting to sea again at the end of the week and working along the English Channel. If we have no success there we might try our luck in the Mediterranean. I hear there are rich pickings to be had there.'

'There will also be a great deal more danger,' said Toby. 'Not only from the French, but from North African pirates. Will Grace be sailing with you this time?'

Matthew smiled. 'Yes, but I have had to agree to give her a share of any prize money we make. Grace sees it as a means of becoming entirely independent. Besides, I would miss her if she stayed behind in England. That woman grows on a man, Toby. One of these days I'm going to surprise myself and ask her to marry me.'

'Why not do it now and allow me to perform the service?'

Matthew shook his head. 'Not yet. I might wake up one morning and find I've regained my senses. Besides, we're both happy with things the way they are at the moment.'

Matthew stood up from his chair and held out his hand to Toby. 'Goodbye. I hope you catch up with your young Quaker girl before too long. I have no doubt at all you'll have found her before I return home for the wedding.'

'The wedding?'

'Oh, did I forget to tell you? Brother Charles popped the question to Parson Trist's widowed daughter yesterday and she's accepted him. They plan to marry sometime in the spring of next year. I've told Charles he should go out and enjoy life a little more before settling down to married life, but he's besotted with her and won't take me seriously. Mind you, Sally is a damned attractive woman. I don't doubt they will both be deliriously happy.'

'I must call on them and offer my congratulations,' said Toby. Ruefully, he added, 'Everyone except me seems to be bringing some order into their lives. I'm more unsettled than I was when I first came to Porthluney. I suppose I could always accept Reverend Trist's offer and go to Veryan as his curate.'

'Don't be in too much of a hurry to make up your mind, Toby. Something will come along. It always does – but I shouldn't need to tell you this. You're the man whose life is based on faith.'

Toby watched with some sadness as the Falmouth ship-owner rode away. He was going to miss him – and Grace too. They had both brought a great deal of colour into his life. Just for a moment he regretted not accepting Matthew's offer of sailing with him in the *Potomac*, leaving someone else to take on the problems of Porthluney.

Then he thought about Bethany. He would not move far from his parish until he had found her again.

* * *

On the Sunday following Toby's return from France, the small Porthluney church was filled to overflowing. Word of Toby's achievements had reached the remotest corners of the rural parish. Men and women who had not attended church for years came to express their approval, or merely to satisfy their curiosity.

In addition there were fishermen from Mevagissey and Gorran who came with their families and friends to thank the curate who had freed them from a French prison.

In keeping with the celebratory nature of the occasion, Toby preached a sermon of hope for the future of the parish. It was coupled with a wish that the war which had brought tragedy and difficulties into so many of their lives might soon come to an end.

Even as he was uttering the words, Toby accepted that it was a vain hope. The Battle of Trafalgar had secured domination of the seas for Britain, but on land Napoleon Bonaparte was as invincible as ever. He seemed able to conquer countries at will.

After the service, men and women stood in line to shake Toby by the hand as they left the church. Inside, on the altar, collection plates were filled to overflowing, thanks to the generosity of the grateful fishermen.

'I don't think Porthluney church can ever have enjoyed such a congregation. It would have brought great joy to the heart of Parson Kempe.'

Caroline Bettison had waited inside the church until all the congregation had filed past the curate. Her words reminded Toby that he had the sad task of officiating at the funeral of the late rector in only a few days' time. That service too would attract a great many people from neighbouring parishes.

Details of the funeral had already been sent to the manor, but Toby made no mention of it. Instead, he asked Caroline about her health and of the situation at Porthluney Manor.

Her immediate change of expression told Toby before she spoke that all was not well with her life.

'I would like to say that all my hopes have been realised, but . . .'

Two of the Mevagissey fishermen had returned to the

church to say something more to Toby. Caroline broke off what she was saying and said, 'Come to tea at the manor today. John is away until mid-week. I would like to have a talk with you.'

'Of course. I'll be there about four o'clock.'

Watching Caroline walk to her carriage, Toby felt deeply sorry for her. To an outsider, Caroline Bettison would appear to have everything a woman could wish for. Yet he thought she was probably the loneliest woman he knew.

It was a fine afternoon and tea at Porthluney Manor was served on the lawn. Initially the talk was of the morning's church service and of Toby's time in France.

Caroline had spent some time in France as a young girl and was very fond of both the country and its people. She had heard that Toby had been accompanied by a female interpreter and joked that had she known, *she* would have volunteered her services.

Replying in the same vein, Toby said he would have asked her had he not believed her to be busily preparing for the arrival of the baby and deciding on the priorities for the future of the Porthluney Estate.

'I am looking forward to the birth of the baby,' replied Caroline. 'Everyone is hoping it will be a son. I would rather like this one to be a daughter. She would be company for me and no one would mind very much if I spoiled her a little.'

'I hope your wish is fulfilled,' replied Toby. 'But what of the estate?'

Caroline shrugged unhappily. 'When I first learned of the baby I had a long talk with John about my father's promise. For a while I believed he was trying hard to please me. Then I found a letter threatening legal action against him if he did not settle his gambling debts. Most had been incurred since we had our talk.'

Fixing him with a direct look, she said, 'I would not be telling you this if I did not regard you as a trusted friend, but it is also the confession of an unhappy woman to her priest.'

'It will remain with me, but is there any way in which I might be of help?'

'There is little you can do about the estate, but . . .' Caroline hesitated as though seeking the right words. 'There is another matter that worries me very much. John's violence when he has been drinking is becoming worse – and he is drinking more. I can cope with it most of the time, but I fear for the baby. If things do not improve, I must consider leaving Porthluney and returning to my father's home until after the baby is born.'

Toby was aware Caroline was a restraining influence upon her wayward and unpredictable husband. Without her presence at the manor, life would be far more difficult for the servants and tenants of the estate.

'I realise your husband holds the Church and its ministers in low esteem, but I will try to speak with him if you think it will help?'

'Thank you for the thought, Toby. Unfortunately, I feel it would only make things worse. You have already helped me by listening to my problems.'

'Do you have no sisters who might come to Porthluney and stay until after the baby is born?'

Caroline shook her head. 'There is only Rupert and myself. The housekeeper at Porthluney is sympathetic, but although she is critical of what she refers to as the "modern generation", she is very defensive of the Bettison name. However, merely expressing my thoughts out loud to you has helped me make up my mind. The next time John is violent towards me, I will leave him. If that happens you will be needed more than ever before. When I move out of Porthluney, the devil will move in. Remember that, Toby.'

Chapter 68

The service held for the Reverend Harold Kempe was not so much a funeral as a thanksgiving for his life. At Rosemary Kempe's request, much of the sombre music associated with such an occasion was omitted. Instead, the organist, brought in from St Stephen's church, played a selection of the late rector's favourite hymns.

The small church was almost as crowded as it had been for the Sunday service a few days before. Rosemary Kempe was deeply moved that so many parishioners had attended to pay a final tribute to their late rector.

Caroline Bettison was also present at the service. She offered apologies for her husband, saying he was away in London.

After the service, Toby and many of the guests made their way to the rectory for refreshments before going on their way.

Rosemary Kempe took the opportunity to wander around the rectory and garden where, she said, Harold Kempe had spent so many happy hours.

While she was making her farewell tour, Toby was very much on edge. Billy still occupied the upstairs bedroom where he had been since his operation. Toby had ensured the door was locked and the key was held by Alice, who was helping out with the refreshments. Billy had been instructed to make no sound while the guests were in the house.

It came as a great relief when the widow announced it was time for her to leave. She was going to live with a sister in London, leaving the following morning, and still had some last-minute packing to complete.

'Thank you for a wonderful service,' she said to Toby,

before climbing into the carriage that was to take her to St Stephen. 'It was exactly what Harold would have wanted. Thank you too for all you have done in Porthluney. It was fully appreciated by Harold. He told me shortly before he died it was only a question of time before you made it a very happy parish once again. I agree with him. The people of Porthluney love you.'

The remainder of the funeral guests also left now and Alice was able to unlock Billy's room before beginning the task of returning the house to its everyday state.

Billy was able to walk about a little now, although he was still in a very weak state. He came down and sat in the kitchen while Alice carried out her tasks.

It was still early in the afternoon and Toby wondered what he would do with the remainder of the day. Then he remembered the *Potomac* was due to sail the following day. He decided he would go to Falmouth to say farewell to Matthew and Grace.

'The Revenue cutter is still lying off Portloe,' said Billy. 'That means none of the men will be out fishing. Go and see my pa. He'll be happy to take you there. It will save you a lot of time.'

Toby thanked Billy for his suggestion and left for Portloe.

It was as Billy had said. With faintly smoking clay pipes gripped between their teeth, the fishermen were sitting around mending nets and lobster baskets and grumbling about the prolonged presence of the Revenue men.

Any one of the men would have been happy to ferry Toby to Falmouth, but they were all aware of the threat of being taken by the Revenue men and pressed into service with the Royal Navy.

'I'll take you,' said Billy's father, eventually. 'I'm too old for naval service. Anyway, they're hardly likely to take me on board and leave you out there drifting in the boat.'

'I hope you're right, Tom,' said one of the fishermen, gloomily. 'But I wouldn't chance it. There's a hefty price on the head of any man who can be proved to have been at sea on the night the Revenue man was killed. It's more than enough to make them stretch the truth.'

* * *

In spite of the gloomy predictions of the Portloe fishermen, the short voyage to Falmouth was completed without incident and as they entered the harbour Toby could see the *Potomac* in its usual berth.

Telling Tom Kendall to berth astern of the privateer, Toby called out to Matthew Vivian who was standing on the deck, talking to a member of the crew.

By the time he reached the gangway of the *Potomac*, Matthew had been joined on deck by Grace. She greeted Toby in her usual effervescent manner, his embarrassment producing wide grins on the faces of the crew members who were watching.

'This is a very pleasant surprise,' said Matthew, as the two men shook hands. 'Does it mean you've changed your mind and have decided to come with us after all?'

'Please say you'll come with us. You are lucky for the *Potomac*. We will return with lots of money and I will not have to put up with Matthew's meanness whenever I wish to buy new clothes.'

As Grace made her plea dressed in clothes reflecting the latest in English fashion, her words carried no sting.

'I'm quite sure you'll do very well without me,' said Toby. 'I found myself with a few empty hours on my hands so I thought I would come and bid you both farewell.'

'That is very kind of you,' said Grace. 'I will miss you while we are away. I will miss Charles and Sally too. I have made some very good friends in England.'

'You could always stay behind with them if you wished,' said Matthew, nonchalantly.

'No, I could not do this,' said Grace. 'I would soon become bored – and you would miss me too much.' She squeezed his arm affectionately before saying to Toby, 'But you must not go to France again until I am able to come along and take care of you. You are an innocent among the French.'

Matthew smiled. 'I think we should avoid a debate on innocence, Grace. Let's go below and have a farewell drink to the success of the next voyage of the *Potomac*.'

After leaving the *Potomac* Toby called in at the Vivian

shipping office. Sir Charles's first question was also about the possibility of Toby's returning to France.

'I've heard nothing yet,' he said. 'And I didn't leave Fox's office filled with optimism about the prospect of negotiating the release of more prisoners.'

Unaware of the contents of the letter Toby had delivered to the British Foreign Minister, Sir Charles said, 'Perhaps he has had a change of heart? When I was in London recently word was going about that Fox was trying to negotiate a peace with France.'

'I'll pray for the success of that,' replied Toby. 'But I came here today to bid farewell to Matthew and Grace, and also because I wanted to offer you my congratulations. I am very, very pleased for both you and Sally. I have grown very attached to Reverend Trist, Sally and Anna during the short time I've been in Cornwall. They are the nearest thing to a family I have ever known.'

'Thank you, Toby. I hope you'll always regard them in the same way. I do know that Sally and Anna are very fond of you too. They were most concerned for you when it was learned you were in France. Talking of which . . . have you learned any more about the whereabouts of your Quaker girl? Bethany, is that her name?'

'Yes to both counts, although I am not much farther forward.'

Toby told Sir Charles all he had learned about her. The baronet made a few notes, saying, 'It's possible this officer has paid a courtesy call on the Bailiff of Guernsey. Most senior officers who visit the island do. I'll write and ask if he knows anything about him. Of course, it's hardly likely they will have discussed the numbers in the officer's family if he was on the island only briefly, but it's worth a try.'

'I'm very grateful to you,' said Toby. 'My own enquiries seem to have come to a halt, but I haven't given up hope. I'd like to have it all settled while I'm still in this part of the country.'

'You're surely not thinking of leaving Cornwall so soon? You've hardly had time to settle in.'

'I don't think I'll be given very much more time.' Toby

told Sir Charles how the death of Reverend Kempe was likely to affect his life.

'Yes. Yes, of course. I hadn't thought of that. Who is your patron?'

'A Mr Fortescue of St Stephen. We have never met. He's been out of Cornwall ever since I was appointed.'

'I know Piers Fortescue. He's a good man.'

Toby thought Sir Charles was about to say something else to him, but at that moment a clerk put his head around the door to say that one of the Vivian ships was entering harbour.

'That will be the *Pride of Prideaux*,' said Sir Charles, excitedly. 'She's returning from a long trading voyage to the East Indies. There should be all manner of exotic goods on board. Come out to meet her with me, Toby.'

'I'd love to, but I must be getting back to Porthluney. I have a Portloe fisherman waiting to take me back and it's already dusk. It's time we set off.'

Chapter 69

The return to Portloe from Falmouth was not to be as straightforward as the outward voyage had been. The small fishing boat gave the Revenue cutter a wide berth – but Tom Kendall had reckoned without the smaller Revenue boats.

As the fishing boat manoeuvred to make the final run into the tiny fishing inlet, they were hailed from somewhere near at hand and ordered to lower their sail, or be fired upon.

'What shall we do?' hissed Tom Kendall.

'Exactly as we're told,' said Toby firmly. 'We've got nothing to hide.'

'That's as may be,' said Tom Kendall. 'But we wouldn't be the first men to have dutiable goods mysteriously turn up in their boat. We could outrun them. I know these waters better than any Revenue man . . .'

'No!' said Toby firmly.

'Do you hear me?' Another call came from the Revenue boat that was no more than a vague shadow in the darkness.

'We're taking the sail down now,' called Toby. 'But we're about our lawful business. I'm the curate of Porthluney, on my way back to Portloe from Falmouth.'

'I don't care who you are. I have orders to pick up anyone who's at sea at this time of night and take them to the chief Revenue officer.'

As the two men in the fishing boat waited for the other boat to come alongside, Toby found his heart beating faster, even though he knew he and Tom Kendall had done nothing wrong. He thought he could understand why young men found smuggling an exciting way of making money.

'Here. Take the rope and make it fast.' A Revenue officer

held a lamp aloft as the rope was thrown towards the fishing boat. Toby caught it and tied it to a ring on the bow of the boat.

The fishing boat was pulled in close to the larger Revenue vessel and two men carrying lanterns clambered on board.

One of the Revenue men lifted the single net that was carried in the boat and peered beneath it. 'You're not carrying much for a fishing boat, are you?'

'I told you just now,' said Toby patiently, 'Mr Kendall took me to Falmouth earlier today, now he's bringing me home.'

'So you say. I doubt whether our chief Revenue officer's going to believe you. You'll need to prove your story – and he's a difficult man to convince.'

'I have no intention of trying to convince anyone,' said Toby. 'I shall tell him where we've been and where we're going, the same as I'm telling you. If we're delayed unduly I shall make an official complaint to London. Now, if you intend taking us to your cutter, do so quickly. I wish to go home.'

The small fishing boat was dropped astern of the Revenue boat and they were towed to the cutter, anchored a short distance out to seaward.

As they bumped alongside the sea-going vessel, a voice called down, 'What have you got there, Harry?'

'A Portloe boat with two men on board. One of them says he's a curate, though what he's doing out here at this time of night I don't know. It certainly wasn't fishing.'

'We'd better have 'em on board and have a look at 'em. I'll throw a rope ladder down.'

'If you want us on board you'll lower the gangway,' said Toby, firmly. 'My days of climbing rope ladders ended at Trafalgar.'

There was a low-voiced conversation on board the cutter, then a voice said, 'Are you the curate of Porthluney?'

'That's right.'

'Just a minute, Mr Lovell, we'll lower the gangway. Pull off, Harry, while the gangway comes down.'

'You *are* a curate!' There was disbelief in the voice of one of the men who had boarded the fishing boat.

'He told you that,' said Tom Kendall.

The gangway was lowered and Toby went on board the cutter, followed reluctantly by the Portloe fisherman.

Once on board, the two men were taken to a hatchway and led down the steps to a cabin. One of the escorts knocked on the door and a voice called, 'Come in.'

When Toby and Tom Kendall entered they found themselves in the presence of the chief Customs officer whom Toby had last seen at the rectory on the night the Revenue man was shot.

'Hello, Curate Lovell, our paths cross once again.'

'You will no doubt recall that neither occasion has been at my instigation, sir.'

'True. No doubt a great many arrested smugglers would say the same.'

'Are you suggesting I am a smuggler?'

'I am suggesting nothing, but you must admit it is suspicious at the very least to find you at sea after dark in a boat that does not appear to have been fishing.'

'I admit no such thing. I have already explained that we were going about our lawful business.'

'Explain it once again to me, Curate Lovell.'

Toby was angry at the attitude of the chief Revenue officer, but taking a deep breath, he said, 'After conducting the funeral of Reverend Kempe this morning, I asked Mr Kendall to take me to Falmouth. I wanted to say farewell to a friend who is setting sail tomorrow. I also wanted to congratulate his brother who is soon to be married.'

'No doubt these friends will verify your story if we all sail to Falmouth now and rouse them from their beds?'

'I doubt if either of them will be pleased at being disturbed so late at night.'

Toby thought he detected a gleam of triumph in the other man's expression when the Revenue officer said, 'A little inconvenience will surely not be resented when it is on behalf of a friend, Curate. Give me their names, if you please.'

'Certainly. One is Matthew Vivian. He will no doubt be spending the night on board his ship the *Potomac* which will be sailing early tomorrow morning. His brother is Sir Charles. No doubt you know him?'

'Vivian? Of the shipping company?'

'That's right.'

'I know of them, of course . . .'

'Then perhaps we can sail for Falmouth right away. They are both busy men to whom sleep is probably almost as valuable as friendship.'

Toby had called the bluff of the chief Revenue officer and both men knew it. The Vivians were a wealthy family with a great deal of influence in the county.

The Revenue officer was aware that if Toby *was* a close friend of the two brothers, his own actions might already be sufficient to bring criticism down upon his head. He did not wish to add to it by hauling either of the brothers from his bed in the dead of night to verify the word of a family friend.

On the other hand, if Lovell was lying . . .

The curate had incurred the wrath of the Porthluney landowner but the Revenue officer remembered the stories that were circulating about the Porthluney curate. Trafalgar . . . France . . . It was also rumoured he had been to London for a meeting with the Foreign Secretary . . .

He turned to Billy's father. 'You, Tom Kendall, is it? What do you know of this?'

'Nothing at all. Parson asked me if I'd take him to Falmouth and wait there to bring him back. That's what I've done. I saw him board the *Potomac* and then he came back from town with a man when that big ship came in. That's all I know.'

'The big ship was the *Pride of Prideaux*, owned by the Vivians. She was returning from the East Indies,' said Toby. 'Sir Charles wanted me to go on board with him to welcome home the captain and crew but it was getting late. I decided to return home. Now, can we set sail for Falmouth? We've already wasted enough time.'

'I'll take your word for the reason you're out in a boat at this time of night, Curate Lovell, but you must understand I have a duty to perform. You have served the king yourself, so I've heard.'

'You've heard correctly. But I fail to see how *you're* serving the king by anchoring off Portloe for so long when there must be a great deal of illegal activity taking place elsewhere along the coast. It smacks to me of intimidation, sir. Our fishermen have a difficult enough time battling against the weather – and the French. They do not need our own people to make it impossible for them to earn a living.'

'I carry out my duty as I see it, Curate. One of my men has been murdered. Someone in the community – one of your parishioners – is harbouring his killer.'

'No, sir. I do not dispute the fact that one of your men has met a tragic death. I doubt if there's a man or woman in the whole community who has not been saddened by his death. But murder? I think not. My understanding is that he was killed by a musket ball. To the best of my knowledge there is not a fisherman in the area who owns a musket. They earn their living by fishing, not shooting. I am not naive enough to claim they never trade in dutiable goods. We all know different. But it's a means of supplementing their main livelihood, no more. It's nothing for which they would kill a fellow man. I know from my own naval service that there are men – desperate men – who *will* kill, but we are talking now of full-time smugglers, not fishermen. You won't find such men operating along this part of the coast. No, sir. The only men carrying muskets that night were Revenue men. Your men. I leave you to draw your own conclusions as to how your man met his death.'

'I would expect you to defend the smugglers, Curate. We both know they are your parishioners . . .'

'My defence is of *innocent* men, sir. Now, we have wasted enough of our time. May we get on our way?'

'You are free to leave whenever you wish,' said the tight-lipped chief Revenue officer, 'but be certain that if suspicion ever falls on you, I shall remember where your sympathies lie and will act accordingly.'

'If such an occasion arises, you can be equally certain there will be a full investigation into the circumstances of an unsuccessful operation which resulted in the death of one of your own men. One cannot pre-judge the outcome of such an investigation, but the word that immediately springs to mind is . . . bungling. Shall we go, Mr Kendall?'

Billy's father said nothing until the small fishing boat had drifted clear of the Revenue cutter. Then he expelled his breath noisily. 'I never thought I'd live to hear a senior Revenue officer given such a dressing down by a parson. It would have gladdened our Billy's heart to hear it.'

Toby wondered whether he ought to have felt guilty when he remembered that Billy was recovering from his wound in the Porthluney rectory even as he was lecturing the chief Revenue officer on the innocence of the local fishermen?

He decided he did not, and would not.

'I can see the white of the breakers against the cliff,' he said, changing the subject. 'I'll stand by to lower the sail when you give the word. I will be glad to get home tonight.'

Chapter 70

It was very late by the time Toby reached the Porthluney rectory. He was surprised to see a light burning in the room occupied by Billy.

With his recent encounter with the Revenue Service fresh in his mind, he felt more concerned than he might otherwise have been and hurried into the house and upstairs to the bedroom.

He frowned when he opened the door to see Alice seated in a chair beside the young fisherman, but he was relieved nothing untoward was happening.

'I'm home much later than I expected. I didn't think to find you still here, Alice.'

Speaking to Billy, he said, 'Your father took me to Falmouth. On our way back, after dark, we were boarded by Revenue men and taken to their cutter. We were questioned by the chief Revenue officer who was here nosing around on the night you were wounded.'

'Is Pa all right? They didn't keep him?'

'He'll be safely tucked up in bed and asleep by now – as both of you should be.'

'There are a couple of things to tell you,' said Alice, 'so I waited. Time's passed much more quickly than I realised. Jacob Hosking called to see you. He said he has some news about Bethany, but he told me to stress that he still doesn't know where she is.'

Toby's hopes had risen and fallen again as she spoke. He wondered what the news could be and what form it had taken. He pulled out his watch. It was after midnight. Far too late to go to Hemmick now. He would call on Jacob in the morning.

Replacing the watch in his pocket, he said, 'You said you had two things to tell me. What is the second?'

Alice and Billy exchanged glances before she said, 'Billy has asked me to marry him. I've said I will.'

'Congratulations! I'm absolutely delighted for both of you.'

Toby kissed Alice on the cheek and shook Billy warmly by the hand.

'You're the first to know,' revealed Alice. 'I haven't even told my parents yet.'

'Do you think they will agree?' Toby was aware that Alice was barely seventeen.

She nodded. 'Ma and I have talked of it quite often.' She smiled at Billy, happily. 'She was married to Pa when she was no older than me.'

'We'd like the wedding to be towards the end of the summer,' said Billy. 'You'll marry us, of course?'

'I very much hope so, Billy, although there might well be a new rector at Porthluney by then.' Observing Alice's expression of dismay, he added, hastily, 'But I'm sure we can arrange something. Now, I really do think you should hurry home and tell the good news to your parents, Alice. I had better come with you.'

'There's no need for that,' she declared. 'The only things about at this time of night are owls, badgers and a fox or two and they don't bother me. You get on off to bed. You've had a busy day.'

Although she had not left the rectory until the early hours of the morning, Alice was back for work again at eight o'clock.

She reminded Toby that it was market day in Tregony and they were short of provisions. Giving her some money, he told her to take Nipper. Inexplicably, the bad-tempered donkey seemed to have developed an affection for Alice. Although as vicious as ever with others, he now made no attempt to bite her. Toby would walk to Hemmick, taking Nap with him.

Toby took the cliff path and it was a pleasant walk. Nap enjoyed it too. After chasing the occasional rabbit, he would return, tongue lolling from his mouth, panting from the pleasure of the chase.

There was another reason to enjoy the walk. Out in the bay, the surface of the sea was dotted with fishing boats. It was a sight that had not been seen since the night the Revenue man had met his death.

The Revenue cutter had sailed from the area during the night. The fishermen were once more able to go about their business.

Jacob was one of the men taking advantage of the departure of the Revenue cutter, but Muriel was at their Hemmick home.

It was the first time she and Toby had met since before he had arranged for Jacob's release from the French prison.

Muriel greeted him more warmly than at any time since Bethany had left Cornwall.

'I am so grateful to thee,' she said, emotionally. 'I always will be. When I thought I had lost Jacob I realised that he means more to me than anything else in this world. It has made me far more understanding towards Bethany, and what she was prepared to do for thee.'

'It's because of Bethany I'm here,' said Toby as he picked up one of the girls who had fallen. Setting her on her feet and dusting down her knees, he added, 'Alice said Jacob had come to the rectory with news of her?'

'It is news of her, and yet it isn't,' said Muriel, ambiguously.

'I'm sorry, I don't understand?'

'I've had a letter from my mother. She says Bethany has been to see her. She refused to say where she was living, but she had heard about Jacob's capture by the French, and of thy part in arranging for his release. My mother wrote that Bethany was impressed by thy courage in going to France, although that was never in doubt. Bethany also told my mother she was overjoyed for me, Jacob and the children. She said that despite what thou hast done, she will pray for thee in gratitude for thy part in reuniting our family.'

'In spite of what I have done?' Toby was more bewildered than before. 'What exactly *is* it I am supposed to have done?'

'I don't know that, Toby. If thou honestly doest not know there is very little that can be done to put it right

– but things are not quite so hopeless as they were before the letter arrived.'

'How have they improved? Bethany still thinks the worst of me – and we don't know why. What's more, we don't know where she is. I can't find her and learn what it is she believes me to have done.'

'That is true, but I believe it will only be a matter of time before we learn where Bethany is. If she has heard that thou hast been to Guernsey and France, and of Jacob's capture, then it means she is still somewhere in the Channel Islands. In view of the time that elapsed between Jacob's release and her visit to Mother, I doubt if she is on Guernsey itself. She is probably living on one of the other islands. We will find her, Toby. I am convinced of it.'

Returning to the rectory, he mused on what had been said by Muriel. He was inclined to believe her theory was right. If so, then the letter sent by Sir Charles Vivian to the Bailiff of Guernsey might bear fruit.

Toby would need to contain his impatience and frustration for a while longer. It in no way lessened his determination. He *would* find Bethany. And when he did, he had no doubt at all that he would be able to resolve their misunderstanding.

Chapter 71

Toby was preparing his church for the next day's Sunday services when Alice returned from Tregony market. She had news of happenings at Porthluney Manor and sought out Toby.

'I've heard something I thought you would want to know about right away, you being friendly with Mrs Bettison, up at the manor.'

Alice sat down in one of the pews, but was too full of her news to sit still and rose to her feet again, immediately. 'I met my cousin Edith in Tregony. She's a kitchen maid at the manor and was buying spices for them at the market. She said there's been a big argument between John Bettison and his wife. Edith said he came home drunk late one night and she wouldn't let him in her room. She didn't open the door until he started trying to kick it down. They quarrelled far into the night and he could be heard shouting at her. Then Edith said the servants heard Mrs Bettison crying and her personal maid tried to go in and see her, but Mr Bettison wouldn't let her in the room and sent her away.'

Alice sat down again and this time she remained seated. 'Edith says John Bettison should be locked away before he kills someone. She says the someone's most likely to be his poor wife.'

'I think you're right, Alice. Thank you for telling me about it.' Toby was concerned at what he had been told, but not too certain what he should, or could, do about it.

'Something ought to be done about him, Mr Lovell.'

'You're quite right, Alice. Is Nipper still saddled?'

'Yes. I left him outside the kitchen door and came straight here after I'd put the provisions in the kitchen. What are you going to do?'

'I'll go up to the manor and try to speak to Mrs Bettison.'

Alice looked scared. 'Do you think that's a good idea?'

'How else can I help Caroline Bettison?'

'I don't know, but be careful. Mr Bettison is a very dangerous man. My cousin Edith said so.'

'I'm sure your cousin Edith is right. But as you say, something needs to be done about him.'

When Toby turned in to the grounds of Porthluney Manor a gardener nudged his assistant. Both men stopped to watch him as he made his way to the house. Parish priests were rare visitors to the Porthluney manor house.

Toby rode up to the front door. He had been seen approaching the house and the news had gone ahead of him. He looped the reins of Nipper around the hitching-rail at the edge of the drive.

The front door of the house stood open and before he reached it, Ada Hambly, the Porthluney housekeeper, put in an appearance.

Toby remembered her from his first visit here as a stern, forbidding woman in complete command of herself and of those about her. Today she seemed flustered and more than a little frightened.

'I think you should go, Curate. This is not a good day to come visiting Porthluney Manor.'

'I'm here to see Mrs Bettison, Mrs Hambly. I've heard you have had some trouble here?'

'It's nothing you can help with. I fear Mrs Bettison has lost the baby she was carrying. I have sent for the doctor. It would not help her were there to be a disturbance in the house. Please go.'

Mrs Hambly's plea came too late. There was a sound in the hall behind her. A moment later John Bettison appeared, demanding to know who had tethered an ass outside his house.

He was very drunk. When he saw Toby, he roared, 'What are you doing here, Curate? I'll have no priests coming cadging at my house. Go round to the kitchen. They might be able to find a few scraps for you.'

'I've come here to speak to Mrs Bettison,' said Toby, swallowing his anger.

'She's not receiving visitors – especially not *you*. It's bad enough having my wife defy my wishes by going to church. I'm not having priests coming whining to the house.'

'I believe it's Mrs Bettison's house too.'

'Oh do you? I'll have you know there have been Bettisons living in this house for more than three hundred years. This is *my* house. A Bettison house. Damned impertinence! *Damned* parsons . . . Where's that butler of mine? I'll have you thrown out, Lovell. No, I'll do it *myself* . . .'

John Bettison went back inside the house, walking none too steadily.

'Please go,' pleaded the housekeeper.

'I came here to see Mrs Bettison. I heard there was a fierce argument in the house. Now you say she has lost her baby. Was it his fault?'

'You can only make matters worse, Curate Lovell, believe me . . .'

Her voice faltered. Looking beyond Mrs Hambly, Toby saw John Bettison return to the hall and the curate's expression registered his alarm.

In his hands the landowner carried a double-barrelled flintlock sporting gun.

Standing in the hall, Bettison put the gun to his shoulder and fired a shot over Toby's head. Pieces of wood splintered from the doorframe and fell to the ground about him.

The sound of the shot terrifed Nipper. The reins had not been secured to the hitching-rail and the donkey pulled them free and took off along the drive at a speed he had never attained with Toby in the saddle.

John Bettison roared with laughter at his success. 'That's one of them gone. Either you follow at the same speed, Curate, or you'll find yourself so weighed down by lead shot you'll need to be carried off.'

Bettison pointed the gun at Toby's midriff and Mrs Hambly moved to stand between Toby and the gun. At the same time, she spoke over her shoulder in a strained voice. 'Please go, Curate Lovell. I'll make certain Mrs Bettison is taken care of.'

Toby knew that if he stayed John Bettison would either have to shoot him or be obliged to back down. The landowner was far too drunk to make a rational decision.

'Thank you, Mrs Hambly. Please tell Mrs Bettison I called. If there is anything I can do . . .'

Bettison shouted for Mrs Hambly to get out of the way or be knocked aside and Toby left hurriedly, though very deeply concerned.

He caught Nipper and rode home deep in thought. He decided he should go to Sampford Courtenay, the home of the Killigrews, to speak to Caroline's father, dismissing the uncomfortable thought that this constituted interference in something that was really none of his business.

He was deeply concerned for Caroline Bettison, believing her to be in great danger from her violent and unpredictable husband.

Chapter 72

Toby decided the quickest way to reach Sampford Courtenay was by horse. The road which carried coaches between Cornwall and London ran close to the village, but he could probably travel more quickly on horseback and it would be more convenient.

He had been toying for some time with the idea of buying a horse for riding. He would keep Nipper for work around the parish, perhaps pulling a small cart that was kept in one of the outhouses. Alice had already experimented with the donkey in the shafts and felt it would work very well.

The problem was, he wanted the horse as a matter of urgency and knew of no horse dealers in the parish. He decided to ask the help of the Vicar of Veryan.

Jeremiah Trist was a riding man and had already suggested that Toby adopt this form of transport, while Sally had also said her father had an eye for a good horse.

It was late in the day by the time Toby reached Veryan vicarage on foot. He found Sir Charles Vivian there and the baronet was present when Toby asked where he might purchase a horse very quickly.

'Is there any particular reason for urgency?' asked the baronet.

'Yes.'

Toby told Sir Charles, Reverend Trist and Sally what had happened that afternoon during his visit to Porthluney Manor. He added that he intended riding to Devon to speak to Caroline's father at his home in Sampford Courtenay, close to Devon's Dartmoor.

'I think *I* might be able to let you have a splendid horse,' said Sir Charles. 'It's the one I rode here. I bred it myself and it is from a first-class blood line. Come out to the stable and see her for yourself.'

On the way to the stable, Sir Charles asked a great many questions about John Bettison and the situation at Porthluney Manor.

'What do you think her father will do when you tell him of what's happened?'

Sir Charles asked the question as he swung open the stable door and both men entered to look at the horse.

'I think – I *hope* – he'll come to Porthluney and take Caroline home. She has threatened to leave Bettison before. I believe she must do it now. If she stays I am fearful for her safety and well-being. She was hoping the baby she was expecting might make John Bettison change his ways. It should have done had he been a normal man. It was a wonderful opportunity to make a new start, but I really don't think anything at all will make him change his ways now.'

'The man is mentally unstable!' declared Sir Charles. 'No normal man would shoot at visitors, no matter how unwelcome they might be!'

'I agree,' said Toby. 'One thing is quite certain. If Caroline's father withdraws his support from Porthluney Manor, Bettison will go under. He'll probably need to sell the manor and his lands.'

'From what I've been hearing of his behaviour, that will come as a great relief to his tenants – and to the Church. Now, here's my mare, what do you think of her? You'll not find a finer one in this part of Cornwall, I promise you that. What's more, if you like her she's yours right away. Reverend Trist will have me taken home in his carriage.'

Toby took to the horse immediately. She was an attractive light chestnut and her temperament seemed to be all that Nipper's was not. He bought her on the spot and Sir Charles threw in the saddle and tack as a present.

It was a good deal and Toby was well pleased with his bargain. But as he was about to ride away, Sally sounded a note of warning about John Bettison. 'Be very careful, Toby. Charles believes him to be unbalanced, and so do I. The next time you meet there might not be a housekeeper around to stand between you and John Bettison's gun.'

Toby set off for Sampford Courtenay early the next morning, but it was not a good time to be on the road. A summer storm was rolling in off the sea, accompanied by thunder and lightning. As Toby rode inland from Porthluney the horse was constantly pricking its ears, worried by the thunder and becoming increasingly edgy.

Toby's route took him across Bodmin Moor, at the heart of Cornwall. It was here, amidst the rock-strewn tors, that he was overtaken by the storm which quickly enveloped the high moor.

It had not yet begun to rain but the lightning was frighteningly close and Toby was relieved when he reached the remote Jamaica Inn at Bolventor. Here he put his newly acquired horse in the stable for safe-keeping while he went in for a meal.

As he ate, there was the sound of a horn, heralding the arrival of the mail coach that linked London with Falmouth.

The coach bumped and swayed over the cobblestones of the inn yard until it came to a halt outside the door. The steaming horses were led away and fresh horses brought out to be placed in the traces.

By now the skies all around the inn were black and threatening and it seemed to Toby the world was waiting for something to happen.

It was not long in coming. There was a sudden sizzling noise, as though water had been poured in a giant cauldron of boiling fat, and the dining-room was illuminated by a dazzling light. The flash of lightning was followed immediately by a deafening bang which rocked the inn and hurt the eardrums of all those inside.

At first, Toby thought the lightning had struck the inn, but a trembling serving-girl, hardly able to control the terror she felt, said, 'It's the smithy, sir. It's been struck by lightning!'

Toby rushed to the window with other guests. Across the road from the Jamaica Inn was a blacksmith's shop. It was a lean-to, attached to a thatched cottage.

In fact, it was the cottage which had been struck. There was a gaping hole in the thatched roof, from which smoke rose in ever-increasing volume.

As Toby watched, fingers of flame licked up through the smoke.

'Is anyone in the house?' he asked

'Yes, sir,' said another of the inn's servants. 'Gladys Hooper and her two young children are there. She's expecting another any day now . . .'

Before she finished speaking, Toby was running from the inn, followed by guests and servants.

As he ran across the road, he could hear the screams of terrified young children inside the burning house.

When he pushed open the front door there was smoke billowing everywhere.

The screams came from a downstairs room. Toby pushed open the door and found himself in what was obviously a kitchen. Seated on the floor was a baby, perhaps a year old, screaming in a lusty voice.

Nearby a girl, perhaps a year older, was also crying, but in a dazed, bewildered manner.

Toby could also hear the crackle of flames coming from a room upstairs.

'Get the children out . . .'

Toby scooped up the baby and handed it to one of the inn servants. At the same time a passenger from the mail coach picked up the older girl and passed her to another servant from the Jamaica Inn.

'Organise buckets of water . . . I'll go and search the rooms upstairs.'

Toby ran from the kitchen, pushing past a couple of inn servants who appeared too dazed to know what they were doing. He made for the stairs which led to the bedrooms.

Someone had gone up ahead of him. A slightly built man appeared from the smoke in front of Toby, cuffing away tears, induced by the smoke.

'There's a woman up here. She's unconscious. I need help.'

Another man had followed Toby and the slightly built man led them to a bedroom. A woman lay on the floor.

She was heavily pregnant and Toby knew they had found the blacksmith's wife.

There was no ceiling to the upstairs rooms, only the thatch above them – and it was burning fiercely.

The man who had first found the woman gripped her beneath the armpits and tried unsuccessfully to drag her towards the stairs. The third man took over from him. With Toby holding her legs, they half-dragged, half-carried her to the top of the stairs.

Along the way they needed to be constantly brushing away tufts of burning thatch, dropping on them from the roof.

At the top of the stairs they were joined by other men and the woman was carried from the house. Meanwhile, his eyes streaming, Toby returned to where he had seen a closed bedroom door. He opened it cautiously and closed it again hurriedly when flames roared out through the opening.

Running back down the stairs, he shouted, 'Does anyone know the whereabouts of the blacksmith?'

He needed to repeat the question before someone replied, 'He went to Launceston this morning. There's no one else in the house.'

It was a great relief to him to know there had been no one in the room he had been unable to enter. Now they needed to get as much water as possible to the house in order to try to put out the fire.

Everyone from the hotel, the coach and the surrounding houses joined in to form a chain, conveying water from the well at the Jamaica Inn to the burning house. Even so, they were fighting a losing battle until there was another flash of lightning and a frightening clap of thunder.

Fortunately, on this occasion the target was a tree some distance from the inn but, as though the latest lightning strike was a signal, it began to rain – and it was a veritable cloudburst. Water poured across the ground and roads and paths became rivers and streams.

The flames rising from the thatch of the blacksmith's house flickered in momentary defiance then died away altogether.

Beams and woodwork inside the cottage were still burning, but by using a variety of pieces of wood and pitchforks, the firefighters stripped the thatch from the roof allowing the rain to pour inside.

It was a drastic but effective method of firefighting. Within half-an-hour, the last of the flames had been extinguished.

The house had been severely damaged, but most of the furniture had been saved and the villagers would set to and have the roof repaired within a week.

Everyone agreed that it was a miracle no lives had been lost in either the lightning strike or the ensuing fire and the landlord of the Jamaica Inn announced that drinks would be provided free to all the firefighters to celebrate the rescue of the blacksmith's family.

Chapter 73

Toby returned to the Jamaica Inn smoke-begrimed and bedraggled and inquired after the blacksmith's wife.

'She came round about five minutes ago,' replied the landlord. 'I think it was the sheer terror of the lightning strike that caused her to faint. She'll be as right as ninepence now, although I don't know what she's going to do when she sees the mess her house is in.'

'She's got more to worry about than her house right now.' The landlord's wife had hurried into the room and heard her husband's words. 'She's gone into labour! This baby's going to arrive a sight faster than her other two did – and I should know, I helped with both of them.'

Speaking to her husband, she said, 'I'm going to need Hettie from the kitchen to help me. She's a good sensible girl.'

'Take her,' said her husband, expansively. With a resigned gesture towards Toby, he said, 'I've already given up any pretence of normality today. Someone's just struggled in, more dead than alive from the beating he's taken from the rain. He says the clapper bridge between here and Temple has been damaged by debris, brought downstream by the rainstorm. The coach is stuck here until the bridge can be repaired!'

The landlord had a drink in his hand. Putting it down suddenly, he said, 'But what am I thinking of, sir? Let me find some dry clothes for you while I have those you're wearing cleaned and dried. I promise you it will take no more than a couple of hours.'

'I have a change of clothes in my bags. I left them in the stable with my horse. But I will be grateful if you could arrange a room in which I might change. I would also be obliged if these I'm wearing now might be dried and pressed as quickly as possible. I'm in a great hurry to be on my way.'

'They'll be ready for you almost before you know they're off, Parson Lovell. In the meantime, I'll have another meal prepared for you, seeing as you never finished the last one. You may take it where you wish, sir. In the dining-room, or in the room where you change.'

'Thank you, I'll take it down here, with the others. You'll be kept busy enough today, without having to cater especially for the needs of one.'

When Toby returned to the busy room where the guests were being given refreshments, there was a great babble of sound. The events of the day had been exciting for all.

A tall, grey-haired man who had been chatting to the landlord came across the room to greet Toby immediately.

'Curate Lovell, am I right in thinking you are from Porthluney?'

'That's right, sir. Have we met before?'

'No, and the fault is entirely mine. I am Piers Fortescue, patron of the parishes of Porthluney, St Stephen and St Denis. I approved your appointment as I was going away.'

'You've heard of Reverend Kempe's death?'

'Yes. It was a very sad business. He's a great loss to the Church in Cornwall.'

'I'm glad I have finally met you, sir. Perhaps you'll be able to tell me what is going to happen in Porthluney? Whether you have already chosen Reverend Kempe's successor? It has a great bearing on my own future.'

'I am afraid that what I have to say is likely to make your future more uncertain than ever. For some years now I've been toying with the idea of leaving England and going to live abroad. My brother has a home in the West Indies and I have invested a considerable amount of money in his business interests there. For a number of years he has been trying to persuade me to go out there and join him. I have finally made up my mind to go. I must admit that a recent offer for the patronage of

Porthluney and the small amount of land I own there has helped persuade me.'

Toby found it difficult to hide his dismay. 'May I ask who has made the offer, sir?'

If the living was to be split there was no way that a small parish of the size of Porthluney could support a rector *and* a curate.

'It's not John Bettison?'

'I fully understand your concern, Curate Lovell, but I very much doubt if the offer will have come from John Bettison. He does not have the money to purchase the patronage. Even if he had, I can assure you I would not sell to him. Actually, I know little more than I have told you. The offer has come through my solicitor. I am sorry that the news has been broken to you in such a fashion. It was my intention to call upon you when I returned to St Stephen. The events of today have precipitated matters somewhat.'

Toby felt as though the patron had dealt him a severe body blow. Nothing he could do now would help his own future. The patronage had probably been bought by someone who wanted to place a relative in the parish as rector. It was a common practice.

It *was* possible he would be an absentee rector who *might* just want to take on a curate to carry out the duties of parish priest, but it was unlikely.

It seemed that once more Toby's future had been thrown into uncertainty. It cast a gloom over his brief stay at the Jamaica Inn.

Toby was eventually obliged to spend the night at the remote moorland inn. His clothes took longer than had been anticipated to be cleaned and dried.

Piers Fortescue left shortly before nightfall, apologising once more for the upsetting news he had imparted to Toby. The bridge at Temple had been temporarily repaired and the Falmouth-bound coach went on its way with the driver determined to make up as much time as was possible.

Toby's gloomy mood was temporarily lifted when the

Bolventor blacksmith returned and went upstairs to see his son for the first time.

When he came down, the blacksmith found Toby and thanked him for his part in the rescue. Somewhat shyly, the big man asked Toby for his name. He was the only one of the rescuers remaining at the inn and the blacksmith stated his intention of naming his new son after him.

Toby declared it to be an honour but at the same time sympathised with the blacksmith over the loss of his home.

'It's all right, sir,' said the smith, philosophically. 'A house can be repaired. I'd find it a sight harder to find another wife like my Winnie. And she's given me a son too. One day he'll take over the smithy – thanks to you and the other gentlemen. No, sir, this day won't be remembered as the day my house was struck by lightning and burned down. It will be the happy day that a son was born to me and Winnie.'

Chapter 74

Toby arrived at the Sampford Courtenay home of Vernon Killigrew soon after eleven o'clock the next morning. He had no difficulty in locating the house. At the mere mention of Killigrew's name, the countryman from whom he was inquiring directions doffed his hat as a token of respect for the Devon landowner. It was a gesture Toby had not met with in Porthluney.

Upon reaching the house, Toby was told that the landowner was out, inspecting the home farm. A servant was detailed to escort him there.

Vernon Killigrew was with one of his herdsmen. They were examining a number of calves, housed in a large barn close to the farmhouse.

Toby was introducing himself to the polite but reserved landowner when he was hailed from the direction of the farmhouse. To his great surprise he saw Rupert hurrying towards him.

Shaking the Porthluney curate vigorously by the hand, Rupert said, 'It's a great pleasure to see you again, Toby, but what are you doing in Sampford Courtenay? It's a long way from Porthluney.'

Turning to his father, Rupert explained, 'This is the curate who saved my life when the *Arrow* was wrecked on the Cornish coast. We owe him far more than we can ever repay, Father. I am absolutely delighted to see him here.'

'I doubt if you'll be quite so pleased when I tell you the reason I'm here,' said Toby, gravely. 'I'm afraid Caroline has lost her baby. It's probably the fault of her husband. I realise that by coming here I am interfering in a private family matter, but I am very concerned for her.'

Rupert, suddenly serious, said, 'What did I tell you,

Father? You should never have allowed Caroline to marry the man. He's mentally unstable.'

Vernon Killigrew made no comment for a moment or two, then he said to Toby, 'Tell me what you know, Curate. *All* you know.'

Toby told the Devon landowner what he had been told by Alice, then he described his visit to Porthluney Manor and the reception he had received there.

'That settles it!' exclaimed Rupert. 'Caroline is not going to remain at Porthluney for another night. I'll return there with you, Toby, and bring her back to Sampford Courtenay right away.'

'We'll *both* go,' said his father, tight-lipped. 'I want to know exactly what has gone on at Porthluney Manor. If Caroline is seriously ill as the result of anything Bettison's done, he'll rue the day he crossed my path. He may think he has had problems before – he'll learn he has had an easy life until today. We'll leave right away, Rupert. Have the grooms make ready the fastest horses we own. If we need to bring Caroline back we'll use a Porthluney carriage. It was probably my money that bought it in the first place . . .'

At Porthluney Manor, Caroline was lying in bed, ill and deeply distressed at the loss of her child. Her condition did not prevent John Bettison from riding off for a liaison with Charlotte.

They met, as they had on many previous occasions, in the hideout constructed by the Revenue man who had been one of Charlotte's many lovers.

The stable hands at Porthluney were aware he was seeing a local girl, even though they did not know who it was. When his horse was left to find its own way back to the Porthluney stables, the servants would say knowingly that within a year there would be another of the master's bastards born in the parish.

On this occasion they were particularly incensed because of what had happened to Caroline Bettison. Yet they dared not allow their feelings to show when the landowner was around.

* * *

Inside the hideout, Bettison adjusted his clothing and prepared to leave. He was not well pleased. Making love to Charlotte today had been a less than exciting experience – and he had told her so.

'You'll need to do a lot better than that the next time we meet, girl. Otherwise you'll be looking for someone else to keep you happy.'

'I was uncomfortable today, that's all,' said Charlotte, sulkily. 'But I've no intention of looking for anyone else. Anyway, I wouldn't be able to keep them for long if I did.'

'Explain yourself,' said John Bettison, arrogantly. 'What exactly do you mean by that? I sincerely hope it is not what I think it might be.'

'I'm pregnant,' declared Charlotte, trying hard to keep the triumph from her voice. 'I'm expecting a baby.'

'I am fully aware of the meaning of the word "pregnant",' said John Bettison, angrily. 'Who is the father? Who else has been having you?'

'No one!' declared Charlotte, indignantly. '*You're* the father! I haven't been with anyone else.'

'Don't lie to me, girl. You were a Revenue man's whore when I first met you – and you're still a whore. You can find someone else to blame for your bastard. I'll not acknowledge it as mine.'

'But . . . it *is* yours. I *swear* it is.'

Charlotte came close to tears. She had not expected John Bettison to deny his paternity so vehemently. This was all going horribly wrong. She was aware she had chosen her moment badly. She should not have sprung the news on Bettison after an indifferent love-making session.

Yes, that had been her mistake. It was purely an error of judgement, but it could be rectified. 'Do you want to do it to me again – now? I'll be better this time, I promise you . . .'

'You've never been anything more than mediocre, girl. A baby in your belly's hardly likely to change *that*. Go off and offer yourself to one of the fishermen, or whoever else it is you've been with before. Tell *him* you're pregnant and need to find a husband before you're taken before a magistrate. Get him to marry you.'

As John Bettison ducked out of the shelter, Charlotte cried, 'I'm not lying to you. There's no one else . . .'

Bettison rounded on her angrily. 'What do you think you're doing? Stay here and hold your tongue until I'm well clear. You should know that by now.'

Choked with chagrin, Charlotte pleaded with him, 'Please . . . when am I going to see you again?'

'When you find someone else to accept the brat you're carrying as his own. When you do you can come to me while I'm out riding. Until then I want nothing more to do with you, do you understand? Now, stop that wretched snivelling and get back inside the hide before I lose my temper with you.'

Inside the hide, Charlotte crouched beside the low doorway sobbing with frustration and pique. There was also an element of genuine distress in her sobs. All her plans had collapsed about her ears – and she was still pregnant.

Far from being able to look forward to a life of reasonable comfort, she was in trouble. Very serious trouble. Local magistrates did not look kindly upon single girls who found themselves pregnant and could neither find a husband quickly, nor supply the court with the name of a man to take the responsibility for its upbringing from the parish.

It was without doubt the worst day of Charlotte's young life.

Chapter 75

Charlotte was not the only one to have a bad day. That evening, John Bettison was drinking in his study when a servant hurried in to tell him that Mr Killigrew had arrived at the house.

Before Bettison had time even to place his glass on the table beside his chair, Rupert entered the room.

'Rupert! From what the damned stupid servant told me, I thought it was your father!'

'We are both here,' said the young naval officer. 'Father has gone upstairs to see Caroline.'

'Oh! He might have had the courtesy to come and see me first, but she is his daughter, I suppose. He's bound to be concerned for her. It's a pity about the baby. A damned pity. But there will be other children. Lots of them. As many grandchildren as the old man wants.'

Even as he was talking, John Bettison was trying to muster his thoughts. It was not easy. He had been drinking for some hours. Nevertheless, he realised someone must have taken news of Caroline's condition to her father.

He thought it probably had something to do with Caroline herself. She must have passed a message via her personal maid. He should have thought of that and got rid of the girl.

He wondered what Vernon Killigrew had been told? It was ominous that he had not bothered to attempt to see him first, but had instead gone straight upstairs to see his daughter.

'I'll take you up to see Caroline. She'll be pleased to see you, I'm sure. It will cheer her up. The poor girl's feeling pretty low . . .'

'No, John. We'll wait here until Father has had time to

talk to her. We were given some very disturbing news about her. Father is most concerned. We both are.'

'So am I, dammit! I would have thought he'd know that and have the courtesy to speak to me first.'

John Bettison's sudden flare up was as much the result of fear as anything else. He was fully aware what would happen if his father-in-law removed all support from Porthluney. There was also the matter of a loan Bettison had received from Caroline's father many years before. He had not repaid it. The Devon landowner had never pressed him about it, but if their relations deteriorated . . .

His temper flared once more. 'This is *my* house! I'm damned if I'm going to hide myself away while my wife is questioned about tittle-tattle that's being bandied about by some troublemaker . . .'

'Calm down, John. If there's no truth in what we've heard you have nothing at all to worry about. Caroline will tell Father so. On the other hand, if she's lost the baby through any fault of yours, you have every reason to be concerned. Father feels you've already had far more chances than you deserve. After what I witnessed during my last visit here, I am inclined to agree with him.'

Uttering a coarse oath, John Bettison said, 'We'll see about this. I'll not be threatened in my own home and told how I should treat my wife. Out of my way!'

Instead of complying with the other man's demand, Rupert moved to place himself between Bettison and the door.

The mounting tension was broken by the arrival in the room of Vernon Killigrew. He looked pale and drawn. Rupert recognised his father's symptoms as those of controlled fury.

Ignoring the Porthluney landowner, Vernon Killigrew spoke to his son. 'Have the servants bring the carriage to the front door, Rupert. Caroline is being dressed by her maid. She's returning home with us.'

'You can't do this!' John Bettison protested angrily.

Caroline's father rounded on him furiously. 'I not only can, but *am*. I suggest you go and find a corner to sit in with your bottle for company, Bettison. If I'm forced to look at you for long enough, I'll likely take my crop to you and give you what you so richly deserve.'

'I don't know what lies you've been told,' blustered Bettison. 'Caroline's my wife and this is her home . . .'

'My daughter has never been a liar, Bettison. A fool, maybe, to have insisted upon marrying you in the first place, but I trust her word. As for this being her home . . . a home is somewhere where love is found. That's the sort of home Caroline knew before she met you and will know again – but not here.'

John Bettison tried to interrupt a couple of times while Caroline's father was talking, but he was ignored. Vernon Killigrew had no intention of listening to him.

'There's been enough talking, Bettison. Far too much. Rupert, the carriage, if you please. We're leaving right away.'

'You can't take a wife from her husband. The law . . .'

'Don't tell me about the law, or I might be inclined to invoke it on Caroline's behalf. I am taking my daughter from a drunkard and a bully. That's not my idea of a husband.'

Rupert was reluctant to leave his father with John Bettison, but Vernon Killigrew jerked his head in the direction of the door, saying, 'I'll be upstairs with Caroline. Come and find me when the carriage is ready.'

'She won't want to come with you,' said Bettison, in desperation. 'You can't force her to leave.'

'She can't wait to see the last of Porthluney – and you in particular. I suggest you begin packing your things too. When I return to Sampford Courtenay I shall instruct my solicitor to call in the loan I made to you some years ago.'

'You know very well I can't pay you right now. I'd need to sell everything I own!'

'As I said, I suggest you start packing your things. You're a fool, Bettison. You had everything any normal man could wish for. A good wife, a fine estate and a comfortable way of life. You've squandered it all with your gambling, drinking and womanising. Even so, you might have survived had you treated Caroline as a wife should be treated. The Lord knows I've bailed you out often enough in the past. It's over now. You've run your course. It's time to pay the price – and you can be quite certain I'll make it a high one.'

Turning from his son-in-law dismissively, Vernon Killigrew spoke to Rupert who had hurried back to the room after speaking to a servant about the coach.

'Once we're on our way you'll need to ride ahead and make arrangements at some inn for us to stay the night. We'll discuss the details once we're on our way. It will be dark before very long.'

'Why . . . why don't you stay here for the night? We can talk things over. I'd like to speak to Caroline.'

The effects of the alcohol John Bettison had consumed were rapidly disappearing and full realisation of his plight was sinking in.

'The time for talking is past, Bettison. It's time for retribution. Goodbye. I doubt very much whether we will meet again.'

Chapter 76

News that John Bettison's wife had left Porthluney and returned to her father's home reached every corner of the small parish in a matter of hours. There was a wide variety of reactions. Those who were aware of the situation at Porthluney Manor agreed it was in the best interests of Caroline. Many more were apprehensive for the future. They saw the action as the final nail in the coffin of the Porthluney landowner and were concerned about what was likely to happen to them.

Charlotte saw in it renewed hope for her own situation. She forlornly hoped that if the landowner was lonely, he might regret what he had said to her and renew their relationship.

She felt the need to discuss what was happening with someone who might sympathise with her predicament. When she saw Toby riding past her house from the direction of the rectory she decided to go to speak with Alice.

The younger girl was her closest friend. They had always been able to talk to each other about anything that was troubling either of them.

Charlotte had no intention of telling Alice *everything*, of course, but there was no one else to whom she could speak – and she urgently needed to talk to someone.

When Charlotte entered the kitchen of the rectory she was taken aback to see Billy sitting there. He was stronger now and he and Alice had been discussing the possibility of his returning home to Portloe.

Nevertheless, he was still pale and weak and Charlotte looked at him uncomfortably closely before saying, 'What are you doing here, Billy Kendall?'

'The same as you, I expect. I've come to see Alice.'

'You've no need to lie to me, Billy. You haven't been seen around Portloe since the night a Revenue man got killed – and look at the state of you! If I blew hard enough you'd fall over. The Revenue men knew they shot someone that night. It was you, wasn't it?'

'Don't talk rot,' said Alice, alarmed at Charlotte's acumen. 'Billy's not been feeling very well lately, that's all.'

'You're wise to want to keep it secret. The Revenue men have offered a reward of five hundred pounds for the capture of the one responsible for killing their man. There are posters everywhere. You must have seen them, Billy? Anyone who's been out and about can't have missed them. There's a couple on the road between Portloe and here – but you'd know that if you've just walked here, wouldn't you?'

Billy had not been told about the wanted posters and looked from Charlotte to Alice in dismay.

'That's an awful lot of money, Billy,' commented Charlotte. 'There's some I know as would murder for a lot less than that.'

'Or go to the Revenue men and have a friend hung for something he didn't do, no doubt,' retorted Alice. In truth, she was horrified that Charlotte should have walked in on them.

She did not believe her friend would actually report Billy to the Revenue men, but discretion was not one of Charlotte's strongest attributes. She had never been able to keep gossip to herself and was quite likely to pass on her suspicions and the news of Billy's whereabouts, regardless of who might overhear.

'That's right, there's them as is likely to think all sorts of things too, but I hope you're not suggesting I'd do anything like that?'

'All I'm saying is that you shouldn't go jumping to any conclusions, Charlotte. Billy's done nothing wrong. Saying anything different can only cause trouble. Serious trouble.'

'Well, *I* won't say anything, you know that. Anyway, two's company and three's a crowd. I'll leave you two together. Cheerio!'

When Charlotte had left the kitchen, Alice said to Billy, 'I want to have a quick word with Charlotte. I won't be more than a few minutes.'

Leaving Billy seated in the kitchen, Alice ran from the house after her friend.

'Charlotte! Wait a minute . . .'

When she caught up with her, Alice asked, 'Why did you come to the rectory? Is there something you wanted to see me about?'

'Not really,' Charlotte lied. 'I just called in to see how you were, that's all.'

'There's nothing wrong? I mean, after what you told me when you last called I've been worrying about you. Everything *is* all right?'

'Couldn't be better! Especially now Bettison's wife has left him. Who knows? Before very long I might be the lady of the manor. That's where I'm going now.'

Charlotte went on her way, leaving her friend looking after her uncertainly.

Alice still felt decidedly uneasy about Charlotte seeing Billy in the rectory kitchen in his present state. She expressed her concern when she returned to him.

'You don't really think she'd say anything to the Revenue men, do you? She's one of us.'

'Is she? I'm not certain any more, Billy. I've known Charlotte for a very long time. It's my opinion she'll find the thought of five hundred pounds too tempting. I wish Curate Lovell were here. He'd know what we ought to do.'

'We mustn't get him into any trouble. Perhaps I should go home . . .'

'No. If anyone came looking for you and didn't find you here, that would be the next place they'd go to.'

'You really do think Charlotte's going to say something, don't you? And you don't think she'll just let it slip without thinking.'

'Yes. Yes, I do.' After a moment's hesitation, Alice told Billy about Charlotte's affair with John Bettison and the fact that she was pregnant by him. 'She's got some stupid notion of going to the manor to live now that Mrs Bettison has left. It won't happen, but if she thinks it will help her, she'll tell him what she knows of you.'

Now Billy too was alarmed. 'I must leave here right away, Alice. I won't stand a chance if I'm taken by the Revenue men. It wouldn't matter to them that I've done nothing. They'll be able to see I've been wounded and will know I was there that night. As far as they're concerned that makes me guilty. They'll also take you – and Curate Lovell. You must warn him. I've got to leave this house right away. But where can I go?'

'I know! There's an old shooting hut in Brownberry Wood. You can go there.'

Billy looked doubtful. The wood must have been at least a mile from the rectory. 'I'm not sure I'm fit enough to walk there, Alice.'

'You won't have to. I'll take Curate Lovell's donkey together with some blankets and food. Come on, we'll do it right away. If we go out the back way, across the fields, there's no one will see us. But I'll need to be back here when he gets home, so I can tell him what's going on.'

Chapter 77

Charlotte hurried straight from the rectory to Porthluney Manor. When she arrived there she was forced to rest until she regained her breath. She was not yet used to the extra weight of the baby she was bearing. When she recovered, she headed for the front door.

After what seemed an age, it was opened by a footman. He was a young man she had known since childhood. Her surprise was equalled by his own.

'Hello, Charlotte, what are you doing here? Shouldn't you have come to the kitchen door?'

'No. I've come to see Mr Bettison. Tell him I'm here, please.'

The footman still hesitated. 'Is it something that can wait? He's not in the best of moods today. If it's not important he'll take it out on me as well as you.'

Charlotte realised John Bettison's mood did not bode well for a reconciliation between the landowner and herself, but she put her misgivings aside.

'It *is* important. Tell Mr Bettison that. It's *very* important.'

'All right, if you're quite sure. Wait out here, I won't be long.'

Aggrieved that she had not been invited to wait in the hallway, at least, Charlotte stood outside the front door of the manor and looked about her at the gardens. They were well-kept and extended almost to the beach of the cove. This was one of the most sheltered little bays along the whole of the Cornish coast.

She was here to inform John Bettison about Billy because he was a suspected smuggler, yet in times gone by this had been one of the favourite haunts of the smuggling fraternity who had always operated with the full knowledge and support of the Bettison family.

Charlotte waited for a long time before the young footman returned. He looked scared.

'Mr Bettison says you're to go away. He doesn't want to see you. What's more, he says if you come bothering him again he'll take you before a magistrate.'

After delivering this threat, the footman would have closed the door on her, but Charlotte stuck her foot inside and prevented the door from closing.

'He's *got* to see me. Tell him . . . tell him it's not what he thinks. I'm here to help him. It's something urgent. Something he'll want to know about.'

'I'm sorry, Charlotte. Mr Bettison's just given me my orders in no uncertain terms. I'm not going to disturb him again unless I know what it's all about. Then I'll decide whether or not it's something worth risking dismissal for.'

Charlotte was in a dilemma. She could not tell the footman why she was here. If she did, the news that she had betrayed Billy would be around Porthluney in no time. Her life would be in very real danger. Besides, it was more important to her in the long term to resume her relationship with Bettison. She doubted whether there would ever again be an opportunity like this.

'I've already told you, it's *very* important, but I can only tell it all to Mr Bettison.'

While the footman stood in the doorway, undecided, John Bettison appeared in the hall behind him.

When he saw Charlotte standing in the doorway, his face showed his fury and he shouted at the unhappy footman: 'I told you to get rid of the girl! Why am I surrounded by incompetent servants? I don't want to talk to her. Do you hear me, girl? I don't want to see you again.'

As he advanced towards the door, the footman hurriedly moved aside but Charlotte stood her ground.

'If you've come here to threaten me, girl . . .'

Bettison suddenly turned on the footman. 'You! Go away. Go to the servants' quarters. I'll deal with you later.'

As the frightened footman scuttled from the hallway,

John Bettison returned his attention to Charlotte. 'I've already said the brat you're expecting isn't mine. Now . . .'

'It's nothing to do with the baby,' said Charlotte, desperately. 'I know who killed the Revenue man, and where he is now.'

'You know? Who is he?'

His rage subsided and Charlotte said quickly, 'There's a big reward out for him. Five hundred pounds.'

'You'll get a share. Where is he?'

'It's not the money that's important to me, it's the baby – and it *is* yours.'

'Don't prevaricate, girl, we can talk about that some other time. Tell me about this wanted man.'

'You will see me again afterwards?'

'Yes. Yes. I'll show my gratitude, if that's what you want. Now, out with it, where is he?'

John Bettison was impatient. The five hundred pounds would give him some breathing space. Time to work out where the remainder of the money he owed might be found.

'It's Billy Kendall, from Portloe. He's the one who was shot by the Revenue man. He's at the rectory right now.'

John Bettison was startled. 'The rectory? Are you quite certain?'

'I saw him myself. I've just come from there. He was in the kitchen with Alice. She works for Curate Lovell.'

John Bettison remembered Alice, but chose not to dwell upon the memory. This was much better than he could ever have anticipated. Not only was there a large reward in the offing, but it gave him an opportunity to avenge the humiliation he had suffered on his last visit to the rectory. It would also remove the curate who had been a thorn in his flesh ever since he had taken over the parish from Reverend Kempe.

'Thank you, girl. I must go and do something about this right away.'

'But . . . I *will* see you again?'

'Of course.'

John Bettison had already dismissed Charlotte from his

plans, but he said, 'When this has been dealt with I'll meet you again at the coastguard's hideout.'

'I thought you might like me to come here sometimes. Now your wife is away I could stay here, if that's what you wanted?'

'Don't talk such arrant nonsense, girl. On your way. There are things to be done – and quickly.'

Charlotte walked from Porthluney Manor with a desperate feeling that her visit had not gone as well as she had planned.

She consoled herself with the knowledge that she would at least have a share of the Revenue Service reward. Besides, John Bettison had said he would resume their meetings at the coastguard's lookout.

She would ensure that on the next occasion they met there, her love-making with him would not lack enthusiasm. John Bettison *would* support her and the child – and despite his words, she had made up her mind that she would be installed in Porthluney Manor, too.

Chapter 78

Returning to the rectory from the wood where Billy had gone into hiding, Alice unsaddled Nipper and turned him loose in the paddock. Then she hurried to the house and removed every trace of occupancy from the recently vacated bedroom.

Downstairs, in the scullery, she put the bedclothes to soak in a large wooden washtub.

She returned to the kitchen in time to witness the arrival of a number of uniformed horsemen, mounted on heavily lathered horses. John Bettison was with them.

Although she was half-expecting them, the speed at which they had reached the rectory took Alice by surprise. It was no more than three hours since Charlotte had left. She must have gone straight to the manor house after seeing Billy.

Alice felt a great bitterness towards her long-time 'friend'. For the sake of the reward she had been ready to see Billy hanged and Alice and Curate Lovell thrown in prison. It was the most despicable thing she had ever done.

When the horsemen dismounted and knocked simultaneously at the front and kitchen doors, Nap ran to the kitchen door barking angrily.

Holding the dog by its collar with one hand, Alice opened the door to find John Bettison standing outside with a number of armed Revenue men.

'Where's William Kendall?' The question was hurled at Alice by the Porthluney landowner.

At the sound of his voice, Nap barked fiercely and tried to break free.

Taking a startled pace backwards, Bettison said, 'Keep that dog under control or I'll order him shot.'

Alice's anger at the treachery of her friend and the arrogance of Bettison overcame her fear of the landowner's power.

'He recognises you as the man who did this . . .' Alice pointed at the scar still plainly visible across Nap's haunches '. . . and who attacked me one night.'

The Revenue men looked at him questioningly, but John Bettison said, 'We've not come here to listen to any of your nonsense. We have reason to believe you are harbouring a wanted felon.'

'I'm not harbouring anyone,' protested Alice, spiritedly, although her heart was beating rapidly. 'Before you come in you'll need to ask permission from Curate Lovell. He's not in right now.'

'We'll not wait for any curate,' retorted the landowner. 'A dangerous criminal is at large. He's already killed one man going about his lawful duty.'

Turning to the Revenue man who appeared to be in charge of the party, John Bettison said, 'Search the house – and shoot that dog if he looks as though he's likely to attack anyone. He's a dangerous animal.'

The Revenue man was not as senior as the officer who had visited the rectory on a previous occasion. A little uncertain of himself, he seemed somewhat overawed by Bettison.

'Go on, what are you waiting for? Kendall is in this house somewhere. Find him.'

Eight Revenue men filed past Alice apologetically as she clung to the collar of the angrily barking dog. When the last of them had passed through the kitchen, Bettison followed after them. He glared at Alice and Nap, but he too gave them a wide berth.

When the men had gone, Alice took Nap outside and tied him to a tree in the garden. There was ample shade here and he was out of the way of the men in the house.

Alice was just telling Nap to settle down and behave himself when Toby turned into the rectory drive from the road. When he saw the horses of the Revenue men, he called to her.

'We seem to have a lot of visitors, Alice. Who are they?'

She hurried to him as he dismounted. 'It's Mr Bettison and some Revenue men. They're here searching for Billy.'

Startled, Toby looked at her in alarm.

'It's all right, he's not here.' Alice spoke quietly, so that her words would not carry to the men in the house. 'They'll find no trace of him either. I've seen to that.'

'Where is he?' Toby dropped his voice to match hers.

'I'll tell you when they've gone, but they won't find him.'

'How did they learn of his whereabouts?'

'It had to be from Charlotte. She called unexpectedly a few hours ago when he was sitting in the kitchen with me. She left in a hurry and I suspected something like this might happen.'

'Are you quite certain they are not going to find him, Alice? If they do . . .'

At that moment two of the Revenue men came from the house and headed for the stables.

Toby looked at Alice questioningly and she shook her head.

'Then let's go and find out what's happening in the rectory.' Toby secured his horse and led the way.

Bettison and the senior Revenue man were in animated conversation in the rectory kitchen when Toby entered. Ignoring the landowner, Toby spoke to the Revenue man. 'Do you mind telling me what you and your men are doing in the rectory?'

'We're searching for a wanted man, Reverend.'

'Who is this wanted man, and what is it he's supposed to have done?'

'We're searching for William Kendall. He shot and killed a Revenue officer – and don't bother to plead your innocence. We know he's here somewhere.'

The reply to Toby's question came from John Bettison.

'I know Billy Kendall,' said Toby, addressing his reply to the Revenue officer. 'He's a good hardworking young man. I doubt if he's ever handled a weapon, far less shot anyone.'

'You would say that,' said Bettison. 'I know differently, and it's no use you saying he hasn't been here. I have it on very good authority that he has.'

'I don't doubt that he's been here,' said Toby, calmly. 'Alice and I both know him and he's always welcome at the rectory. There's no reason at all why he shouldn't come visiting. I can't say the same for you, Mr Bettison. I seem to recall that on the last occasion you were here you assaulted Alice. I'd like an explanation of what you are doing in the rectory today.'

'Don't you start throwing such accusations around in front of witnesses, Curate, or I'll have you in court. I'm here with the Revenue officers, seeking a man who has committed a murder.'

'Any accusations I make can be substantiated, Mr Bettison. The archdeacon was a witness – or had you drunk too much to remember? As for Billy committing a murder . . . The idea is too preposterous for words. Besides, having Revenue officers carrying out what they consider to be their duty is one thing. Your presence in the rectory is another. You will leave, please . . . immediately!'

As the two men had been talking, other Revenue men had entered the kitchen in ones and twos.

'I won't be spoken to in such a manner, Lovell. You'll regret this . . .'

'I think we should all leave, sir,' said the senior Revenue man. 'There's nothing to be found here. I don't know where your information came from, Mr Bettison, but I would check it out thoroughly before you come to us in future. I'll put it in my report that the information was given to us with good intent, but we have wasted a great deal of time here today.'

'Damn you, don't treat me like a foolish child! I tell you, William Kendall is your man. If he's not here it's because someone has warned him. Go to his home. He lives at Portloe. See what he has to say.'

'I'll leave it to my superior officer to do that, sir. We've done what we came here for, I think we should leave now.'

Speaking to Toby, he said, 'I am sorry for any inconvenience we may have caused you, sir, my men and I were only carrying out our duty.'

'I appreciate that, but I hope that in future you'll bear

in mind that any information given to you by Mr Bettison about me will undoubtedly have malice at its root.'

'You've not heard the last of this, Curate. You're in this business up to your ears and you'll pay for it in the end.'

Even as he made the threat, the Porthluney landowner was thinking of the way in which the information about Billy Kendall had been given to him. He now believed it was a deliberate attempt on Charlotte's part to take revenge on him for the way he had treated her. The girl had made him look foolish in the eyes of the Revenue officers and Curate Lovell. She too would learn that it did not pay to play silly games with John Bettison.

Chapter 79

'Where *is* Billy?' Toby put the question to Alice as soon as John Bettison and the Revenue men had left the rectory.

'I took him to a hut in Brownberry Wood. We set off immediately after Charlotte left this morning. She saw how ill Billy looked and guessed what had been wrong with him. She left in such a hurry I felt certain she'd go straight to Porthluney Manor and tell Mr Bettison.'

'But why, Alice? Why should she betray Billy to Bettison of all people? I know there's a large reward for the capture of the man who shot the Revenue man, or for anyone involved in the incident, but Charlotte will get very little of it. Bettison will make certain the bulk of any reward goes *his* way.'

'Charlotte is pregnant. Bettison is the father. She's expecting him to keep both her and the baby. She'd also like him to put her in Mrs Bettison's place, up at the manor.'

'What a very foolish girl she is! Bettison of all people. He'll never do that! As for keeping her . . . I doubt he has enough money to keep himself for much more than another week or two. Does her mother know about this?'

'So far as I know, she's told no one except me.'

'I'm going to have to speak to the girl, Alice – but her problems are of her own making, Billy's are not. What are we going to do with him? He can't stay in a hut in the woods for very long, but now Charlotte has given his name to Bettison and the Revenue men he won't be able to show his face anywhere in Cornwall. The problem is to find somewhere he can go that will be safe.'

'I was hoping you would have some idea,' said Alice, unhappily. 'He's still not fit. I gave him blankets and enough food to last him for a couple of days, but I'm worried about his being there on his own for too long.'

Toby thought about the problem for some minutes before saying, 'You've said that Billy and you are to be married, Alice. When did you plan it to be?'

'We haven't talked about dates or anything,' she said. 'Only that we want to get married.'

'Are your parents aware of this?'

She nodded. 'They said they've always known we would marry one day.'

'That makes things easier. As I see it, the only way Billy can avoid arrest is to go away from Cornwall. Right away. He should leave England and go to another land. If it can be arranged, are you willing to go with him and marry him when you reach your destination?'

Alice looked at him wide-eyed. 'You mean . . . Never come back to Cornwall?'

'You'd certainly need to stay away for some years.'

'But . . . where could we go? We know nobody outside Cornwall!'

Toby was reminded that Alice had spent all her life in Porthluney. It was a small community where she knew everyone, and they knew her. She could not imagine a life among strangers in a new country.

He said sympathetically, 'You and Billy would soon get to know people, Alice. Young people like yourselves, who'd be carving out a new life for themselves. I'm not saying it will be easy, but so much depends upon how much you and Billy love each other. If the bond is strong enough you'll succeed. If you have any doubts at all you mustn't even consider it. We will think of something else. But Billy is not going to be safe anywhere in England.'

'Where do you think we could go?'

It was an empty question. Any place outside Porthluney would be as foreign to Alice as any other.

'I really don't know at the moment. I'll need to discuss it with some friends of mine. Canada, perhaps, or America – although they're not particularly friendly towards us at the moment. People are beginning to settle in New South

Wales too, but that's a penal colony and conditions are harsh there. Don't worry, we'll find somewhere.'

'What would Billy and I do there? How would we earn a living?'

'I'll give you money before you go. Enough for him to buy a boat to enable him to fish. That would be something familiar for him.'

'I think we have enough for that anyway. I've got a little money put by. Billy has too. Eli left him some. All the same . . . I'll need to talk about it to Billy.'

'Of course, but we have very little time. The Revenue men will go to Portloe and search his father's house. When they don't find Billy there they'll extend their search. They know he's around here somewhere.'

'I'll go and see him tonight. Then I'll return home and have a talk with my ma and pa.'

Toby set off for Falmouth early the next morning. He left a note for Alice telling her he would return that afternoon. She was to wait for him at the rectory.

The horse made the journey much faster than Nipper and by mid-morning Toby had reached the busy port. There were many ships anchored in the Roads and the harbour was a veritable forest of masts.

Toby had hoped he might find *Potomac* here, but realised he had been too optimistic. He made his way to the shipping office where Sir Charles Vivian was working and asked about his brother and the privateer.

'I expect them to return to Falmouth in another week or two,' said the baronet. 'I've just received word that they've taken a prize into Sheerness. Matthew must be trying his luck in the Eastern Channel. Was there some special reason for wanting to speak to him?'

'Yes, there's a little matter I had hoped he might be able to help me with. However, the more I think about it, the more I realise it would be asking too much of him.'

'Would you care to tell *me* what it is? I might be able to assist.'

Toby hesitated. He did not know Sir Charles as well as he did Matthew. 'To be honest, I'm not at all certain it's something you would want to know about. You might feel obliged to repeat what I say to the Revenue Service.'

Sir Charles chuckled. 'Toby, I am a shipowner, remember? Try me.'

'It's a young parishioner of mine. He's in trouble with the Revenue men and I'd like to see him safely out of the country. They are convinced he killed one of their men during a fight between smugglers and the Revenue men. I am equally certain he did not. Neither he nor any of those with him carried guns. He wouldn't even know how to use one. The only men carrying firearms that night were the Revenue men themselves.'

'Then why doesn't he give himself up and tell his story? Surely, if he's innocent he has nothing to worry about?'

'That's what I thought at first, then I realised I was being naive. If nobody but the Revenue men were carrying guns, it means their man was killed by one of his colleagues. They are hardly likely to admit to such a tragic error. My parishioner is an unsophisticated and basically honest young man. When questioned he would undoubtedly admit to smuggling. He was also wounded in the encounter. In the circumstances, I don't doubt that will be enough to hang him.'

'What were you hoping Matthew might do – take him on as crew?'

'No, there's a young woman involved. She's been keeping house for me. They want to get married. I'd like to see them make a fresh start in a new country. They are a decent, hardworking young couple. If they were able to leave the country I would ensure they had sufficient money to make something of themselves.'

'You're a romantic, Toby. Are you quite certain this young man had nothing to do with the death of the Revenue man?'

'I would stake my life on it. You might just remember him. He brought me across to Falmouth on one of my visits.'

'Hm! Well, one of my ships is due to sail to Nova Scotia within a few days. I have an agent there who should be able to help them to settle in . . .'

'That would be absolutely marvellous, if you're willing to help him? I swear that if I thought for a moment he was guilty I would never have asked you to do such a thing . . .'

'Tell them to be ready to come to Falmouth at a few hours' notice. They had better come by sea. Around dawn would be the best time. There will be no Customs or Revenue men awake then.'

'Thank you, Sir Charles. Thank you very much indeed. I doubt if anyone in the Revenue Service would agree, but you really are serving the best interests of justice.'

'I hope neither of us will need to use that in our defence in a court of law. Now, I have a couple of pieces of news for *you*. I trust both will please you. First of all, I have received a reply to the letter I sent to the Bailiff of Guernsey.'

'Does he have any news of Bethany?' Toby asked, eagerly. Sir Charles had hinted at good news.

'Possibly. He seems to think she may be nursemaid to the young children of a Major Cecil. He is garrison commander on the Island of Alderney. The Bailiff is fairly certain of his facts. The girl came to his attention by showing great courage and commonsense when Alderney was raided by the French during the absence of Major Cecil and his troops. It appears that by her actions she saved the lives and properties of many of the islanders.'

'She wasn't hurt?'

Sir Charles shook his head. 'I feel sure the Bailiff would have said. Apparently, Major Cecil calls on the Guernsey military commander every couple of weeks. The Bailiff is going to speak to him on his next visit and make certain of his facts.'

Toby thought of all the scraps of information that had come his way about Bethany. They all added up. Alderney was close enough to Guernsey for information to be received of events on the larger island. At the same time, it was remote enough for a woman to escape the attention of those on the neighbouring island.

He wondered how soon he might make his way to the small island. There were so many things requiring his attention at Porthluney right now, chief among them being the need to arrange for Billy's flight to safety.

'I am very, very grateful to you, Sir Charles. I think you're probably right. If Bethany is living on Alderney so many things that have happened fall into place. I'll have to think of a way to get there . . .'

'My advice to you is to wait until the Bailiff has spoken to this Major Cecil. Everything points to his nursemaid being the young woman you're seeking, but until we're certain you can't go running off on what might turn out to be a fool's errand.'

'You're right. Besides, I'm likely to have more time on my hands soon, when a new rector is appointed to Porthluney.'

'I wouldn't count on that, Toby.' Sir Charles gave him a knowing smile. 'I told you I had *two* pieces of news for you. Don't you want to hear the second?'

'I'm sorry, I was so excited at the thought that we might have located Bethany at last, everything else went out of my head.'

Toby waited politely, believing that nothing Sir Charles could say to him now could be as exciting as the information he had just been given.

Sir Charles thought otherwise. 'I am hoping that what I have to tell you now will prove almost as important to your future as Bethany, Toby. I have purchased the patronage of Porthluney from Piers Fortescue of St Stephen. The selection of a new rector now rests in my hands. I have written to Bishop Fisher to say *you* are the man I want.'

Chapter 80

Toby rode away from Falmouth with his thoughts in turmoil. His curacy at Porthluney had so far been a turbulent one. Now, as the result of his visit to Sir Charles Vivian, it seemed everything was likely to take a turn for the better. It was unlikely that the bishop or Archdeacon Scantlebury would object to his being appointed rector of the parish. Once installed, he would have security of tenure for the remainder of his life, if he so wished.

There was still the problem of John Bettison, of course, but Sir Charles seemed to agree with Toby's own assessment of the situation. It was only a matter of time before the occupier of Porthluney Manor was forced to sell up and move away.

If only he could find Bethany now and resolve their misunderstanding it would mean he had all in life he could possibly wish for – and this too seemed to be resolving itself.

But for the moment there were other, more immediate problems to be faced. As he rode along the driveway to the rectory, Alice came to the door, her anxiety showing.

'It's all right, Alice, I have come to an arrangement for you and Billy to be taken to a fishing community in Canada. There will be someone there to help you and to arrange for you to be married.'

For a few minutes delight and fear fought for possession of Alice. Dismounting from his horse, Toby took her hand and squeezed it reassuringly. 'Everything will be well for you both, Alice, I promise you. It's a wonderful opportunity for two young people.'

'When are we to go?' she asked, tremulously.

'It will be sometime in the course of the next few days.

We will only get a few hours' notice, I am afraid, so all will need to be ready.'

Alice seemed to be having difficulty finding her breath. 'It gives me a funny feeling in my stomach just thinking about it. I . . . I think I'm a little frightened.'

'Of course you are. But if you feel you're not ready to go just yet it can always be arranged for Billy to go alone. You could follow when he's settled in there.'

Alice thought about it for only a few moments then shook her head. 'It's taken me a long time to make up my mind exactly what it is I want. Now I know it's Billy, I don't want to risk losing him. Besides, he still needs someone to take care of him. I wish he didn't *have* to go, but there's nothing can be done about that now. We'll go together.'

'I honestly believe you're making a wise decision, Alice. Billy is a good man. He won't let you down and it will be the beginning of a great adventure for both of you in a wonderful new country.'

Releasing her hand, he said, 'We must bring Billy back to the rectory tonight. They've already searched the house once, they won't do it again.'

'I'll go to fetch him and tell him what's happening once I've made a meal for you.'

Alice turned away before suddenly putting a hand to her head and facing him once more. 'I'm sorry, in all the excitement at your news I forgot to tell you – you've had a visitor while you were away. A Mrs Cecil.'

'The wife of Major Cecil – from Alderney? Where is she now?' Toby could hardly contain his excitement. 'Was Bethany with her?'

Alice shook her head. 'I don't know anything about her husband, or about Bethany. She came on her own, riding in a very smart light carriage that she said belonged to a friend. I told her you wouldn't be back until very late, but she stayed for a cup of tea. I gave it to her in the lounge and she made me stay there with her and answer a whole lot of questions.'

'What sort of questions?'

'About you mostly. She also wanted to know whether I was the girl who was in the house when Bethany came to call, after being made to leave her Church. I told her it was Charlotte who was working here at that time. Then she wanted to know all about her. Who is this Mrs Cecil?'

'She's the wife of the army officer who commands the garrison on the Isle of Alderney. I heard only today that Bethany might be nursemaid to their children. I think this confirms it. Where is she now? Did she leave an address where I can find her?'

'No, but she said she would return tomorrow.'

'This is absolutely wonderful news, Alice, but I wonder why she came here asking you so many questions?'

'Would Bethany have asked her to call?'

'Perhaps, but if that's the case why should she be asking so many questions about the day Bethany called here? Surely she would have the answers for herself?'

Toby felt he was moving closer to an answer to the question of why Bethany had left so suddenly and unexpectedly. He wondered what it could be?

Alice said suddenly, 'I don't know whether it has anything to do with her questions, but that day when Bethany called here, Mr Bettison was in the house.'

Toby looked at her sharply. 'How do you know that? Did they meet?'

'I can't say whether or not they actually met, but Charlotte told me of the places where she and Mr Bettison used to see each other. She said she thought they had been found out when Bethany called while they were in one of the bedrooms upstairs. I know she answered the door to Bethany. Afterwards, she was worried Bethany would tell you about it. I believe that's the real reason Charlotte stopped working here for you.'

Toby was puzzled. Why, if Bethany had found out about Charlotte and John Bettison, should it have caused her to leave Cornwall in such haste?

It was a question to which he had no answer at the moment. He hoped Mrs Cecil might be able to throw some light on the matter.

Billy returned to the rectory later that night, brought back by Alice. He seemed none the worse for his brief sojourn among the birds and animals of Brownberry Wood and was very excited about leaving Cornwall for Canada. His only regret was that he and Alice could not be married before they went. He also told Toby he would like to see his father before leaving the country.

'It's going to be very sad leaving him behind,' he said, 'but I'll pass the net-making business on to him. He'll find it a lot easier than going out fishing for a living. He's not getting any younger.'

'Do you want me to go and tell him to come here to speak to you?'

'No. I'll go there to see him, tomorrow night. Alice can come with me. The Revenue men have already searched Portloe, as they have here. I'll be safe enough.'

'Safe you may be, but are you up to walking such a distance yet?'

'Yes,' said Billy, confidently. 'I've been walking about in the woods while I was there. I'm a lot fitter than I realised. By the time Alice and I reach Canada, I'll be ready to take on anything that needs to be done.'

'Well, if you're quite certain, I think we should have a celebratory drink. Then I suggest Alice goes home and asks her parents to come here, to the rectory. We all need to have a talk about the future.'

It was an emotional meeting. Afterwards, Toby felt he had been justified in calling Alice's parents to the rectory and not leaving it to her to go home and tell them what was happening.

Her mother dissolved in a fit of weeping. With some justification, she declared that her daughter had little experience of life. Marriage in itself would be a big step for her. Marriage *and* emigration to a country of which she had hardly heard was like stepping off a cliff in the darkness.

'I'll look after her, Mrs Rowe,' promised Billy. 'She'll not want for anything while I'm capable of working for her.'

'That's not saying very much at the moment, Billy Kendall. You look as though you need someone to take care of *you*.'

'That's not fair, Ma.' In spite of her own reservations,

Alice sprang to Billy's defence. 'Billy's much better than he was. He was close to death. That was when I realised I wanted to be with him more than I want anything else in the world. You should know all about that. How old were you when you realised you wanted to marry Pa?'

'Things were different then,' argued her mother, albeit without conviction.

'No, they weren't,' said Alice. 'And I'm only doing what you would have done had you been in the same situation.'

'Don't let's have a family argument at this stage,' said Toby. 'For what it's worth, I think it's a wonderful opportunity for Alice – and it's the only course open to Billy.'

'Isn't it possible for you to marry them before they set off?' asked Alice's father.

'Both Billy and Alice have already said that is what they would like,' said Toby. 'Unfortunately, there are very definite Church laws on the subject of banns. It just isn't possible. However, if you write a letter confirming that Alice has your permission to marry, I will endorse it and ensure they are married within a month of arriving in Canada.'

Eventually, Alice's parents agreed to this course of action. When they left the rectory they were reconciled to their daughter's leaving Cornwall for far-off Canada.

Before Alice returned home, Toby asked her if she would come to the rectory the next day, to be present when Mrs Cecil came to visit. He was aware Mrs Rowe wanted her daughter to spend as much time as possible with her before setting sail for Canada, but Toby felt Alice knew far more than he did about what had gone on in the rectory on the day Bethany had called.

He hoped that between them they might put everything right between Bethany and himself.

Chapter 81

Alice arrived at the rectory the following morning shortly before noon. She brought with her a pie cooked by her mother. It would only need to be heated.

She also brought news from Porthluney Manor. John Bettison had dismissed almost all the servants who worked at the house. In addition, he had sent most of his horses to market, together with the livestock from Home Farm. It was evident the landowner was now desperately short of money.

The tenants and remaining employees of John Bettison were fearful of what he would do next. Few of them had any respect for or loyalty to him, but their whole livelihood depended upon the occupant of Porthluney Manor. If Bettison became bankrupt there would be no money coming into their houses.

Toby sympathised with the tenants. However, today other matters needed to be dealt with before he could tackle the problems facing his parishioners.

He was so nervous about the imminent visit of Mrs Cecil he was unable to do justice to the pie which he shared with Billy. The excitement of what the future held for him and Alice affected Billy's appetite too. As a result, much of the pie was put aside for their supper.

Jennifer Cecil arrived early in the afternoon and Toby liked her immediately. In answer to his first question, she confirmed that Bethany was in her employment. However, he was disappointed to learn Bethany had not asked her to visit him. She was not aware that Jennifer Cecil was visiting Cornwall.

Jennifer explained she had come to England because she had been informed her mother was seriously ill. When she reached her mother's home, it was apparent the illness was not as serious as had been feared. Jennifer was able to leave her mother in the care of a sister and make the journey to Cornwall, to the home of a family friend.

'Does Bethany ever speak of Cornwall and of me?' Toby asked hopefully.

'She talks a great deal of Cornwall and of the sister who lives at Hemmick with her young family. Which reminds me, you must explain how I can visit Hemmick before I leave. My friend had never heard of it, so I gather it is not very large. Bethany never spoke of you at all until we learned you had been to France and to Guernsey. Mind you, I was aware there was something in her background that had made her very unhappy. I was certain it was the reason she had left Cornwall and returned to the Channel Islands. Eventually she told me the full story and I was able to understand her unhappiness.'

'I wish you would tell me about it. Bethany left Cornwall without saying anything to anyone of her reason for going. It has remained a complete mystery to everyone who knows her.'

'I can understand that,' sympathised Jennifer Cecil. 'From all the enquiries I have made, I feel quite certain she was mistaken in what she saw – or *thought* she saw – when she came to visit you here. Alice has already told me you were not here on that particular day.'

'That's right. I was in Exeter, with the bishop and the archdeacon. But, tell me, what is it she *thought* she saw?'

'When she arrived at the house she was most surprised to find both the rectory doors locked. After knocking for some time, the door was opened to her by a young girl in a dishevelled condition. She had clearly just risen from bed and had not even had time to fasten her buttons correctly. Although your donkey was in its paddock, the girl told her you were not at home. Bethany was puzzled. Then, as she was walking from the house, with the girl still in the doorway, she saw a curtain move in a bedroom window and glimpsed a face. She believed it was you. I understand it had been a very emotional day for her and this was the final straw. At any other time I am convinced she would have returned to learn the truth of what she had seen. As it was, she jumped to a logical conclusion, albeit a wrong one.'

'So that was it!' Toby was distressed. 'How could she possibly believe I would have been in bed with Charlotte?'

'As I just said, Bethany was in a distraught state. She admitted that to me herself. All she could think of was to get as far away from here as she could, and as quickly as possible.'

Jennifer looked from Toby to Alice and back again. 'Do you know the identity of the man who was in the house with your servant-girl that day?'

'Yes, Charlotte told Alice. It was John Bettison from Porthluney Manor.'

'My friend was telling me something about him. Isn't he married?'

Toby nodded. 'Yes, although his wife has been taken away from the manor by her father. Charlotte is now expecting his baby, or so she says.'

'You're the priest of the parish, have you confronted Bettison with this?'

'The last time I confronted Bettison with anything he tried to shoot me. He has been in dispute with the Church since before I came to Porthluney. It was as a result of a complaint made by him that I was in Exeter the day Bethany called. I tried to get word to her of where I would be, but everything seemed to conspire against me.'

Toby shook his head in pained disbelief once more. 'It hurts that Bethany could have believed this of me.'

'Of course it does – but I doubt if it hurts as much as it did Bethany when she believed you had been false to her.'

Toby nodded. 'Yes, in the state she must have been in, it would have been the final blow. Poor Bethany, she must have felt as though her whole world had collapsed about her. After giving up so much for me . . . I must come to Alderney and speak to her. To put things right between us.'

'It makes me very happy to see you are sorry for Bethany and not for yourself, Curate Lovell, but might I prevail upon you to leave this to me, at least for the time being?

To clear any obstacles that may be in your path, if you care to see it that way.'

Toby's every instinct was to throw everything else to the winds and go off to find Bethany. To tell her how wrong she had been about him. That all was well between them – but he could not do that right now. First he had to see Alice and Billy off to Canada. He would also like to have his appointment as Rector of Porthluney confirmed. Then he would have something worthwhile to offer her . . .

'All right, but I would like to write a letter to Bethany for you to take with you. Perhaps you could give it to her after you have explained what really happened here?'

'Of course. I am absolutely delighted to have been able to sort out this awful muddle – although I really shouldn't be. It means I will need to find a new nursemaid!'

Jennifer Cecil smiled in resignation. 'I will never find another like Bethany.'

'I don't know how to thank you, Mrs Cecil. After a number of really dreadful months here in Porthluney, it would seem things are finally going my way at last. Now, while Alice makes us some tea, please tell me what Bethany has been doing while she has been working for you. Then, if you will allow me time to write my letter to her, I will take you to Hemmick to meet Muriel, Jacob and their children. They too will be delighted to see you and to learn the misunderstanding between Bethany and me is about to come to an end.'

Chapter 82

The arrest of Billy Kendall by Revenue men was as much a surprise to them as it was to Billy himself.

When Toby returned from Hemmick after he had taken Jennifer Cecil there, he, Billy and Alice enjoyed a pleasant evening together in the rectory while they waited for darkness to fall. Billy and Alice intended making a farewell visit to his father, in Portloe.

When it became dark, the two young people set off to make the short journey to the small fishing village. Talking happily, they were about to turn off the lane to follow a path across the fields, when suddenly a number of men rose from the shadows on either side of them.

Alice gave a brief, startled scream and one of the men surrounding them said, 'That's no smuggler, it's just a young girl.'

'Who's that with her?' asked another voice.

'It's my young man,' said Alice, quickly. 'We're going to be married.'

One of the unseen men chuckled. 'Then don't leave it too long, young lady. Traipsing around in the dark with a man can only lead to trouble, even if he's the one you're going to marry. Get wed and you'll be able to enjoy each other's company in front of a nice warm fire. That's where I'd be tonight if I had any sense.'

There was considerable good-humoured banter between the men before one of them said, 'Where are you going now?'

'We're going home, to Portloe,' said Billy. 'We've just been for a walk, that's all.'

'Let them go on their way,' said another voice. 'We're not interested in them.'

'Let's have a look at their faces first,' suggested the man who had asked most of the questions. 'Strike a light to that lantern.'

'I'll get into trouble at home if I'm late in,' said Alice, desperately. 'Can't we just go?'

'You won't be kept for more than another minute or two, miss,' replied another of the men. 'We'd just like to know who we're talking to, that's all.'

From somewhere behind Alice there was the sound of a flint being struck, then a faint yellow glow as a lantern was lit. In its light Alice could see what she already suspected. The men who had stopped them wore the uniform of Revenue officers.

'Make it quick,' said one of the men. 'We don't want the whole world to know we're here.'

The lantern was briefly held up first to Alice's face, and then to Billy's.

It was being lowered again when one of the men said excitedly, 'Hold that up to his face again. Quickly!'

The lamplight played upon Billy's face once more and the man who had just spoken said, 'It's *him*. It's William Kendall. Grab him!'

Billy charged at the man with his shoulder, at the same time shouting, 'Run, Alice. Run . . .'

Fortunately, the men were too intent upon capturing Billy to bother with Alice. She obeyed Billy automatically and took to her heels in the darkness.

She knew this area well and made no attempt to follow the path. Instead, she ran off across the field to where she knew there was a gate. Beyond it was another path, which led along the cliff edge.

As Alice tumbled over the gate, she stumbled. Picking herself up quickly, she ran along the path. She was not heading towards Portloe now, but away from the village. The direction she was taking would lead her back to the rectory eventually.

She had not gone far, running much faster than was wise along the narrow and dangerous path, when she ran headlong into another group of men and was held fast before she could escape again.

'Steady on . . . steady on. It's a girl, isn't it?'

At first, Alice had believed these men to be Revenue men too, but she saw the outline of laden ponies with them and recognised the voice of the man who had spoken.

'Solomon? Solomon Crago?'

'Shh! We'll have no names that others might recognise,' admonished the man. Lowering his voice he said, 'What are you doing here, Alice? Who are you running from?'

'Revenue men. They were waiting by the path to Portloe from the Porthluney lane. They've taken Billy.'

'You were with Billy? How many Revenue men are there?'

'I don't know. Six, or maybe eight. They seemed to have been waiting there for someone else.'

'Us, probably,' said the man she had called Solomon. 'The Mevagissey men have had a big shipment landed tonight, more than they could handle themselves. They brought us and the Gorran men in on it. Trouble is, it seems someone has talked. The Revenue men knew all about it. Word's gone about they were lying in wait offshore for the Mevagissey boat. We believe all the men got away, but the boat and its load has been captured. They've taken it to the old salt store at Gorran Haven. That's where they'll most likely take Billy too.'

'What can we do about it?' asked Alice, desperately. 'If I try to go and see him there they'll arrest me too, but if they keep him, he'll hang – and he's done nothing. You know that.'

'There's not much we can do alone,' said Solomon, 'but the Mevagissey men are angry, and they've never yet allowed the Revenue men to better them. I'll go and find them. George, Harry, Moses, Digory . . . you come with me. The rest of you take the ponies. Get off the paths right away. Go across the fields to the manor woods. Hide the loads there, then turn the ponies out in a field – any field. When you've done that make your way to Gorran Haven to join us.'

'What can I do?' asked Alice, eagerly.

'Nothing!' declared Solomon. 'Go back to the rectory and wait there until you hear from us.'

'But . . .'

'No buts, just do as you're told. Now, we all know what we have to do. Let's get to it.'

Back at the rectory, Toby listened to Alice's tearful story in growing dismay.

'This is a calamity, Alice. Tonight of all nights! A rider from Falmouth left here only minutes ago. He must have passed you in the lane?'

Alice shook her head. After guiding Solomon Crago's men and ponies across the fields to the manor woods, she had returned to the rectory from the opposite direction to that a Falmouth rider would have taken.

'He came to say the ship will be leaving for Canada on tomorrow morning's tide. The captain sent word to say you and Billy should go on board as soon as possible.'

Alice let out a loud wail of despair. As Toby took her in his arms, she began to cry.

As he held her shaking body, he wondered what he could do to help Billy. He realised he would not be able to secure his release. The Revenue men would want to know how he had heard of the arrest so quickly.

All he could do was go to the Revenue headquarters at nearby Fowey first thing in the morning and ensure Billy had everything he needed for his comfort. He would also arrange for him to have the best legal advice possible. Even with such help Toby knew there was little chance Billy would be acquitted of killing the Revenue man.

Alice's sobs were subsiding a little when there came a knock at the door of the kitchen in which they were standing.

Before Toby could make any move towards it, the door opened and Alice's mother hurried into the house.

One look at Alice's tear-stained face and puffy eyes and Mrs Rowe opened her arms. Alice went to her.

'You've heard what's happened?' asked Toby. It was an unnecessary question.

Mrs Rowe nodded. 'There can't be anyone between St Austell and the Roseland who doesn't know by now. Fishermen are going around the houses calling out the men to join them. Alice's pa has gone. I doubt whether they'll find anyone who will dare to refuse.'

'What are they going to do?' Toby was alarmed. Civil disobedience on such a scale could fetch in the army from the garrisons at St Mawes and Fowey. If this happened there would most certainly be bloodletting.

'From what was said, they're all heading for Gorran Haven. The Mevagissey men intend getting their goods back. The men from these parts aim to set Billy free.'

'I'd better get to Gorran Haven right away. We want Billy freed, but there must not be any more bloodshed. I'll take the horse. You and Alice remain in the rectory until I return.'

Chapter 83

It was no more than three miles from the Porthluney rectory to Gorran Haven, but the night was dark and Toby dared attempt no more than a trot on his horse.

As he neared the small village he strained his ears for the sound he hoped he would not hear: the sound of shooting.

The Portloe men might carry no firearms, but the Mevagissey men had no such scruples. There was a hard core of professional smugglers in the village, men who regarded smuggling as their time-honoured right. They were prepared to defend that right, using every means at their disposal.

This would not be the first occasion on which they had launched a counter-attack against the Revenue men, in order to recover undutied goods they considered to be rightfully theirs.

The only difference tonight was that if what Alice's mother had said was true, they had the whole of the countryside marching with them.

Toby suddenly became aware he was among a large number of men. He pulled his horse to a halt as they blocked his way.

'Who's that?' he called into the night. If these were Revenue men he knew he would be able to go no farther.

'Curate Lovell?'

'Yes. Who's there?'

'There's no need for names, Curate, but we've got young Billy here with us. He's unhurt, but there's very little strength in him. Can he ride your horse?'

'Billy!' Toby slipped from the saddle to the ground.

'How have you managed to rescue him? Was there a fight? Is anyone seriously hurt?'

'Not a blow was struck, Curate. Nor was one needed. So many men marched upon Gorran Haven from Mevagissey that the Revenue men got scared and took off like rabbits. They left Billy and a whole boatload of goods behind them. Not that I blame 'em. The Mevagissey men were armed to the teeth and were very angry. By the time we got there they were loading up their boat and Billy was standing there wondering whether he should go with them or head for home. Not that he'd have made it on foot. I'd say he's had enough walking about the countryside for one night.'

'I'm all right,' declared Billy. 'I've just got out of the habit of it, that's all.'

'You've a few more things to do before the night is over,' said Toby, meaningfully. 'I'll get on my horse. Will a couple of you help Billy on behind me?'

As the men surged about the horse to help, Toby said, 'The rest of you get on home as quickly as you can. After what's gone on tonight the Revenue men will call in the army to help them. If they pay you a call, let them find you in bed.'

As Toby was about to guide the horse away from the men, Billy asked, 'Where are you taking me, Mr Lovell? Alice was with me when I was taken. I think . . . I *know* I called out her name. If they don't find her at home they'll come to the rectory looking for us.'

'We'll tell them nothing.' The voice was that of Alice's father. Toby had not realised he was among the crowd and standing close enough to hear what Billy had said.

'There will be no need for anyone to say anything,' said Toby. 'Both Billy and Alice will be safe – but I think you should say goodbye to each other now. I doubt if you'll meet again for many years to come.'

'Is it . . . tonight?'

'Yes.'

Alice's father reached up and grasped Billy's hand in a strong grip. 'God bless you, Billy. Take good care of Alice. You'll not find a finer girl anywhere.'

'I know that, Mr Rowe. Try not to worry too much about her. I'll look after her, I promise.'

On the way to the rectory, Billy told Toby of his night's adventures and what he knew of all that had been going on.

The night's landing of smuggled goods had taken place on Hemmick beach. The Revenue officers who had taken him prisoner had been posted outside Portloe to prevent any smugglers making their escape in that direction.

Others had been posted at various spots along the coast, while the main body of Revenue officers had been in a boat, lying off the beach at Hemmick.

The operation had been well planned and executed. The boat lying off the coast had intercepted the smugglers, as planned, and driven them ashore, where they captured the boat and its contents. Unfortunately for the Revenue officers, the very scale of the plan had defeated its objective. Their resources had been spread too thinly, and too far. Nowhere were they strong enough to oppose the smugglers and their friends when they turned out in unprecedented force. The government men could not even put up an effective fight. All they were able to do was recognise the superior strength of their opponents – and run.

When the smugglers entered the salt store Billy had been recognised immediately, and released.

'Well, our success has been absolute so far,' said Toby. 'Now we need to get you and Alice to Falmouth tonight and on board the Vivian ship in time to catch the morning tide. I think the best way we can do that is to get you both to Portloe. Your father can take you to Falmouth and put you on board. In view of all that's happened I think it will be better if I remain in the rectory and deal with any Revenue men or soldiers who come searching for you. Do you think you have the strength to begin your voyage to Canada tonight?'

'If Alice is with me, I'll be able to do all that's needed,' declared Billy. 'We both appreciate all you're doing for us, Mr Lovell. We'll never forget how much we owe to you.'

* * *

When Toby arrived at the rectory with Billy, Alice's joy dispelled any doubts her mother might have had about the two young people being right for each other. Soon they had gathered all Billy's belongings and set off for Alice's home. Here they collected the bags she had put together for the voyage to Canada.

They took the paths across the fields to Portloe, meeting up with none of the Revenue men who were supposed to be guarding this area.

The strength of local feeling against the Revenue Service had shaken the government men to the core. They had abandoned their positions and retreated upon their Fowey headquarters to assess their future role in this area.

From Portloe, Billy's father ferried the young couple to Falmouth and put them on board the ship that would carry them to a new life in Canada.

Meanwhile, Toby spent a couple of hours in the small Porthluney church praying for their future success and happiness.

Behind him, Nap lay stretched in the church aisle, his head resting on his forepaws. It was a scene that would have taken Alice back to the very first time she had seen the young curate of Porthluney.

Much had happened since that day, but there were still difficult days ahead for Toby.

Chapter 84

In a desperate bid to remain solvent, John Bettison sold everything it was possible to put on sale at short notice from both his home and the lands of Home Farm. It was not enough.

He had dismissed most of the servants employed at Porthluney Manor, but he was not yet ready to admit all was lost. In a final moment of desperation, he appealed to a spinster aunt, Lavinia Bettison.

The sole surviving member of his father's family, she lived a reclusive life in the far west of Cornwall and was a stern critic of his way of life.

In a letter sent in the care of the only remaining groom, John Bettison set out the stark facts of his present predicament. If he could not raise some money immediately, the manor house and its lands, which had been owned by the Bettison family for centuries, would have to be sold off.

He pointed out that if the property was to be retained for future generations, money was urgently needed. He reminded her he was the only male representative of the Bettison line. It would survive at Porthluney only through him.

Bettison hoped family honour would override his aunt's dislike of him.

He thought she might write a letter immediately upon receipt of his plea and send it back with the Porthluney groom, but the servant returned empty-handed.

For three days the Porthluney landowner waited. On the third day he received a letter, but it was not from the maiden aunt. It was from the office of a London solicitor, giving him the date when he was required to appear before a debtors' court in the capital.

John Bettison responded to this summons by raiding the cellars of the manor house, well stocked by Bettisons in better days.

By late-afternoon he was dangerously drunk. When a young and inexperienced maid was sent to the study where he was drinking, Bettison made a determined attempt to rape her.

Her screams brought the housekeeper and butler, the last of the house's senior staff, to the room. When the butler remonstrated with his employer, Bettison knocked him to the floor with a savage punch to the face.

The housekeeper now added her disapproval to that of the butler. In a fit of rage, Bettison dismissed the butler, then the housekeeper and the maid. In a final grand gesture he said he no longer needed any staff in the manor house. They should all go.

The butler and the maid took him at his word, as would the remainder of the staff, but Ada Hambly refused to accept dismissal from Porthluney.

'You're not throwing me out of the home I've enjoyed all my life, John Bettison,' she said defiantly. 'In case you've forgotten, it was written into your father's will that I be provided with a home for life here.'

'If I'm forced to sell Porthluney you'll have nowhere to go. You might as well leave now as then.'

'A new owner will need someone who knows all there is to know about Porthluney Manor, the estate, and the staff,' retorted the housekeeper. 'I have no worries about that. What I am concerned about at the moment is your state of mind. Striking a servant is unforgivable, as was your attack on that poor young girl. It was despicable.'

'Go away, Ada. You've been the self-appointed voice of my conscience for long enough. I'm bored with it. The best thing you can do now is go – and take the servants with you. There's no money to pay anyone, and there's not likely to be any.'

'Perhaps you could sell off some of the drink you have in the cellars? You'd at least make enough to give the servants what they're due. You have a responsibility towards them . . .'

'Go away, woman! I'm tired of your constant whining

about what I should or shouldn't be doing. All my life I've had to listen to it. I've had enough.'

Pouring himself another very large drink, he waved it in her direction. 'Now, either join me, have a drink and be less critical, or get out of my sight.'

Ada Hambly had no intention of sharing a drink with her employer. She made her way to the kitchen where the butler was using a series of cold compresses in a bid to stop his nose from bleeding.

Meanwhile, the young maid snivelled her way through the task of wiping off empty shelves in a kitchen pantry.

Soaking the cloth in a bowl of cold water, the butler said, 'What's going to happen to us, Mrs Hambly? Master Bettison seems to have gone completely out of his mind since the mistress left.'

'He was out of his mind before then,' declared the housekeeper. 'Had he been sane he would never have let her go. She was all that was keeping Porthluney together – and keeping her husband together as well. There's nothing any of us can do right now. There's no money to pay anyone and he's dismissed you all. Return to your homes and keep yourselves as best you can. Porthluney won't be in the Bettison family for very much longer. When the house is in new hands I'll speak to the owner with a view to having you back at the house again.'

'What do you think Mr Bettison will do when Porthluney's sold?' asked the girl who had been cooking for the household since the regular cook had departed.

'Don't worry yourself about that,' said Ada Hambly. 'He certainly doesn't care what happens to any of us. I've no doubt he'll get by. They do say that the devil looks after his own. Now, when you've all finished up here and left everything tidy, you can come up and see me. Unbeknown to Mr Bettison I still have some of the housekeeping money put by. I'll pay you what you're owed, plus a little bit extra. You'll need to make it last for as long as you can, because we don't know when there'll be any more. And don't dawdle. Mr Bettison is still drinking and it's not going to make him any better humoured.'

* * *

John Bettison sat in his study until it was too dark to see. Then he rose unsteadily to light the lamp, refill the brandy decanter and search unsuccessfully for some tobacco.

He was returning to his seat when he heard a sound from somewhere in the house. It sounded as though it was in the hall.

Frowning, Bettison was heading for the door when he had a sudden thought. He went to a cupboard in a corner of the room. Unlocking it with a key kept in a nearby desk, he took a double-barrelled flintlock fowling-piece from the cupboard. After checking the powder in the pan, he went in search of the source of the sound.

He found the intruder in the hall, detected in the darkness by a faint movement close to the door.

Throwing the gun to his shoulder, he called, 'Who's there? Speak quickly or I'll shoot you.'

'It's me, Charlotte. Don't shoot!'

'You!? What are you doing here, girl? You've made a laughing-stock of me. Sending me off on a fool's errand with the Revenue men. I ought to shoot and be done with you.'

'It wasn't a fool's errand. Billy Kendall *was* at the rectory with Alice. The Revenue men caught him last night, but he was set free by the Mevagissey fishermen. Alice was with him when they caught him, but she ran away and I don't think they know her name.'

'Where is Kendall now?' John Bettison lowered the fowling-piece.

'I don't know – but I'll find out for you,' said Charlotte, eagerly. 'I'll talk to Alice. Sooner or later she'll let it slip. She's not very clever.'

Bettison was not thinking too clearly. This girl irritated him, but there was still the chance she might put a very acceptable windfall his way. 'What are you doing here now, creeping around in my house like a thief?'

'I heard you'd dismissed all your servants. I wondered if you'd like me to cook a meal for you, or something?'

'If I'd wanted someone to cook for me, I'd have kept a servant on.'

'Well, I thought you might like some company.'

Charlotte had moved closer to him and he was reminded of the hours they had spent together in the Revenue lookout and other places.

'Come and have a drink with me, then we'll go upstairs to bed. That's the only company I want tonight.'

'I can stay here? Sleep in your bed with you?'

'For tonight. But I don't want to hear a single word about that brat you're carrying. Mine or anyone else's. Is that clear?'

'Yes.' Charlotte could hardly contain her delight. She would be spending the night in Porthluney Manor – with John Bettison. It was what she had wanted. True, he had said it was only for tonight, but she hoped she might be able to persuade him to change his mind.

'You're having an awful time. I'll help you forget about all your troubles. I'll be 'specially nice to you . . .'

Chapter 85

Toby was standing on a step-ladder, cleaning the inside of one of the church windows when, through the glass, he saw Charlotte. She made her way along the lane past the church before turning in at the rectory.

Curious, he descended the ladder and made his way to the house. He entered quietly, expecting to find Charlotte in the kitchen.

She was not there. When he walked along the passageway towards his study, he heard someone upstairs, closing a door.

He was halfway up the stairs before Charlotte put in an appearance in the hallway above him.

'What are you doing here, Charlotte?' he demanded.

Seemingly unconcerned at being found in the rectory by its occupier, she replied, 'I'm looking for Alice.'

'She's not here.' Toby did not believe her explanation. She might have come to the rectory hoping to speak to Alice, but she had taken the opportunity to have a look around. He suspected it had something to do with Billy.

'Where is she?'

'Right at this moment, I couldn't say.'

This was certainly the truth. She and Billy had been taken to Falmouth in the boat belonging to Billy's father on the night of his brush with the Revenue men. The two young people were now somewhere on the high seas.

'Isn't she working for you any more?'

Charlotte continued her questioning as she followed Toby down the stairs.

'Working here was only a temporary arrangement, until your mother was well enough to return. I was at your house earlier this morning. Your mother will be coming back here to work tomorrow. She would have come in today had she not been so concerned for you. She says you didn't return home last night.'

'She doesn't need to worry about me. I can look after myself. I'll be able to take care of her too, one of these days.'

'That isn't what I've heard, Charlotte. I believe you're already in trouble.'

'Then you believe wrong,' she retorted, her chin coming up defiantly. 'I suppose Alice has been speaking to you about me. She wasn't supposed to tell *anyone*.'

'Oh? I don't think we should talk about loyalty between friends, Charlotte, it's likely to cause some embarrassment to you. Let's discuss your condition and what's to be done about it.'

'There's nothing to talk about. I'll be taken care of.'

'By John Bettison? He's too deeply in trouble to take care of himself. He can't take on any more responsibility, even if he were willing to, which I doubt very much.'

'Well, you're wrong – and so is everyone else. I'm living up at the manor now and Mr Bettison has an aunt who's going to give him all the money he needs. But I didn't come here to be told how I should live my life, or to listen to a lot of lies about Mr Bettison. I'm looking for Alice. If she's not here I'll go to her house.'

Toby did not tell Charlotte she would be wasting her time there too. Alice's parents would say nothing to her. The less she knew of what her friend was doing, the better it would be for Alice and Billy.

As Charlotte went on her way and Toby returned to his church, he thought of what Charlotte had said about Bettison's aunt coming to his rescue. He wondered who she was and why she had not helped him before.

Charlotte spent the next four nights at the manor. She told John Bettison that Billy had gone into hiding but that she would find out where he was before too long.

It was not difficult to fool him. During the whole of this time he was rarely sober. Day or night no longer made any difference to him. He would drink until he fell into a drunken stupor.

Sometimes Charlotte was able to coax him to bed. At other times he slept where he was sitting. No matter where he was, the moment he woke he called for her to bring him a drink.

It was not the way of life she had envisaged when she dreamed of moving into Porthluney Manor – but she could still make-believe.

During John Bettison's periods of drunken sleep she would wander about the great house, running a finger across the surface of highly polished furniture, ignoring the film of dust that grew with each passing day.

She would walk from room to room imagining she was the lady of the manor, giving orders to imaginary servants and greeting phantom guests.

Her favourite room was the bedroom once occupied by Caroline. Here were silks, satins and frills to delight the most discerning woman.

Charlotte had tried to persuade John Bettison to sleep with her here, but he refused to even enter the room. When he took her to bed it was in his own bedroom, farther along the same corridor.

Lying in bed, with John snoring noisily beside her, Charlotte was trying to decide whether or not to get up. She had just heard the huge grandfather clock in the hall downstairs strike eleven. The light showing through the chinks in the curtain told her it was morning. They had not come to bed until dawn, after a night's carousing. She was wondering what she might find to eat that day. There was more than half of a huge cheese in the dairy, but there was no bread to go with it.

There was also the chance that if she went downstairs in the daytime she might meet up with Ada Hambly, the housekeeper. Their paths had crossed only twice during Charlotte's stay at the manor.

On each occasion the housekeeper had left Charlotte in no doubt of how *she* felt about having what she referred to as a young 'village whore' staying in the manor house.

When Charlotte complained to John, he had merely laughed, declaring he was able to enjoy Ada's acerbic tongue more now he was no longer paying her a salary.

Suddenly, Charlotte heard the crunching of carriage wheels on the gravel in front of the house. She leaped naked from the bed and peered from the window but was unable to view the space in front of the main door.

As she looked she could hear a bell ringing in the servants' quarters, the sound softened by the distance.

She wondered whether she should dress and go downstairs to answer the door, but decided against it. When the bell was rung once more, she thought she should try to rouse John.

It was no easy task. For a long time she might have been shaking a dead man. When her efforts finally began to succeed, he tried to fight her off, mumbling for her to go away and leave him alone.

Not until she thought she could hear voices on the main staircase did she turn to the water standing in a jug on a marble-topped wash-stand in a corner of the room. Soaking a flannel in cold water, she squeezed it out on his face.

'Wh . . . what!' He came awake trying to brush the water from his face. Struggling to a sitting position, he said, 'Damn you, girl! What do you think you're doing?'

'There's someone come to the house.'

Voices were outside the door now. Suddenly, it was flung open without warning. Ada Hambly stood in the doorway beside an elegant, elderly woman. Behind them was a young girl dressed in a maid's uniform.

As Charlotte dived for her clothes and crouched beside the bed, clutching the dress in front of her to hide her nakedness, John Bettison pulled the sheet up about him.

Giving them both a contemptuous look, Ada Hambly said triumphantly, 'There you are, Miss Bettison. You wanted to find your nephew. Now you have.'

'Who are you?' Lavinia Bettison jabbed a finger in Charlotte's direction.

She was too terrified to reply and Ada Hambly spoke for her. 'Her name is Charlotte. She's one of the village girls.

According to a rumour I heard from the servants, she is expecting a child.'

'John's child?' Lavinia Bettison's expression showed stern disapproval.

'It's possible – although knowing the girl as I do, it could be anybody's.'

'That isn't true . . .' Ada Hambly's assertion stung Charlotte to a reply.

Before she could say more, Lavinia Bettison said, 'Get out, girl! Out of this room and out of this house.'

'I . . . I . . .'

'THIS MINUTE!'

John Bettison's aunt advanced across the room with such an angry expression on her face that Charlotte scooped up her clothes and fled from the room, startling a young, uniformed footman who was standing at the top of the staircase leading to the hall.

Behind her, Lavinia Bettison said to the Porthluney housekeeper, 'You may go too, Ada. I have a few things to say to my nephew. Unladylike things. It won't take long. Please tell my footman to be ready to escort me back to my carriage. I don't want to remain here one minute more than is necessary. Porthluney Manor is no longer the house I loved so much in my childhood. Sadly, I feel it is time the old place had a new owner.'

Chapter 86

Holding Toby's unopened letter in her hand, Bethany listened in stunned silence as Jennifer Cecil told her of the visit she had made to Cornwall, and of her meeting with Toby and Alice.

Bethany remained silent for a long time after her employer had finished talking, before asking, 'Do you believe Toby was telling you the truth of what happened that day?'

'I am convinced of it. The young girl who works in his house confirmed it. She seemed to know a great deal about the girl who was at the rectory when you called there.'

Bethany nodded. 'She would. Alice and Charlotte are friends, although they are not at all alike. Alice is a kind and honest girl. Charlotte is . . . well, she is no better than you were told.'

'What I find difficult to comprehend is the part played in this by the lord of Porthluney Manor,' said Jennifer. 'This Mr Bettison.'

'He's a thoroughly evil man,' explained Bethany. 'He has been in dispute with the Church in Porthluney for many years.'

'So I was given to understand. What with this Bettison, Toby's suspension from his duties, and your sudden inexplicable disappearance, I would say he has had a very unhappy time.'

Once again there was a long silence before Bethany said, unhappily, 'Poor Toby. I have behaved very stupidly, haven't I? I wouldn't blame him if he never wanted to see me again.'

'I think he was terribly hurt at the thought that you did not trust him. However, he realises that you had not known each other for long and you had just had a very upsetting experience. He probably explains all this in his letter. Had I been in your situation, I think I would have arrived at the same conclusion. Whether or not I would have had the courage to leave, as you did, is another matter. What is quite certain is that he is still very much in love with you.'

'I really don't know why. Not after what I have done to him . . .'

'Yes, you do. It's for the same reason you have never stopped loving him, even after what you *thought* he had done.'

Close to tears, Bethany pleaded, 'But . . . what can I do now?'

'You must go to him, Bethany. Return to Cornwall. However, I would very much appreciate it if you could possibly stay with me until I have found another nursemaid.'

'Of course I will. I . . . I really don't know how I can thank you for all you have done.'

'My dear, all I have done is show my gratitude for everything *you* have done for the Cecil family.'

Suddenly, Jennifer went to Bethany and hugged her. 'I really am happy for you. I know you do not need my approval, but I must say that I took an immediate liking to your Toby. He is a very fine young man.'

'Yes. Yes, he is. I always thought so. I should have trusted him. He really deserves someone better than me.'

In spite of her words, Bethany was thinking of Toby without suffering the misery she had known for so long. It was the first time for many, many weeks. Once again she was able to think of a future shared with him. A happy future.

It was ten days later that Bethany said farewell to Jennifer Cecil and her children. It was a tearful parting.

Bethany had become very fond of the major's wife and her four young children, and they of her.

Jennifer was extremely emotional and promised she would bring the children to see Bethany in Cornwall when they were next in England.

The children's new nursemaid was some years older than Bethany, but a very gentle person. Coincidentally, she too had once been a Quaker, who had left the Society of Friends many years before, when she married an army surgeon.

He had died when he was stationed in Guernsey, but his widow had felt so at home on the island, she remained there. She had been living on an army allowance, supplemented by teaching children at a local school.

Major Cecil was accompanying Bethany to Guernsey. They were taking passage on board a small naval vessel. It was used to take him there for his regular meetings with the Commanding Officer of the Channel Islands forces.

In Guernsey, Bethany first made a visit to see her parents. Her father was not at home and she was able to enjoy a few hours talking with her mother and exchanging news.

Bethany learned that in spite of the difficulties of her last birth, Muriel was expecting another child. She was also told that Muriel's letters indicated Toby had been trying very hard, through the Quaker family at Hemmick, to discover Bethany's whereabouts.

'I know this is true, Bethany,' said her mother. 'I think he must care for thee very much.'

'Yes,' she agreed, humbly. 'I believe he does. I do not deserve it.'

'I liked his manners when he called here,' said her mother. 'I know thy father wouldst be angry if he heard me say this, but if thou art determined to marry outside the Society, thou couldst not have made a better choice. Thou hast not forsaken God, only chosen a different path to walk on thy way to Him.'

Hugging her mother, Bethany slipped easily into her former mode of speech when she said, 'I thank thee with all my heart. If only Father would see it that way I would be very, very happy.'

Her mother shook her head sadly. 'Thy father is one of the last of those Friends who confuse bending with breaking. It is what made martyrs of so many of our people. But go now, Bethany, and remember, for all his apparent harshness, thy father loves thee too.'

Major Cecil had arranged a passage to England for Bethany,

in a Portsmouth-bound ship that was leaving the following day, but her plans were thrown into confusion that evening.

The Bailiff of Guernsey had been present at the talks between the Islands' military commanders. Speaking with Major Cecil afterwards, he learned that Bethany was in St Peter Port.

Remembering her as the woman whose presence of mind had thwarted the French raid, he expressed a wish to meet her. Major Cecil promised to bring her to the Bailiff's house that evening.

It was an ordeal for Bethany. She arrived at the house to discover the Bailiff had hastily organised a reception for dignitaries and senior army officers, and that she was to be the guest of honour.

Fortunately, the Bailiff's wife proved to be very supportive. It was she who upset Bethany's plans for a return to England.

All the talk about the table had been of Bethany's thoughts on the night of the French raid. When she admitted her main concern had been for the safety of the Cecil children, the Bailiff's wife said, 'Thank goodness you came through the experience safely. But now you are leaving Alderney. When are you actually sailing for England, my dear?'

'Tomorrow. Major Cecil has booked me a passage on a ship to Portsmouth.'

'I wish you a safe voyage, but what a pity you won't be here when that nice young curate arrives from Cornwall, though I believe he is actually the rector of his own parish now.'

Bethany's heart missed a beat. 'Of whom are you talking? Not Toby Lovell?'

'Lovell! Yes, that's his name. The curate who came here seeking you and went to France to release all those prisoners. My husband has received a letter from the English Foreign Secretary. It seems that Curate . . . sorry, *Rector* Lovell is making another journey to France to arrange an exchange of prisoners. We don't know exactly when he will arrive, but we have been told to expect him any day now. My husband has been asked to arrange for a vessel to convey him to France. He is also to provide an interpreter to accompany him.'

Chapter 87

Two letters were delivered to Toby by different messengers on the same day.

The first told him he had been confirmed as Rector of Porthluney, now officially separated from the parishes of St Stephen and St Denis. It was the confirmation for which he had been waiting and it delighted him. At last he felt able to plan for a secure future.

The second letter was quite different and took him by surprise. It came by a special messenger from the Foreign Office, in London. Charles Fox, the Foreign Secretary to whom Toby had delivered Minister Fouché's letter, was dead.

His successor had been made aware of the letter and the part played by Toby. He wished to meet the newly appointed rector in London, as a matter of some urgency. He hinted that Toby might be required to make another journey to France on behalf of the British government.

Toby realised the letter was a thinly disguised indication that the new Foreign Secretary was interested in discussing peace with the French Minister of Police.

It was a summons he could not, and would not, ignore.

Rose Henna was once more housekeeping at the rectory. Toby's disclosure that he had been summoned to London by the Foreign Secretary impressed her almost as much as if he had received a personal command from God Himself. To Rose, London was so far away it had to be close to Heaven.

That same day Toby rode to Falmouth to inform Sir Charles Vivian of the contents of both letters.

The shipowning baronet was pleased that the Bishop of Exeter had confirmed Toby's appointment. He also agreed his new rector could not ignore the summons to London and approved Toby's suggestion that he should travel to the capital by carriage the next day.

He added that had Matthew been in harbour with the *Potomac* he would have sent Toby to London in the vessel. It was a much more comfortable mode of transport.

Toby travelled to London on the mail coach from St Austell. It was a fast, at times hair-raising, journey, but the coach was in London long before dark the next day.

There had been much to occupy his mind on the journey and he had not slept. He found a small inn close to the Foreign Office and after a somewhat indifferent meal, went to bed and fell asleep immediately.

The following morning, Toby was at the Foreign Office before the arrival of the Foreign Secretary who had succeeded Fox.

Unlike his previous visit here, Toby was received with a great deal of deference from the clerks in the Foreign Secretary's office and shown into the minister's presence within minutes of that official's arrival.

Rising to his feet from a seat behind a huge, polished desk, the new Foreign Secretary extended his hand. 'I am delighted to meet you, Mr Lovell. It is very good of you to come and see me at such short notice. I have been intrigued by the stories of your adventures in France. I understand you actually met with Minister Fouché? A very powerful man – and also an extremely dangerous one. However, I believe you successfully negotiated the release of a number of English prisoners?'

'They were civilians who should never have been taken by the French in the first place.'

'Quite. However, you succeeded in securing their release when others had failed. I feel your feat should have received acknowledgement in the right quarters at the time. It is my intention to release the story to the newspapers of the land immediately. I want everyone to know what you did – and what I hope are about to do once more.'

'I'm sorry, I don't understand . . .'

The Foreign Secretary smiled. 'What will not be disclosed is the fact that you also acted as a courier for tentative peace negotiations between France and England. This time I would like you to take a letter from England to France, Mr Lovell. To be delivered personally to Minister Fouché.'

'It was Minister Fouché's express wish that nothing should be put in writing, sir.'

The British Foreign Secretary inclined his head in acknowledgement of Toby's statement. 'I am aware of that, Mr Lovell. However, there are a great many questions for which I need to have answers. There are also many points that must be clarified before any serious peace negotiations can take place. There is a certain amount of danger for you in undertaking such a mission, of course. If you feel inclined to refuse, it will bring no discredit upon you.'

Toby shook his head. 'I'll go, of course. If there is any chance of bringing this war to a close, it must be taken. I was merely repeating Minister Fouché's instructions, especially as I am likely to have my baggage searched frequently when travelling through France.'

'Of course. Before you leave this office, your coat will be taken and a letter stitched inside the lining.'

Smiling once more, this time at Toby's expression of surprise, the Foreign Secretary said, 'Yes, I have already written the letter. You see, I found out a great deal about you before summoning you to London, Mr Lovell. I was confident you would not refuse this most important mission.'

'I thank you for your confidence, sir, but what of the exchange of prisoners? There will need to be one.'

'Yes, indeed! I will ensure your mission to exchange prisoners is public knowledge long before you set off. I can assure you it will be known to Minister Fouché in Paris before you reach your home in Cornwall, such is the efficiency of his secret police. We are aware they are operating even here, in London.'

The Foreign Secretary placed both hands on the desk in front of him and paused for a moment before speaking once more. 'There is also a very effective exchange of information between the Channel Islands and France. I suggest you go to Guernsey or Jersey and make it public knowledge there that you are on your way to France. Spend a day or two on the islands. By the time you arrive in France you will find they are expecting you.'

'Who am I to exchange? Is there anyone in particular you would like back in this country?'

'It would please me very much if I could bring home every Englishman in French hands to this country, Mr Lovell. However, that would not be realistic. I will leave the details to you. Exchange whoever you can. We have many wounded French officers here at the moment. No doubt they have many of ours. You have a free hand in your negotiations and will carry an open letter to this effect, written in both English and French.'

The Foreign Secretary's ready smile showed once more. 'Now, Mr Lovell, may I divest you of your coat?'

Toby made the return journey to Cornwall in a happy and excited frame of mind. Not least because it meant he was going to the Channel Islands once more.

This time he was convinced he would find Bethany. Hopefully, he would return to Cornwall from France with all their misunderstandings finally settled.

Chapter 88

Before making his plans to set off to the Channel Islands, Toby went to Falmouth once more to tell his patron what had happened in London. He gave him details of his proposed visit to France, to arrange the exchange of prisoners.

If Sir Charles wondered why it had been necessary for the Foreign Secretary to summon a Cornish parson to London for an undertaking that might have been arranged at a much lower level, he kept such thoughts to himself.

Instead, he offered to do all he could to facilitate Toby's mission.

'I will make enquiries and arrange a passage for you to the Channel Islands. I had expected that Matthew and the *Potomac* would be back in Falmouth long before this, but I have had no word from him for some time. He would have been the ideal man to take you to the Channel Islands.'

Giving Toby a sly smile, he added, 'And, of course, Grace might once more have volunteered to accompany you as interpreter.'

'Yes. I'll miss her enterprise and charm. She could probably achieve far more on her own than I will. Perhaps I should have suggested to the Foreign Secretary he send her in my place?'

'Had you done so we might never have seen her again, although perhaps I underestimate my brother's charm! How long do you expect to be away from the parish?'

'I hope to accomplish my task within a couple of weeks. Three at the most. Much depends on the efficiency of the French authorities.'

'Return as swiftly as you can, Toby. Upon your return Sally and I will have the banns called and arrange our wedding. Her father will perform the ceremony, with your assistance.'

'That's wonderful news! Please give my congratulations to Sally. I hope it won't be too long before I follow your example. While I'm in the Channel Islands I intend to find Bethany and clear up the misunderstanding between us.'

Extending his hand, Sir Charles said, 'I trust your travels will be successful on all counts, Toby. As soon as I have news of the vessels sailing to the Channel Islands, I will send word to you.'

Toby returned from Falmouth with an unaccustomed feeling of well-being.

Rose was once more firmly in charge of the rectory and made a great fuss of him, insisting that he sit down and enjoy a drink while she prepared a meal for him.

Toby carried his drink to the kitchen and sat down at the table. While she busied herself, he told her something of his plans.

She was concerned that he would be returning to France once more. 'You be careful how you go among those French people, with their fancy language. We had some of them land in Portloe many years ago, before we were at war with them. Their ship had sprung a leak and they beached it there. They could only speak their own funny language, but whenever they said anything to us local girls we all knew what it was they wanted. Not all of 'em was kept at arm's length, neither. There's one or two fishermen in the village who should be speaking French today if they took after their natural fathers.'

Toby smiled at her gossip. He thought she might have conveniently forgotten the behaviour of her own daughter – but he was wrong. Charlotte was very much in the forefront of her mother's thoughts.

'Talking of such things, sir, I'd be obliged if you would find time before you go off to France to have a talk with my Charlotte. I'm worried about her. I thought she'd got all foolish thoughts about him up at the manor out of her head, but she's up there staying with him now. Mind you, what they're living on I couldn't say. The servants who used to be there say there's no food left, and no one about here will give John Bettison any credit to buy more.'

Rose paused to brush back a lock of hair that had fallen in front of her face as she leaned over the fire. 'I'm worried about Ada Hambly too. I know she's living in the lodge and not in the house itself, but she hasn't been seen about for some days. There's no one in the house to care about her now.'

'I've already spoken to Charlotte,' said Toby. 'I'm afraid she will take no more notice of me than she will of you. She believes I have no right to interfere in anything she is doing. Ada Hambly is different. I'll go along to speak to her first thing in the morning. She might be able to tell me what's happening up at the house.'

When Toby arrived at the lodge, he found Ada working in the manor's small vegetable garden.

In reply to his asking whether she was able to manage now there was no longer work for her at the manor, she replied, 'You don't have to worry about me, Mr Lovell. I've been at Porthluney Manor for most of my life and the farmers hereabouts see I want for nothing. Mind you, I don't know what they're living on up at the house. There was cheese and a little salted pork left there, but that won't have lasted very long.'

'It's something that's occurred to Rose Henna. She's concerned for Charlotte and wanted me to go up to the house and speak to her. After what happened the last time I was there, I wonder whether it would be wise?'

'It would be *most* unwise!' declared Ada, emphatically. 'Master John would kill you. He never moves anywhere without that gun of his. When he's been drinking – and that is most of the time these days – there's not a scrap of sense in him.'

'Have you seen anything of Charlotte recently?' he asked.

'No, and I don't want to,' replied the housekeeper, sharply. 'She's a little whore and always has been. It's her mother I feel sorry for, not the girl.'

'She's only young, Mrs Hambly. Having the lord of the manor pay her attention is enough to turn her head.'

'Don't you believe it! She's the one doing all the running. It suits her to have things up at the manor the way they are. She can spend all day wandering around the house making believe she's Mistress of Porthluney. It's a dangerous game she's playing, you mark my words. Master John's unbalanced and as likely to turn on her as on anyone else.'

'She ought to be warned, Mrs Hambly. That's a task I should be carrying out.'

'You'd be wasting your time, Mr Lovell. She wouldn't want to listen to you. You know that already.'

'All the same . . .'

'Don't waste any sympathy on that girl. Besides, you wouldn't know when she's likely to be about the house. They don't keep normal hours up there. You never know whether they're awake or sleeping. The only thing you *can* be certain of is that, day or night, they'll both of them be the worse for drink. Stay away from there, Mr Lovell, if you value your life.'

Toby knew the housekeeper spoke the truth. 'Well, if you do see her, tell her of her mother's concern. You can say too that I would like to have a few words with her.'

'I'll tell her if I see her, but don't wait in for her. She won't come to see you. There's nothing you're likely to say that she wants to hear.'

Chapter 89

In Porthluney Manor, Charlotte came awake with a start. Something had woken her but she was not immediately aware of what it had been. For a minute or more she lay in the darkness of the bedroom, trying to gather her senses together.

It was not easy. For some moments she could not even remember where she was, or whether it was day or night. It was a dull throbbing inside her head that finally helped her to put the pieces together.

Remembering, she reached out beside her. John was not in the bed. She could not remember whether they had come to bed together, or whether she had been alone. Not that it mattered very much. He was usually too drunk to do anything anyway.

Although John had not yet acknowledged the baby was his, she believed it was no more than a matter of time before she was ensconced in the manor as his mistress.

Even so, the way of life they were leading could hardly be regarded as in any way normal. Nor was it as she had imagined life would be, here in the manor house.

It grieved her particularly that her lover would not allow her to call him by his Christian name and treated her more as a whore than as a mistress.

Indeed, when they had last come to bed together, some time in the late-afternoon, or perhaps it was early-evening, he had actually called her a whore. He had also struck her. It had happened when she protested that his rough and clumsy love-making was hurting her . . .

The sound of a gunshot echoed through the house and she realised this was the sound that had woken her.

She sat up in the bed and gingerly put her feet to the

ground, fighting against the nausea she had come to accept as part of the penalty of pregnancy. She was also fully aware it was aggravated by the amount she had drunk with John before coming to bed.

Another shot made her push thoughts of her malaise to the back of her mind. Dressing hurriedly, she left the bedroom and made her way along the unlit corridor in the darkness until she reached the head of the stairs.

There was a single lamp burning in the downstairs hall. By its light she could see John seated on a chair in the centre of the hall. In his hands he held his favourite double-barrelled fowling-piece which he was clumsily reloading.

As Charlotte watched he completed the task. Priming the gun, he raised it to his shoulder, aiming it unsteadily in her direction.

For a few terrifying moments, Charlotte thought he was about to shoot *her*. Then the gun went off with a deafening report and the pellets tore through the canvas of a portrait on the wall above her head, splintering the wooden panelling behind it.

Downstairs in the hall, John Bettison laughed uproariously. 'Did that frighten you, my little whore? Shall I fire again and see if I can hit something a bit closer this time?'

'No.' Charlotte hurried down the stairs until she was in the hall. 'And I wish you wouldn't keep calling me that.'

'Why? Are you trying to say you *aren't* a whore? Are you trying to tell *me* that? Well, I can tell you that's what you bloody-well are. A little village whore. But who cares? You're *my* whore right now and so long as that suits me, it should suit you too. Right?'

Charlotte realised he was in one of his dangerous drunken moods. She nodded her agreement.

'I should damned well think so too. Now, go and see if you can find something for me to eat. I'm hungry.'

Charlotte could have told him there was virtually no food left in the kitchens, but she said nothing. It would only make him angrier than he was right now.

She would try to find something. There was still some cheese left. She could cut off the mould. If she took a lantern she might also find an onion and perhaps a lettuce in the kitchen garden . . .

She was still in the hall when the front door was flung open and Ada Hambly hurried in.

She looked at John Bettison as he reloaded the barrel of the gun that had just been fired.

Looking up at her for only a moment, he said, 'Go away. What are you doing here?'

'I came here to ask you the very same question. I can hear the shooting from the lodge. What on earth do you think you're doing?'

'I'm venting my feelings on my ancestors for leaving me with insufficient money to run Porthluney. Like this, Ada . . .'

Raising the gun, he peered along the barrel and pulled a trigger.

The report startled both women, but Ada recovered first. Looking up at the ruined portrait, she demanded, 'Have you taken leave of your senses? Those portraits are irreplaceable. They provide a record of every Bettison who has ever lived at Porthluney.'

Reloading again, Bettison said belligerently, 'So? I have just blasted Great-great-grandfather Charles out of existence. What difference does it make to anyone? Will I be rid of my debts? Will the world come to an end? No, everything will go on exactly as it was before, except that I will have had a few moments of amusement. There hasn't been much of that in my life recently. Everything and everyone has been against me.'

'Oh! So it's time to be feeling sorry for yourself now, is it? You deserve everything that has happened to you, Master John. You've never done anything right since you were a young boy in this house. The only thing that ever brought pleasure to you was hurting others. Usually the servants. Men and girls who dared not stand up for themselves because they knew if they did they would be dismissed. You've been no different since you grew into manhood. When your poor father died, he left you a good, well-run estate. It's your own gambling and profligate ways that have reduced things to their present state. You have no one to blame but yourself. Your aunt was right. The best thing that can happen to Porthluney is for it to have a new owner.'

'She might have been more sympathetic towards me had you not done your damnedest to turn her against me. She would have paid up to keep Porthluney in the family.'

'Never! She read your character right very many years ago. It's time Porthluney had a new landowner. I'm only thankful your dear mother never lived to see her son turn out to be a wastrel and a scoundrel.'

'Shut up! I want to hear nothing you have to say. You never have liked me.'

John Bettison pointed the gun in the housekeeper's direction. 'You've always turned the servants against me and now you've done the same thing with my own aunt.'

'I've never had to turn anyone against you. You've always done that very well yourself. The best chance you ever had in your miserable life was when you married Mistress Caroline, but you treated her as you've always treated everyone else. Now you've discarded her for this young slut.'

Ada jerked her head in the direction of Charlotte who still stood in the hall.

'I said, shut up!' John Bettison was unused to being spoken to in such a manner and was trembling with rage, the gun in his hands shaking alarmingly.

But Ada Hambly was not to be intimidated. 'All I can say is that you and Charlotte Jane deserve one another. Neither of you . . .'

She never completed the sentence. The gun in John Bettison's hands was suddenly discharged.

When the cloud of white smoke cleared, Charlotte could see Ada Hambly lying on the ground, a red stain spreading around the holes peppering her dress in the region of her stomach.

Aghast, Charlotte ran to where the housekeeper lay on the hall floor. Ashen-faced, she looked up at John Bettison. 'You've killed her! You deliberately shot her!'

'The gun went off by accident,' mumbled the landowner, almost incoherently.

'No, you deliberately killed her,' Charlotte repeated. 'I'm not staying here.'

Turning from him, she ran for the door.

It was the worst thing she could have done. Raising the gun in an instinctive reaction, John Bettison shot her. It was what he would have done to any fleeing rabbit, deer or fox.

Charlotte gave a scream of pain, and collapsed to the floor.

She lay still, moaning, as John walked over to her. Charlotte raised her head to look up at him, panting hard. 'Help me! Help me . . . please!'

He looked down at her for a full minute. Then he turned and walked from the house.

Chapter 90

Toby was in bed when he was awakened by a loud and persistent hammering on the front door of the rectory. Wondering who wanted him so urgently at this time of the night, he pulled on some clothes and hurried downstairs to the door.

He opened it to find a man standing there. Toby had seen him among the congregation at his church services, but could not recall his name.

'Parson Lovell! I'm Michael Grose, from Porthluney Home Farm. I've got Ada Hambly up at my place. She's been shot.'

Startled, Toby said, 'Shot! How?'

'By Mr Bettison, up at the manor. She said he's gone mad. He shot her first, then shot down young Charlotte Jane. Ada said I was to come and warn you. She said Mr Bettison's likely to come after you next.'

'How badly is Ada hurt – and what of Charlotte?'

'Ada was left for dead. Mr Bettison shot her in the stomach, but she was wearing a corset with a metal busk in front. She's got a few pellets in her and she's bled a lot, but she'll live to testify against him.'

'What of Charlotte?' Toby repeated.

'Ada reckons she's dead. She tried to run away after he'd fired at Ada. He shot her in the back. Charlotte pleaded with Bettison to help her but he left the house. Ada had been pretending to be badly hurt, but after he'd gone she went across to see how Charlotte was. She was unconscious by then. Ada doesn't think she would have lived for more than a few minutes.'

'I'll come out there right away. In the meantime we ought to call out the constable – and a magistrate.'

'I've already sent one of my farmhands to call out the constable. He'll then ride on to tell Magistrate Tremayne over at Heligan House what's happened. He should be well on his way there by now.'

'Give me a moment or two to saddle my horse and we'll go to the manor. We've got to find out if there's any possibility that Charlotte's still alive.'

The other man looked doubtful. 'Shouldn't we wait until Magistrate Tremayne gets here? Or until we've spoken to the constable?'

'The most important thing is to see if there's anything that can be done for Charlotte. Do you have a gun?'

After a moment's hesitation, the farmer said, 'I've got a musket I use for keeping down troublesome foxes. It hasn't been used for some time.'

'We'll call at your farm and collect it on the way to the manor. If Bettison is waiting there for us we'll have some form of defence, at least.'

The farmer seemed dubious, but he said nothing. Ten minutes later he and Toby were riding hard for Home Farm.

While the farmer checked the loading and priming of his gun, Toby spoke to a pale but undaunted Ada Hambly. She confirmed all that the farmer had told Toby. She also suggested that if they met with John Bettison on the way to the manor, the farmer should shoot the Porthluney landowner on sight – before he had the opportunity to fire at either of them.

The two men were halfway to the manor house when they met up with a group of men. One was the constable, a nervous young man named Harold Mitchell.

'I've never had to deal with anything like this,' he confessed to Toby. 'When I took on the post of constable I never thought I'd be called upon to arrest the lord of Porthluney Manor on a charge of murder.'

'If we hurry up and get to the manor we might find Charlotte still alive,' said Toby. 'Then it won't be murder.'

'Shouldn't we wait until Magistrate Tremayne arrives?' asked the constable, anxiously. 'He'll know more about this sort of business than we do.'

'Not while there's a chance that Charlotte might still be alive. Come along, we're wasting time.'

When John Bettison staggered into the night from Porthluney Manor he was still clutching the fowling-piece. Convinced he had just killed two women, he stumbled about in the garden in the darkness as he tried to think what he should do next.

Sooner or later the bodies would be found. When they were he would be a wanted man. A hue-and-cry would go out for him. He needed to put as many miles between himself and Porthluney as he could.

He made his way to the stables which, until recently, had held more than a dozen horses. Now only one remained: his own hack.

Clumsily, John Bettison saddled the animal. It was not used to being woken at this time of the night and prepared for riding. Nevertheless, it was a good horse. By the time the sun rose the landowner believed they would both be far away.

Far enough to leave any pursuit behind, even if the bodies of the two women were found tonight, which in itself was highly unlikely.

Suddenly, Bettison stopped short. He was preparing to flee on the assumption that the bodies would be found. But why should they be found at all? He could bury them both in the extensive gardens of the manor. Among the bushes at the side of the house, for instance.

The soil was loose there. He would have to dig only shallow graves. No one would ever find them and he need not become a fugitive.

Leaving the horse saddled, he took the lantern from the stable and made his way to the gardener's hut in the walled kitchen garden.

He came away from the small store house carrying a spade and returned to the house.

He felt more sober now, although the incidents of the night still seemed blurred. Almost as though they belonged in a dream.

The dream became a nightmare when he entered the

hallway. He had intended dragging both bodies outside to the shrubbery where they would be buried – but there was only one here.

Charlotte lay in a pool of blood that was already beginning to dry around the edges.

For a few frantic moments, Bettison ran around the hall, holding the lantern up high so he might peer into the shadows of every dark corner.

He thought he must have mistaken the spot where Ada Hambly had fallen, remembering once again the blood he had seen coming through the dress from her body.

Having shot her in the stomach, he was convinced she could not have survived. However, if she was not quite dead he knew she was determined enough to have dragged herself out of the house.

She was most likely lying dead or dying somewhere outside. He had probably walked past her on his way to the house.

He was heading for the door once more when he came to a halt. Finding Ada's body could wait. His first priority was to bury Charlotte and clean up the hallway.

Before he made a start, he checked the loading of his gun once more, just in case anyone came nosing around while he performed his grisly task.

Chapter 91

Digging even a shallow grave was not as easy as Bettison had imagined. He conceded that he was nowhere near as fit as he should be.

Working in the darkness, it was taking him much longer than he had anticipated. When he thought he had probably dug deep enough, he went inside the house. Skirting the body lying grotesquely upon the floor, he picked up the lantern and hurried with it to the shrubbery.

By its light he realised he would have to make the hole at least twice as deep as it was at the moment.

Cursing, he put the lantern down and resumed digging. He was encountering roots now and cursed each one as he chopped at it viciously with the blade of the spade.

Eventually, he was satisfied that the hole was now deep enough. Leaving the lantern on the earth excavated from the hole, he returned to the house.

He tried to drag Charlotte along by lifting her beneath the arms, but found this too difficult. She was heavier than he thought. It was easy enough pulling her across the marble floor of the hall, but more difficult when he reached the doorway.

He laid her down on the top step and grasped her by the ankles. He found this easier as he did not need to bend so low.

Her body bumped down the steps to the gravel driveway and then he dragged it across to the lawn.

He had almost reached the shrubbery when he heard voices and the sound of horses treading the gravel of the driveway as they left the lane.

Fortunately, from where they were they could not see the

lantern. Leaving Charlotte where she lay, he hurried to the shrubbery and extinguished it.

Picking up the fowling-piece, he went back to where he had left the body and crouched down beside it.

Among the voices of the men who were now standing in front of the house he recognised that of the Porthluney curate, and felt a blind rage come over him. His finger touched the trigger of the gun, but moved away. This was not the time.

Some of the men cautiously entered the manor. One must have known the lay-out of the house – it was probably a servant – because he knew where to find a tinder box.

A lamp flared into life and he heard the sound of excited voices inside the hallway. He could not hear all that was being said, but one word was repeated more than others.

That word was 'blood'.

The men came out to the doorway and he could clearly distinguish the outline of Curate Lovell. If he fired now he could not miss. But Bettison held his fire. He could hear the men more easily now.

'We need lanterns to search the grounds.'

'No, it would be too dangerous. He is no doubt still armed. It's best if we wait until dawn. It's not very far away now.'

The men extinguished the hall lamp and went away.

As they rode towards the lane he wondered what had brought them here. He did not believe Ada could have reached help. Not after being shot in the stomach.

Perhaps someone else had heard the shots and told Charlotte's mother out of concern for the girl? She would have gone straight to the rectory and asked for Lovell's help.

It was a pity the young parson had not come to the manor on his own. He would have shot him and buried him in the same grave as Charlotte.

In the darkness, John Bettison allowed himself an amused smile. They would have made good grave companions, the parson and the harlot.

Thinking of Charlotte reminded him of what still needed

to be done. Dragging her the remainder of the way to the shrubbery, he awkwardly rolled her inside the grave.

Before replacing the earth, he returned to the house and lit the lantern. Taking it outside he made a search for Ada, but she could not be found.

Puzzled, he returned to the house and had a few more drinks before going outside once more. He could not understand what could have happened to Ada's body. But he would bury Charlotte now and have another search when daylight came. He was convinced she would not be far away.

After filling in the shallow grave, he discovered there was far more earth left over than he had anticipated. He worked hard to spread it all around until he was satisfied that in a day or two no one would ever know it had been dug over.

It was light enough now to do away with the lantern. He carried it back to the house, then fetched a pail of water to wash away the blood in the hall.

He had not completed this task when he heard the sound of voices outside once more.

Looking through the window he saw Lovell and some other men returning to the house. There were more of them this time, perhaps a dozen. One of them was the constable.

He suddenly remembered he had left his fowling-piece near the spot where he had buried Charlotte and ran from the house to fetch it.

The men saw him and spurred their horses forward, but Bettison had retrieved the gun and was backing towards the house by the time they reached him.

One of the party carried a gun in a saddle holster but made no attempt to draw it, and all the men pulled up their horses well clear of him.

John Bettison backed his way up the steps to the doorway. Here he stopped.

The men would have moved closer, but he brought his gun up and said, 'Stop right there. What is it you want?'

'You, Mr Bettison,' said the constable, uncertainly.

'We're here to arrest you for the murder of Charlotte Jane.'

'What are you talking about. I've murdered no one. Where is she? Where is the body?'

'If you've murdered no one then you won't mind coming with me to speak to Magistrate Tremayne while the others look around here.'

'I am not going anywhere – and no one is coming inside my house.'

The men outside the manor looked at each other uncertainly and began whispering among themselves.

There was apparent agreement and after much nodding of heads, the constable said nervously, 'I'm very sorry, Mr Bettison, but I am the parish constable. In view of what we already know, it is my duty to arrest you in the name of His Majesty the King.'

The young man edged his horse forward slowly but stopped when John Bettison shouldered his gun and aimed it at him.

'Stay where you are or I will shoot you.'

'Don't be a fool, Bettison, you'll only make things worse for yourself.'

As Toby spoke, the gun swung around to cover him.

'How? You say I have killed someone. If I have, how can I possibly make it worse? I can only be hanged once. But if I go, I'll take you with me.'

Toby saw the expression on John Bettison's face and dived off his horse as the gun went off and pellets flew through the air.

The report caused chaos among horses and men. Fortunately, Toby had retained his reins and was able to maintain a grip on his mount.

Meanwhile the front door had slammed shut as Bettison ran inside, not certain whether or not he had shot the Porthluney parson.

Bettison did not remain inside the house for long. Sprinting through the house, he emerged from the kitchen door and ran to the stables.

He was leading out his horse before he was spotted – and then it was by a man who was on foot.

The man sent up a shout immediately but Bettison swung himself into the saddle and was gone before anyone else came around to the rear of the house.

He did not head for the road but made off through the extensive grounds of the manor, making for the woods that stretched inland.

Chapter 92

Magistrate Tremayne was a brisk and efficient man. He had left Heligan House at first light, accompanied by four grooms.

On the way he met up with a messenger sent by the Porthluney constable and was acquainted by him with what was going on in and around Porthluney Manor.

The magistrate immediately sent his grooms and the messenger off to rouse the countryside. They were to put armed men on every road leading from Porthluney.

He also called out the huntsmen and those who rode to the hunt. They would scour the countryside under his direction in a search for the fugitive landowner.

Magistrate Tremayne knew the woods where John Bettison had last been seen. He had hunted over this countryside for very many seasons and was confident their quarry would be found.

One of the first men he met when he reached Porthluney was Toby. Tremayne asked whether the facts of the case as reported to him were accurate.

'I'm afraid so,' said Toby. 'Bettison murdered young Charlotte Jane and at the same time shot and wounded his housekeeper. She pretended to be dead but managed to escape from the house. She is a thoroughly reliable witness.'

'Have we found the body of the girl yet?'

Before Toby could reply a shout went up from some of the men outside. It was a grim answer to the magistrate's question.

One of the manor's dismissed servants had discovered Charlotte's body. He had found signs in the shrubbery of recent digging. He had scraped away some of the earth with his bare hands – and located her.

'Right!' said the magistrate, briskly. 'Now we are quite certain of the facts. Porthluney has gamekeepers, of course?'

'It had until Bettison dismissed everyone.' Looking about him, Toby pointed to where he could see Alice's father. 'Harry Rowe is one.'

Magistrate Tremayne called Harry to him. 'I understand you were one of Bettison's gamekeepers? Do you know this particular wood?'

'As well as I know my own back garden, sir.'

'Good. Can you raise some beaters quickly?'

'Many of 'em are already here, sir. I can send off for others right away. They'll all be here within the hour.'

'We can't afford to wait that long. We'll use the men we have and send for the others. They can join us as we go along. I want these woods beaten thoroughly. You flush Bettison out and we'll be waiting for him at the other side.'

'Be careful,' warned Toby. 'He's probably still armed.'

'We'll be armed too,' said the magistrate. Sweeping back his coat, he revealed two pistols tucked inside his belt. 'I want armed men with each party. If it's necessary they will use their weapons. I want no one else hurt by Bettison.'

The gamekeeper paused beside Toby before hurrying away. 'I just thought I'd tell you that my wife has gone with a couple more women to comfort Rose Henna. Charlotte wasn't exactly a good daughter to her, but she was all Rose had.'

'Thank you, Harry. I'll go to see Rose myself when this is sorted out.'

A growing line of beaters swept through the wood, making the sort of noise that was traditional when they were putting up pheasants.

Ironically, in view of the search he had once instigated for young Billy Kendall, John Bettison was hiding in the shooting hut. He heard the hullabaloo of the beaters as they made their way through the woods towards him, their ranks constantly swelled by more men from neighbouring farms and houses as word of the hue-and-cry spread.

Soon the estate and farm workers would be joined by

fishermen from Portholland and Portloe. None had any liking for the Porthluney landowner.

Retreating ahead of the line of beaters, John Bettison had almost reached the edge of the extensive wood when he heard men calling to each other in the pastureland beyond the trees.

He was in grave danger of being trapped between beaters and the waiting men.

John Bettison decided he would show them he was not to be caught so easily. Mounting his horse, he rode it at right angles to the line of beaters.

Fortunately for the hunted man he came out of the woods at a spot where Magistrate Tremayne had not yet posted guards.

He cleared the first field and had jumped the hedge into the next before he was spotted by one of the beaters who had just emerged from the woods.

The man set up an immediate shout, but with all the other beaters making such a din, it was some time before they responded to the urgency in his voice.

By the time the latest sighting was reported to the magistrate, John Bettison had long since disappeared from view, but now the hunt began in earnest.

Messengers were sent out to report the last sighting to the various groups who were augmented by farmers and others who rode horses. They began to flush out every copse and spinney.

For the next hour there were frequent sightings, and even more false alarms, but it became clear that Bettison was making his way eastwards.

Huntsmen were sounding their horns each time he was sighted and this became more frequent. The pursuers were closing in upon the desperate landowner in countryside on the high cliffs between Gorran Haven and Mevagissey.

The area in which he was hiding shrank in size until it was less than a half-mile in diameter, bounded by cliffs on one side and a ring of armed countrymen preventing his escape inland.

Magistrate Tremayne rode up beside Toby and halted his horse. The animal was well-lathered, both horse and rider having covered almost twice the distance of any others involved in the pursuit of the wanted man.

Pointing to a small copse in the centre of the area, the magistrate said, 'He's hiding in there.'

Standing up in his stirrups, he waved on the men riding to either side. 'Come along. Let's go in there and fetch him out.'

Some of the men cheered his words and began advancing upon the copse in an undulating crescent.

The nearest horseman was perhaps thirty lengths distant from the copse when John Bettison and his mount broke cover.

The horse left the copse at a canter which was almost immediately extended to a full gallop.

As the pursuers took up the chase, one of the huntsmen sounded a 'tally-ho' on his hunting horn. It was taken up by others.

Suddenly, the rousing sound faltered and died away. At the same time the men riding with Magistrate Tremayne reined in their mounts.

Only John Bettison's horse maintained a full gallop – heading straight for the cliff edge!

The men of the pursuing party watched in horrified disbelief as Bettison urged his horse on to even greater speed.

Even now, every man present believed this was the landowner's last act of bravado. They waited for him to turn his horse at the very last moment and ride back to surrender to the magistrate.

John Bettison proved them all wrong.

His horse never slackened speed. When it reached the cliff edge it stretched out as though taking a wide ditch. At the same time Bettison rose in the saddle and let out a last, loud shout of defiance.

Then horse and rider vanished from sight.

After a momentary hush, men began dismounting and hurrying to the cliff edge.

'Bodrugan's Leap!' muttered Magistrate Tremayne. He might have been talking to himself.

'I beg your pardon?' asked a puzzled Toby.

'I said "Bodrugan's Leap",' repeated the magistrate. 'It's the name of this particular section of cliff. Hundreds of years ago one of Bettison's ancestors rode his horse over the cliff when he was being pursued by the king's men. It was a high tide and he was picked up by a boat waiting offshore and carried off to safety in France. I don't think John Bettison will enjoy the same luck. It's low tide and the sea is too rough for there to be a boat close inshore.'

Turning to the other men, he said, 'I think justice has been served, gentlemen. We have seen the last of John Bettison. I thank you all for your assistance.'

'And may God have mercy on his soul,' said Toby, crossing himself. Then he too turned away from the cliff edge and set off to return to Porthluney.

Chapter 93

As the Vivian ship *Lady Felicia* entered Guernsey's St Peter Port harbour, Toby stood on deck, thinking of all that had changed in his life since the last occasion he was here.

He was now Rector of Porthluney. True, it was only a small parish, but his future was secure, especially now that John Bettison was dead.

Thinking of the late landowner caused him to remember the last sad duty he had performed before leaving his parish to undertake the voyage to France.

It had been the funeral of Charlotte Jane. The service had brought almost the whole parish to the church. Even those who had disapproved of her in life came to express sympathy for the manner of her death.

It was a very sad occasion . . . but all that was now behind him.

Toby allowed himself to feel excitement at the prospect of meeting Bethany once more. He wondered whether they would both still feel the same when they saw each other again.

He would be the first to admit there had been very little time to get to know each other as well as most couples contemplating marriage.

He had always hoped they would have time together in Porthluney, but that had not come about.

He also hoped Jennifer Cecil had been able to convince Bethany of the truth of what had happened on that fateful day at the rectory.

Tragically, the events of the past week would serve to confirm his story of Charlotte's liaison with the Porthluney landowner.

'Do you have a list of the men you hope to bring back to

England, Reverend Lovell?' The master of the *Lady Felicia* came to stand by Toby and broke in upon his thoughts with the question.

Toby's intended mission to France for the purpose of exchanging prisoners was no secret and had roused a great deal of interest among the crew.

'No, but I expect there'll be many wounded soldiers and army officers among them. It will be for the French to make the choice – unless you happen to know where any non-combatants are being kept?'

'As a matter of fact, I've been told of a prison where they are holding fishermen and merchant seamen.'

'Where?'

'In a town called Arras, not far from the Belgian border. The mate's brother is being held there. He's a Wesleyan preacher. Does that make any difference to you, Reverend?'

'The only thing that matters is that he's not a serving soldier or sailor. If he isn't, they shouldn't be holding him prisoner.'

'He was master of a ship working out of Falmouth. It was bound for Portugal with a cargo of smoked fish from Mevagissey when it was captured. A letter received by his brother says there are nearly sixty of them being kept in the same place.'

'Does he have the letter on board with him?'

'Yes. He showed it to me only yesterday.'

'Ask him if he will let me have it before I leave the ship. I'll specifically ask for the release of the men at Arras.'

'I wish you luck with your mission, Reverend. The mate will be delighted to hear you'll try to help his brother.'

When the *Lady Felicia* berthed in St Peter Port, one of the harbour officials came on board and enquired whether Toby was being carried as a passenger.

When he learned the Porthluney rector was on board, he asked Toby to remain on the ship until the Bailiff of Guernsey had been notified.

The instruction puzzled Toby. However, less than half-an-hour later a liveried servant came for him. He was told he was to be a guest of the Bailiff during his stay on the island.

At the house, he was shown to the study. Here the Bailiff greeted him with a warmth that Toby found somewhat surprising.

'It gives me great pleasure to meet you again, Mr Lovell, and to know you are undertaking another mission on behalf of those unfortunate Britons in French hands.'

Toby expressed his surprise that news of his mission had reached Guernsey already, but the Bailiff explained.

'I received a letter from the Foreign Secretary. He wishes me to give you every possible assistance. I have made the necessary arrangements for your journey. You will be sailing from here to Le Havre, where an escort will be waiting for you. They will take you to Paris to meet with M'sieur Fouché. I understand he wishes to discuss with you personally the proposed exchange of prisoners.'

'Will I have my own interpreter or will the French provide one for me? If it's possible I would rather have someone with me I can trust.'

'Of course. I think I have found the right person for you. I have arranged for them to be here to meet you this morning. No doubt you will want to be on your way as soon as possible. I thought I might arrange a passage to Le Havre for tomorrow.'

Toby was startled at the speed with which events were moving. 'That's rather sooner than I'd anticipated! I had thought I would go to Alderney before setting out for France.'

'I do understand.' The Bailiff acknowledged Toby's request with a nod of his head. 'Actually, Major Cecil is in Guernsey right now. I will arrange a meeting with him for you, but I don't think we will need to change my arrangements.'

The Guernsey Bailiff left Toby somewhat confused. The Bailiff had said Major Cecil was on the island . . . and there would be no need for him to change the arrangements he had made for Toby. What could he have meant? Was Bethany no longer on Alderney?

He was still wondering some time later when there

was a knock on his door. It was one of the Bailiff's servants.

'The Bailiff would like you to go to the study to meet the interpreter who will be accompanying you to France, Mr Lovell.'

As Toby followed the servant, he thought of his last interpreter and could not help smiling wryly to himself. There would never be another quite like Grace.

However, the personality of the new interpreter would be of vital importance to the success or failure of the mission he was undertaking. Both the stated aim, and the clandestine purpose, of his journey to France. One thing was certain: the interpreter would need to be someone he could trust implicitly. He would also have to be very careful not to antagonise the French authorities.

When the servant knocked on the door of the study it was opened by the Bailiff himself. Smiling at Toby, he said, 'Ah, there you are! Thank you for coming. I will leave you to get to know your interpreter. No doubt you will have much to talk about. In the meantime, I must prepare myself for another meeting I have this morning.'

Before Toby could indicate surprise that an introduction was not being effected, the Bailiff had gone.

Entering the study, Toby did not immediately see the figure standing to one side of the room, partly hidden from view by the open door.

Then a voice he had been longing to hear for very many months said, 'Hello, Toby.'

It was Bethany.

Chapter 94

'Bethany!'

Toby took a couple of paces towards her. Then he stopped, suddenly uncertain of her, and of himself.

She too hesitated, and the opportunity was gone. Had they both followed their heart, the barriers that divided them might have been swept aside. But such impetuosity would have been alien to the life each had led in the past.

'I . . . I've been seeking you for a long time, Bethany.'

It was not at all the way Toby had envisaged their reunion, although, in truth, he had not thought a great deal beyond the need to find her and put things right between them.

He had always somehow believed that once this aim had been achieved everything else would fall into place and all would be right once more.

'I know and I'm sorry. It's all my fault. I've behaved very stupidly.'

'You can't be blamed for thinking as you did. It looked bad . . .'

'Mrs Cecil told me what you confirmed in your letter – about Charlotte and John Bettison. I should have known you wouldn't have behaved in such a way with a girl like that.'

'She's paid very dearly for what she did, Bethany.' Toby told her of all that had happened at Porthluney Manor and of the end of John Bettison.

Bethany shuddered. 'I disliked Bettison intensely. Even so, I wouldn't have wished him to end his life in such a manner. But after what he did to Charlotte there was no way things could have worked out happily for him.

It's fortunate he didn't try to shoot you too. He had a passionate dislike of everything to do with the Church.'

'He did try,' said Toby, then exclaimed: 'But . . . you no longer talk like a Quaker, Bethany!'

She gave a wry smile. 'That's partly because I am no longer a member of the Society of Friends. It is also because Major Cecil was not happy that the children were beginning to imitate my way of talking. I thought it better to speak like everyone else.'

There was an awkward silence between them that lasted many moments. It was broken when Toby gave an embarrassed laugh. 'The Bailiff played a little joke on me. He sent for me to come to his study pretending I was to meet the interpreter who will be accompanying me to France. I must take him to task about it.'

'Why? You wanted to meet your interpreter. Now you have.'

For a brief moment, Toby did not comprehend what she was saying. When it sank home, he exclaimed, 'You! The Bailiff has suggested *you* should come to France as my interpreter?'

'No. *I* suggested it. He agreed. Is it unacceptable to you? I thought you took a woman along as your interpreter on the last occasion you went to France. Do I not meet your requirements?'

'There's no one I would rather have with me all the time,' declared Toby, fervently. 'But it might prove dangerous. Besides, Grace is . . . well . . . she's seen a great deal more of the world than you.'

Bethany raised an eyebrow. 'Really? You must tell me more of this woman with whom you spent so much of your time in France! Would you rather the Bailiff appointed someone else to accompany you?'

Toby did not even have to think about his reply this time. 'No, Bethany. There's no one I would rather have with me. Besides, it has taken me a long time to find you, I don't think I want to let you out of my sight again. Not for a very long time.'

'Thank you, Toby.' Bethany's voice sounded shaky, even to herself. 'I was hoping you might say something like that.'

* * *

The journey from Guernsey to Le Havre was to be made in a small coastal craft and would take twenty-four hours. The boat normally operated between the various Channel Islands.

Accommodation on board was somewhat cramped and both Toby and Bethany were thankful the sea was moderately calm for the voyage.

That night the boat sailed around the Cap de la Hague before changing course to steer eastwards. It was heading for the port that guarded the mouth of the Seine, the great river that flowed through Paris on its way to the sea.

On deck, Toby and Bethany sat side by side, looking across the narrow stretch of water that separated them from France.

They told each other of much that had happened to them during the time they had spent apart, speaking of family and friends, and of mutual acquaintances they had known in Cornwall.

'I must have added a great deal to your troubles at a time when you needed support,' said Bethany unhappily. Toby had just told her of being summoned to Exeter to answer the charges laid against him by John Bettison, and of his subsequent suspension.

'I was very concerned for you,' he admitted. 'So too was Muriel. She also had Jacob to worry about.'

After a minute or two of contemplative silence, Bethany said, 'Tell me something of Grace, the interpreter who accompanied you on your last journey to France?'

Toby told Bethany of his first meeting with Grace and of the way she had been able to help him during his French mission. He left much unsaid about the manner in which she was able to influence the decisions of French officials, but Bethany was an astute young woman and was able to fill in many of the unspoken details for herself.

'You grew fond of this woman . . . of Grace?'

'Yes, I did,' agreed Toby, honestly. 'She managed to secure my release from prison when I was beginning to give up hope of ever getting out. She is a very warm-hearted woman and knew how desperate I was to find you.'

The silence between them lasted longer than any that

had gone before. It ended when Bethany asked, 'Where do we go from here, Toby? Now you have found me?'

'Have you changed in the way you think about me?' he countered.

'I . . . I don't think so. But it distresses me that I was able to think what I did of you. Would I . . . *should* I think such things of a man if I loved him enough?'

Toby thought deeply before replying to her. 'We barely knew each other long enough to discover how much we could trust each other. I realised when I was searching for you that I had not got to know you as well as I would have liked. I never had doubts about the way I felt. Never. But I didn't know you well enough to understand why you thought or behaved the way you did. Perhaps I never will, but I *do* know that neither time nor logic can change the way I feel, and I would not have it any other way.'

Once again there was a long silence between them and Toby wished he could have seen Bethany's face, but it was far too dark.

When she spoke it was in a carefully controlled voice. 'I thank you for that, Toby. But it makes me feel even more humble than before. You cared enough to search for me in an enemy country, even when you did not understand why I had gone off and left you.'

Suddenly, she reached out a hand and touched his cheek. 'I wonder how many men would have done the same for a woman who ran off without explanation?'

Removing her hand, she said, 'I am going below to my cabin now. You should do the same. I think it will be a very busy day for both of us tomorrow.'

When she had gone, Toby put a hand to his cheek where she had touched him. Her words had warmed him. It was only when he too left the deck to make his way to his cabin that he recalled she had not felt able to declare unequivocally that their time apart had not altered the way she felt about him.

It troubled him for much of the night as the ship ploughed through the waters of the Channel, on its way to Le Havre.

Chapter 95

The small Guernsey vessel, flying the British ensign, attracted a great deal of attention from the crews of ships lying at anchor in Le Havre as it was escorted in.

The boat had been intercepted in the Seine river estuary by a French gun ship and a boarding party sent on board.

After inspecting the letters signed by senior English, French and Channel Islands officials, a French officer told the ship's captain to lower the British ensign before following the French vessel into the harbour.

The captain refused to lower his flag, pointing out that he was not a prisoner of the other man. The French officer eventually gave way and the two boats proceeded.

Le Havre was a busy port, although since the war most was river traffic linking the port with Paris and the interior. Nevertheless, French ocean-going ships did occasionally evade the patrolling British men-o'-war, as did American blockade runners.

'Are you feeling nervous?' Toby had been watching Bethany closely as they sailed closer to the quayside.

'Not exactly,' she replied. She waved her hand in a gesture which encompassed all the houses stretching down to the harbour's edge. 'I just feel sad that all these people should be our enemies.'

'Fortunately, this war won't last for ever,' said Toby. He wished he might have been able to share the secret of the letter stitched inside the lining of his coat with Bethany. He felt the need to have her think more highly of him than he believed she did. He desperately wanted to know he had her respect once more.

Waiting on the jetty were a small number of green

uniformed *Chasseurs*, sitting their horses patiently as the Guernsey boat docked.

There was also a growing crowd of onlookers and it was this that disturbed Toby most of all. Remembering some of the incidents that had occurred on his earlier visit to France, he told Bethany they would remain on board until their escort came on the ship and accepted official responsibility for their safety.

For a while after the ship berthed it seemed they had reached an impasse. They remained on board the ship, while the soldiers stayed on the jetty.

Eventually, the lieutenant in charge of the *Chasseurs* lost patience. He sent his sergeant on board to inquire when Toby was coming off the ship.

With Bethany interpreting, he said he would come off when the officer had cleared the onlookers from the quay and could guarantee their safety.

The sergeant looked contemptuously at Toby. Then he shrugged and let loose a torrent of French, accompanied by much gesticulating.

'He says our countries are at war with each other,' explained Bethany. 'If you have come to France expecting to be among friends, perhaps the British have sent the wrong man.'

Toby nodded his acknowledgement of the translation. 'Tell him I am aware I am in an enemy country, but I am here on a mission of peace: to arrange for prisoners of both countries to be returned to their families. It is something I have done before. I have also felt the anger of those whose loved ones will never return to them. It is an experience I have no intention of having you subjected to. He can tell his officer that if he is unable to ensure our safety, I will return to England. From there I will inform Minister Fouché that I will not come to France again until he can find an officer who is not too inept to perform his duties.'

Somewhat hesitantly, Bethany translated this ultimatum. Meanwhile, to show he meant what he said, Toby told the master of the small ship to have his men ready the vessel for leaving port.

The combination of words and deeds had the effect of

stirring the French cavalry officer to action. The sergeant who had come on board began calling upon the crowd to move away from the ship.

They were reluctant to obey and he was forced to repeat his request, informing them of the nature of Toby's mission to France.

The reaction of many in the crowd was exactly as Toby had predicted. Someone shouted that *his* son would never return, adding that his memory would be sullied if an Englishman were allowed to set foot on French soil.

Even as Bethany translated what she could hear of the heated exchange on the quayside, a howl went up from the crowd.

Now the officer moved forward. He shouted for them to disperse, only to have his words greeted with shouts of derision.

The lieutenant's response was to order his men to draw their swords. Then he lined them up, facing the crowd.

There was a moment of silence before the men and women nearest to the horses tried in vain to move back against the pressure of those behind them.

Suddenly, there was a shout from someone in the midst of the mob and a stone sailed through the air, aimed at the *Chasseurs*.

A roar of approval went up and suddenly missiles were flying in all directions. Some were aimed at the cavalrymen, many more began raining down upon the Guernsey ship.

'It's time we went below,' said Toby, and called for the captain and his men to do the same, while urging him to leave a couple of armed men at the top of the gangway, ready to take action should the angry mob attempt to storm the ship.

'How did you know that would happen?' queried Bethany, as they waited below deck for things to quieten down on the quayside.

'Did you see the missiles that were being thrown on board? It was not a spontaneous attack. Many of those in the crowd were carrying them when they arrived. I saw stones, lumps of wood and even iron spikes taken from railings among them. As the French sergeant said, we are their enemies. Some of those among the crowd have lost relatives. This is a sea port, many men from here would have been lost in sea battles.'

'What will happen now?' Bethany's eyes looked wide in the dim light below decks.

'I should imagine the French officer will send for reinforcements to guard us when we leave the ship. Hopefully they will remain with us until we are well clear of Le Havre.'

Once more, Toby's prediction proved accurate. A full company of blue-coated infantrymen was despatched from the town's garrison to the harbour. They quickly beat back the crowd and then a coach arrived for Toby and Bethany.

Escorted by the cavalry troop and the infantrymen, they were taken along the Paris road. Not until nightfall did the infantrymen turn about and return to Le Havre, leaving the others to make speedier progress to Paris – and Minister Joseph Fouché.

Chapter 96

Bethany and Toby spent two nights on the road to Paris, arriving in the French capital late on the third day after leaving Le Havre.

The first night on the road, Toby discovered his baggage had been thoroughly searched. When he mentioned it to Bethany, she said she suspected the same had happened to hers, although she was puzzled that they should want to go through her belongings.

The French officer also spent much time talking to Bethany, although he never once asked Toby a direct question.

Toby thought this was because the Frenchman had taken a liking to her, but when he made a joke of it, Bethany shook her head.

'There is nothing romantic in his questioning. He seems more curious that a French minister of M'sieur Fouché's stature should interest himself in the exchange of a few prisoners-of-war. He wants to know whether you are a particularly important man in England. I have a feeling he has been ordered to ask such questions. He seems more interested in M'sieur Fouché's involvement than in your presence here.'

While Toby was pondering on what she had said, Bethany asked, 'Is there something about this mission to France you haven't told me, Toby? Something I should know?'

He did not enjoy lying to Bethany. 'We are here to arrange an exchange of prisoners, Bethany. The more messages that are exchanged between the ministers of our two countries, the more chance there is of one day bringing about peace. If it will help to satisfy the curiosity of the young lieutenant, you can tell him I am already acquainted with Minister Fouché. I once arranged for the release of his brother-in-law in exchange for some British prisoners. Consequently, he is the man who has been approached on this occasion.'

If Bethany felt Toby was not giving her the full story of what was going on, she made no comment and passed his information on to the lieutenant of the *Chasseurs* when he next questioned her.

When the small party reached Paris, they were taken immediately to the magnificent home of Fouché. Here they were put in the care of the minister's servants.

Remembering the antagonism shown towards him by Fouché's wife, Toby was relieved to learn she was away, holidaying in a villa owned by Minister Fouché on the Mediterranean coast.

Not until a servant came to Toby's room to inform him that the Minister of Police had returned home did Toby unpick the lining of his coat. Carefully, he removed the letter entrusted to him by the British Foreign Secretary.

He delivered it personally to Monsieur Fouché in his study. The minister thanked him, asked after his welfare, and said he needed to read the letter and reply to some urgent correspondence. He would meet Toby and his interpreter over dinner that evening.

At dinner, Minister Fouché played the part of the perfect host. He was in a jovial mood, giving his approval to Toby's present interpreter.

'I really must commend your choice, M'sieur Lovell. You have a penchant for attractive young ladies.'

'Bethany is the one I was seeking when I came to France before,' explained Toby, not wanting her to gain the wrong impression from the French minister. 'As it happened, she was not in France at all, but on one of the Channel Islands.'

'I am so glad you have found her,' said Fouché. 'I trust you will not lose her again.'

'I sincerely hope not,' said Toby, not looking at Bethany.

It was an excellent meal and the vintage Champagne provided by Fouché helped to create a warm and relaxed atmosphere about the table. Not until dessert was about to be served did the minister bring up the subject of the exchange of prisoners.

'Do you have any particular prisoners in mind?' he asked casually.

'As a matter of fact, I do,' said Toby. 'You are holding a number of English prisoners in a military prison in Arras . . .'

'Ah!' Minister Fouché sat back in his chair and wagged a finger at Toby. 'I was waiting for you to mention Arras, M'sieur Lovell. You must let me into the secrets of your English intelligence service. I only heard the news myself yesterday. You are talking, of course, of the delectable Grace?'

'Grace, M'sieur Fouché?'

'Yes, your last interpreter. Do not act as though you are surprised. Why else would you request the release of the prisoners held at Arras? She was taken, together with many of the crew of a ship that was driven aground not far from Ostend. I had hoped to keep the fact a secret. Perhaps persuade her to take up residence here in Paris. However . . .'

Fouché shrugged. 'Perhaps it is as well you have arrived. Had it become known, it would have caused trouble between myself and Madame Fouché. Besides, had Madame's brother learned of Grace's presence in France, he might have pressed his claim to her. In French law she is still legally his slave, I believe. You would do well to return her to England quickly, M'sieur Lovell. Calais is the nearest port to Arras. You will, of course, return to Paris and give me a list of all prisoners who have been released. I will in turn provide a list for your own government of the prisoners we wish to have released. There will no doubt be others – wounded officers perhaps – whom you may wish to repatriate as a gesture of good-will towards France.'

Later that evening, Toby and Bethany took a walk through

the streets of Paris. Behind them, keeping a discreet distance, were two of Minister Fouché's secret policemen. They were present only to ensure that the minister's English guests did not run into any trouble.

As they walked beside the River Seine, Bethany said suddenly, 'Tell me more of this Grace? The woman who came with you on your first visit to France.'

'I have already told you most of what I know about her.'

'You also, if I recall correctly, told me you are very fond of her. Is she attractive?'

'Yes, very,' said Toby, honestly. 'It's also very probable she had an affair with Minister Fouché while I was in prison.'

'And with you too?'

Toby looked at her with a delighted smile. 'Do I detect a trace of jealousy? No, Bethany, not with me. We were in France searching for you. She was my interpreter and my friend. If I can secure her release from prison it will make me very happy.'

More seriously, he added, 'I am also concerned for the man she was sailing with, and for his crew. Matthew Vivian was master of a privateer and I came to know him very well. I hope he was rescued too. Anyway, we'll soon know. Hopefully we'll set off for Arras tomorrow. It's another two-day journey. I hope Minister Fouché details a different officer to take charge of our escort. I didn't like the *Chasseur* lieutenant.'

'He was resentful that he had been detailed as our escort,' explained Bethany. 'He thought it was a task for an old soldier. He wanted to be with Napoleon, fighting in the wars.'

'No doubt he'll be fighting soon enough,' sighed Toby. 'I had hoped peace might have moved closer by now. It was rumoured in England that Napoleon had offered to return Hanover to the throne of England if a peace could be arranged between us. But Minister Fouché says there are too many differences remaining between England and France. Still, like me, he remains hopeful.'

Suddenly, Bethany linked her arm through his. 'If you

and Minister Fouché are both seeking peace, I have no doubt it will come about sooner or later. One day you have a lot of explaining to do to me, Toby Lovell – and I am not only talking of your other interpreter! But we are in Paris together. I want to enjoy it. Look! Isn't that Notre-Dame over there? What a wonderful building. Can we go and have a look at it?'

Chapter 97

Paris was a turning point in Toby's and Bethany's relationship. They regained much of the easy companionship they seemed to have lost since their parting in Cornwall. Each felt comfortable once more in the other's company.

They arrived in Arras riding in Minister Fouché's personal coach. They had been given a change of escort too. For this journey they were provided with a party of uniformed policemen. It seemed the minister wished his part in the exchange of prisoners to be as public as possible.

The coach and escort ensured they received prompt and willing service along the route. The only problem they encountered was the weather. It was wet and blustery for the whole of the journey.

It was perhaps the weather which made the military gaol appear so grim and forbidding when they reached it, although Bethany believed it would have looked no more inviting whatever the weather.

Toby wanted to go inside the gaol immediately, but the officer in charge of the escort refused to consider it. His orders were to take them straight to the hotel where they were to stay.

Once there, their coach and escort again ensured they received a warm welcome from an innkeeper who spoke good English. He told them he had worked at a Paris hotel popular with their countrymen in pre-Revolution days.

However, the hotelier's manner underwent a change when he was told the purpose of their visit.

'You are going to the military gaol? I am sorry, M'sieur and Mam'selle, I regret you cannot remain in my establishment.'

His change of attitude was so sudden it took both the travellers by surprise.

'Why not? It will make no trouble for you. Minister Fouché's men will remain here.'

'I am not concerned about trouble. The people of Arras are used to seeing Englishmen in the town. Sometimes, on special religious occasions, a few prisoners are allowed out on parole. They neither cause trouble nor meet with it from our people. The reason I cannot allow you to stay in my hotel if you visit the gaol is because they have the fever there. Many have already died. So many that most of the guards have fled from the town rather than work in the gaol and risk bringing death to their families. You are both very welcome to stay here. Most welcome. But not if it is your intention to visit the gaol.'

When Toby and Bethany talked the matter over with the officer in charge of the escort, he offered the opinion that they should forget all thoughts of visiting Arras gaol. He suggested returning to Paris immediately, adding cynically that they could find any number of English prisoners in many gaols in France.

Toby would not even consider such a course of action. Grace and, hopefully, Matthew were inside the gaol. He would not leave without securing their release. However, he did suggest that Bethany return to Paris with the police escort.

'And leave you here in the company of the delectable Grace? No, Toby. We will both go to the gaol and see if there is anything we can do for the men there.'

The hotel keeper relented sufficiently to agree they could return after only a single visit to the Arras military gaol, but he still insisted they must leave if it was their intention to pay regular visits to their countrymen.

The police escort took them as far as the great, iron-studded entrance gate, but there did not appear to be a gaoler on duty. Toby was forced to pull the bell rope many times before there was any response from inside.

Then, through a small opening in the door, a French gaoler enquired what they wanted. When told they wished to come in, he replied that no visitors were allowed, for fear they would take the gaol fever out to the city.

When told by the police inspector they had the authority of the Minister of Police, the gaoler reluctantly asked them who it was they wished to see.

Toby explained they wished to see the woman Grace, and the gaoler's manner changed immediately.

'Ah, she is a wonderful woman. She works day and night for those who are ill. Everyone calls her the Angel of Arras! But she is sleeping.'

'She will be delighted to see us and hear the news we bring. Let us in.'

After much arguing and a great deal of grumbling, the door opened and Toby and Bethany were allowed inside.

Before leaving the French police escort outside the gaol, Bethany had a long conversation with the commanding officer. When Toby asked what they were talking about, Bethany explained she had told the French policeman she wanted one of his men to remain outside the gate. They would relay all their needs and plans through him. She added anxiously, 'He told us that everything we ordered would need to be paid for. Do you have any money?'

Toby nodded. He had been given a generous sum by the Foreign Office in London. He also carried quite a large amount of his own money, much of which had been exchanged for French money when he was in Guernsey.

'Good. Then let's find this woman I have heard so much about.'

Toby had thought the prison at Morlaix left much to be desired, but it was a palace when compared with the one they were visiting now.

The Arras military gaol was very much older. It smelled as though damp and decay seeped from every stone of the ancient building.

Today the foul atmosphere was further polluted by the menacing miasma of disease that seemed to hang in the very air.

They passed a couple of communal cells, but they appeared to be empty except for a deep layer of dirty straw covering the stone floor.

Eventually, the gaoler stopped at an iron door in which

there was a small grille. Peering inside the cell, the gaoler confirmed that Grace was inside, and still asleep.

When Bethany translated his words, Toby said, 'Tell him I am sorry to have to disturb her, but I want to speak to her.'

The warder shrugged. To the surprise of Bethany and Toby he pushed open the door. It was not locked.

'Madame . . . Madame Grace!'

While the gaoler was speaking, Toby looked down at her pityingly. This was not the elegant, silk-clad woman he remembered. True, her dress might have been of silk, but it was very dirty. She was untidy too and most unlike the woman he had last seen on board the *Potomac*.

Grace woke up reluctantly and with considerable difficulty. Sleepily, she murmured something in French before opening her eyes. They suddenly grew wide when she looked up and saw Toby.

Scrambling to her feet with a cry of disbelief, she flung her arms about him. 'Toby! Toby . . . it *is* you. Tell me I am not dreaming?' Suddenly and unexpectedly, she burst into tears.

Toby held her for a few minutes, uncomfortably aware that Bethany was watching them silently.

Grace pulled away from him, saying, 'I am so sorry, Toby, but it has been too terrible . . .'

She became aware of Bethany and the warder standing behind Toby. Her hands brushed her dress quickly, before travelling up to her hair.

'Grace, I would like you to meet Bethany.'

'You have found her!'

Grace's obvious delight would have satisfied all but the most jealous woman. 'I am so happy for you, Toby. Happy for you both.'

'What of Matthew? Was he saved?'

Grace's expression changed to one of concern. 'Yes, he was saved, but he is very ill. So are many of the men in here. Some have already died . . . but why are you in France? You should not have come here. The gaol fever . . .'

'Right now we're here to see what can be done for you and the others, Grace. I have a letter from Minister

Fouché authorising your release. When the fever has been contained we will all go home. To Cornwall.'

A wide variety of expressions passed across Grace's face. 'At any other time that would be wonderful news. As it is . . . I only hope some of us will survive to see Cornwall once more. But come, I will take you to Matthew.'

Chapter 98

Toby was shocked when he saw Matthew Vivian in the Arras prison cell. Lying on straw with eight other sick men, he barely had strength enough to raise his head. Nevertheless, he managed a tired smile for Toby and reached up a hand for Grace to hold.

'What are you doing here?' he asked Toby, breathlessly.

'I've come to take you and the others in your crew home to Cornwall,' replied Toby, trying to sound cheerful. 'But I can't take you until you're well enough to travel, so you'd better hurry up and get better.'

Matthew's expression registered disbelief and he turned to Grace for confirmation. 'Is Toby telling the truth? He's not just saying it to make me feel better?'

'I have a letter here from Minister Fouché,' said Toby. 'It authorises the release of all British prisoners held in Arras and directs the prison authorities to arrange repatriation as soon as is practicable.'

Matthew closed his eyes and seemed to relax. 'Thank God – and you too, Toby. It means that no matter what happens to me, Grace will return safely to Cornwall. She still has this threat of being a French slave hanging over her here, you know?'

Opening his eyes once more, but wearily now, he added, 'She has a copy of my will, Toby. All I own in Cornwall is to go to her. Should the will be contested, you are a witness to my wishes.'

'I'll be a witness certainly, Matthew. But you'll return to Falmouth and put it in the hands of a solicitor yourself. Meanwhile we're going to set to work to have this gaol cleaned up and get some good food and drink sent in for you. Grace, is there any clean straw anywhere?'

She shook her head. 'None. I have been trying to persuade the gaolers to obtain some, but they are no longer interested. They say, "Why should we waste good money on men who are going to die anyway?" It has made me very angry sometimes.'

'We'll have some sent in. Soap, water, and limewash too. We also need the services of a doctor. Has anyone been in to treat the sick men?'

'A naval surgeon was one of the prisoners, but he was among the first to die. Since then we have received no medical help whatsoever.'

'I think this requires the attention of the prison governor. Bethany, will you ask the gaoler where we can find him?'

'I can tell you the answer you will receive,' said Grace, aggrievedly. 'He is "away". That is the answer I am always given. He has not been near the gaol since the outbreak of the fever.'

'Where does he live?'

The question was put to the gaoler, but although he went into considerable detail, Toby was none the wiser.

'Tell him he must take us there,' he said to Bethany.

This provoked a torrent of animated talk from the gaoler.

'He says he has no time to take us on a wasted journey,' explained Bethany. 'There are few enough gaolers here as it is. Were he to desert his post for us, the governor would dismiss him on the spot.'

'If we do not make some immediate changes here, it will be the governor who will be dismissed,' said Toby. 'Tell him I am here at the express wish of Minister Fouché. The minister is an impatient man. If something is not done immediately, the governor will not only lose his position, but most probably his head – and no doubt others will suffer with him.'

The implication for the gaoler was clear, and Minister Fouché's reputation was enough to make the man reassess where his duty lay. Minister Fouché was notorious for his ruthlessness throughout post-Revolutionary France.

'He says he will take us,' said Bethany. 'But we will please inform the governor it was a direct order from an emissary of the minister.'

* * *

The Paris policeman on duty outside the prison accompanied Toby, Bethany and the gaoler to the prison governor's home, a very large mansion on the edge of town.

At first, the governor was extremely angry that anyone from the gaol should visit him here, especially in view of the fever raging within the prison walls.

His manner underwent an immediate change when Toby repeated the warning he had given to the gaoler. He then handed the governor the letter from Minister Fouché, ordering him to release all the British prisoners held in Arras.

Suddenly anxious to please, he signed requisitions for everything Toby demanded: provisions, straw, cleaning materials. He promised that a doctor would attend the prison on a daily basis, commencing that very day.

The prisoners were also granted unlimited access to the exercise yard inside the prison. The governor hesitated only on the issue of granting their freedom. He eventually agreed they could go – but only when the doctor confirmed that they posed no danger to the people of Arras and the inhabitants of the towns and villages through which they would pass on their way to the coast.

Toby left the governor's house well pleased with all he had achieved. It meant that within the walls of the gaol, the English prisoners were free to do more or less as they pleased.

He decided that in view of the hotelier's attitude, he and Bethany would also remain in the prison, to supervise all they had planned.

Back inside the gaol, Toby called all the English prisoners together and told them what had been agreed. It gave them all new heart, and with a return to England within sight, they set out to do all within their power to bring it about as quickly as possible.

Within forty-eight hours the prison had been cleaned thoroughly and its walls limewashed. The French doctor proved to be a dedicated man and worked hard for the sick men. Meanwhile, Bethany and Grace helped to cook and supervised the cleaning in addition to nursing the sick.

Understandably, Grace devoted much of her time to

Matthew and after a couple of worrying days, he began to respond to her care.

Yet, despite all their efforts, seven more prisoners died before the outbreak of gaol fever was brought under control. It was not until eleven days after Toby's arrival that the doctor gave him the all clear. In his opinion, the English prisoners were now well enough to make the journey home to their own country without posing a threat to anyone else.

Chapter 99

The English prisoners in the Arras military gaol were preparing themselves to leave within a few days when their departure was precipitated in an unexpected manner.

An important messenger arrived from Minister Fouché in Paris. He was accompanied to Arras by a police escort comprised of men of Fouché's own élite guard. They were commanded by an officer who was surprisingly senior for such a duty.

The messenger was the minister's personal secretary and he brought alarming news. Fouché had learned he was suspected of negotiating for peace with England without consulting Bonaparte.

It seemed rumours had reached the Emperor that his Minister of Police was plotting to overthrow him while the country's leader was fighting his foreign wars.

Toby was suspected of acting as go-between with the British government. The personal secretary had ridden in great haste to Arras to tell him he must leave the country immediately if he was to avoid arrest.

Toby's reply was that he would not go until the prisoners were ready to leave with him.

His reply exasperated the messenger. 'Never mind the prisoners. You must leave immediately! It is of extreme importance to everyone that you are not taken prisoner by the army.'

Toby refused to be panicked into doing as the messenger wished. 'If I leave France hurriedly without taking the prisoners with me it will appear that the Emperor's suspicions are justified. On the other hand, if they go too, then Minister Fouché can always say I did what I came for. It will add strength to his argument that there is nothing sinister in my mission to France.'

After thinking it over for some moments, the Minister of Police's personal secretary agreed. 'All right, but you must leave immediately, M'sieur Lovell. You will take my escort with you. The officer who commands them is to be trusted.'

Bethany had not been present at Toby's interview with the personal secretary, but realised the visitor was a man of some importance.

When Toby came from the meeting and said the prisoners had to be ready to leave immediately, she guessed something untoward had happened and asked Toby the reason for the urgency.

'Minister Fouché appears to be falling from favour,' he replied, keeping as close to the truth as was possible. 'If he is brought down, the exchange of prisoners will most likely be halted.'

'Does Fouché's fall from grace have anything to do with your mission to France?' she asked.

'We'll discuss it later,' said Toby. 'Right now we must get the men ready to leave.'

'How will they reach the coast?' persisted Bethany. 'They are not fit to march any distance. Some are still so weak they can hardly walk at all!'

'I'll have a word with Fouché's private secretary,' replied Toby. 'While I'm doing that, will you and Grace have the men gather up any belongings they may have with them? They should take the best of the blankets, too. We'll be travelling overnight and they may feel the cold.'

When Toby tackled the private secretary, he learned that plans to obtain transport for the prisoners were already in hand. Minister Fouché's police were scouring the town, commandeering carriages and horses for the journey. Meanwhile, an officer had been sent ahead to Calais. He would charter a ship of sufficient size to make the short journey across the Channel.

Unaware of the drama behind their sudden departure from the prison where some of the men had been incarcerated for years, the freed Englishmen set up a cheer as the small convoy of carriages moved off.

Once clear of the town they began singing. The celebrations continued in the vehicles for much of that evening and into the night.

The policeman in charge of the escort proved to be a very efficient organiser. Men had been sent on to requisition fresh horses and they were waiting at various points along the route. As a result, the carriages rolled into the ancient sea port of Calais only a couple of hours after dawn.

There had been no problem finding a suitable ship to carry the Englishmen. In common with other French ports, the blockade by British men-o'-war was almost total. Most ships in the harbour had been bottled up in the port for very many months. The soldier organising the charter was able to choose from a couple of dozen vessels.

As the men boarded the ship, Toby saw the commanding officer of the police escort talking animatedly to a man in civilian clothes who appeared to be well-known to the others of the escort.

The conversation came to an abrupt end and the officer hurried to the ship where he beckoned urgently to Toby.

When Toby hurried down the gangway to him, the senior police officer said, 'You must hurry! Soldiers have arrived in Calais, seeking you. Get under way immediately. I will post my men at the entrance to this particular quay. If the soldiers arrive I will delay them for as long as I can.'

The last of the sick men had been hurried on board when a large troop of French cavalry cantered up to the policemen guarding the quay. A fierce argument ensued between the two commanding officers.

On board the ship, Toby said to Bethany, 'Quick! Tell the captain to cast off and get under way.'

Bethany spoke to the French captain but he gave her an abrupt reply, seemingly more interested in the developments on the quayside.

'He believes the army officer is trying to attract his attention,' said Bethany, suddenly pale-faced. 'He is sending a man to find out what he wants.'

Matthew, still not fully recovered, was standing nearby and Toby turned to him in desperation. 'Can your men sail this ship?'

'I've yet to find the ship they couldn't sail.'

'Right! We've got to overwhelm the crew and put the ship to sea as quickly as we can. If the army get here first there'll be no return to England for anyone.'

Many of the survivors from the *Potomac* were standing close enough to overhear what was being said.

As they hesitated uncertainly, Matthew told them, 'You heard what the parson said.' Raising his voice, he shouted, 'All of you. We need to put this ship to sea ourselves – and do it quickly. Go!'

The *Potomac* men were the first to spring into action, casting off the ropes connecting them with the shore and raising sails to catch the wind. Not until the French crew began disputing their right to take over the working of the ship did the others take part in what was going on.

Some of the ship's crew were laid out with hastily seized weapons, others were flung over the side into the harbour. By the time the French soldiers broke through the police lanes, there was half a ship's length of water between the vessel and the quay.

The Englishmen fought with the desperation of men who knew their freedom, and probably their lives, depended upon success.

By the time the ship was clear of the harbour, the French crew was battened down in one of the holds, although every so often another Frenchman was discovered hiding somewhere on board.

Fortunately, it was not necessary to sail very far. Less than two miles from the French coast they were intercepted by a seventy-four-gun English ship of the line.

When the two ships were tied alongside each other, Toby told as much of his story as was necessary to the captain of the Royal Navy vessel.

In the captain's cabin, Toby wrote a letter explaining what had happened in France. Using the captain's seal, Toby addressed it to the Foreign Secretary in London. The naval officer promised he would take it to England immediately and have it delivered to London by one of his lieutenants.

The naval ship also took on board those recently released

prisoners who did not wish to sail to Cornwall. They would be landed at Dover, with the lieutenant.

Toby and the many Cornishmen on board intended sailing the French vessel to Falmouth. A party of marines was placed on board to help guard the French crew until their destination was reached.

Once there, the crew would be allowed to sail their ship back to Calais. They would take with them the French prisoners Toby was authorised to repatriate from the naval hospital in Plymouth, and from working parties engaged in building a huge prison at Princetown, on Devon's Dartmoor.

Toby felt he owed this gesture, at least, to Minister Fouché. It would strengthen his hand against those who sought to topple him.

For the rest . . . Toby believed the Minister of Police was wily enough to talk himself out of trouble, but he hoped he might never again be called upon to journey to France to meet him.

Chapter 100

The French ship slipped into Falmouth harbour almost unnoticed. Not until a Customs party came on board was it learned the vessel had been brought into port by returning English prisoners-of-war.

The Cornish port erupted in a frenzy of celebration. Ships in harbour fired off their cannons and townsfolk descended upon the ship with gifts of food. A local brewery sent a cart containing barrels of ale for the men on board.

Somehow during the voyage Grace had managed to clean the only dress she possessed and wash and arrange her hair. It was a return of the woman Toby had first seen on board the French merchantman captured by Matthew's privateers. Bethany was moved to say that she was an extremely beautiful woman.

When Sir Charles Vivian heard the party was headed by a clergyman, he guessed it was Toby and hurried from his office to the harbour. He was astonished to see Grace and Matthew on board. Despite his questioning, he was able only to gain a bare outline of what had happened to the *Potomac* and its crew before another batch of town dignitaries arrived to offer congratulations to the returning men.

Before leaving his brother at the centre of the crowd, he said, 'As soon as you're able to get away, we'll take you and Grace home. You can enjoy a long convalescence while we decide on your future. I think perhaps it's time we found you something to do in the office.'

'Nonsense!' replied Matthew who had regained much of his vitality in the excitement of the town's welcome. 'We'll buy another *Potomac*. It's the only way I can keep an eye on Grace. That reminds me, before I do anything else I have some business to conduct with our solicitor . . .'

Further conversation became impossible with the arrival of the Sheriff of the county. Soon afterwards, Toby, Bethany and Sir Charles made their way to the office of the Vivian shipping company. They passed through celebrating crowds making their way to the harbour to cheer the returned men. Many hoped to catch a glimpse of the enemy seamen, released from the ship's hold.

Once in the office, Sir Charles said, 'I am very pleased to have you back in the county, Toby, and to know you have finally managed to find your Bethany. I hope her influence will persuade you to settle down to the quiet life of a country rector.'

'It is sad that John Bettison should have met such a tragic end,' said Toby, 'but his death has made life much easier for me. Though I suppose much will depend upon the new lord of Porthluney Manor.'

'Ah!' Sir Charles beamed at him. 'I don't think you have any worries there, Toby. You see, *I* have bought Porthluney Manor. Sally and I will live there when we are married. Right now workmen are making a few alterations. They should be completed within the month, by which time I hope Sally and I will be married.'

Smiling at Toby's delighted expression, Sir Charles added, 'It made sense, really. I am patron of the church, so I thought I would buy the house and land. I have taken on all the staff who worked there before and the employees who worked on the estate. I must say, I am looking forward to life as a country squire – and to entertaining my rector at the house. With his delightful wife too, I hope.'

'I am absolutely delighted, Sir Charles. I can't tell you how much . . .' Toby found it difficult to express the elation he felt at the shipowner's revelation.

'Good! I promise not to fight you over the Church tithes. In fact, I intend foregoing the first year's tithes due to the manor, to celebrate my marriage.'

Riding home with Bethany, Toby would have passed the rectory by and taken her on to Jacob and Muriel's cottage at Hemmick, but Bethany insisted they go inside.

Wandering about the house, touching the furniture, she said, 'This will be a very happy house now, Toby.'

'I sincerely hope so,' he said.

'It's a wonderful place in which to bring up a family.'

Toby could think of nothing to say immediately so Bethany continued: 'So much has happened since I first came here. You were seeking a new life then, and mine has changed far more than I would ever have believed possible.'

'Do you have any regrets, Bethany?'

'Sometimes.'

Her reply dismayed him. 'You mean . . . you're still not certain of me? Of us?'

'How can I be certain, Toby? So far as I can recall, you have never said in so many words that you want me to marry you . . . That's if you *do* want marriage?'

'But . . . I thought you had taken that for granted!'

'Toby Lovell! Many things a woman may take for granted, but not THAT!'

'Very well. Bethany Poole, will you marry me and become the mistress of Porthluney rectory?'

'Why?'

The question took Toby by surprise. 'What do you mean . . . why?'

'I mean, why do you want to marry me?'

'Because . . . because I love you, that's why.'

'That's better. Now say it again.'

'I love you, Bethany, and I desperately want you to become my wife and come here to live with me.'

'That's *much* better. If you practise saying it to me often enough, I think you could become quite good at it.'

Suddenly her mood changed and she became more intense than he had ever seen her. 'I love thee too, Toby. Please, can we be married soon?'